UNCHARTED

A NOVEL

JANET M HOWLE

Published in Australia in 2020 by SisterShip Press Pty Ltd

www.sistershippress.com

Copyright © Janet M Howle 2020

Editor Shelley Wright

This book is a work of fiction. Names, characters, some places, and incidents are used fictitiously. Any resemblance to actual persons, living or dead, is entirely coincidental.

Cover photo: Wayne Beardsley

Cover design: Annie Seaton

National Library of Australia data:

SisterShip Press Pty Ltd, 2020, Uncharted

ISBN: 978-0-6489856-0-0

Digital ISBN: 978-0-6489856-1-7

Large Print ISBN: 978-0-6489856-2-4

www.sistershippress.com in collaboration with www.seascribebooks.com

To my husband and partner in everything who taught me all I know about blue water sailing.

To the people of the Bahamas who demonstrate such resilience in the aftermath of hurricanes, I donate my royalties from the first year to hurricane relief efforts.

CHAPTER 1

Carter McDowell dropped *Wind Chaser's* anchor disrupting the flat turquoise water. Before the sea regained its clarity, the rippling surface sparkled in the late afternoon sun. Leaning over the bowsprit on the foredeck, he pushed sun-streaked hair out of his eyes and stared vacantly at conch and starfish on the sandy bottom. This was not his usual stop when crossing the shallow water of the Great Bahama Bank to Nassau. What little wind there was had died, sailing was not an option, and Carter wanted to conserve his remaining fuel. There was no land in sight and he was confident this anchorage placed him safely out of the path of any freighter headed through the Bahama Islands during the night.

The newly oiled teak was hot under his bare feet as he walked back along the deck to the cockpit. He shifted into reverse to pull against the anchor, digging it into the sand. Shutting down the engine, he sat in the open air, absorbing the silence and remoteness. Despite having sailed these waters for seventeen years, Carter continued to be captivated by this magical and mysterious expanse of translucent ocean. Miles from anywhere, The Bank, as it was called, was never more than twenty feet deep. The opportunity to anchor with no breeze and a calm sea was rare. Too often, the wind came up, and waves bounced *Wind Chaser* around, preventing sleep and causing Carter to pull up anchor and head for a protected harbor.

Running his callused hand over the smooth varnished cockpit table, Carter collapsed against the padded seat along the starboard side, and popped open a beer. He wished he had gin or rum but his sudden departure hadn't left time for shopping. The sky reddened with the sinking sun and soon stars appeared. At times like this, his longing for Becca and Claire blocked out the brilliance of sunsets and left him alone with an emptiness in his chest that would never go away.

Wind Chaser was a charter yacht; his livelihood, home, and the only love he had left. Carter wanted this sail to last as long as possible, but the repo men were in pursuit, and most likely, it would be his last before they caught up and seized the boat. As darkness closed around him, he stripped off his worn shorts and sun-faded t-shirt and dove into the warm water. Toweling off on the swim platform, he focused on the faint glow of green starboard lights, two boats passing him in the night, but so far away he couldn't hear their engines; perhaps freighters headed for Nassau.

Carter retreated to the aft cabin, the largest of *Wind Chaser's* three staterooms. The wide centerline berth was a luxury he took advantage of when he didn't have a charter. The hatch and ports were open, welcoming any breeze that would cool the humid night air. The generator, needed for air conditioning, sat idle. He wouldn't waste fuel for that.

In the dark, Carter bolted upright, awakened by a disturbing sound that left him in a cold sweat. He shook his head, trying to clear his grogginess. He often slept fitfully, but this was so real. He swore he heard Claire calling him. "Just a stupid seagull," he muttered, flopping back on the bunk. The hands on his watch glowed two twenty-one, still a long time until daylight. Restless and uneasy, he tossed side to side and hoped not to be awake the remainder of the night. Nightmares often robbed his sleep.

The cry again. It sounded like a human voice. Racing through the pilot-house, Carter scooped up his spotlight, switched on the deck light, and stumbled up the steep companionway stairs. Sweeping the spotlight in an arc over the dark water, he held his breath, listening. "This is insane. No way someone's out here." Was he hallucinating again? Even with his doubts, he continued to search with the spotlight. The moon had risen, illuminating the ocean, but the sea plays tricks at night and sound travels across open water with few clues for direction or source. Shining the light on the compass, his best guess was the shout came from the north.

"I'm coming," he yelled, still not convinced there was anyone to hear. His heart raced. *Please, let me get there this time.* He ran forward to pull up the anchor by hand, avoiding the clatter of the diesel or whine of the electric windlass which might drown out the voice. Straining, he slowly hauled the heavy anchor on deck.

Once more, the cry, more desperate this time. Carter dashed back to the wheel, checking the direction of the response; definitely from the north. He fired up the engine and pushed it to full throttle without any warm-up. The old John Deere protested the sudden exertion by belching so much smoke from the exhaust he could see it in the moonlight. He knew better than to treat his engine this way. Sweeping an arc with the spotlight as *Wind Chaser* moved forward, he saw nothing. After a couple of minutes, Carter shut down the engine.

"Where are you?"

"Over here."

"Holy shit!" He wasn't hallucinating; someone was out there in the open sea and it sounded like a girl. Aiming the spotlight, he caught a glimpse of a person in the dark water. In what must have been a last burst of energy, she splashed aimlessly, struggling toward the boat.

"I see you. Stay there, I'll come to you." Carter restarted the engine, turned the bow, and eased toward her. Shifting to neutral, he coasted the last short distance. He threw the life preserver with its line attached to the stern and pulled her over to the boat. With no lifejacket and heavy with exhaustion, she could barely lift her outstretched arm. His heart pounded as he reached over the rail and pulled what appeared to be a waif of a girl onboard. She collapsed on the cockpit seat and threw up sea water. Pixie-like dark hair plastered against the sides of her cheeks, framing her face. Her soaking wet t-shirt and shorts clung to her like a second skin, outlining the curves of her body. She was older than he first thought. It was the haircut, her small size, and her face washed of any makeup that made her look so young. He wasn't good at guessing ages, perhaps mid-twenties? Relief that she was alive so overwhelmed him that he said nothing as he knelt beside her.

"Thirsty." Her voice was hoarse.

"Is there anyone else?" Carter felt the slight shake of her head, so he scrambled to his feet and dashed down into the galley. Fumbling in the refrigerator, behind a carton of eggs and a package of cheese, he found the last Diet Dr. Pepper. A sugary drink or orange juice would be better, but this would have to do. She hadn't moved when he returned. Holding her head, he forced her to drink slowly.

"I'm going to put you in a cabin. Can you sit up?" His lanky frame towered over her as he half carried her down the companionway stairs before she could protest. She winced and moaned when he lifted her onto a bunk. As he started to cover her with a light-weight blanket, the light from the cabin revealed bruises on her upper arm and shoulder, welts around her wrists, and blood on her knees. A ball of anger clenched his stomach and mixed with a sense of helplessness; feelings he knew too well.

"Who did this?"

"Hide me." Her voice was hardly more than a whisper, but the strength of her grip on his forearm surprised him. Hiding wasn't a problem; it was what he was already doing.

Carter's mind swirled with questions. "Who's after you?" he asked. Nothing. The answer would have to wait; she'd passed out. Crossing the hallway to the head, he found his first aid kit in the cabinet behind the toilet and bandaged her knees. She was lucky the blood from her legs hadn't attracted a shark. He watched her exhausted sleep, her arms and legs jerking as she moaned. He knew about running from demons, real or imagined, but he didn't know if he should wake her from this nightmare or not. Finally, he decided sleep was what she needed. He quietly closed the door.

None of this made sense. In all his years of sailing, Carter had never pulled anyone out of the water. He'd heard stories of boaters picking up Haitian refugees whose overloaded, dilapidated boats sank, and of men falling overboard while pissing over the rail, but this was different. She was white, sounded American, and was brave. That touched something deep inside him; a place he thought no longer existed. For the first time in months, he felt a connection to another human being, and until he knew more, he would hide her. After all, what was at stake? She posed no threat to him.

Back behind the wheel, Carter turned off all the lights except the compass. He didn't know if she was being pursued, so he revved up *Wind Chaser's* engine and set a course to the southeast. There was a risk moving without running lights, but this was an uncharted route and it was unlikely he would encounter another boat. Reefs surrounded the shallow Bahama Bank and there was only one way to cross it safely. Carter could maintain this heading for three hours before having to change direction or risk putting *Wind Chaser* aground on coral heads. For now, it was a safe course as long as he kept his eye on depth and time.

Adrenalin coursed through him, but Carter knew that wouldn't last. Now underway, he would be on watch the rest of the night. With the autopilot in control, he went below and fixed a pot of robust coffee, the way he liked it on night watch. Pouring the dark, steaming liquid into his thermos, he grabbed a mug and climbed back to the cockpit. Carter listened to the smooth, reassuring rumble of the engine as the sloop cut through a flat sea under a boundless canopy of stars. Surrounded by a landless horizon, it was as though *Wind Chaser* was in the middle of a shallow bowl, and infinitely small. As he stared over the water, he could only imagine the fear she must have felt swimming toward the unknown with only his anchor light to guide her. She must have been desperate.

Carter watched the phosphorescent glow of his wake and the dim red light of the compass, and after verifying his heading and the absence of traffic, he decided to check on his guest. She was still out but breathing evenly. Her t-shirt read 'Enjoy Life'. *God, I wish I could*, Carter thought. Then he realized her shorts and shirt were soaking both her and his mattress, so he tried to rouse her. As a charter captain, he was well aware of the threat of hypothermia, and this girl had no extra padding to guard against the cold. He touched her shoulder and raised his voice.

"Hey, you need to get out of those wet clothes."

There was no response. He checked her pulse and found it strong and steady. He knew he should get her into dry clothes, but he just couldn't do it. Already he felt like a voyeur. He rolled her gently side to side, tucking the blanket tightly around her. It would have to do.

Looking at her sleeping so deeply, he let his imagination run, but he couldn't come up with any scenario that would put her in the water, miles from anywhere, swimming for her life. Had she jumped overboard to avoid—what? Or been thrown? That stuff was only in movies or cheap novels. Who was she running from? He knew the Bahamas had pirates, but these modern-day thugs were into drugs and stealing fast boats, not tossing young women overboard. All he knew about her was that she was probably ten years his junior, slim, and wore a wedding ring. Obviously, she was a strong swimmer; if another boat had passed close, he would have heard it. A captain, like the mother of an infant, has a sixth sense that sleep doesn't close off.

Still leaning against the arched door frame, Carter glanced at his watch and realized two hours had passed since he'd set his course. He needed to change direction and head toward the Northwest Channel Light and back on the route to Nassau. On deck, he entered a course that would steer him through the narrow opening in the reef north of the light and into deep water. Carter hoped he'd avoided the usual route long enough to evade whoever might be after the gutsy young woman, if someone was. The moon had set; stars filled the darkness. Then he focused on something that surprised him. For the first time in months, he was clear-headed; the sluggishness that sapped his energy was gone. His sailing had a purpose. He would get her to Nassau where he now had to stop for fuel and where she would be safe.

Many people told Carter they were envious of his ability to find a way to make a living doing what he loved. He was proud of his yacht charter business: McDowell's Charters. It was different from the nuke and puke catamarans operating out of Nassau. Those boats took twenty or thirty college kids, operated on loud reggae music and lots of alcohol. They kept a tight schedule and never shut down the engine. Putting up sails was only for show. Carter took guests who were disappointed when he had to start the engine. Since the winds in the Bahamas were predominantly from the east, he offered a one-way charter. He would motor out against the wind from Fort Lauderdale while the guests flew into a location of their choice in the southern Bahamas. Then, they would island-hop back through the many cays that made up the Exuma chain.

Meeting new people and sailing to his favorite places was exciting, when he had his wife and daughter. Although Becca occasionally took the helm, she mostly took care of their guests. She was an excellent cook and created meals in the small galley that continued to surprise him. Claire was home-schooled. Her constant enthusiasm for adventure was contagious, and paying guests caught her mood. She was a fearless swimmer, and even at nine, she could run the six horse-power outboard on the hard-bottom dinghy. Along with Carter, she led their snorkeling trips. It worked well for everyone.

Then everything changed. Maybe it was a mistake to keep the charter service going on his own, but it was all he knew. Now guests snorkeled or explored isolated beaches while Carter remained onboard to prepare meals, wash dishes, maintain the engine and generator, and scrub saltwater from the teak deck and brightwork. There were always chores and repairs, and he couldn't afford crew.

Memories of Claire haunted him. The Bahamas were filled with them. There was no island he could visit without dredging up visions from their many escapades. Night sailing with Claire was etched in his mind. There was nothing but the sea, the sigh of the wind in the sails, and the gentle slapping of the waves against the hull. Claire would sneak out of her bunk and into the cockpit to sit in his lap. He'd let her take the wheel as they sailed under a blanket of stars undiminished by city lights. He'd give anything to have those days again, but time doesn't move backward. Now, even if it was only temporary, he was glad not to be alone on the boat.

CHAPTER 2

Carter watched the sky grow lighter. First, nautical dawn, then the rising sun back-lit the scattered clouds, shifting the horizon from gray to shades of pink and orange. They were still two hours away from the passage north of the channel light. Going below, he found the young woman sleeping peacefully, a more natural flush of soft pink covered her cheeks. Carter poured hot water over fine grounds and the cabin filled with the rich aroma of a fresh brew. As tired as he was, he savored the salty scent of summer mixed with fragrant coffee that he always enjoyed in the early morning light.

It was nearly eight when the woman appeared in the companionway hatch wrapped in the blanket, her salt-encrusted brown hair sticking out in all directions. She looked so young, but all Carter could think about was how fearless she'd been. She was staring and he shifted self-consciously. He ran his hand over his chin and cheek; he hadn't shaved after his saltwater bath. Unruly hair nearly touched his shoulders, and his over-washed khaki shorts and t-shirt were so faded they defied description. He hadn't expected to have anyone onboard. At least the long hours of managing the boat left him tanned and trim. Carter waited for her to speak.

She moved cautiously, lowering herself onto the cockpit cushion.

Running her hand over the striped fabric, she said, "Blue. White. Lime. Nice."

It wasn't a remark he expected. She seemed as tired as Carter felt, his hazel eyes bloodshot from lack of sleep.

"You saved my life."

"It was just by chance I was anchored there," Carter responded. "That's not usually where I stop, but it's what anyone would have done."

"I'm so thankful you were there and when your boat lit up, I was sure you heard me yelling, but…" Her voice trailed off.

Carter held out the thermos. "Coffee?"

"Oh, yes. Please."

"I don't have cream or sugar."

"That's fine."

As she sipped her drink, Carter plunged ahead. "Why were you out there?"

"It's a long story." She scanned the horizon, pulling the blanket over her shoulders, trying to hide her injuries.

"We're alone. I haven't seen another boat all night," Carter said, following her gaze.

"This is a big boat for one person to handle."

Carter shrugged. "Fifty-four feet. Not so big. I'm used to it. And the pilot-house lets me steer from inside if the weather turns sour. I admit it's easier with crew."

"We're alone on the boat?"

"Yes." She seemed to shrink inside the blanket. Carter wanted to offer some reassurance, but he wasn't sure what words would help. Finally, he said, "You're safe here."

She didn't respond.

"Would you like some dry clothes?" Carter offered.

She nodded.

"If you'll sit at the helm, I'll find something for you. Do you know anything about boats?"

"A little."

"Nothing to do except watch for traffic. You don't even have to touch the wheel, autopilot's on. That keeps the course." Carter pointed to the throttle. "Pull that handle back if you see anything, a sudden change in speed always gets my attention."

As Carter stepped below, he realized she didn't trust him. After whatever she had been through, it was no wonder. He went into his cabin, rummaged through his locker, and pulled out a t-shirt. Holding it up, he realized his clothes would swallow her. Becca's would be better. There was still a blue-striped t-shirt and denim shorts in the drawer under the bunk. He kept them there for…what? He held them to his face, closed his eyes, and inhaled what he still imagined was her scent: sunshine and perspiration. It seemed a sacrilege to let someone else wear them. He started to put them back in the drawer. *Be practical*, he told himself.

Returning to the deck, he handed the clothes and a towel to the young woman who took them without comment. Carter was relieved. He didn't want to explain why he had women's clothing onboard. "If you'd like a shower, there's one in the head across from the cabin you were in. You'll find ibuprofen and more bandages in the first-aid kit in the cabinet." When she didn't move, he added, "The door locks from the inside. Just don't use up all my water. I don't carry much, and it's expensive in the islands."

"I remember that. I used to come to Bimini on my father's sportfishing boat. He always complained about the cost of water."

She seemed to relax as the conversation turned away from questions about her current circumstances. Carter continued, "I'm Carter McDowell, by the way."

"Mary Katherine Deano. I prefer Kat. You don't happen to have an extra toothbrush, do you? My mouth tastes like I've eaten rotten jellyfish wrapped in decaying seaweed."

Even if it was only a momentary distraction from her trauma, Carter was relieved to see that in some deep place, she still possessed a sense of humor. "Let me look."

Carter went below, searched drawers, and found a spare intended for Claire, still in the wrapper. As he handed it to Kat, she examined the character on the small pink toothbrush.

"Ariel, The Little Mermaid."

Carter's eyebrows pinched together in a puzzled expression.

"You rescued me from the sea. In the fairy tale, I rescue you."

Carter watched as she turned and gingerly made her way down the companionway stairs. *I wish you could.*

He heard the fresh-water pump cycle on and off. She had spent time on a boat; she knew how to conserve water. However, the polish on her fingers and toenails, and lack of suntan suggested not recently.

When Kat reappeared, her brown eyes were clear and wet bangs swept across her forehead. Usually, Carter didn't like short hair on women, but somehow it suited her.

"Feeling better?" he asked.

"Much, thanks. Guess I wasn't very appreciative last night. I've never been so exhausted, but that coffee already helps."

"You weren't very talkative. I made an omelet. You must be hungry. I am."

Kat looked at the glossy teak table where Carter had set eggs, toast, and coffee. "You eat well for a solo sailor."

"Sometimes. I take charters. If I fed my guests crap, they wouldn't come back."

Kat smiled in response, the first one Carter had seen, but as she carefully eased herself down on a cockpit cushion, she hunched forward and clenched her hands between her knees.

"I had just about given up. The current had turned and was pushing me away from what I hoped was your anchor light. I was losing ground but something drove me on, maybe anger, maybe fear. I felt desperately alone. You can't imagine my relief when I heard your engine." She dropped her eyes and ran her hands over the welts on her wrists. "I don't have words to describe how I felt then, or now."

"I know what it is to be alone, but nothing like that." Carter spoke from experience but he wouldn't share his story. This wasn't about him. "Now, tell me, who's after you? Before you passed out, you said, 'hide me'. Who am I supposed to hide you from?"

Kat twisted her wedding band, struggling with a decision. "You'll be better off if I don't involve you."

"Too late for that. I am involved." Carter pulled out his phone. "Whoever it is, we need the police."

Kat snatched the phone from his hand. "The police won't help." She took a breath and held out his phone in her palm. "Sorry, I shouldn't have done that; it's just they won't help."

"Of course they will." Carter fiddled with the phone in his hand.

"No, they can't afford to. I was thrown off *Navy One.*"

Carter nearly choked on a mouthful of food. "God! No way, that's the Prime Minister's boat."

"I know."

"You were with Rollins?"

Kat ran her hands through her hair; her words came fast. "He wasn't onboard. I'm a journalist. I'd been invited to his fundraiser in Bimini—well, sort of. When I asked about my brother, who's missing and presumed dead after a boating accident, suddenly I was persona non grata."

"Wait, I'm confused. Were you there for Rollins' fundraiser or your missing brother?"

"Both. But when I began to question people about my brother, the Prime Minister's bodyguard, this huge ox, took me onboard *Navy One* then threw me overboard."

"That can't be the whole story."

"Well, that's the short version. Maybe Buddy was into something and they think I'm involved in it."

"Buddy?"

"My twin, Dwight. Everyone calls him Buddy. He's now missing— or dead."

"But trying to kill you?" Carter knew that a former prime minister had been indicted for corruption, but Rollins could never risk being connected to murder. He was up for re-election.

"I'm not saying Rollins was behind it. I don't know, maybe his bodyguard."

"Isadore Jones. He has a reputation for being a crook, but murder? I don't think even he'd cross that line."

"My brain's not working." Kat sighed as she sank back against the cushions. "I know this doesn't fit, but I can't give you any explanation, and you have no reason to believe me."

Carter changed the subject and scanned the horizon for other vessels. "What would you have done if you hadn't seen my anchor light?"

"Died." They both stared over the endless expanse of water.

"I know Isadore. He's the PM's son-in-law," Carter finally said. "You're lucky if he was put in charge of killing you. He never gets anything right." Carter shook his head. "So, if they've trumped up some charges against you, I'll be in trouble too if I don't turn you in."

Kat's hands were in her hair again. "I'm scared."

"Yeah well, I would think so. I don't know how much danger you're in, but I don't want to throw you to the wolves—or sharks. Any bright ideas?"

"No."

Carter stood up to clear the dishes, then sat back down.

"I know some things about the Bahamas. I've spent a lot of time here," Carter said. "Murders of inconvenient people have happened. Money changes hands, and these crimes are left unsolved. Obviously, you don't have your passport. Maybe you can find someone who will be willing to sneak you back into the U.S. There are plenty of people who take questionable cargo into the States, but it's going to cost plenty up front. The more desperate you are, the more it will cost."

"Are you one of those people?"

"No. But I know some. I don't plan to go back to the States. I'm heading to Nassau to refuel and then on south."

"I'm not heading back either. I came over to find out about my brother and I intend to do that."

After her near-death experience, her tenacity was appealing, but Carter also felt a bit irritated. She should be looking out for herself.

"Haven't you gotten the message?" he asked. "It should be obvious that someone doesn't want you to find out what happened."

"All the more reason I want to know."

"You'd be safer doing it from the States," Carter said.

"My father already hired a lawyer and a detective, and they didn't find out squat. That's why I flew over here. I'm an investigative journalist."

"And you're going to be a dead journalist if you keep at this."

"It's not the first time I've taken a risk."

Kat rolled her coffee cup between her hands. "I know this is asking a lot, but can I hide on your boat until I get help? It will only be for a couple of days. My husband's a lawyer. In Florida. He can't practice here, but he can help me find a top-notch Bahamian attorney and bring me money. I can pay you."

"I have to keep moving." *And I don't need a pretty little brunette— someone else's wife no less—to distract me with her problems.*

"Just a couple of days."

"Look, the bank is after my boat," Carter said, his voice sharp. "I borrowed money and put it up as collateral. I fell behind. I guess you could say I ran out on the bank that holds my title. I haven't even cleared customs here. I can't spare the $300.00 fee. Not if I'm going to eat and keep *Wind Chaser* fueled. I'm hoping I can be south of the Bahamas before customs finds out. No one usually checks."

"Can a U.S. bank claim your boat here?"

"I don't know. Never been in this situation, but I do know that the U.S. Coast Guard patrols these waters. I guess they can confiscate it."

"There's a way I can help. Stewart can get the answer to that question and the money to pay you. How soon do you need it?"

"I need to pay customs within twenty-four hours after I dock in Nassau."

"Can I use your phone?"

"Sure." He looked at his phone. "The signal's weak, but it'll probably work."

Carter handed the phone to Kat and watched her go into the cabin and close the door. He knew his emotions were inappropriate, but he felt shut out. At the very least, she needed a lawyer, and that wasn't him. Carter wasn't in that league. He'd quit college after the second year and didn't have a degree of any sort, let alone law. He should be glad that she had a husband who would drop everything and come to her. *Wind Chaser* was his priority, he couldn't risk losing his boat sticking around to help Kat. She'd have to work this out on her own. Carter was only an accidental part of her life, and he certainly hadn't planned for Kat to be part of his.

There was something else gnawing in his brain, something he tried to ignore. Kat was brave where Becca was a coward. The very thought made him feel guilty, disloyal to Becca. That was absurd; he had known Kat for less than twenty-four hours. It didn't matter that Becca was gone. He still loved her and missed her.

When Kat returned to the cockpit, she handed the phone to Carter. "No luck. Stewart's in the middle of an important trial; he's the lead counsel. If he wins, he's a shoo-in for partner. He can't just walk out on his client."

Carter shook his head. "And his wife is about to be thrown into a jail in Nassau. He's got this backward."

"He'll come when the trial is over."

"How long will that take?" Carter asked.

"You never know."

"Do you have anyone else you can call?"

"My father. But he's already had one stroke; his only son is missing and may be dead. I don't want him to worry about me. I'm not that desperate."

"You should be. I'm in no position to help. I told you. I've got to keep moving."

"Where are we now?" Kat asked.

"In about an hour we'll reach the passage off The Bank and into deep water."

They sat, each with their own worries. As if to fill the silence, the radio squawked. "*Reel Time, Reel Time.* Dis be *Fish Story.* Come back."

"*Reel Time* here, go to our workin' channel."

These were Bahamian sport fishing boats headed for Chub Cay, hoping to pick up a charter. Carter knew these fun-loving captains and their questionable catches. Guys you'd want on your side in a fight, but they walked a thin line with authorities. He keyed the radio to channel seventeen knowing this was their working channel.

"*Reel Time*, come back. *Fish Story* here."

"I with you. Where you at?"

"'Bout five miles west a da Northwest Channel."

"We at da light. Lots goin' on. Police boats boardin' every boat comin' off da Bank. Never seen dis before. We behind a little sailboat but des guys take der own sweet time. You probably catch up wid us. Hope you sort out your catch before you get here or da police sort it for you."

"Thanks for da heads up. We be clear. Back to sixteen."

Carter frowned. "Don't think they're looking for undersized lobsters or grass. My guess is they're looking for you. I can't take you past that light." He shifted into neutral and let *Wind Chaser* coast at idle.

"Isn't there another way off The Bank?"

"Not without going north of the Berry Islands and not without wind so I can sail. I don't have fuel for that distance." Carter fell silent, then something occurred to him. "You know, a couple of years ago, I was talking to a Bahamian captain at the End of the World Bar in Bimini. He was bragging drunk. Told me he knew a way through the coral reefs about four miles south of the light, near Mackie Shoal. Said it was complicated. You needed good light to watch depths and spot the coral heads. Claimed at high tide, there was six feet of water. The guy pulled a piece of paper out of his wallet and showed me the coordinates. I didn't really believe him, just drunk talk, but I did write them down and put it on my chart. Thought I'd check it out sometime. Figured it'd be a short-cut to Nassau, if it's even possible."

"How much depth does your boat need?"

"Five feet, nine inches. Probably less right now, she's so lightly loaded. I'm willing to try it. As long as we get there before high tide, even if I run aground, I can get off."

"Why are you willing to take that risk?"

"Well, staying this course, we both lose. My boat. Your freedom. I said I'd get you to Nassau, and it's not so much of a risk. *Wind Chaser's* strongly built. I'll plot our course if you stay here and watch for traffic. Never could teach Captain Auto-Pilot to do that. He doesn't multitask. Good with keeping the course, but shit as a look-out. Don't take chances; call me if you spot anything."

Carter went below and searched his worn chart until he found the three sets of coordinates. He plotted the course; 113 degrees, 8.4 nautical miles. The tide table showed the next high tide at ten fifty-six and indicated this one was three inches above the average high.

"Need to get there about ten-fifteen to give me a margin." Carter was talking to himself as he often did alone on the boat. "Might as well see if she's going to be any good at the helm." He called Kat on the intercom.

"Shift into forward, 1600 rpm, course heading one, one, three degrees."

"Roger that." He felt the engine shift into gear, rev up, and the boat swing to starboard. Walking forward to the inside steering station, he looked at the instruments. She was dead on course, and the engine was turning 1600. He came back to the companionway.

"Was that a test?" she asked.

"Yup. You made an A-plus. I'll need you at the wheel when we go through the coral. You okay with that?"

"I think so."

"I'll stand on the bow and give you hand signals to indicate which way to turn," Carter said. "We'll go through dead slow. Engine at idle."

"Roger, Captain." She smiled as she said it.

Carter looked at his instruments. They showed an ETA of ten thirty-two. "Give her 200 rpm. more."

CHAPTER 3

Carter knew the dangers of taking a sailboat into shallow Bahamian waters. Sooner or later, a weather forecast would be wrong and an unexpected storm could destroy his boat. Or, he might collide with an uncharted coral head and take a chunk out of the hull. Worse yet, was the possibility that drug dealers might board in the night, rob and kill everyone. He lived by the sailors' code. They helped each other in distress, even at risk to themselves. It was not purely altruistic; Carter knew the time would come when his survival would depend on a returned favor. But the help he was offering Kat went beyond this. That wasn't selfish either; he honestly didn't care what happened because, for the first time in months, he felt useful.

Carter was worried about one thing; where to hide Kat if necessary. He unlatched the dinette back cushion that covered the storage space that was usually stuffed with canned goods and other non-perishables. Now it was mostly empty. The latch that released the back cushion was hidden by plush upholstery. Without close examination, it wasn't evident that there was enough room for a person. He called up to her.

"I think I have a hiding place for you in case we need it. Come take a look."

Kat frowned. "Hope I don't need that for long."

"Yeah, it could get hot back there real quick. The engine's right below you."

"There's no latch on the inside. You will let me out, right?" Kat asked.

"Well, if I don't, you could kick it open."

"I couldn't even straighten my legs in there."

"Then let's just hope you don't need it." Carter said as he pushed the cans to one end of the compartment.

They thought they were alone as they approached the waypoints that routed them between the coral heads, then a speck appeared on the horizon behind them, quickly growing larger. From the engine sound, Carter identified it as a cigarette boat, the fastest vessel in these waters, other than the Bahamian Defense boats. "You'd better try out your new quarters."

The cigarette boat flew past, obviously on the same course that Carter had set. A fast-moving white hull was an excellent camouflage in the ocean; from a distance, it looked like the crest of a wave. He wondered if they were carrying drugs; they had no interest in him.

As Carter closed in on the passage, he could see the speed boat dead in the water tied alongside a sixty-foot Royal Bahamian Defense Force vessel with its distinct black and gold RBDF crest. Blue lights on the bow and stern flashed. The defense boat was specifically designed to intercept drug and weapon smugglers, and human traffickers. Carter's mouth was dry as he focused on the machine gun mounted midship. He was well-aware these boats carried additional automatic weapons and a host of handheld firearms. They were authorized to stop, search, and detain anyone deemed a threat to Bahamian security.

Forget the repo men, Carter's days at sea would be over if they discovered he was hiding Kat. Through his binoculars, he counted three policemen crowded into the cockpit of the cigarette boat. Two other officers were on the defense force vessel. One appeared to be Captain Manny, someone Carter knew. It was too late for Carter to turn away; Manny was standing on the flybridge, his binoculars focused on *Wind Chaser*. Carter heard a voice on the radio.

"*Wind Chaser, Wind Chaser,* dis is *Nassau Intercept.*"

Carter recognized Manny's voice. "*Wind Chaser* here. Pick a channel." Manny could talk on sixteen if he wanted to, and while he couldn't keep it private over any radio frequency, he could be more discrete by changing to a low-wattage channel.

"How 'bout goin' up two?"

Carter switched to eighteen.

"Dat you, Carter?"

"It's me, Manny."

"Thought I recognized dat beautiful gal. Don't make 'em like dat anymore. It's a job keepin' all that teak shiny and lookin' new. What are you doin' down here? Dis ain't no place for you. Nothin' but drug runners come through here. We're gonna plug dis hole. How you know about dis?"

"Some guy at End of the World Bar told me a while back. Can't remember his name."

"Dat be Capt'n Willie. He talk all da time."

"Sounds right."

"He already in lock-up. Dis can be a dangerous place. You don't wanna be here, mon."

"Thanks for the warning. Capt'n Willie said it was a short-cut to Nassau. I'm dead-heading so thought it'd be a good time to check it out."

"Yeah, short-cut to Nassau jail, he mean." Carter could hear Manny's deep-throated chuckle. "Say, you anchor out on da Bank last night?"

"That's a roger."

"Didn't see anything of a gal swimmin' out there did ya?"

Carter was forced to make a quick decision. "You're kidding. There're miles of ocean out there. And with jellyfish, sharks, and those currents, she'd have to be a mermaid or superwoman to survive that."

"Dat's what I think. I was told she fell or jump off *Navy One*. My opinion, she'd be shark bait by now. We wanted to question her about a few tings."

Carter felt guilty about misleading Manny. He was twenty years older than Carter, short, dark, and wiry like most Bahamian men. Carter hadn't exactly lied, and if he played this right, he wouldn't have to turn Kat over to the police. He'd promised he'd get her to Nassau and she was just beginning to trust him.

"Capt'n Carter?" Manny again. "Since you're here. How about I lead you while my officers finish dat conversation with des down-island boys. It's hard to get through here with no look-out on your bow."

"Much appreciated, Manny." If this hadn't been Manny, Carter knew his boat would have been boarded and searched. Fortunately, Manny owed Carter; he had once provided information that led to a big-time arrest and a promotion for Manny. But Carter wondered, why was Manny here? He wasn't in drug enforcement anymore. He was a captain in the homicide unit.

Once through the maze of jagged coral heads, Manny waved Carter off and watched *Wind Chaser* continue to Nassau. Something was bothering him. He had known Carter for a long time, and he knew he was honest and trustworthy. But there was something in his voice. He seemed hesitant, indirect. He hadn't actually said "No" when Manny asked about seeing a girl, and he hadn't even seemed curious about why she was on *Navy One* or why she was wanted for questioning. Maybe he was reading too much into it. After all, it hadn't been that long since Carter's intense police grilling. Even after the newspapers lost interest, Manny continued to follow the police reports. There never was any evidence pointing to Carter, but Manny knew how an unfounded accusation could ruin a man. Some people were never the same; the damage was done despite being cleared of the crime. The entire ordeal had badly bruised Carter. He had lost so much; healing would take time. It shouldn't surprise Manny that Carter seemed a bit edgy about being questioned, but it did.

Right now Manny had a job to do, but he intended to keep an eye on Carter. He wouldn't say anything to the Prime Minister about Carter being on The Bank last night, not now. He didn't have any facts to report, only an unsettled feeling. He wasn't going to pull Carter in unless he had hard evidence. Why Rollins wanted direct reports about that girl was another thing that bothered Manny. Normally he struggled to keep the PM's attention. And so far, he didn't have proof this American girl was guilty of anything criminal. It was just circumstantial. Just because she was seen running out of the Compleat Angler confirmed nothing. Who wouldn't run from a burning building? What possible motive would she have? Why was the Prime Minister personally insisting that Manny use all his resources to verify the girl's drowning and wrap this up quickly? Manny could think of better ways to spend his time than taking the PM's calls. God, the man was becoming a pain in the ass. He let out a deep breath. As much as he hated to, he needed to call Carter back.

CHAPTER 4

Carter set the autopilot. *Wind Chaser* was now in the dark blue sea of the North East Providence Channel, the deep water that would take them to Nassau. He went below to let Kat out.

"All clear," he said as he removed the settee's back panel.

Kat groaned as she untangled her limbs from the small space. "Thanks. It was beginning to feel like a sauna, and that didn't do anything for my bruised body."

"There's a fresh breeze outside. Come on. Did you hear that conversation?" Carter asked.

"Part of it. Why didn't you turn me in?"

"Maybe I should have." Carter shrugged. "But I didn't lie."

"A lie of omission. But for a second time, thanks. Mind if I fix a sandwich? I can do one for you too if you like." She seemed eager to change the subject.

"Sure. That'd be great. Help yourself to whatever's in the fridge. Might not be much. I wasn't planning on company."

Carter watched as she started down the stairs, favoring her right knee. Even Becca's clothes were too big, and Kat had tied the t-shirt in a knot at her small waist. If he had to guess, he would have said she was a runner or at least worked out regularly. Her legs were toned and firm, and even with her injuries, she balanced confidently on the boat. He heard bacon sizzling, and the smell made his stomach growl.

Carter looked at his wind instruments. North-northwest, twelve knots, time to put up sails. All the lines led back to the cockpit; it was a job he could single-hand. As he sheeted in the jib, he heard the radio again.

"Capt'n Carter? One more ting you need to know, dat girl's accused of arson, maybe murder. I know it's a big ocean, but boats have to follow along da same route. You sure you didn't see her?" Manny was broadcasting on sixteen and didn't give Carter the option of switching to a low-wattage channel.

Before Carter could answer, Kat appeared at the companionway stairs, holding a plastic plate with sandwiches. For a few brief seconds, the person Carter saw was his daughter Claire. Claire, who did not even celebrate her first double-digit birthday. Claire, who would never have to imagine trusting her life to some stranger. Claire, who was as courageous as Kat. Carter gave Manny an answer with far-reaching consequences. Looking directly at Kat, he said, "No, Manny, just running lights from a couple of boats passing in the distance about ten, that's all."

But Manny wasn't done. "Carter, we go back long time, if you hear anythin', you let me know. I'm gettin' a lot of flak from da big guy. They say she burnt down da Compleat Angler. Piccolo Pete's dead. Crushed by a timber when da building cave in. You help me here?"

Carter was still staring at Kat. "Will do Manny." He slowly replaced the radio mic. No doubt others heard the full power radio communication as all boaters were required to have their radio on channel sixteen for emergency broadcasts. Manny offered Carter a final chance to set a different course, and he hadn't taken it. His fate was now linked entirely to Kat.

Kat's eyes were wide. She covered her mouth with her free hand and tripped at the top of the companionway stairs. The plate clattered on the deck. Bacon, lettuce, and tomato flew everywhere. Kat dropped to her hands and knees frantically picking up the pieces from the cockpit floor, her legs bleeding again.

"Let it go," Carter yelled, but Kat continued to grope for the food, scrambling as though cleaning up would block out Manny's words. Carter grabbed her arm. "It's not important. Let it go."

Kat flinched at his grip. Tears overwhelmed her as she sat back on her heels. "He was my friend. I've known Piccolo since I was a child. I was locked in my room. He saved me from that fire. It was my fault." She pulled away from Carter's grasp and hugged her arms around her body, rocking back and forth.

"What was your fault? The fire? Piccolo's death? What do you mean, 'Locked in your room'? I'm trying to be reasonable, but you're beginning to sound like a nutcase. You owe me some explanation. Piccolo Pete was my friend too. I'm in enough trouble already. I'm not covering for this." Carter knew he was scaring her, but he didn't care. Standing, he stepped over Kat, retrieved a trash can from the galley, and shoved it at her.

"Talk," he ordered and sat back down at the helm.

Still shaking, Kat continued to pick up the mess, looking everywhere except at him. "Where…what to begin with?" She bit her lip trying to keep it from trembling.

"Talk, or I'm calling Manny back."

CHAPTER 5

Two weeks earlier, Kat jogged along the raised boardwalk over the marsh grass, past the commercial fishing docks, and down to the marina. She loved her town with its pungent odor of brackish water and decomposing marine life. In the low country of South Carolina and Georgia, this unique smell was affectionately known as Pluff Mud, but here, along the coast of Florida, it was the smell of home. Once the hideout and stomping ground of pirates and bootleggers, Fernandina was the only town on Amelia Island.

Despite the increase in tourism, Fernandina remained a quaint village of just over eleven thousand people. Elegant resorts, built in the style of old plantation homes with sweeping lawns and formal gardens, occupied the Atlantic side of the island, but Fernandina fronted the Intracoastal Waterway and didn't depend on beachgoers. Center Street was lined with bookstores, antique shops, and cozy restaurants that were popular with locals and vacationers willing to get off the interstate or away from the all-inclusive hotels to explore real life on the island. For much of the year, Fernandina belonged to the residents who made their living shrimping or supplying the pleasure boaters cruising the waterway.

Kat and Stewart owned a rambling dark-green clapboard house

with white trim, a tin roof, and a big screened porch. It had been modified and added on to by previous owners so that now, it was hard to identify which rooms were part of the original structure. Someone described it as arrogantly shabby. It suited Kat, but Stewart already planned to move to the fashionable historic neighborhood once he made partner. Kat loved the live-oak trees hanging with moss that shaded the house and separated it from the waterway. As she made her way up the walkway, she was surprised to see The General's black Mercedes in the drive and her father sitting in the swing on the porch. Although retired for some years, people still called him The General. Kat was thrilled; he rarely came by and never unannounced. It wasn't his style. Seeing her approach, he stood. She bounded up the steps and swung her arms around him. "Daddy, what a nice surprise."

Kat knew immediately something was wrong; he stood rigidly, leaning heavily on the cane he was usually too proud to use. Stepping away, she saw his eyes were red, and his hand shook as he silently handed her the letter he was holding. Her stomach constricted as she read the letterhead: Commonwealth of the Bahamas, Office of High Commission, Nassau, The Bahamas. It was dated August twenty-third, addressed to General Mark Edwards. She scanned the first paragraph.

```
"We regret to inform you of a boating
accident involving Dwight David Edwards. The
sixty-foot research vessel, Ocean Pearl, with
Dr. Edwards and two Bahamian captains
onboard, ran aground on a coral reef and
burned."
```

It went on to say that The Bahamas Air-Sea Rescue Association had come to their aid, but apparently all three onboard perished.

```
"The bodies of the captains have been
recovered, but we have not yet located the
body of Dr. Edwards."
```

Looking up, Kat saw tears in her father's eyes. She continued to read. "The owner of the vessel, Oriental Mineral Resources, is being charged with damage to the fragile reef eco-system and there is an ongoing investigation into the cause of the accident." It ended with the normal condolences and indicated that he should contact the office of the High Commission with any questions. It was signed His Excellency, The Honorable Basil Starkweather-Post, MP, Governor-General.

Kat stumbled across the porch and sank into a wicker chair, absently stroking the cat rubbing against her leg. The General followed. His limp, the residual from a stroke two years ago, was more pronounced, a sure sign of stress or fatigue. Pulling another chair closer, he waited in silence, clenching and unclenching his jaw. Finally, he couldn't contain his anger. His knees cracked as he pushed himself out of the chair and resumed his uneven pacing.

"God damn it. What a bunch of assholes." His knuckles were white as he gripped his cane and hammered the floorboards. "Not one word from Oriental Minerals. I've had my lawyer trying to reach them all morning. No success. And that Honorable Basil Starkweather-Post guy doing this by mail. There's nothing honorable about that. The U.S. Army would never handle such a sensitive issue like this. Did you read that part about damage to the reef? They're more interested in their fucking coral than in the people who died. Do I care if The Bahamas National Trust and the Agency of Environmental Services are involved? We're talking about my son."

Kat lifted her tear-streaked face. "Daddy, this is my fault. I could have stopped him. He called in the middle of the night a couple of weeks ago and left a message saying he had landed a $500,000 contract in the Bahamas. I didn't pick up because Stewart gets so angry when Buddy wakes us like that."

Her father sank on the chair beside her and took her hand. He sighed deeply, his voice gentle. "It's not your fault. You know how Buddy obsesses on things. If he'd wanted to go, you couldn't have stopped him."

Kat still held the letter. She re-read it. "It doesn't make sense. No time or place of the accident, nothing from Oriental Mining—Minerals, whatever. No body . . .maybe?" The cat jumped into her lap and nuzzled her arm. She shook her head. "I'm not ready to admit that he's…" Her tears started again.

"I'm canceling my trip next week," her father said.

"No, don't. I think you should go. Buddy would want that. He knew how much your hunting trips mean to you. Let me take care of things here. I have a key to his apartment. We'll plan a memorial service once we have details. First, I'm going to make some calls, maybe even go to Nassau."

"What good will that do?" Her father ran his hand over his eyes. "You want me to stay with you until Stewart gets home?"

"Thanks, but I'll be fine. Moose will keep me company." She looked at the big gray cat purring contentedly in her lap and attempted to smile.

Kat wanted to be alone. Numerous questions raced through her mind. Was Buddy involved in something illegal? Why were they willing to pay him so much? She planned to check her computer, and she didn't want to upset her father with what she might find. Buddy could be duped so easily. He believed almost everything he was told. She changed the subject. "The only thing I worry about is you being alone at the cabin. I wish you'd take Gerald or someone."

"Yeah, and I wish you wouldn't go to Nassau alone. So, I guess we're even." He leaned over, kissed her gently on the forehead, stroked her hair, and patted the cat. "I wasn't a good father for him. We were so different."

"He knew you loved him."

"Sometimes love isn't enough. Maybe if your mother had lived. She seemed to understand him." His voice broke. "Be careful; you're all I've got."

She stood, cuddling Moose in her arms as her father made his way cautiously to his car. "Call me when you get home." He waved dismissively over his shoulder, not committing to her request, but she knew he would, especially now. She stood on the porch holding the screen door open with her hip, absently rubbing the cat's ears until his car was out of sight.

Kat sat back down on the porch swing, not quite ready to search her computer. All she could think about was ignoring Buddy's midnight call. At least she hadn't erased his message. Maybe there were some clues there that would direct her search.

Buddy, her Buddy. He was the one who had first called her Kat, unable to pronounce Mary Katherine and the nickname had stuck with everyone except their father. As different as they were, they looked alike with dark curly hair and brown eyes. Born prematurely, they remained small for their age. This worked to Kat's advantage since no one expected a tiny girl to be so assertive and stubborn. It was not the same for Buddy. As adults, Buddy had retained his slight frame and the delicate features inherited from their mother.

The General expected his son, named for the WWII hero, to become a hardened military man like himself. Much to his annoyance, Buddy considered working out pointless and the fitness equipment that The General constantly upgraded, sat unused. The only interest he sincerely shared with their father was sharp-shooting. Buddy's obsessive nature matched the attention and precision needed for success on the rifle range. His firearms skills eventually exceeded his father's; however, he flatly refused to go on any of The General's hunting trips.

Buddy had never fit in. While bright and verbal, he couldn't keep friends. Initially, kids were fascinated by his nearly total recall of everything he read and his ability to recite details about almost any subject. But he missed their jokes and soon they just considered him weird. It didn't help that they were Army brats and moved every three years or so as their father advanced. Buddy struggled to understand social interactions, bursting into conversations, and blurting out opinions that most people learned to suppress out of politeness by adulthood. He understood logic, but missed the subtle intent of exchanges. Buddy was content being alone, digging in the dirt, and Kat wasn't surprised when he graduated with honors, a Ph.D. in geology. Initially accepting a faculty position at Florida State, Buddy's inability to focus on the research and writing that he deemed nonsense, led to his dismissal. That and his drinking. One thing Kat knew; he didn't lie, not even little social lies to make someone feel good. He was so unlike Stewart, who said whatever people wanted to hear to make his goal of partner. As much as she hated to admit it, there was no possibility that a legitimate company would hire a socially inept, alcoholic, out-of-work geologist for such a lucrative contract. Buddy was distorting reality.

CHAPTER 6

Kat spent the next few days walking the waterfront, unable to concentrate. She should have been writing and missed deadlines. Grief was hard enough, but Kat couldn't move on until she knew the truth.

Daily, she checked the *Nassau Guardian* online, reading through the archives starting the day of Buddy's midnight call. There was no mention of any accident involving a research vessel. She called the Office of the High Commission in Nassau repeatedly but got nowhere. Each time she was promised a call back that never came. Eventually, she learned that since her inquiry involved a non-resident, it had been turned over to the Ministry of Legal Affairs. Neither she, her father's lawyer, nor the detective he'd hired, had been able to get any contact information for Oriental Mineral Resources. It was as if they didn't exist. Then Kat discovered a message from Buddy that shocked her. It was in the spam file of her business email. He never used that address; she didn't even know he had it. It was dated August twenty-first.

. . .

**Desperate. Need help. Meet me at the old air terminal on North
Bimini at 10:00 p.m. on the 28th. Urgent.**

Her head throbbed. God, what if she hadn't checked her spam? Was it
possible that Buddy was alive and in trouble? But something didn't fit.
She remembered distinctly; the High Commissioner's letter to their
father was dated August twenty-third. This email had come on the
twenty-first. That meant the accident must have occurred either on
the twenty-first or twenty-second. She'd never known any official
investigation of this magnitude to be wrapped up in one or two days.

As a reporter, she had contacts in the Bahamas. She sent an email
to Barracuda Bob, her most reliable source, asking about Oriental
Minerals, but oddly there was no response. The run-around she was
getting increased her suspicions and determination. Frustrated by
sitting home waiting on calls, Kat booked a flight to Bimini. She'd
sidestep Nassau for now; she had their official report.

Kat could think of several people on Bimini who might be able to
point her in the right direction. As children, and later as teenagers, she
and Buddy often went to Bimini with The General on his sports
fishing boat, *Even Keel*. Last year she had received an offer from a
literary magazine to write a series of articles about the time
Hemingway spent in Bimini, sometimes writing, but mostly drinking
and shark-shooting from *Pelar*. It wasn't her usual line of work, but
she'd spent fascinating hours on the island digging up details and
talking to people who knew Papa—or claimed to. This led to a
surprising offer from the infamous Bahamian resident; Carlos Lehder,
requesting she write his memoir. His only stipulation was, he would
write the last chapter.

Lehder was the Colombian drug king who operated out of
Normans Cay back in the late 1970s. It was slow going. She was
continually waiting on the first-hand information Lehder promised to
supply, and Buddy's well-being was far more critical than any
potentially lucrative royalty payment. She'd put this aside for now.

As expected, Kat and Stewart argued as they often did over Buddy.

Finally, Stewart agreed to go with her if she would wait until his current court case was over. Kat wasn't willing to wait. She knew that with each passing day, the trail grew colder. Buddy was her twin, and she was determined to be at the abandoned air terminal as he requested.

Stewart was already out of the house early on the morning that Kat was due to leave. There was a note beside the coffee maker: *If you get yourself in trouble, work it out on your own.*

Kat crumpled the note and scooped up Moose, who was rubbing around her ankles begging for his breakfast. "You're going to have to remind Stewart to feed you. I'm going to be gone awhile."

She headed for the airport to fly to Miami. From there she took a twenty-seater passenger plane to the small airstrip on South Bimini. Outside the bright green cinder-block airport, she boarded the rusty, rattletrap van covered with stickers expressing every opinion of the driver. Yellow and blue flags, the colors of the Bahamas Progressive Party, flew from each side. The taxi dropped her at the small open ferry which operated much like a bus service to North Bimini. It was filled with school children and adults who lived on the south island but worked on North Bimini; a quick ten minute ride across the smooth bay.

The ferry tied up at the concrete commercial dock behind the mail boat from Nassau. When Kat disembarked, she stepped into the middle of a frenzy. Bahamian flags flapped from the telephone poles in Alice Town. Store windows and signposts along the waterfront were adorned with Prime Minister Rollins' re-election campaign posters. Speakers in the straw market were belching distorted Bahamian music at a volume well beyond their intended capacity. With no hotel reservation, Kat hoped she hadn't landed in the middle of some celebration that would make it challenging to find accommodations. Hotel space was limited in Alice Town; most vacationers stayed on boats they brought over for fishing or diving.

Kat walked directly to the Compleat Angler Hotel and Bar carrying her backpack and duffle. She loved this rambling old building with its arched stone entrance. Every famous and infamous person who escaped to Bimini had stayed here. The first floor housed the bar, dance floor, and the Hemingway Museum. The walls were lined with framed black and white photos of Papa Hemingway in various sports fishing tournaments in the 1930s, posing with prized sharks and beautiful young women.

Kat pushed open the swinging doors that led directly into the bar where she hoped to find Piccolo Pete, bartender, hotel manager, singer, and friend. Piccolo claimed to have been Hemingway's chair boy, but Kat knew it wasn't so, that would make Piccolo over ninety. She also knew that Piccolo was eager to be the center of any gossip, and he loved an audience so he would tell what he knew—with or without embellishments. If he knew anything about Buddy, he'd talk to her.

Piccolo hadn't heard her come in and she smiled as she watched him stocking the shelves above the bar. He was darker than many Bahamians but Kat knew there was a lot of mixed blood in these islands which had first been settled by the Lucayans Indians and later by Spanish explorers, African slaves, and American loyalists. Skin tones reflected this rich heritage.

Finally, Piccolo saw her reflection in the mirror and spun around. "Mz. Kat, What a surprise. I sure is happy to see you." He reached across the bar and took her small pale hand between his dark ones. His face grew sober. "But I'm sorry for da reason you here. I told dat boy to stay away from them Chinese, but dey money talk too loud to him. And they got plenty of dat. Dey rent out da whole Big Game Club and park a boat so big it can't hardly turn around in Bimini Bay." Piccolo lowered his voice even though there was no one else in the bar. "They got guards to stand at da gate to keep everyone out." Finally, he took a breath.

"Good to see you too, Piccolo." She pulled out a bar stool and dropped her duffle on the floor. "You got a room for me?"

"Mz. Kat, you lucky. I still got Papa's room up on da top where you stay last time. Don't give it out to most folks, only those who respect it. Kinda hot up there now, but lots of people here today. I almost filled up. In fact, now you here, I am filled up."

"Chinese you say?" Kat asked.

"Look like it with them eyes and all."

"Piccolo, I don't know about you, but I'm hot. Can I buy you a beer?"

Piccolo looked around the wood-paneled bar. "Ain't nobody here. Think I might as well." He reached into the cooler and pulled out two Kaliks, pushed one across the bar to Kat, and leaned in toward her.

"Let me tell you Mz. Kat, something big comin' down. I don't rightly know what it is, but Rollins is up for re-election."

"I saw all the campaign signs and flags," Kat said.

"Well, you don't know dis. The Bahamas National Movement is chargin' him with takin' bribes. Gonna be a hot election. Rollins gonna be here dis afternoon with his big-shot boys. *Navy One*, with his bodyguard, already here. He come in here for a Kalik. I think he suppose to be checkin' out security. Mostly he check out hisself in das mirror over da bar. Maybe he want to be sure da beer ain't poison. Course they all stayin' down at Big Game. Guess dis ole place only good enough for drinkin'.'"

Kat took a swig of her beer but didn't say anything.

"You can bet Rollins here ta talk to da Chinks and ta figure out how to line his own pocket with whatever they givin' out. Just like da last PM did in Nassau when them Chinese build dat big ole marina and casino down on Coral Beach. My cousin drive a cab there, and he tell me they even change da road around to make room for dat casino. Ain't no other reason for da PM to come here. He don't ever come to Bimini. Ain't enough votes here."

Kat didn't want to talk about the problems in Nassau. "And the Chinese? Are they staying on their boat?"

"Now Mz. Kat, don't you go gettin' involved with dat. I warnin' you. You brother already dead, along with two of our own."

"I don't know that Buddy's dead. A letter from the High

Commission's Office said they hadn't recovered his body." Kat wrapped her feet around the rungs on the stool.

"Oh, come on now Mz. Kat. Don't go chasin' no dream. He dead alright. I feel it in my bones, and I don't be wrong about death signs. My Mama from Andros, and I got da gift too." He leaned close again. "I also know it weren't no accident."

Even though Kat and Buddy were fraternal twins, Kat believed their twin telepathy was as reliable as Piccolo's gift and her instinct told her Buddy wasn't dead.

"How do you know it wasn't an accident?" she asked. "Who would want him dead?" But Piccolo was finally done talking. He picked up the ashtrays from the bar, wiping them vigorously.

"It don't feel right. Da spirits talk to me, I tell you. Just leave it be."

"Thanks for the warning, Piccolo, but I'm a big girl now. You don't have to look out for me anymore."

"I was always lookin' after you cause you always so busy lookin' after Buddy dat you don't look after yourself. After your Mama die, your Daddy should have found another woman, is what I say. A Mama who mighta take after you with a stick sometime. Not let you and dat boy run wild over dis island while he fish. You betta be happy you got me around."

"I am, I really am, Piccolo." She laughed. "I guess we did get into our share of trouble around here."

"Well, dat Buddy did, along with dat Bimini boy."

"Elliot. Haven't thought about him in a long time. Whatever happened to him?"

"Don't know. What I do know is you was always coverin' up for dem boys."

CHAPTER 7

No one could miss Prime Minister Rollins' arrival. His noisy helicopter set down onto the landing pad, kicking up sand and sweeping clean the rarely used tarmac. The abandoned air terminal was where the little twelve-seat seaplanes from Chalk's airline had once unloaded passengers from Miami. Even before the tourists saw the sign for customs and immigration, they would read the plaque boasting that this was the place where the final scene in *Silence of the Lambs* was filmed. A chilling thought, and in Kat's eyes, hardly a promotion for the fisherman's paradise that Bimini advertised. Now that Chalk's air service was gone, if tourists didn't come by private boat, the only way for them to get to North Bimini was the circuitous route by plane, taxi, and ferry that Kat had taken.

The PM and his talking suits formed a slow-walking entourage heading down to the Big Game Club and Marina. He waved and shook hands as he walked, his smile flashing white teeth against the background of his dark face. A rag-tag band with drums and whistles kept pace and beat out the Goombay rhythm that was unique to the Bahamas.

Kat stepped away from her third-floor window, pulled on her yellow sundress then darted downstairs, and out onto the street. As she ran toward Rollins, an ox of a man wearing an earpiece and mirrored sunglasses stepped between them. Kat took in his gym-built body, wide neck, and shaved head. *He's been watching too many cop shows.* She sidestepped the bodyguard and raised her voice.

"Prime Minister Rollins, I'm Mary Katherine Deano." She grasped his outstretched hand. "You may have seen my articles on the Bahamas in travel magazines."

The PM waved his bodyguard away. Kat was glad she'd remembered to stuff a dress into her duffle bag at the last minute. "Yes, yes, of course, some outstanding writing there, young lady."

Bullshit, but I think I'm in. Kat fell in step beside him. "I wonder if I can take a few minutes of your time to interview you about the election." She gave him her most disarming smile. "I understand you have some exciting new programs to promote tourism and I'd love to be part of that. I think of the Bahamas as my island home."

"Yes, yes, indeed. Absolutely correct. But you're a step ahead of me on that. I'm about to announce my new economic program right here on Bimini. Tonight. Tell you what, I'm hosting a fundraiser down at the Big Game Club. You know where it is, don't you?"

"Of course. I came here often as a child. My father always docked his Cabo 52 at that marina. Love the place."

"Good, good. I'd like you to come as my guest. Don't worry about the one-hundred-dollar donation. I'll see to it your name is on my personal guest list. Most of my cabinet will be there too, including my minister of tourism. You might want to interview him. Give me your card. Starts at six."

Two can play this game. Kat pulled her card from her pocket and handed it to Rollins, dropping her sunglasses as she did. She only partially covered the top of her scooped-neck sundress with one hand as she leaned to pick them up. The PM's eyes focused precisely where she wanted them to. He handed the card to his bodyguard. "Be sure she's seated at my table so we can talk." Then he turned back to Kat. "Perhaps I can give you an exclusive."

"Oh, that's asking too much. But I'd love it, thank you," Kat said, taking his hand. *Politicians with big egos are so easy.* "I look forward to this evening."

She withdrew her hand and moved back into the crowd. *Good first step. Now to steer this from politics to my agenda.*

Kat planned to review the government website which, as she remembered, included photos of all the cabinet members. The six o'clock dinner would give her plenty of time to get to Chalk's old terminal by ten. She was here to find out about Buddy. She needed to stay focused.

At the Big Game Club, Kat was stopped by the guard at the entrance. He checked his clipboard and frowned as he looked her up and down and asked to see her identification. Kat produced her passport and stepped through the scanning device. It all seemed a bit pretentious to her; who on Bimini would be a threat to the Prime Minister? The host's name tag read, Jolton Pinder-Cooper, Family Island Administrator. Dressed in a tuxedo, he politely escorted her to the head table. No one was seated. She glanced at the embossed place cards, only hers was hand-written. She recognized the name beside her. The Honorable Franklin Albury, Minister of The Interior. *At least I won't be the only white face at the table.*

A band was on a makeshift stage at the far end of the room. Kat wasn't surprised to see that Piccolo Pete was the lead singer. He was legendary. Balloons, in the colors of the PM's political party, hung from the ceiling. Kat accepted a flute of champagne and waved to Piccolo Pete who frowned and shook his head as he continued singing into his microphone. The room was hot. The air-conditioning could not compete with the crowd of men dressed in dark business suits, long-sleeved pastel shirts, and bright ties. The women were equally decked out in colorful low-necked gowns. Wearing her short sundress and sandals, Kat was definitely underdressed, but she hadn't expected to attend anything that required more formal attire. No wonder the guard had scowled when she arrived, it wasn't only her white skin and American passport, she had violated the dress code. Kat wondered if the guests, along with most of the band, had been imported from Nassau or Freeport. She had never seen much evidence of affluence on Bimini.

Rollins spotted her and came over with another man. "Let me introduce you to the Honorable Oswald Saunders."

"Minister of Tourism," Kat said before the PM could finish. "I'm glad to meet you." She held out her hand.

"Please, it's Ozzie. Dance?" Ozzie grabbed her hand and pulled Kat onto the floor. Together they moved to the distinctive rhythmic Bahaman sound Kat remembered from the times she and Buddy danced when they were children. Fortunately, the conversation was easy. No questions about what she planned to include in her report. Ozzie was more interested in her than in politics or tourism.

When the music ended, Kat wandered the room, introducing herself, and quizzing the guests about where they were from. As she had surmised, only a few were from Bimini. She hoped to find someone who might mention the boating accident so she could discreetly ask a few questions, but it was not part of any conversation. It was either old news or no news at all. Boating accidents in these waters were not uncommon and were headlines only for a day. But she had a distinct impression that someone was suppressing this particular incident.

Finally, Rollins moved to the head table and clipped a microphone to his lapel. In his booming voice, he called out, "Distinguished guests, ladies, and gentlemen, please be seated." The room became quiet except for the scraping of chairs against the polished wood floor. Rollins pulled some folded papers from his jacket pocket and smoothed them out on the podium.

"Before we begin this beautiful dinner, I have an announcement of economic magnitude for our fortunate, God-blessed islands." He raised his hands as though he was about to receive manna from heaven. "This announcement is so important that I have invited Ms. Mary Katherine Deano, a distinguished member of the American press, to attend our celebration." He turned and nodded at Kat. She smiled weakly and waved in recognition.

Kat was embarrassed to be singled out, but this might work to her advantage. The Bahamas always sought positive attention from the American press; it was good for their economy, and she had learned that people loved to be interviewed with the hopes of seeing their names in print.

Rollins turned to three men on his right. "I present to you, these distinguished representatives from the Korean-based company, Oriental Mineral Resources."

So, Korean, not Chinese. Kat refocused on the PM's speech.

"Oriental Mineral Resources has found rich deposits of rare-earth minerals, especially dysprosium, on one of our family islands." Rollins looked down at his notes. "For those of you who might not know the significance of this find, these minerals are essential for the development of wind turbines, hybrid gasoline-electric cars, electric motor production, and a long list of other green energy industries. The Bahamas will now be part of the future of clean energy!" Rollins bellowed like a seasoned revival preacher. He waited for the expected applause to die down.

"But that's not all. Oriental Mineral Resources has paid the people of the Bahamas very generously for a tract of undeveloped land where they will soon set up mining operations. Unlike China, who mines these minerals for greed, our Korean partners are concerned about our clear, clean, fish-filled waters and the pristine beaches of our archipelago. My Minister of the Interior, The Honorable Mr. Franklin Albury, will ensure that appropriate safeguards and pollution controls are carried out to protect our sacred environment." Rollins acknowledged Albury with a nod. "You have my personal assurance on this." Again, he smiled at the applause, then waved his broad, expressive hands for silence.

"But more importantly, the money will be used to improve the social infrastructure of all the family islands, including, I am pleased to say, the first high school on Bimini." This was followed by long, loud applause. "No longer will our children have to be shipped off to live with relatives in Nassau, Freeport, or Georgetown to finish their education." More applause.

God, who's his speechwriter? Kat had attended many press conferences, and this had all the elements of a well-rehearsed press release. No need for a member of the Bahamian press to cover this; Rollins' office probably had already faxed a copy of his speech for tomorrow's morning edition.

"Where will this mining take place?" A question from the audience. *Ta-da!* Kat held her breath. *This is what I need to know.*

The PM smiled like a teacher addressing a curious but dull student. "Because of the magnitude of this find, the Bahamian government has agreed to keep the location secret. Certainly, you understand the potential conflicts that would arise if this information were made public. We would be swamped with a gold-rush mentality and would find ourselves unable to control mining by improperly licensed companies using open-pit mining, scarring our country, and disregarding the importance of our islands in the sun with their shining waters and sparkling sands. Or worse yet, the onslaught of thieves and crime rings setting up operations within our borders to steal these precious metals from our land and leaving only a black stain on our country. No, fortunately for us, Oriental Minerals have made a very generous offer to our little country, and we will hold the terms of that contract dearly as they move forward in their pursuit of a clean energy future."

Shit. That was planted. Even the questions and applause are part of his script. Kat was sure most of the audience heard these kinds of political promises before or was she being cynical?

"Now, let us all enjoy this wonderful dinner before we break out our best champagne and celebrate with music and dancing."

The air carried a hum of excitement, with the guests more interested in discussing the PM's big news than in the lobster dinner set before them. As the guava duff pudding, coated with hot, sugary-sweet rum sauce, was served, a chorus of school children, all in their uniforms, marched in, stood behind the PM's table, and sang *One*

Nation Moving On. As they filed off, Rollins stood up with a flute of champagne in his hand.

"I'd like to offer a toast to the new future of the children of Bimini."

It had all been well choreographed. As soon as the PM held up his glass, tuxedoed waiters came through the room with trays of champagne. The band broke in with *Red, Red Wine* and guests left their tables to dance. The fanfare cut off any more questions.

Kat danced with several Bahamians she didn't know, but when the band took a break, she made her way back to the head table where the Koreans sat alone, solemnly watching the sensuous dancing. Kat sat down next to the man who had been talking with the Prime Minister. She read his name tag.

"Mr. Lee. I'm Mary Katherine Deano. As the Prime Minister announced, I'm writing an article about his economic programs, and I'm wondering if you'd answer a few questions about the importance of rare-earth minerals to the Bahamas."

"Most certainly," Lee said, smiling broadly.

Kat continued. "Can you elaborate on the value of this discovery?"

She listened impatiently as Mr. Lee repeated much of what the PM had already covered and then said. "I know this has not come without cost to you. I heard the *Ocean Pearl,* ran aground and burned, killing everyone onboard."

"A regrettable accident." Mr. Lee nodded solemnly. "But we have many reports from geologists who assure us of the wisdom of continuing our research and exploration."

This was the opening Kat was waiting for. "I don't know anything about the reports, sir. The Bahamian government has informed me that my brother, Dr. Edwards, was onboard that vessel. He's missing, presumed dead. I hoped you could give me the details about the accident."

Mr. Lee abruptly turned away and conferred with his colleagues. While Kat couldn't understand the words, their expressions said it all.

"The Prime Minister has made a serious mistake." Mr. Lee stood abruptly. "Your presence is not beneficial here." He snatched her arm, led her over to the PM, and interrupted a conversation Rollins was having with his constituents. He spoke softly directly into Rollins' face.

"Prime Minister, this woman is Dr. Edwards's sister. We have what is perhaps a serious problem."

"Is that true?" The PM glared at Kat.

"Yes, but…"

"Let's you and I finish this conversation on the balcony," Rollins said. Without being asked, the Koreans followed them outside.

"Are you trying to make me a fool?" Rollins turned to face Kat. "Trying to pin some unfortunate accident on me? Give Buckley and his Bahamas National Movement reason to accuse me of, of…"

A cover-up? Murder?

"…something that would advance *their* political agenda."

"No sir, this isn't about you. I'm trying to find out about my brother. But if you have any information, I think it's only right that you tell me. I'm not leaving until I get to the bottom of this." She glared back at him.

Rollins took a white handkerchief from his breast pocket and wiped the sweat from his forehead. "I have nothing to say to you. Nothing. Do you hear me? I don't need trouble from your kind. We're trying to do something good here. And I can even assure you that the American government is fully behind this." He paused, breathing rapidly, his nostrils flaring.

I've certainly pushed his button.

The PM turned to his bodyguard, who had finally located them on the balcony. "Isadore, take her out of here. Make sure she stays in her room. I'll talk to her later. You know how to handle this."

"How?" the big man asked. The PM seized his arm, pulled him closer, and whispered in his ear. A shiver of dread spread down Kat's arms. If she made a scene, no telling how much trouble she'd be in. She needed to cooperate and leave the party. It was getting late anyway, and she had to meet Buddy. If he wasn't there, she'd start digging tomorrow and hopefully find more to go on.

The bodyguard grabbed her elbow roughly. "It go better if you don't make no scene."

Kat snatched her arm away. She attempted to cover up the shakiness in her knees with a strong voice. "I'll walk by myself, thank you." She started toward the exit, unaware that Piccolo's eyes had been on her the whole time.

"Where you stayin' at?" Isadore asked. "I'm to take you there."

"I can go by myself. There's only one road, you know."

"Da PMs say I'm to take you. Make sure you stay there."

"Compleat Angler. Know where it is?" She couldn't keep the sarcasm out of her voice.

"Course I do. Been there lots a times."

"Are you always so obedient?"

"Da PM's my boss. I do what he say."

"And what'd he say about me?"

"He say you to stay in your room 'til he come."

CHAPTER 8

The hotel was dark. Isadore's forceful grip around Kat's wrist had numbed her fingers. As Kat stumbled up the stairs beside him, Isadore spoke in a harsh voice. "You be quiet. We goin' to your room. Where da key?"

Isadore snatched the room key from Kat's hand, unlocked the door, and pushed her with such force that she stumbled and fell to her knees, scraping them on the hardwood floor. He slammed the door and locked it from the outside. The old-fashioned lock couldn't be opened without a key, and she no longer had one.

Kat realized the depth of her trouble. Rollins wouldn't want her to report on what she now surmised. Somehow he was linked to Buddy's accident. Was he on the take from Oriental Minerals as Piccolo had suggested? Pacing back and forth, she tried to formulate a plan. Her watch now read nine-fifty, only ten minutes until she was to meet Buddy. Frantically, she dug through her backpack for her phone. *Shit! Totally dead.* The charm of no phone in the hotel room was suddenly a liability. Whirling around, she ran to the window and looked down at the quiet street. The whole town must be at the reception. She slipped off her dress and pulled on shorts and a t-shirt. If she had to run to the old air terminal, shorts and running shoes would be more comfortable. Pressing her ear to the door, she heard whispered voices. The sounds faded, followed by the thud of heavy footsteps in the hall. Gasoline seeped under the door and burst into flames.

"Help! Help! Get me out!" Kat screamed, banging on the door with her fists. Coughing, she stumbled to the window and struggled to haul it up. Her breath came in short bursts. Jumping seemed her only escape. She felt dizzy as she looked down three stories and nothing to break her fall. Piccolo Pete's voice cut through the roar of the flames.

"Mz. Kat, you in there?"

"I'm locked in." Panic filled her voice.

Piccolo burst through the door, a fire extinguisher in one hand, spraying the flames. "Come on. Dis fire start up here. It gonna spread fast but da stairs still open." On the next landing, he shouted. "I gotta stop on da second floor. Make sure no one else here."

"Let me help," Kat coughed.

"No, you don't know all these hallways. I be right behind you. Go on now." He pushed her toward the stairs. "Hurry."

Flames licked the walls as Kat raced down the flights of stairs. Bursting through the door onto the street, she doubled over, gasping for air as two policemen grabbed her roughly and twisted her arms behind her.

"What are you doing?"

"Takin' you to Nassau."

"I haven't done anything," Kat protested.

"Uh-huh. Just start dis fire."

"I didn't start it. Let me go. I was locked in my room." Kat struggled, trying to free herself from their grip.

"Den how come you da only one come out dat door? No one else here."

"Listen, please. Get someone in there. Piccolo Pete's inside." Kat coughed. The air, thick with smoke, burned her eyes and nose.

"Uh-huh, and Santa Claus too. Piccolo's down at the PM's party. He da lead singer. Nobody here but you, girl. You just hush up and be still." The policeman jerked her backpack off and slapped handcuffs on her wrists. "Dis will stop your squirmin'. Dis ain't da U.S. You can get ten years for what you done. Dis ain't gonna go easy on you. Da Hemingway museum is in der."

The fire cast an eerie light over Kat's hot face as she watched the burning building in horror. She hoped Piccolo had escaped through a back door. *Please, God, make sure he gets out safely.* A fire truck was parked nearby and the firefighters were struggling to connect the hose to the rusty old hydrant. They were going to be too late. God, she hoped Piccolo had gotten out some other way.

The police launch roared out of the harbor in the inky darkness. Kat sat in the cockpit with her hands cuffed behind her. The boat turned north skirting the shallow water, and then at North Rock headed east and sped toward Nassau. Kat had no way to brace herself, and each time the boat bounced off the top of the waves, the handcuffs chafed her wrists, and her spine pounded against the hard seat. Soon her head and jaw ached. She tried to reason, but another thought filled her head; she'd missed her rendezvous with Buddy. This was insane, but Piccolo could verify her story. She lost track of time, then she heard massive diesel engines behind them.

The two-way radio hissed "*Intercept Four, Intercept Four,* dis is *Navy One.* Ya read me?" She knew the voice; it was Isadore.

"We read ya."

"Kill da engines, drop fenders, and prepare lines to raft up."

Navy One thumped against the side of the police boat with such force that Kat lost her balance and fell to the floor, banging her already bleeding knees. Isadore dropped a metal boarding ladder to the smaller boat and yelled down. "I'm takin da woman from here. Give her to me and head back to Bimini. Those da orders from da PM."

One of the policemen pulled Kat to her feet, and as he unlocked her handcuffs, she rubbed her raw wrists. "Listen to me," Kat pleaded. "He started that fire. He locked me in my room."

"Now dat be a good story. Da PM's right-hand man. He head of security. Who you gonna blame next? Well, you got lots of time to make up a story on your ride to Nassau. Have fun." The policeman laughed and shoved her toward the ladder.

As Kat reached the top, Isadore seized her arm and hauled her onboard. He threw her across the deck and slammed her against the side of the cabin. Her shoulder burned from pain. She watched as the policemen on *Intercept Four* cast off the lines, re-started their engines, and turned back. *Okay. Breathe. He's got to get me to Nassau in one piece. How bad can it get?* Isadore answered her unspoken question.

"Say your prayers. You goin' overboard, shark bait."

Isadore grabbed her around the waist. Kat snatched the rail on the cabin top with both hands. "I can't swim!"

"Wouldn't matter no way." Isadore yanked her hands loose and tossed her overboard. Kat thrashed around and then sank. Surfacing, she struggled, took a deep breath, and then sank again.

Through the dark water, she heard the throb of the engines and used all the strength in her legs to push away from the hull, away from the lethal propellers. She kicked off her shoes, surfaced for another breath, and watched *Navy One* gain speed.

Kat lied about not being able to swim. Treading water, she scanned the surface, hoping desperately to see something, anything. Bobbing under a mantle of stars, Kat spotted one light near the horizon brighter than the others. She remembered her father telling her sailboats couldn't cross The Bank in one day. *Could it be the anchor light of a sailboat?* It was her only chance. Trying to calm the panic rising in her chest that choked off her breath, Kat repeated in her head, *It is a sailboat. It is a sailboat.* She had to believe it or the fear of failure would threaten the smooth, steady strokes she needed for survival. As the sound of the big engines faded into the night, she felt lonelier than she had in her entire life.

That was the story Kat told Carter.

CHAPTER 9

"Now you know everything I do. Everything that happened before you picked me up," Kat said. Carter was silent, adjusting the sails. *Wind Chaser* heeled comfortably to starboard and the sails filled with an easterly breeze.

"Say something," Kat begged.

"Unbelievable," Carter responded.

"You don't believe me." As tense as she was, her shoulders collapsed.

"I didn't say that. I just said what happened to you was unbelievable. Just as a start, the police never should have accused you of setting that fire without some evidence. But as they said, this isn't the U.S., and with Rollins on the island, I think they were looking for a quick fix."

"And Piccolo Pete is dead," Kat said. "What are you going to do when you get to Nassau?"

Carter knew she meant; are you going to turn me over to the police? He could check her story on the internet; she'd given him enough details. But he had no way to verify any of her statements until he was docked in a marina.

Carter pushed his hair out of his eyes. "I think for the moment the best thing is for you to hide on my boat until we figure something out. Everyone thinks I'm alone on *Wind Chaser*, we'll leave it at that."

Kat went below to nap, leaving Carter at the helm mulling over his options.

If her story doesn't match up, I can turn her in. I've lied to Manny, but if I help capture her, he should go easy on me. If I let her off and she disappears into the slums of Nassau or manages to get out of the Bahamas, I lose my bargaining power. And if she's telling the truth, maybe her money will help me keep Wind Chaser, *at least for a while longer. There's got to be some alternative to dropping her and moving on.*

By four o'clock Carter spotted the new monstrous casino-resort on Cable Beach which dominated the skyline west of Nassau. Then the garish pink Atlantis hotel on Paradise Island came into view. Through his binoculars, he picked out two multistoried cruise ships and the two high bridges that spanned the harbor. He called Nassau Harbor Control for permission to enter before he passed every sailor's true mark of the northwest entrance; the familiar whitewashed lighthouse on the tip of Paradise Island. He and Claire had climbed it every time they hung around Nassau while Becca provisioned for the next charter. Even though it was abandoned and in crumbling decay, Claire never tired of pretending she was the lighthouse keeper guiding clipper ships in the 1800s.

Carter was told to stand off, one of the cruise ships was about to leave. *Wind Chaser* would have to wait until the floating hotel cleared the channel. Carter visualized the sunburned tourists with beaded corn-rows in their hair crowding the decks laden with souvenirs from the straw market, cheap t-shirts, and Cuban cigars. The ship's horn echoed the entire length of Bay Street, but it wasn't the regular three blasts this horn played. It boomed *It's a Small World*. Claire used to love it, and the first time Carter heard it he laughed, but it got old very quickly and made him feel like he was in Disney World rather than Nassau.

Carter pulled *Wind Chaser* alongside the empty fuel dock at Nassau Harbor Club and filled with diesel. The current running through harbor made docking difficult even in light wind, and his exhaustion made it worse. He handed the diesel hose back to the dockhand. "I need a slip for just one night. Got one?"

"No problem, mon, Go into slip twenty-four. Westside. Put's your bow into da wind, it be easier dat way."

"Can you give me a hand with my lines? I'm solo."

"You got it mon, I be on da finger pier. If you can throw 'em, I can catch 'em."

With *Wind Chaser* safely tied in the slip, Carter plugged in the power cord, walked up the dock, and signed in at the marina office. The next thing he wanted to do was discreetly see what he could find out about Mary Katherine Deano and maybe her twin, Dr. Dwight Edwards. As tired as he was, he couldn't sleep until he had more information about his fugitive.

The opaque privacy shades were lowered over the ports; Kat was washing the lunch dishes. He looked at her bare feet and realized she'd need clothes and shoes, but that could come later.

"Kat, I'm going across the street to Harbor Thyme Cafe to check my email, internet's not reliable here. I'll be back shortly. Stay out of sight."

The rich aroma of fresh ground coffee filled the café. Boaters checking email or Bahamians conducting business occupied almost every table. Carter placed his order with an eager, smiling barista who seemed disappointed that all he wanted was black coffee. He found an unoccupied table in the corner and unpacked his computer.

Online, he found that the first part of Kat's story checked out. She was a very prolific and respected investigative reporter, frequently wrote on events in the Bahamas, married to Stewart Deano, and the daughter of the famous General Edwards. More importantly, for Carter, she probably did have money. He scrolled further down. There was a link to her writing about Hemingway, but he didn't take time to read it. What did catch his attention was the mention of her name in an article in a local Florida paper entitled *Youthful First Offenders: Jail Time or Rehab?* The report was several years old. It was probably something minor; she hadn't mentioned it. He skipped over it and typed in *Compleat Angler.* There was no mention of the fire or Piccolo's death; the website hadn't been updated. Apparently, Bahamians still depended on the paper or TV for breaking news.

Before he left the coffee shop, he swiped a *Nassau Guardian* from an empty table. There it was. The lead story on the front page was all about Rollins' visit to Bimini, and on page two the headline read: *Compleat Angler Burns.* There were pictures of the building before it burned and another one after the fire; just a stone chimney and fireplace left standing among smoldering timbers and ruins.

Embedded in the article was a picture of Peter "Piccolo Pete" Moxey stating that he died in the fire while attempting to rescue tourists staying at the hotel. The possibility of arson had been raised, but there was no lead to any suspect and no mention of anyone seen leaving the building. Were the police assuming Kat had drowned and were covering this up? Or was this a ploy so she would unwittingly show her whereabouts? He didn't know, but for the moment, he was inclined to believe Kat was telling the truth. He tucked the newspaper into his backpack and headed back to the marina.

As he started down the dock, two men dressed in gray slacks, sport coats, and hard-soled shoes, walked toward him. Definitely not tourists or yachties, they looked out of place. *God, the bankers.* There was no way Carter could pass them or turn around without raising suspicion.

"Hey there," the first one said, flashing an over-friendly smile. "You have a boat here?"

"Yeah, why?" The man flashed his I.D. and handed Carter a business card.

"Can we ask you some questions?"

Carter looked at the card in his hand; Agent Brian Scofield, U.S., Drug Enforcement Administration, Caribbean Field Division, Miami. Carter was momentarily relieved. This wasn't about his boat.

Scofield handed him a photo. "Have you seen this girl?"

"Why are you asking me?"

"We're asking everyone, in particular, anyone who appears to be American."

White, you mean. Carter thought to himself.

"She may be in a bit of trouble. She's American, and we think it's logical that she will try to contact other Americans for help."

"Really? Why wouldn't she go to the U.S. Embassy?"

"She may have the impression that the embassy won't help her. She's been on our watch list in the U.S., but suddenly she skipped out to the Bahamas, and we've lost her."

"Terrorist watch list?"

"No, nothing like that, but if you run into her, best not to approach her; it might just spook her. Call us. Honestly, we're here to protect her."

Something didn't seem right to Carter. There was nothing in the paper about her. How had they tracked her? Were they really DEA? He had certainly never heard of a Caribbean Field Division. And protecting her from what?

Carter studied the photo again. "She looks like a lot of the American girls crewing on boats around here. But if I see anyone who looks like this, I'll let you know."

"That would be a big help. That's my cell phone." Scofield pointed to the card. "You can reach me at any time."

Carter remained where he was and watched the two men continue down the dock, stopping to question another cruiser. He wasn't sure what to tell Kat. At the very least, the encounter left him doubting the wisdom of his decision to hide her, even for a couple of days. He climbed down the companionway stairs and silently handed Kat the newspaper. As she read the articles in detail, Carter thought over his conversation with Agent Scofield. What would bring in the U.S. DEA? It wouldn't be about the fire. He wanted to believe that Kat, or perhaps her brother, had inadvertently stepped into something sinister, possibly an international drug operation, but this Scofield guy acted like she was already involved in something in the States.

Carter wished he'd read the article that mentioned her as a youthful offender. He hardly knew her and knew nothing about her brother except what she'd told him. She seemed sincere, but her presence was becoming a threat to him. He didn't want any unnecessary focus on himself or *Wind Chaser.*

"I don't get it. Why no mention of me?" Kat asked.

"Huh?"

Kat waved the paper at him. "This says no suspect. They were certainly ready to blame me yesterday. Why's my name not here? You heard that police captain, what's-his-name…"

"Manny."

"Yeah, him. He certainly considered me a suspect." She paused, drumming the table with her fingers. "Maybe it's good if they think I'm dead; it could make my investigation easier. And I do intend to investigate this, both Buddy's disappearance and this fire. I don't want to go back, but right now, I don't see any safe way to stay in the Bahamas. I need to convince Stewart to come soon."

"If you tell him the whole story, I'm sure he'll change his plans."

"Maybe." Kat twisted a lock of her short hair.

Carter made a decision. He wasn't going to mention his encounter on the dock. After all, it wasn't his problem. He had a better plan. "I think I can make you a deal that will benefit both of us," Carter said. "I desperately need money, and you need a safe place to stay until your husband gets here. After I provision and pick up stuff for you at the shopping center, I'll go out to Rose Island and drop anchor. It's close enough for cell phone coverage so you can be in touch with Stewart and it's unlikely that anyone will bother us there. I can always bring you back in the dinghy. If you can get Stewart to bring enough cash, I know a pilot who will fly you back without a passport. Just don't ask any questions about his other cargo. Are you willing to get dropped at an abandoned airstrip in Florida?"

"Sure."

Carter watched her reaction; flying with a drug runner didn't faze her.

"But the problem is, Stewart would never agree to risk his stellar reputation," Kat said.

"He can fly back commercial. It's getting you out that's the problem."

"I don't want to go back without answers, but if I have to, I'm willing. It could be fun."

"It won't be cheap," Carter said.

"Any idea how much?"

"A couple thousand at least."

"And staying on your boat? What will that cost?"

"A thousand a day."

"I only want to charter, not buy it."

"For a boat this size with a captain, that's quite fair. I'm taking a risk having you onboard."

"And as you pointed out, it's off-season. Eight hundred."

"Deal."

Before Carter could say anything more, he heard a familiar voice outside.

"Capt'n Carter? You onboard?" It was Roosevelt, the dockmaster.

Carter knew Roosevelt well; he had managed the marina for as long as Carter had been coming to Nassau and was the most competent dockmaster Carter knew. He could catch a line and tie up a boat under any weather conditions. Not wanting to put Roosevelt in a compromising position, Carter stepped onto the dock. Roosevelt grabbed him in a bear hug, slapping him on the back.

"Capt'n Carter, sure is good to have you back. But I do miss dat little brown-eyed gal a yours."

"I know, it's not the same." Carter quickly changed the subject. "What's happening around here?"

"Can't rightly say, but police been down here goin' on boats. They gone now, but I reckon they be back tomorrow. Don't say what they after."

"Drugs probably."

Roosevelt shook his head. "Don't think so. Des guys from da detective unit, not drug enforcement. I know all dos guys." Carter was one of the few people who knew Roosevelt was a police informant intent on cleaning up the never-ending drug trade in Nassau. Carter wanted to tell him about his encounter with the DEA, but not within earshot of Kat.

"Maybe somethin' on da TV tonight." A voice crackled over Roosevelt's handheld radio. "Dat be *Bright Star* comin' in now. Dey definitely not bright and not a star neither. Gotta run before dey try to tie up on their own and ram my dock and tear it up like last time. Catch you later, mon. We grab a Kalik."

CHAPTER 10

Carter ducked into the cabin where Kat was chewing the end of a pencil, still studying the paper. She looked up. "So, Capt'n Carter," she said, imitating Roosevelt's accent. "A little brown-eyed gal, sounds like you have a girl in every port. I should've known, as much time as you spend island hopping. Hope I'm not cramping your style."

"I don't have any style," he snapped. "You don't know anything about me and I sure as shit don't know anything about you." He turned abruptly and climbed the companionway stairs. Kat felt the boat rock as he jumped onto the dock and was gone.

God. What brought that on? She hadn't meant to provoke his anger. He was right, she didn't know his style, but he had seemed so unflappable. She didn't dare go after him, that would only endanger both of them. Anyway, he'd have to come back sooner or later; *Wind Chaser* was his home.

As seven o'clock approached, she made spaghetti Bolognese and picked over the last of the vegetables to put together a salad. She wasn't much of a cook, but this she could do, and after all he'd done for her, maybe it would make him see how badly she felt teasing him.

By dark, he still wasn't back. Was he hoping she'd be gone or asleep before he returned? If he had changed his mind about taking her to Rose Island, she'd leave. She had no idea why he was so angry, but she wanted the chance to apologize. A thought struck her. As children, she and Buddy dressed in each other's clothes. It was a child's game, but worth a try. She dumped out the cold noodles and searched through Carter's clothes. She found a hoodie and a cap that said *Treasure Cay, Abacos* across the front, slipped on a pair of his jeans and gathered them around her waist with a short piece of line. Dressed in the oversized clothes, pants dragging on the ground, she could pass as a teenage boy. Avoiding the dock lights, she headed first to the marina bar.

Kat found Carter leaning against the scarred counter, nursing a beer. Two shot glasses and empty beer bottles filled the space in front of him. He rolled another bottle between his hands and ignored the couples dancing on the sand floor.

"Uncle Carter! I've been lookin' all over for you. You ain't got shit to eat on that boat. I'm hungry. Buy me some food or give me some money."

Carter looked up, blinked slowly, and tried to focus. He stared at the kid who took his picture with a cell phone.

"Jesus, you look, like, wasted man. Mom's gonna love this. She sends me on this boring trip because you'd be a good influence on me. Can't wait till she sees this. I'll be on a plane home tomorrow."

Carter stared. With the baseball cap covered by the oversized hoodie, he really couldn't see her face, but it had to be Kat, and she seemed intent on making a scene. She swiped the nearly empty beer from Carter's hand, tipped it up, and took a swig. As she wiped her mouth on her sleeve, she pointed at the ceiling. Bras and panties hung from the bare rafters, many of them signed and dated. "Lots of bare ta-tas out there somewhere. Now I get why you like it here."

By now the exchange had the attention of the tattooed bartender who turned from the bleached-blond tourist who was chatting him up. "Hey kid, you can't be in here. Go on now."

"Don't call me, kid," Kat said. "I'm not the one shit-faced drunk. Tell him to go." Kat jerked her thumb toward Carter.

"Okay, that's enough," the bartender said. "Show a little respect. We all have bad days."

"Whatever. I'm out of here." Kat slammed the beer bottle on the bar. "You comin' or what?"

Carter continued to stare. Kat leaned close to his face. "Blink if you hear me."

"Right," Carter mumbled. He threw some money on the bar and stumbled after Kat. From under the hood, she glared at him.

"Do you even know where the boat is? Jesus, think you can manage without falling in the water? I swear, I'm not pulling you out."

Back in the privacy of the boat, Kat pulled off the hoodie and cap. Carter sat down at the dinette and put his head in his hands. Now Kat's anger was real.

"Okay, I know that was risky, but if you're going to get all black on me, I deserve to know what I'm doing wrong. What topics are off-limits? Remember, we made a deal. If you've changed your mind and want out of it, say so."

Carter raised his head, clenching his hands as though that would hold him together. "Roosevelt was talking about my daughter Claire. She died nearly a year ago, a brain tumor. Friday would have been her tenth birthday."

"Oh God." Kat put her fist in her mouth, her eyes wet with tears.

Carter took a deep breath and started. "When Claire started treatment, we moved off the boat and rented a small house on one of the canals in Fort Lauderdale. She was so brave through all the chemo and radiation. I think she knew she wasn't going to get better even before either Becca or I were willing to admit it. She made one last request. She wanted to go dancing in Bimini. She insisted on staying on *Wind Chaser* one more time.

"Before we went, Becca took her shopping to buy a wig. Her own hair had been long and straight, brown like yours, but now she wanted to look like Little Orphan Annie. She thought she looked adorable, but all I can remember is that pale little face under all that curly red hair. I tied up the boat at Brown's dock, walked down the street to clear customs, and stopped at the Compleat Angler to make sure the *Calypsonians* were playing that evening. Claire loved to dance, and Piccolo Pete always played her requests."

"Carter, I was a jerk."

Carter didn't hear her interruption. "We arrived early so she could be close to the band and sat on one of the benches that lined the walls. After listening for a while, she requested *Yellow Bird* and asked me to dance with her. She couldn't make it through the entire song, so I picked her up, and she wrapped her thin little arms around my neck. The words to that song are now unbearable. That one dance exhausted her, but she wanted to stay to hear Piccolo sing. She lay down on the bench and put her head in my lap. Since Piccolo was singing, some other asshole was in charge, a man whose ambitions matched his poor judgment. He told us in no uncertain terms that lying on the bench was not allowed. She was nine years old, for God's sake! Not some drunken college kid. I wanted to slug him. I just picked her up and carried her back to the boat to spend what was to be her last night on *Wind Chaser*."

Carter's words tumbled out. Once he started talking, he couldn't stop.

"The tumor was deep. Soon she couldn't walk without help or even feed herself. Her speech was affected, and her swallowing. But the light in her eyes never went out—not until the end. I'd sit next to her bed and watch her whimper in her sleep. She was just a little girl, she didn't deserve this. Finally, the doctors said there was nothing more to do, and we brought her home. We had gone through our savings. I took out a loan and put *Wind Chaser* up as collateral. I had a chance to bring a boat back from Nassau for good money. It would only be for three days. Becca encouraged me to go; pushed me to go. Said I needed the break, we needed the money, and there was nothing I could do for Claire. She slept most of the time and Becca would be with her.

"I rethink that decision so often. It's a mistake I can never put right. How many times I wish I hadn't agreed, but I convinced myself I would still have time with Claire or maybe I did want to get away. I managed to rouse her before I left. Her speech was slurred, but I understood every word she said. 'Don't worry Daddy, I'll wait for you. I'll be here when you get back. I love you.' Those were the last words she ever said to me. I flew to Nassau to bring that boat back. On the return, I anchored on The Bank, not so far from where I picked you up. That night around two o'clock, I heard the lonely scream of a seagull. I knew she had slipped away from me. I couldn't reach Becca; I had no phone coverage. All I could do was lay on the bunk and sob until daylight."

The cabin was dark, the only glow was the dock light shining through the hatch and the only sound, the muted lapping of the water against the hull. Hesitantly, Kat touched his arm.

"Carter, maybe it doesn't mean much to you, but if you hadn't been out there last night, I wouldn't be sitting here today. You couldn't save your daughter, but you saved me. Do whatever you need to do to keep *Wind Chaser*. I won't stand in your way."

Drunk and emotionally drained, Carter fell into an exhausted sleep. Kat couldn't sleep. They had come full circle; she knew his ghosts, and he knew hers. Maybe it would be better if they only knew a bit about each other. She couldn't imagine what might result from the weight of what they'd shared so early in their relationship. Would it bond them, or tear them apart? Since pulling her from the water, he had appeared so competent, so knowledgeable, so in control. Now she was witness to his vulnerable side, a side he probably never intended to share with her. But life had thrown them together and, at least for now, they were dependent on one another.

CHAPTER 11

Carter woke to the smell of coffee. His head ached, and his mouth was dry. Despite feeling hungover, some part of him was eager to get up, and the thought of strong black coffee drew him out of his cabin.

Bacon popped in the frying pan as Kat cracked eggs into another one. Carter sat at the dinette quietly looking over the rim of his mug nursing the coffee Kat had set before him. She didn't need to do this. Was this how she dealt with stress? He didn't know. He was the one who needed to apologize. He felt guilty about unloading on her last night, embarrassed by his mood swing that had nothing to do with her. She didn't need to know his problems; she had more than enough of her own. He choked up when he looked at her; bare feet, same clothes as yesterday, bruised and cut, a missing twin, and criminal accusations. Yet she hadn't complained.

For now, there was nothing but him and his boat standing between her and no-telling-what. Such a slender reed to lean on. At best she'd go to prison in Nassau. Maybe her husband or father could pull some strings and arrange a change of venue to the U.S. He didn't know about these things. But he did know the women's prison in Nassau was no place for her, not even for a short time. He'd heard plenty of stories. She'd be bullied, assaulted, even raped.

"I've been thinking," Carter said. "That was a pretty good act in the bar last night, but you took a real risk. From what Roosevelt said yesterday, the police may be hunting for you. They're searching the marinas." The conversation with the DEA was still lurking in Carter's mind. "I think it's best if I take you back to the States as quickly as possible. You shouldn't wait on Stewart. Whatever you need to do, you can do it from there. If you get caught here, I'm caught as well. We both go to jail."

"I'd never snitch on you. You saved my life."

"That's beside the point. If the authorities find you in Nassau, it won't take long before they realize I brought you here. Unless they think you swam eighty miles. You heard that radio transmission; all the boats coming off The Bank were searched. *Wind Chaser* is probably the only one that wasn't. And it's not just you and me. By all rights, Manny should have searched my boat; he'll be in trouble too."

"So what's your plan?" Kat asked, placing the dished-up breakfast in front of him.

Carter's stomach growled in anticipation. He hadn't realized how hungry he was. They had both missed dinner.

"I'll leave here tonight out of the east end of the harbor, as I said, but instead of anchoring at Rose Island, we'll stay in the wide, deep water north of the Berry Islands and head back. That takes longer, but it's less traveled and safer."

"You said you'd lose your boat if you go back. I don't want to get in your way."

"You won't. I'll come in at night, quietly drop anchor, and take you ashore in my dinghy. After that, you're on your own. I'll slip back out and be on my way again before anyone knows I'm there."

"Where will I be?"

"I think Lake Worth Inlet will work best. It's easy to navigate in the dark. You'll be in Rivera Beach, unless you'd prefer to wade ashore at the Breakers in Palm Beach."

"Don't think I'm dressed for that."

"Since I fueled yesterday," Carter continued. "All I need to do today is buy some food and pick up some stuff for you."

"I can't thank you enough."

"My money won't go far, but you'll need a change of clothes. And sneakers. Better yet boat shoes, if I can find them."

"Sunglasses. I lost those too. Can you find sunglasses?"

"Probably. Becca would have known where to shop."

"You'll do fine."

At nine that night, Carter started the engine. Leaving it to warm up, he stepped onto the dock to throw off the lines. The lights and music from the Poop Deck momentarily distracted him. A noisy mix of tourists and Bahamians filled the open-air marina restaurant. He imagined Kat and himself among them enjoying a dinner of fresh grouper, peas and rice, and coleslaw, listening to island music, and drinking cold beer. Instead, they were heading out, facing an exhausting forty-eight hours at sea.

A voice behind him made him jump. "Where you goin' dis time of night?"

"Hey Manny, I thought I'd anchor out at Rose Island, save a little money."

"Before you go, we need to talk. Can I come aboard?"

"I need to get out while the tide's slack. Can we talk here?"

"Tide ain't slack yet," Manny said. "Besides, I think dis be better said in private."

"Okay." Carter spoke loudly. "Let me retie these lines. Won't take me more than a minute." Carter took as long as possible retying his lines, stepped onboard, and shut down the engine. He heard scuffling below and hoped Manny hadn't noticed, but he was afraid his behavior was too obvious.

It wouldn't have mattered. Manny already knew about the scene Carter's nephew caused at the bar, and he also knew Carter didn't have a nephew. Carter quickly glanced around as they climbed down into the cabin. He didn't see Kat, but Manny walked straight to the galley and picked up the two plastic wine glasses that were lying in the sink, traces of red wine in both of them. He cocked his head and looked at Carter while holding the glasses.

"You and Mz. Deano need to come with me."

Carter stared.

Manny returned his gaze. "You gotta trust me on dis, Carter."

"Give me a couple of minutes."

"No more than dat. I'm in a white Toyota Corolla in front of da marina. Mz. Deano might want to put dat hoodie on again. Not everyone know she here."

Carter felt the boat shift as Manny stepped onto the dock. He waited until his footsteps faded before he unlatched Kat's hiding compartment.

"God, I'm sorry," she whispered. "This is my fault."

"Come on, we've got to meet Manny." He tossed her his hoodie. "Put this on."

As Kat followed Carter up the companionway stairs, she grabbed his cell phone from the table and slipped it in her pocket.

Carter tried to keep his bearings as Manny drove the old non-descript Toyota at speeds that wouldn't attract attention. They drove away from Bay Street, leaving the tourist area, and made their way south of town, down narrow, dusty streets lined with small frame houses, sagging porches, and yards scattered with children's toys. The area, still known as Over-the-Hill, was built by descendants of freed African slaves. Most of the people who lived here now were maids, kitchen help, or laborers, and rode the hot, crowded buses back and forth to work in the wealthy parts of the city. This was the part of Nassau tourists didn't see. Manny continued to a deserted industrial area that Carter didn't know and pulled up in front of a large concrete warehouse surrounded by weeds.

Manny keyed a garage door opener clipped to the sun-visor and a heavy metal door rolled up. After pulling the car inside, he slid out and opened the back door. Kat flinched as he tugged on her already bruised arm. "Come on, you 'bout to meet up with Prime Minister Rollins. Again."

"This has nothing to do with Carter, let him go," Kat said.

"That's not my decision," Manny replied.

They entered a room that looked like it had once been a boardroom for a down-and-out corporation; flickering recessed fluorescent lights, water-stained ceiling tiles, and cheap, light wood-paneled walls. Manny motioned to them to sit at the side of a long, battered conference table. He paced back and forth glancing at the wall clock, the only decoration in the room.

Kat looked around but didn't sit. "Can I go to the women's room? Or are we prisoners here?"

"No one's under arrest. Right down da hall on da left. But hurry, dis go better if you don't keep da Prime Minister waitin'."

CHAPTER 12

As Kat returned, she heard the warehouse door open, a car drive in, and its engine shut off. The entrance to the conference room opened, and she immediately recognized the man in faded khaki pants and navy windbreaker. Pushing back her chair, she whispered, "Prime Minister Rollins." Carter stood.

"You know Mz. Deano," Manny said to the PM. "And dis is Carter McDowell, owner of da sailboat, *Wind Chaser.*" Rollins didn't offer his hand; he only nodded and motioned for Kat and Carter to be seated.

"Thank you, Manny. You can wait for them at the weapons vault." The PM dropped heavily into the chair and ran his hand over his graying hair. He switched on a recorder and stared at Kat a moment before he spoke. "Do you know why you're here?"

"No."

"Let's start with you giving me your version of what happened after you left the banquet."

"You mean when I was escorted out—at your request?"

Rollins ignored her comment. "I want to hear what happened. I don't know all of it."

"If you're accusing me of something, I want to have a lawyer present." Kat stood. In her line of work, she was used to confrontational questioning, but she was usually the one framing the questions. She wasn't about to cave in, not even to a Prime Minister.

"Sit back down. You're not accused of anything young lady, and you're not in the U.S. Please listen a minute. We think what happened after you left the banquet may be a part of a much bigger problem."

"Bigger than an attempt to murder me?"

"Will you listen?" Irritation sounded in the PM's voice. "To answer you, yes, this well may be bigger than an attempt on your life. I want your help, but first, are you willing to keep this conversation confidential? At this point, very few know anything about what I am going to tell you, and I want to keep it that way." His gaze shifted between Kat and Carter.

Kat placed her elbows on the table. "What do I get out of it?" she asked.

"There will be no charges brought against you, and I'll do my best to find out what happened to your brother. I assume that's still your interest."

"You know it is. He's the reason I came here in the first place."

"So you say."

"I want one more thing," Kat continued.

"Go ahead."

"I want your guarantee you won't bring any charges against Carter McDowell."

"Done."

The PM looked at Carter. "Captain Carter, we're going to need your help, so I need your word that you'll keep this confidential also."

Carter hesitated; he wasn't sure he had a choice. Both Manny and Rollins knew where *Wind Chaser* was and that he hadn't cleared in. "I'm not sure what's going on, but I agree."

Rollins turned back to Kat. "Mrs. Deano, describe to me in detail what happened from the moment you were notified of your brother's accident until now."

"Why is all of this so important?" Kat asked.

"I'm not sure, but humor me. Your description of these events may be significant."

Kat told Rollins a shorter version of the one she had related to Carter, leaving out the personal details and focusing on what had happened on Bimini and *Navy One.*

As she finished, Rollins took off his glasses and wiped his tired eyes. "We may be dealing with people who don't understand western values. In our country, we don't murder people because they become inconvenient."

"Well, Isadore Jones sure tried to murder me, at your direction it seems—twice."

"I gave no such order, and for your information, Isadore and *Navy One* are missing."

"Am I supposed to be upset about that?"

Rollins didn't answer.

"Have you questioned your Korean partners?" Kat asked. "And are they North Korean by any chance?"

"Yes they are, and no we haven't questioned them yet. We have to be very careful here. North Korea has recently begun investing in other countries. They've promised to inject millions into our economy. We can't cause them to be offended or lose face unless we have substantial evidence. And at the moment we don't have any motive."

"Oh, unlike arresting Americans on trumped-up charges," Kat said, leaning forward again. "Whose country has been supporting the Bahamas for years now?"

"Can you *please* let me finish? First, you're not under arrest and secondly, why would the Koreans do anything to undermine their project? After you fell overboard, do you know which way *Navy One* headed?"

"After your *Ox* threw me overboard."

Rollins exploded. "The election is only a few weeks away, and I have some powerful, unethical competition. You may think this is self-centered, but if I lose that election, the Bahamas lose. Let's get this straight. You must be aware that, so far, there has been no mention of you in the news. None at all. Who do you think has made sure your name hasn't come up? Now, please ignore how you got overboard and answer my question."

"I'm relieved to know I'm working for the good guys. I'd hate to think what might happen if the bad guys were in office. But, which way *Navy One* headed was not my primary focus at the moment I was *thrown* in the water. I don't remember it turning, so Isadore probably continued east. That's all I know, so keep your promise and let us go."

"You must know more than that. Think. Why would anyone want you dead?"

"Because I had become politically inconvenient to your re-election?"

The PM slammed his fist down on the table. Kat jumped. "I told you I gave no such order." He leaned toward her. "If I had wanted you dead, there would have been other ways. I would never authorize burning the Compleat Angler. We lost a national treasure. Ernest Hemingway, Martin Luther King, Adam Clayton Powell, Jimmy Buffet, Gary Hart, Donna Rice; the list goes on and on."

"And don't forget Piccolo Pete," Kat added.

Rollins leaned back in his chair. "Okay, here's what I think; Isadore, my asshole son-in-law, is or was on the take from someone. Maybe the Koreans, maybe not. Whoever they are, they want you dead. Why? For your safety and for me, tell me what you know."

"I know there are no rare-earth minerals where the Koreans were searching. My brother is a competent and honest geologist. He was confident there were none."

Rollins pursed his lips and drummed the table. "Impossible. They have to be there."

"Well, not where Buddy was working," Kat said. "I had a text from him about a week or ten days before the accident telling me how disappointed he was that there were no rare-earth minerals and he would be flying back as soon as he booked a flight. Obviously, that didn't happen."

Rollins rubbed his temples. "We already have their first payment of fifty million dollars. North Korea may be an isolated county, but they're not idiots." He hesitated. "If your brother is…was…correct, this is totally beyond my comprehension. Understand, I'm not accepting your statement, just adding it to an already puzzling mix. Anyway, it doesn't change my plan for you and Captain Carter."

"Which is?"

"I want you to serve as a decoy."

"Oh, death by fire, drowning, and now I can add shooting to the murder plots."

"I'll give you adequate protection. The CIA is sending two top-notch U.S. federal agents. They'll pose as a couple who have chartered the boat. You'll pick them up in Georgetown."

Carter had been listening to the back-and-forth argument. He had never met Prime Minister Rollins, and while he assumed Rollins had been educated in the U.S., he was surprised that Rollins had no trace of his native Bahamian dialect, at least not while talking with them. Carter slid forward in his chair, his shirt clung to his back from the heat or nerves, he wasn't sure which. He started to say something, then stopped. Kat seemed to be doing fine on her own. She didn't need his support.

Rollins continued, "We want you to be conspicuous. Draw out whoever is behind this. Then we'll know if it's the Koreans or someone else. As you heard me say in Bimini, mining rare-earth minerals here could be very lucrative for the Bahamas and whoever has mining control."

"And if I'm not willing?"

"We still have the ongoing investigation into the fire and Piccolo Pete's death."

"This sounds like blackmail."

"You weren't very straightforward either about your reason for coming to the banquet. Writing for a travel magazine and interested in my incentives to promote tourism, if I remember correctly." They glared at each other.

"Just a minute," Carter broke in. "I have a say in this too. Why me and my boat?"

"I have my reasons," Rollins said. "So, don't even think about leaving the Bahamas until we get this sorted out. Your bank would love to know where you are on that boat."

"Then you also know I don't have the money to just wander around these islands with Kat and two spies onboard."

"I was coming to that. We're prepared to pay off your loan once this investigation is finished and give you the necessary money to cover expenses. After all, there's a minimal risk involved."

"Minimal?" Kat interjected.

Rollins continued to address Carter. "Here's $10,000. Cash." He opened his briefcase, pulled out a large stack of U.S. currency, and put it on the table. "This is for the first month."

Carter eyed the money. Owning *Wind Chaser* free and clear was beyond anything he ever imagined. All he had to do was agree to provide transportation for Kat while she carried out her investigation. That sounded simple enough.

"Your website says you have a crew member. You can use Kat for that. Oh," Rollins said, reaching back into his briefcase, "Here are your papers showing you cleared in. You may need these."

"So," Kat said. "Let me get this straight. If we don't cooperate, I get charged with arson and manslaughter, Carter is an accessory after the fact and loses his boat, but I splash your threats all over the media, and you lose the election. If I do cooperate, I get to wash dishes and make beds for two friggin' spooks, sit around on the deck in a bikini, wait to get shot at, and maybe find out about my brother. You catch the bad guys and get re-elected. How can I resist?"

God, she's sassy. Carter was at a loss for words. Whatever made him think she needed his help?

"We're wasting time here. Are you two onboard or not?"

Carter looked at the stack of money and then at Kat, but didn't answer.

"Okay, Carter, save me here," Kat said.

"Saving you is getting harder. You weren't so assertive the first time as I recall. But sure, why not? Solves my problems," Carter answered.

"Yes, yes, indeed. This will benefit everyone. Thank you."

Kat reached into her pocket, pulled out Carter's cell phone, and put it in speaker mode. "Daddy, did you get all that?"

"Think so. Shall I switch off the recorder?"

"Sure. Keep it to yourself unless I let you know otherwise, or I miss one of our scheduled calls. It would make a great story for the *Nassau Guardian*. I can see my byline now. Love you. Enjoy your hunting trip. Stay safe."

"Me? I'm worried about you. Be careful."

"I will. Bye Daddy. I have to go."

She shut off the phone and looked at the recorder on the table. "So, no need to sign an agreement; we both have a copy of this conversation." She handed the phone to Carter. "You'll need to recharge that."

Carter couldn't believe he was looking at the same girl he had felt so sorry for just that morning.

Rollins stood. "Mrs. Deano stay seated. I want a few words with you—alone. Captain Carter, there's a lounge just down the hall. Wait there for us." Escorting Carter to the door, he added, "Captain Carter, a sailboat can be a pretty small space. I'm glad it's you onboard with her and not me."

CHAPTER 13

Rollins watched Carter walk away, sat down across from Kat, and switched off the recorder.

"I'd prefer you leave that on," Kat said. She felt a knot form in her stomach. Her bravado was gone now that she was alone with Rollins.

"I don't want any record of this, and you won't either," Rollins said. "Now, you asked for my help, that's why we're here. But this deal includes you helping me too."

Kat was confused. "I never asked for your help, sir. I would never have had the audacity to ask for help from you."

"You've been doing an excellent job of covering the Bahamas for some time now. A very professional job."

That seemed like a non sequitur to Kat, so she just said. "Thank you."

"Who's your source?"

"That's not part of any deal."

"Hum. Do I need to remind you of the potential charges against you?" Rollins asked.

"No, you don't. You can charge me with whatever you want and throw me in jail, but I never reveal a source."

"Who's Barracuda Bob?"

"I don't know what you're talking about."

"You've been getting information from him for four years now. The last email he sent was on March twelfth; it contained information about a casino scam in Freeport. An excellent exposé, I must say. Allowed us to clean up a very dirty deal. Then you sent an email to ask for Barracuda Bob's help on August twenty-fourth, the day before you flew to Bimini."

Kat sat silently. Suddenly she knew. "Oh, my God."

Rollins smiled. "Who else did you think would have all that information? Sorry about the threats. I had to know how serious you were about maintaining confidentiality. Incidentally, I know you didn't burn the Compleat Angler. I don't know how you did it, but I was so relieved when I heard you survived both the fire and Isadore's idiotic attempt to drown you. You truly must be a Kat with nine lives."

"I wouldn't have survived without help. Piccolo Pete saved me from that fire, and if Carter hadn't anchored out there, I would have drowned." Kat crossed her arms, dropped her head, and fought back tears. There was silence, except for the clock, until she lifted her head.

Rollins cleared his throat and continued, "I planned to talk to you after the banquet, but you jumped the gun on me, asking the Koreans about your brother. I had to get you out of there and make sure you stayed in your room until I could get to you. I hope I've convinced you that I had nothing to do with the events that happened after that."

"I am," Kat said with a weak smile.

"You want to know about your brother, so I'll start there." Rollins took a deep breath. "There's no evidence that he died in that boat accident and we did a thorough search. He may have gone to ground, and if he did, he had his reasons. Best to let everyone think he's dead. That's all I know at the moment."

Kat tried to interrupt, but Rollins waved for silence.

"Maybe I'm wrong, but I think all these things are connected and that's why I need a competent outside investigation. It's critical that I am re-elected and I'm not sure I'm objective about any of this. Some of my cabinet members would like to see me voted out of office. The police force and the detective unit leak like sieves. That may even include Captain Manny. I have to assume my computer has been hacked, so I didn't dare answer your email. It seems whenever I tell anyone anything in confidence; it appears in the news the next day. But on the occasions I have given you confidential information, requesting it remain off the record, and only used as deep background, you have always honored that. I'm expecting the same professional standard from you now."

"You can be assured of it." Kat sat up straighter. She had read the details of the Bahamas National Movement's platform. They would promote the Bahamas as one big gambling casino and tax haven. Their platform would destroy the very things that bring boaters, fishermen, and divers to these islands, and she would hate to see that happen.

"But what about Carter?" Kat continued. "I've told him everything. I was all about saving myself and finding Buddy. I told him there were no rare-earth minerals here."

Rollins left the question about Carter hanging. "I'm confused on that issue. Oriental Minerals paid a bundle for that land. I have the three independent evaluations from the geologists they hired; they all say the minerals are there. Here are copies for you. I blacked out the location of the property in case these got into the wrong hands. You'll see even your brother's report confirms this."

Rollins slid the reports across the table. Buddy's was on top. "This isn't what he told me," Kat said, scanning the documents.

"I know his history, but giving him the benefit of the doubt, could it be forged?"

Kat flipped to the last page. "It looks like his signature." There was no way to know if someone had changed the report. Kat had never doubted Buddy's word, but now she didn't know what to think.

"If Oriental Minerals commissioned these surveys, why don't you hire geologists to confirm them?" Kat asked.

"Same thing I said earlier. I can't afford to offend Oriental Minerals unless I have solid evidence."

Kat looked over the three letters. "What would be a normal fee for a geological survey like this?"

"I don't know exactly," Rollins said. "Perhaps fifty thousand. Why?"

"I was just wondering." Kat knew where Buddy had gone wrong. Buddy took things literally and didn't read between the lines. The message he had left on the answering machine said Oriental Minerals was paying him five hundred thousand dollars. Kat wouldn't forget the amount. They undoubtedly had asked him to confirm the existence of the minerals, or some such wording. He wouldn't have understood he was being bribed to misrepresent his findings. But this was something Kat was unwilling to say to Rollins yet. He wanted proof, and all she had was a theory. Like Rollins, she couldn't comprehend why the Koreans would want false data and the fact that they had paid so much to get it added to the mystery.

Kat gathered the pages spread out on the table. "If you don't think this is about rare-earth minerals, what do you think it's about?" she asked.

Rollins pushed his glasses up on the bridge of his nose. "This is going to sound like a politician talking, so you don't have to believe me. But here's what I think. They've started dredging a large, deep water marina and have put in an airstrip. My Minister of the Interior receives regular updates. I'm told they need the marina to bring the ships in to transport the ore out. On one hand that makes sense, but it could be the start of a high-end marina-casino complex with another 18-hole golf course, larger than the one the Chinese built on Cable Beach. Everyone knows I opposed that construction and promised to prohibit future developments that would include golf courses. Gambling ruins people, but golf courses ruin the very stuff our economy is based on. Grass doesn't grow on sand or limestone and the extensive use of herbicides and pesticides needed to maintain all those lush greens, destroys our reef's ecosystems. We have solid evidence of that."

Kat was only half listening. Rollins did sound like a politician, and she wondered where this was headed.

"If I weren't in office..." Rollins looked at Kat who was absently thumbing through the reports again. "Guess you know all this."

Kat nodded. "I follow. But this hardly seems the kind of stuff that people are murdered over and my gut feeling is that the same someone who wanted Buddy dead also wants me dead."

"Add this. The Bahamas National Movement suddenly has lots of money to spend hosting elaborate dinners, cruises, and parties. Someone is intent on funding my defeat."

"Add to that a sexual assault charge and it would be a scandal equal to those in U.S. politics."

"Don't jump to conclusions. You dig up the evidence, and I'll make a move. I promise you that. But back to Carter, does he trust you?"

"Probably not entirely."

"Until he does, tell him as little as possible. He's in this by accident. I really wish he wasn't in the picture at all. I've paid him off, but I don't know how firm his commitment is. With what he already knows, he could cause a problem. That's why you must stay with him."

"Use him." Kat eyes followed a cockroach meandering up the electric cord toward the clock.

"Well, I wouldn't go so far as to say that. He's getting something out of this, and he knows his way around these islands. He can be helpful."

Kat faced Rollins. "He saved my life."

"I know," Rollins said. "And now you have a chance to save your own, and maybe your brother's too. Carter's obviously infatuated with you so you should be able to persuade him to keep his mouth shut."

"I don't think that's quite the right word." Kat shifted uncomfortably in her chair. "Responsible is better. Since he was the one who pulled me out of the water, he now feels responsible for me."

"Don't underestimate yourself. You know, I do think you could have wormed your way into my banquet by flashing your knockers, even if I hadn't known who you were."

They both laughed. "Well, I did think you were pretty easy," Kat said. "I apologize. I had no idea...but you think I'm capable of being that manipulative?"

Rollins roared with laughter, tipping back in his chair. "Oh, and about the recording your Daddy made. Any chance of asking him to destroy it? Manny underestimated you. I really can't believe that he let that one slip through."

"Not to worry. I'll keep Daddy Warbucks under control."

"I guess that's the best I can expect." Rollins stood up and unlocked a cabinet. "Here's your backpack. I think everything's there. Fortunately for you, it was left on the police boat, not *Navy One*. I've taken the liberty of adding the name, address, and phone number of Millie Pascal in your phone."

"Should I know Millie?"

"You should. She can be quite helpful. You read nautical charts, right?"

"Of course."

"If you look at every digit in Millie's address and phone number, what you're looking at are four coordinates, four digits each, of the four corners that define the land that the Koreans own. Latitude first. It's on Andros. You are now the only one, besides Franklin Albury, my Minister of the Interior, who knows where it is. Until we have proof of some cover-up, it's essential that you keep this absolutely secret. There has been no announcement of its location, and I've promised Oriental Minerals I won't reveal this."

"You have my word," Kat said.

"You may need to get in touch with Barracuda Bob before we get the agents in. They won't be here until early next week. I suggest you hide out in the Exumas. Lots of small uncharted islands there. I'm sure Carter can come up with an isolated anchorage." Rollins reached into his briefcase and handed over his card.

"This has my direct phone line, but cell phone coverage is spotty in the islands. If you're near Highbourne Cay, they have a very high, long-range radio transmitter tower. There's another in Georgetown. You should be able to reach me with VHF channel sixteen with the call sign *Silver Girl*. It's not as good as having agents onboard, but the best I can do for the next few days. As you know, there are no private channels, so be careful what you say."

"*Silver Girl*, from 'A Bridge Over Troubled Water.' Seems appropriate." Kat continued, "I think I'll start by interviewing the other two geologists. Is this contact information current?" She pointed to the letterheads on the reports.

"I thought you might want to start there. Louis Woodside lives in Georgetown. That's why I'm having these agents fly in there. Carter doesn't need to know that you have a second reason to go to Georgetown. I guess that's it, except to say I always repay my debts. To quote from one of my favorite movies, 'This can be the start of a beautiful friendship.' It's not really the start, but it's good to put a face with the name."

"Same here, 'Bob,'" Kat said.

As she reached to shake hands, Rollins took hers between his, as close to a hug as protocol allowed. "Watch your back."

CHAPTER 14

Rollins accompanied Kat to the lounge where Carter was waiting, then directed them down a dimly lit corridor to meet Manny.

"I didn't want to leave you alone with Rollins, but I didn't know what else to do," Carter said. "He practically threw me out."

Kat stopped and looked at him. "Carter, you saved my life, and I'll always be grateful, but it's not your job to be my bodyguard."

"What did he want?"

"Um… He wanted to be sure I wouldn't write anything negative. He's determined to be re-elected."

"That's all?"

"He gave me his direct phone line in case I need to reach him."

Carter's forehead creased with doubt. "Certainly took him a long time."

Manny was waiting inside the weapons vault. It looked like something from a small bank. Vertical gray metal cabinets, rather than safety deposit boxes, lined the walls. An opened ledger rested on the table that was fastened securely to the far wall. Manny reached into a cabinet and handed Carter a Glock 9mm pistol and fifty rounds of ammunition.

"Unlike da States, possessin' guns is very restricted here. So keep des out of sight unless you need 'em." He motioned toward the ledger. "Write down da serial number of your gun and sign for it. Da ammo also."

Carter did as instructed, as Manny asked, "Do you know how to use dat?"

"Yeah, I've fired one before." Carter kept an old Colt 38 on the boat, but it wasn't registered, wasn't legal, and he preferred Kat not know about it. He had mixed feelings about her. She certainly had shown a very different side this evening.

"Okay, Mz. Deano, you get one too. We'll go to da firing range, and I'll give you some instruction. First, you need to keep dis safety on except when you're about to fire it." He demonstrated with his gun.

Kat clicked her safety off and back on. "Don't do dat," Manny said. "It's loaded. You might hurt someone."

"I thought that's what it was for."

"Well, just leave da safety on 'til I give you more instructions."

"Don't I get ammo too?"

"No, fifty rounds is plenty for both of you. Dis isn't the Middle East; we're not planning a war."

After Kat signed the ledger, Manny put it in the desk drawer and locked both it and the gun cabinet. He set two analog timers on the inside of the vault door for eight in the morning and they stepped out. After the heavy door closed, Manny turned the large three-handle crank and spun the combination dial.

The firing range was across the hall. Unlike the dim hallway, it was a vast brightly lit space without windows. At the far end, the wall was lined with rectangular bales of hay with heavy paper targets tacked to them. Hearing protectors hung on the wall near the entrance. Manny put one on, and Kat and Carter did the same.

"This is quite a setup," Carter said. "How many people know about it?"

Manny ignored Carter's question. "Okay, Mz. Deano, if you want to fire dat, you click da safety off."

"You already told me that." Kat clicked off the safety.

"Careful now, keep it pointed toward those targets."

Kat raised the pistol, braced her right arm with her left, and squeezed off a round. The bullet hit about an inch right of the bullseye.

Manny jumped as though an electric shock hit him. "Damn woman, you got my respect. Carter, could you do dat?"

"Not hardly. You?"

"Not with a gun I'd never fired before. Don't know why we're bringin' in agents."

Kat squinted at the target. "I've done better." Looking at the sights on the gun, she added, "It may be the windage needs to be adjusted."

It was after midnight when Manny drove them back to the marina. As they walked down the dock, Carter said, "Looks like you've figured out a way to stay, that is, if you don't mind being bait. We'll hang out here for another day so I can provision and buy clothes for you. Make a list of what you want. Might as well use some of Rollins' money for that. I don't know about you, but I could use a good night's sleep. Looks like we're going to be together longer than either of us expected. If the police come around, you might have to spend some time in your hiding place. You okay with that?"

Kat avoided answering and asked, "Can I use your phone again? I need to call Stewart. I don't need him."

CHAPTER 15

The day already promised to be hot and humid. East Bay Street had barely yawned to life as Carter quietly untied his lines. Across the water, the engines of heavy equipment rumbled, unloading the commercial ships at Potters Cay. Located between Nassau and Paradise Island, the cay housed docks used exclusively by the barges, freighters, and inter-island ferries. In contrast, Nassau Harbor Club sat silently. Cruisers did not usually leave this early. Following his original plan, Carter slipped *Wind Chaser* out of the east end of the harbor. He didn't radio Nassau Harbor Control as required, that meant declaring a destination, and he didn't want to do that. Maybe he was paranoid, but Carter couldn't shake the feeling that someone was watching their departure, Manny, or someone else. Kat remained below until they were out of range of the strongest binoculars.

As Nassau faded into the background, Kat came up the companionway stairs balancing two mugs of coffee. She handed one to Carter and settled in beside him. "Rollins said to hide in the Exuma Cays until those agents come. Could we go to Normans Cay?"

"Why Normans?"

"I've never been there; I want to see it."

"Not much there now. There was a time when it was really active. It was a drug haven, and no cruiser in his right mind went there." Carter sipped his steaming coffee. "There's still the wreckage of a plane in the lagoon. Rumors say it crashed overloaded with cocaine. The island's been basically abandoned since. Over the years, there's been on-again, off-again development. It always goes belly up. The story is a cocaine-crazed dark-spirit walks the shore and scares off developers."

Kat shook her head. "That was Carlos Lehder's operation. That's why I want to go. I told you I'm writing his memoir. I know a lot about him, but I'd love to walk those roads and see it for myself."

"It's kind of spooky. Lots of torn-up houses, some still with bullet holes in them, others destroyed by hurricanes."

"Well here are some journalistic details you might not know," Kat said, running her finger around the top of her mug. "Lehder was linked with Pablo Escobar, and from the late seventies through the early eighties, eighty percent of the cocaine from Colombia heading to the U.S. came right through Normans Cay. Planes that were large enough to fly from South America to the States without refueling ran the risk of detection. So they off-loaded into smaller ones that could fly under the radar to out-of-the-way grass strips in Florida, Georgia, and the Carolinas. Lehder changed the way drugs were transported and made billions of dollars."

"You sound like you admire the guy."

"Not unless you consider revolutionizing cocaine transport and heading one of the biggest criminal enterprises worthy of admiration. But his story is amazing. He operated in the open and got away with nearly every violent crime imaginable. Lots of people knew what he was doing, right down to the U.S. DEA. He was successful because starting with the first elected Prime Minister, Sir Lynden Pindling, politicians and the police force turned a blind eye. Go figure."

The mention of the DEA sent a shiver through Carter. "Why'd he pick you?"

"Who?"

"Lehder. Why'd he pick you to write his memoir?"

"I guess he reads the papers. Saw my byline and my interest in the Bahamas. He said with my background as an investigative reporter I'd get the facts right. That's all."

"You sure that's all?"

"What else would it be?"

"Nothing, I guess. I'm surprised you haven't been to Normans."

"I planned to go this fall, but then all this came up and here I am. I understand some of Lehder's house is still standing."

Carter pushed his hair back behind his ears and checked his heading. "I've seen it. It's called The Volcano because of a huge stone fireplace in the center of the living room. It's not so special. At least not anymore. Most of the roof is missing, floors too. It does have a great ocean view."

"I want to see it myself. The way Lehder described it in his writing; you'd think it was a palace. I thought this might be a good place to hang out for a couple of days. I could do my research, take some photos, and we could wait for our support staff."

"Actually, it's not the right place for us. There's not much on land, but there's a pristine well-protected harbor and lots of sailboats making the passage through Normans Cut on their way out to San Salvador anchor there while waiting on a weather window. They bring their dinghies to shore to roam the island and chances are we'd never be alone."

"That's disappointing."

"Well, maybe another time." The jib luffed. Carter leaned across Kat, sheeted it in, and stopped the flapping.

"What's your suggestion then?" Kat asked.

"I'm thinking of Mango Cay. It's very isolated. The entrance isn't even in the Cruising Guide. I've never taken any of my charters there. I reserved it for Becca, Claire, and me."

"I'm honored."

"There's no settlement. There was a plantation, but that was abandoned more than a hundred years ago," Carter said. "We can explore it tomorrow if you want. Becca, Claire, and I always took a picnic lunch up to the house. It's a special place to me with a spectacular view. I've got paté, cheese, crackers, olives, and fruit salad. I've even chilled a bottle of wine."

"Where'd you get all that?" Kat was surprised.

"I shopped at the gourmet food store across the street while you were passing the time, twiddling your thumbs on *Wind Chaser* yesterday. I told you I eat well when I have paying guests, and Rollins paid your charter fee."

"You can thank me now," Kat said.

"There's still a granite patio with a stone table and benches behind what's left of the plantation house. We have to climb up through some dense bush, but you'll see why they put their home where they did. You can see the bank on one side and ocean on the other in every shade of blue you can imagine. It's a breath-taking view."

"Sounds like it's worth doing."

"In all the times I've anchored there, there's never been another boat in the small bay. Much of the bottom is grassy and not good holding. You have to know where to set an anchor. The entrance is tricky, but the light should still be good when we get there, and if you take the helm, I can guide you through from the bow."

At three in the afternoon, they were passing through Highbourne Cut with the Exuma Islands close on either side. The water changed from light green to dark blue, and the bottom disappeared. A light wind was on the stern and Carter set the main and headsail to sail wing on wing.

"I'm glad to be outside. I'd forgotten how humid it is here in the summer," Kat said. She ran her hands through her hair, letting the breeze toss it.

"This is my favorite cruising ground," Carter said. "If we weren't trying to hide, we could wander down through the shallow Exuma Bank to Georgetown, the way most cruisers go. We'd probably spot lots of sea life, turtles, dolphins, sharks, maybe even manatee. Plus it would be a smoother ride, but this way we'll be seen by fewer boats. Meanwhile, enjoy this sail as long as this wind stays steady, nothing could be better."

Carter was standing at the helm when he spotted a sizable ship closing in on their port side. "Go below until I sort this out. I think that's a U.S. Coast Guard cutter. If they come much closer, they'll be able to spot both of us in the cockpit and read the name on the stern."

A few minutes later, the radio crackled to life. "*Wind Chaser, Wind Chaser*, this is the U.S. Coast Guard cutter *Escanaba*."

"*Escanaba, Escanaba, Wind Chaser* here. Do you copy?"

"We copy, *Wind Chaser*. State your last port of call and destination."

Nothing like broadcasting to the world. Carter keyed the radio. "Last port of call, Nassau. Not certain of destination. Over."

"*Escanaba* back. Declare destination."

"I repeat. Destination unknown," Carter answered.

"*Escanaba* back, *Wind Chaser*. How many souls onboard?"

Carter could taste acid at the back of his throat. He knew they would next ask for names and they were talking on channel sixteen. If he told the truth, every boat within twenty miles would know where Kat was. But if he were caught lying to the Coast Guard, they would confiscate his boat, in spite of Rollins' promise.

"Only one. I'm Captain Carter McDowell."

"This is *The Escanaba*. Maintain your speed and direction and standby for a boarding."

"Shit." He picked up the intercom. "Kat, Get Rollins on the phone right now. He's got to stop this." Carter keyed the mic again. "*Wind Chaser* standing by for boarding."

Kat appeared at the bottom of the stairs holding her phone to her ear. "It's ringing. What are you going to do?"

"No questions now. Follow my orders. Get Rollins and get this stopped. And stay out of sight. I'll stall them as long as I can. Go."

Carter watched the Coast Guard lower a giant inflatable tender into the water. The clock was ticking, and the phone was still ringing.

The rigid center-console with five American coast guardsmen pulled alongside *Wind Chaser* and matched her speed as three of the seamen vaulted into the cockpit. Carter hoped this was only to practice their maneuvers and nothing more. The other two pulled the tender away and seemed to enjoy racing around in circles while they waited. To Carter, these guys looked so young, probably not yet twenty. They wore carefully pressed short-sleeved navy-blue uniforms, and orange life vests. Handcuffs and pistols swung from their belts.

One pimply-faced guardsman stepped forward and looked sternly at Carter. "I'm Petty Officer First Class Ronald Higgins. I'll need your passport and cruising permit. Can we go below?"

"I'd rather do this out here. With this wind direction, I need to be where I can watch the sails. I'll just be a minute."

Carter went below and quickly grabbed his passport and the ship's papers, thankful once again for the meeting with Rollins. He quietly opened Kat's door. She had the phone at her ear but shook her head. Closing the door, he returned to the deck.

The wind had picked up, and the young officer had trouble holding his clipboard and paper in place as he carefully copied the information from the ship's documents. Carter was secretly pleased it was taking so much time. He fiddled with the lines making small and unnecessary adjustments to the sails. Fifteen minutes passed.

"I think we're done here," Higgins said. "Everything seems to be in order. Just a quick search of the vessel and you can be on your way."

"If everything is in order, why the search?" Carter asked, his mouth suddenly dry.

"Just following procedure," Higgins said.

And I'm about to lose my boat and Kat her freedom. "Are your men capable of managing these sails?" Carter was delaying. He hoped he sounded like a man in charge.

"They can call you if there's any problem."

Carter turned to the other two sailors. "The wind's astern. Sailing by the lee can be tricky if the wind picks up or the direction changes at all. Watch out for a flying jibe and keep your heads down. That swinging boom can crack your head open like an overripe watermelon. I've seen it happen."

"Yes, sir," replied the wide-eyed sailors.

Suddenly the autopilot cut out, and the boom slammed over. "Duck," Carter shouted. He grabbed the wheel, taking valuable seconds to bring the sails under control. The nerve-shattering racket from the rigging finally stopped when he got the sails filled and the boat back on course. Carter switched the autopilot back on. It was working again.

"That shouldn't have happened. I don't know what went wrong," he said to the pale guardsmen. "One of you needs to take over the helm and watch that autopilot. Don't leave it unattended. You saw just how dangerous that is."

The young seamen looked at Higgins; neither wanted the responsibility. Before Higgins could delegate a helmsman, his radio squawked.

"Petty Officer Higgins, Petty Officer Higgins. This is Captain Westerman. Abort your mission immediately. I say again, abort your mission immediately and return to the *Escanaba*. Acknowledge transmission."

Higgins pulled his radio off his belt. "Higgins here. Understood. Returning to *Escanaba*." He turned. "Captain McDowell, thanks for your cooperation. That will be all." All three sailors were eager to disembark *Wind Chaser*. The crew in the tender, also having heard the transmission, swooped over and the three coastguardsmen jumped on. Carter went below to look for Kat. She was sitting at the navigation station, next to the inside controls for the autopilot.

"That was close. I thought I might have to switch that thing off a second time." Kat grinned up at Carter.

"I don't know whether to tell you off or thank you." Carter said, trying not to sound irritated. "You saved our asses, but do you realize how risky it is turning off the autopilot under those wind conditions and no one at the wheel?"

"I didn't know what the wind conditions were."

"My point exactly. Sailboats aren't like Daddy's powerboat," Carter said. "When the boom on a boat this big slams over, it has the force to kill someone or break the goose-neck that holds the boom up, and we'd be headed back to Nassau for repairs. I'm convinced you can handle the helm under calm conditions, but I think I'd better teach you something about sailboats."

"Oh, are there things I don't know?"

"A little testy, aren't you?" Carter asked. "Because as I see it, there's a hell of a lot you don't know. Sailing takes a whole different set of skills than those needed for managing a powerboat."

"You make it look so easy."

"Experience helps. It's not hard once you know what you're doing."

"Lesson one. Listen to the skipper," Kat said.

"That's a start. And don't question my decisions during a crisis. I'm happy to explain anything you want to know *after* things have settled down." Carter checked to see that the sails were filled. "I take it you reached Rollins."

"I did, but I was still afraid he wouldn't reach the Coast Guard in time."

"Did he say anything else?" Carter asked.

"Only that he still had some clout here and not to worry, the U.S. Coast Guard won't bother *Wind Chaser* again."

Their self-congratulations didn't last long; someone else keyed a mic. "*Escanaba, Escanaba,* dis is *Lady Jane*. Over."

"*Escanaba,* back to the vessel calling."

"*Lady Jane* here. Our chartplotter give out. We near you. Please give your location." It was a Bahamian dialect.

The Escanaba read off her coordinates.

"Damn," Carter said.

"Did that sound like Isadore to you?" Kat asked.

"Doesn't matter whether it was or not. That was all on channel sixteen. Anyone listening now knows *Wind Chaser's* approximate location. I'll head for Mango Cay as quickly as possible. The island nearly surrounds the harbor so there's no way anyone would see *Wind Chaser* at anchor."

"Except from the air," Kat added.

"Well, even if people know *Wind Chaser's* there, no one, except Rollins and Manny know you're onboard."

"As far as we know."

CHAPTER 16

A storm was brewing. Afternoon squalls rolled through frequently in late summer, but to Carter, the towering thunderheads forewarned of more than a typical summer storm. The sky darkened by the minute and the seas kicked up. The interval between the swells shortened, and waves grew meaner. As soon as Carter saw it coming, he dropped the sails, hoisted the storm jib, and lashed the deflated dinghy on the foredeck.

Carter and Kat huddled in the shelter of the pilot-house, wearing foul-weather jackets, safety harnesses, and inflatable life vests. There was little point keeping watch; they couldn't see through the wall of water, and for the moment, the autopilot was in control. Carter hoped the storm wouldn't spawn a waterspout. He wouldn't see one coming. Each wave buried the bow and slammed into the windshield of the pilot-house fully twenty-five feet back. The force of the waves stopped the forward motion. *Wind Chaser* shuddered and struggled slowly forward again, only to be slammed by the next monster wave. They had stowed everything that could move, but that didn't stop the nerve-racking banging inside the drawers and cabinets.

Carter considered his options. Checking his instruments, he noted gale-force wind gusting over fifty knots and the wind direction, while mostly over the bow, varied greatly with either a westerly or easterly component. As far as he could see, hoving-to was out. This variation in wind speed and direction meant setting the sails to keep the boat in place would require constant adjustment and the possibility of drifting into Lightning Shoal and shallow water north of his position a dangerous possibility. That left two options; hammer-on, or drop anchor.

He looked at Kat leaning against the bulkhead hugging her knees to her chest. "If you're going to be seasick, get a bucket." At that moment, Kat threw up all over the floor. At the smell of vomit, Carter barely had time to grab the trash can before he was sick as well.

"You too?" she said with a weak smile.

"I was fine until you puked all over the floor."

"Can you get me out of this alive?" she asked, her smile gone.

"Seems to be my job."

She hardly heard him above the roar of the wind in the rigging. Then a rogue wave hit with an ear-splitting crash. The left windshield cracked into a thousand spider-web pieces but remained in place. Hard running in the big seas had caused the safety glass to flex away from the frame and water showered into the cabin around the pane.

Kat was curled up on her side, her arms over her head. "Kat, get up. I need your help. Start mopping." Giving her something to focus on would subdue her sickness and her fears. Kat grabbed a towel, and on her hands and knees, began cleaning up. Each new wave sent more water cascading over her, but she was back in control.

Carter kept an eye glued to the red lights flashing on and off on the instrument panel indicating that the two bilge pumps were keeping up with the water streaming in. So far, so good, but Carter didn't know how much more the windshield could absorb before the entire glass pane gave way. *Wind Chaser* had wooden boards to cover the windshields of the pilot-house under storm conditions, but attempting to manage the heavy storm panels on deck with the unpredictable pitching of the boat would take both of them. That left no one to man the helm and he couldn't imagine attempting this underway. *I hope I'm making the best decision,* Carter thought.

"I need to get the storm jib down and set an anchor," Carter shouted.

"Should I call a Mayday?" Kat yelled as Carter started across the pilot-house. "Are we sinking?"

Carter looked back at her wet hair plastered to her face, a flashback to the first time he had seen her. "No to both. *Wind Chaser's* built for the North Seas, and I'm not going to let her go down." As captain, he had to at least pretend he had a plan.

"Good," Kat said. "I didn't swim all the way to her to just be dumped back in the sea."

"You've got a weird sense of humor. Hand me that flashlight and close the hatch once I go out. Certainly wouldn't want any rain to get in." He pointed to the control panel. "Let me know if those bilge pump lights stay on."

Carter stepped carefully over the wet floor and climbed the companionway stairs. On deck, he snapped the lanyard of his safety harness onto a jack line and groped his way back to the wheel.

Kat poked her head up. "Those lights are both on." She disappeared back inside.

Shit! He opened the lazarette behind the helm, found the manual bilge pump handle, slipped it into place, and began madly pumping.

"Kat. I need you out here," Carter called on the intercom. Kat was still on the floor mopping but scrambled out, responding to his command. "Tether your harness to that safety line," he said, pointing to the stainless steel line running along the deck. He was screaming over the howling wind. "I need you to man this pump."

Sickly pale, Kat did her best to keep up the pace he had set at the pump. He squeezed her shoulder. "That's great. Keep it up as long as you can. I've got to furl that storm jib then free the anchor so I can drop it."

Carter looked at his watch. Fear muddled time, minutes seemed like hours but hours passed in a blink. If the anchor dragged, the depth finder would announce shallow water and the wind and waves would push them onto the shoal where *Wind Chaser* would come to a terrifying halt. She was solidly built, but no boat could stand up to a jagged coral reef for long.

Before he left the cockpit, he drew back the hatch. One bilge pump light blinked off, then the other. One problem solved, at least for now. "Kat, stop pumping and take the helm while I go forward. The auto-pilot's on, but I don't know if it will continue to hold the course. If it doesn't, switch it off and maintain this compass heading."

"How long will this go on?" Kat asked as she wiped the water dripping into her eyes.

"I don't know. It wasn't in the forecast."

"Is your life raft in good shape?"

"Yes," Carter answered. That was all he was going to say. If things got that bad, he'd put Kat in the life raft, and he'd stay with *Wind Chaser* where he belonged. Abandoning *Wind Chaser* and activating his EPIRB, the Emergency Position Indicating Radio Beacon, would alert every other vessel. The situation was not that dire, yet. If the wind and seas picked up more, he could always change his mind.

"Can you manage while I go forward?"

"I think so."

Carter moved over to give her the helm and waited to make sure she could handle it. Her eyes were focused on the compass, her forehead creased in concentration.

"That's good. Watch the chartplotter, if that depth changes, you may have to throttle up. I'm going forward."

Carter went below, grabbed a pair of pliers and a marlinspike. Back on deck, he fought the urge to hurry, time was running out, but he couldn't make a mistake. Fastening himself to a jack line, he worked his way forward on hands and knees along the lurching deck to the bow. Tethered to the safety line would keep him with the boat, but not necessarily on deck. If he washed overboard and Kat left the helm to help him get back onboard, *Wind Chaser* could swing around and probably take a knock-down. He couldn't think about it. Crouching near the bow, he freed the halyard and dropped the storm jib. The sopping wet sail refused to cooperate with his cold, wet hands as he attempted to bundle it. The boat pitched suddenly, and he slipped, falling onto the deck, and banging his ankle into a cleat. He yelled in pain, but Kat didn't hear him above the sound of the furious wind beating the halyards against the mast.

Once he managed to haul the sail back to the cockpit and dump it through the hatch, he called to Kat. "I've got to go forward again. I couldn't contain the sail and free the anchor."

"Don't go. I saw you fall. These waves are getting bigger. I can't do this." The unnatural pitch of panic filled her voice.

Carter took her chin in his hand. "Look at me. You can do this. We're a team." As he wiped the rain from her face, his hand lingered on her cheek. *God, I want to kiss her! How inappropriate is that right now?* Aloud he said, "We don't have a lot of time. Just keep control of that wheel." He turned and made his way forward again. Crouching on the foredeck, he forced the marlinspike through the knot in the line securing the big anchor and staggered back to the cockpit.

"Got about a hundred-fifty foot of chain there, enough to hold us when the depth drops to fifteen or twenty feet, even in this storm." His voice was drowned out by the wind. He wasn't sure Kat heard him or even grasped what he meant, but it didn't matter. Her hood had blown off, water streamed from her hair, but she was intent on maintaining the boat's direction, and that was what he needed. He noticed blood as he took over the wheel. He didn't know where it had come from. His hands? What mattered now was staying off the razor-sharp coral.

"What's that depth finder say?" Carter asked.

"Fifty-three feet, and falling rapidly," Kat shouted.

"Cross your fingers and pray that she grabs and holds. It's like an underwater cliff down there." Carter trusted the holding power of his eighty-pound anchor with its roll bar and skids. Designed to orient regardless of how it hit bottom and then bury rapidly, it had never failed him and that's what he needed now. He would only have one chance to get this right.

Because he had modified *Wind Chaser* to single hand, he could drop the anchor from the helm station. His stomach was in a knot as he switched off the auto-pilot, held his breath, and released the anchor. They both watched as the depth dropped to forty feet, and the anchor attempted to grab. The boat jerked as the chain pulled taut, but the anchor let go and they slipped backward, pushed by the relentless waves. Carter could visualize the swinging anchor and the damage it could do to the hull.

"Shit," Carter screamed. His hands shook as he grabbed the control and throttled up. Cold spray ran down the inside of his foul-weather jacket, chilling him more. When the depth flashed twenty feet, he reduced speed. "Got to give that anchor a chance."

The direction of the boat was now impossible to control, and *Wind Chaser* swung at a dangerous angle to the pounding waves. As Carter struggled to control the boat, the anchor grabbed in earnest this time, throwing Carter against the wheel and Kat onto the floor of the cockpit. He couldn't help her; *Wind Chaser* needed him now. He slowed the engine but left it in forward to reduce the load on the anchor. The depth reading bounced up and down, but never below ten feet.

"She's holding," Carter yelled over the violent wind. He lashed the wheel so the waves wouldn't damage the rudder. Kat climbed onto the cockpit seat, bracing herself for stability, but she was smiling.

"You did it. Go *Wind Chaser*." She grabbed Carter in a wet hug.

"No, we did it. If you ever decide to quit your job, you'd make a great first mate. You've now been initiated by the storm of a lifetime, and you hung in there. Good going." He felt high.

"Was this my intensive immersion sailing course?" Kat asked.

Carter laughed. "Intense is right, and it almost qualified as immersion too. I'll tell you now, I've never been through a storm like that."

"Later I'll tell you how scared I was," Kat said.

"Well, if you hadn't managed the helm like you did, with those seas, we could have had a knock-down or run up on the reef with disastrous results. This may be the best it gets until this system passes, but as long as that anchor holds, we won't go aground. It's not very comfortable, but we're safe for the moment. We'll take turns keeping watch tonight, checking the depth and the anchor chain. As long as the wind is this strong, we'll have to keep the engine at low speed, but we don't want it to take over and swing the boat around if the wind drops." Carter looked at Kat to see if she understood. She was shaking.

"Are you cold?"

"Yeah," she said through clenched teeth, "but I think it's mostly emotional. I'll be okay."

"Well, I couldn't have done this without you. Becca couldn't have done any better. Go below. There are sweatshirts in my cabin. The one with the hood looks good on you. Cover up with anything you find that's dry. The bunks should be okay. Try to get some sleep." He had no intention of sharing the responsibility at the helm when he saw how exhausted she was. She'd been great; he'd do this alone.

Several times during the long night there were distress calls on the radio, but they were all too far away for Carter to help, even if *Wind Chaser* had been in a condition to do so. Some of those boats would be going down. He heard what sounded like the faltering engine of a plane, probably soon to be another casualty.

In the early morning darkness, the wind dropped, and the rain abated to a drizzle. Carter shut off the engine and let the anchor carry the full load. He had been nodding off at the helm, but there was one more thing to do before he could rest without worrying. He woke Kat, surprised she was so soundly asleep. She had put her trust in him. The seas were calmer, and in the blackest of night, Carter turned on the deck lights, and they carried the wooden panel that would cover the broken windshield forward. With two screwdrivers, they worked together, carefully, but quickly fastening the board in place. Kat's hand brushed against Carter's as she reached for the last screw. Neither said a word, their eyes locked. Carter took her hand. They made their way back inside and tossed the screwdrivers into the toolbox. He lifted her onto the bunk in the master cabin, and they tore off just enough clothes. Still covered with salt and the residual smell of fear, he entered her.

"How did that happen?" Carter asked when they could both breathe again. They were entwined, still in their yellow foul-weather jackets and not much else.

"How could it not happen? You were right about pulling me out of the water; anyone would have done that. But I watched the way you handled this storm. This was life-threatening, and you knew exactly what to do to get us through it and *Wind Chaser* safe. You never lost control. Count me in your fan club."

"But I did lose control. We shouldn't have made love."

"Believe me," Kat said, "We didn't make love. That was survival sex. Emotion-driven, out-of-control sex. That doesn't count."

"So it has to be out-of-control?"

"Shut up, Carter." She got up, kissed him on the lips, and went to her cabin.

CHAPTER 17

Dawn arrived reluctantly and late with dim light below the soggy cloud cover. Carter slid back the hatch. The storm had cooled the air, but the lumpy sea was still an angry gray. As he scanned the low white caps, his vision froze. A few hundred yards to their stern was a big motor yacht.

"Hand me the binoculars," he called out. "There's another boat out here." Carter focused the glasses and tried to steady them. "They're heeled away from us and riding low in the water. Obviously aground, driven onto that shoal and taking on water. I'll try to raise them. They must see us; I'm surprised someone hasn't called." Carter checked to be sure his radio was on and tuned to channel sixteen.

"Maybe their radio's out," Kat said.

"Could be." Carter keyed the mic. "Motor yacht at Lightning Shoal, this is the sailing vessel …" He hesitated. He couldn't risk naming *Wind Chaser.*

"*Silver Girl,*" Kat whispered.

"This is the sailing vessel, *Silver Girl,*" Carter transmitted. No answer. He called a second time. Still no response.

"I need to launch the dinghy and go over," Carter said. "There's some reason they're not responding. Could be someone's badly hurt." Carter was trying to keep his voice calm, but his heart was pounding.

Amazingly, the dinghy survived the storm and was still lashed on the foredeck. Together they inflated it and boosted it over the life-lines. Carter tied the line to the stern, lowered the outboard, and locked it in place.

"I'm going with you," Kat said. Carter wasn't going to take up precious time arguing with her.

The seas were still choppy and pushed by the six-horsepower Evinrude, Kat and Carter were soaked again. "Where'd you come up with *Silver Girl?*" Carter called over the hum of the outboard.

"'Sail on *Silver Girl...*' Do you remember that folk song, Bridge Over Troubled Water? Maybe you should rename *Wind Chaser.*"

Carter shook his head. "Bad luck." *And Claire chose the name.*

They circled the stricken boat but saw no sign of life. As they rounded the stern, the name they saw stopped them cold. "My God, *Navy One,*" Kat said as she reached for the boat to steady the dinghy.

"Don't touch it. This is way beyond our pay grade."

"You were so eager to help a few minutes ago. We need to take a look," Kat said. "The tender is still on its davits. Dead or alive, someone is on that boat. So what if it's Isadore; he might be seriously hurt or unconscious. We can't just leave him."

"I won't. But I want to get my gun." Carter's priorities had changed. He swung the dinghy around and headed back to *Wind Chaser.* "I'll raise help by phone or radio. There's a limit to what I'm willing to do. He tried to kill you twice. My guess is he was following us when he went aground."

"I need to question him. This might be my best chance."

"Quit being so stubborn. Think about your own safety."

Back on *Wind Chaser,* Carter was able to reach Davis Harbor at the southern tip of Eleuthera on the marine radio. "Mayday. Mayday. *Navy One* is aground and taking on water at Lightning Shoal. Do you copy?"

"Dis is da dockmaster at Davis Harbor." They could hardly hear him over the static. "You breakin' up. What's da nature of your distress?"

"Davis Harbor, *Silver Girl* here," Carter lied. "*Navy One* is aground and taking on water. No one responds to my radio. Can you patch me through to the Prime Minister's office or the police in Nassau?"

"Davis Harbor, back. Negative on a patch. Da storm took down da relay tower north at Hatchet Bay. Telephones out. We and Highbourne Cay got VHF with repeaters. Will try to get through dat way soon we get da antenna back up. Give me information on your vessel. Over."

Carter wasn't about to offer anything else. "We're fine. It's *Navy One*, the Prime Minister's boat, that's in trouble. A motor yacht, about eighty feet. Aground on coral. Radio Nassau. *Silver Girl* out."

Kat knew if the Prime Minister got any of this transmission, he would know who called it in. "We've got to get back there," she said.

An alarm began to scream, and a bright red light flashed on the control panel. "Now what?" Kat asked.

"It's the high-water alarm," Carter said. "Only one bilge pump is working. I've got to get in the bilge and see how serious this is. I hope it's only a hose that has come loose from all the pounding we took, but it could be something more."

"What about Isadore and *Navy One?*"

"I have to save us first. This will go faster if you stay put and hand me tools once I discover what's wrong." Carter opened the teak panel in the floorboards next to the dinette and eased himself into the engine compartment.

Once he was out of sight, Kat left her post and quietly stepped into the dinghy. Without starting the engine, she paddled toward *Navy One.* The Glock was in the pocket of her foul-weather jacket, the safety off. *If Isadore is on that boat, he's going to talk or die. Maybe both.*

Ten minutes later, Carter hoisted himself out of the bilge. "Lucky us, it was just a hose clamp on the water intake. All done." When Kat didn't respond, he stepped on deck. Kat was almost at *Navy One.* He slammed his hand against the cabin top in frustration. "Shit."

As Kat reached the motor yacht, she could hear the grinding of the hull against the coral, a sound like a thousand fingernails on a chalkboard; it sent chills down her arms. The fiberglass hull could break up at any minute. She'd have to work quickly. She tied the dinghy to the stern, hauled herself out of the rocking inflatable, and crawled unsteadily onto the swim platform. Holding on to the stern ladder with both hands, she felt the sickening vibration as the big boat shuddered each time a wave pushed it further onto the reef. Pulling the Glock out of her pocket, she cautiously climbed up the ladder. A teak table was wedged under the railing of the large open deck, and the chairs were missing. As she scanned the aft deck, she saw the cables used to launch the tender from the stainless-steel davits were hopelessly tangled, whether from the storm or an unsuccessful attempt to launch it. Holding her gun on the ready, she braced herself against the cabin and cautiously stepped through the door leading into the main saloon. The noise of the stranded boat scraping the reef masked any sound she made.

Furnished with soft green leather and beautifully varnished teak, the main saloon was empty. The only noise was the slapping of water and chafing of the hull against a solid surface. The water covering the cabin floor of the once luxurious craft was strewn with debris and had a pungent odor that stung her nose and made her eyes burn. She searched every cabin and splashed through seawater in the engine room. A film covered the surface that Kat assumed was diesel fuel. Then it hit her. There was a pod for an inflatable life raft on deck. No longer attempting stealth, she made her way to the pod. It was open. The life raft was gone. *So I'm not getting any information from Isadore. Maybe he left something useful behind.*

The boat suddenly shifted to starboard with a loud crunch and Kat fell against the rail. Time was against her. Wrenching open drawers and lockers, Kat frantically searched through the main saloon, galley, and pilot-house. She lifted the hinged top of the table at the navigation station. Nothing. No charts, not even the logbook.

Isadore had either taken it with him or more likely, thrown it overboard.

What had she missed? Frustrated, she glanced around the pilot-house one last time. Leaning on the steering wheel, she bent to check the cabinet under it but was thrown to the floor as the wheel spun freely. As she dragged herself back up, she flipped the wheel in the opposite direction. She had been at *Wind Chaser's* helm enough to know there should be some friction turning the wheel. Was this damage from the storm or something else? No wonder Isadore had run aground. She needed Carter to take a look. He would be angry, but she had to convince him to come back with her.

Carter heard the outboard and came out on deck as Kat pulled up to *Wind Chaser's* stern. She threw him the line but remained seated in the dinghy, the engine running. "Carter, I need you to come back to *Navy One*."

Carter turned away.

"You can be mad later. We don't have much time. No one's on the boat, but something doesn't look right."

"What did you expect? A storm and a grounding."

"The wheel just spins like it's not attached to anything. Can that happen from the storm?"

Carter shook his head. "I don't like this."

"Okay, then move out of my way. I don't know enough about mechanical stuff. I need photos." She grabbed the stern rail and started to climb out of the dinghy.

"Forget it." Carter went below, grabbed a flashlight, his phone, and his gun. Once more they made their way through the choppy water to the stern of *Navy One*.

Kat scrambled to grasp the ladder and held the rail to brace herself on the badly listing deck. "Looks like Isadore first tried to lower the tender," she said, pointing out the twisted davit cables. "When that didn't work, he left in the life raft. I checked. It's gone." They splashed through the main saloon and steadied themselves against the cabin wall to manage the three steps that separated the saloon from the pilot-house. "Here's what I want to show you." She spun the wheel. "See, there's no resistance. Even I know that's not right."

Without speaking, Carter moved toward the engine room. "I'm going to take a look at the steering cylinder." A close examination revealed a partial cut at one end of the ram, enough to cause a failure at some point. Whoever did this hadn't counted on the storm and the additional stress that put on the system. This was not an accident, it was sabotage.

"Let's get off this boat," Carter announced.

Carter was quiet on the trip back to *Wind Chaser*. Once inside, he turned to Kat. "That cut was incomplete. The steering would not fail suddenly. Under normal circumstances, Isadore could have maintained steerage for hours, but not in this storm."

"Do you think Isadore did it?"

"What would be the point?"

"So no one could drive the boat if they got it off the reef."

"I'm inclined to think the reverse; he ran up on that reef because he couldn't steer."

"Why would someone mess with the steering? Was someone trying to kill him?" Kat asked.

"More likely sending a message, if I were to guess. I'd say someone wanted to put a scare in him knowing they were capable of getting on the boat. The storm was not part of their agenda."

"Who? And why?"

"Hey, I'm just the skipper. You're the investigative reporter. What do you think?"

"I'm thinking those agents had better be waiting in Georgetown," Kat replied.

CHAPTER 18

Carter and Kat were re-energized by the time they approached Mango Cay. In spite of the choppy sea, they had taken turns on watch and napped throughout the day. Now the island blocked the wind and the water smoothed out. Carter furled the jib and mainsail and started the engine. Kat took the helm, and he went forward to *Wind Chaser's* bow to guide her in. Through the clear water, Carter could see the bottom. It was as he remembered, first a turn to starboard to avoid the sand bar marking the narrow opening in the reef and then a sharp turn back to port, favoring the east side. Finally, they were through. Carter walked to the helm, throttled back to idle, and eased into the protected anchorage. Shifting into neutral, he let *Wind Chaser* drift closer toward shore before setting the anchor.

"Look, two rays. Spotted ones." Kat pointed over the starboard side. "They appear so docile gliding along like that."

"They're eagle rays, quite skittish, but their tail barb is lethal," Carter said. "They're pretty content here because there rarely is a shark to prey on them in this shallow water."

"Lehder should have set up his operation here," Kat said. "He might have stayed in business longer."

"Maybe, but he'd have to dredge this channel, and unlike most of the southern Bahama Islands, there's no flat area to build a runway."

"Why don't boaters come here?"

"Well, partly because there are over 300 cays in the Exumas, lots of them with great beaches, plenty of fish, and much easier to get to. This entrance is uncharted and most boats can only get in here at high tide like we did. But I love this one. It has great memories for me. Each time I came here with Becca and Claire, we pretended we were the first explorers to discover it. Sounds silly, doesn't it?"

"I'm glad to know you have a silly side. What's next? Can we swim?"

"After we get those wet settee cushions out into the cockpit so they can dry or the entire boat will soon smell like mildew."

"That and vomit," Kat said.

"But, I've got a better idea," Carter said. "Rather than swim, let's get the snorkel stuff out and see if we can spear lobster for dinner. We've still got enough daylight. There are always some hiding under the ledges along the shoreline. He handed her fins and a mask. "You do snorkel?"

"I grew up on the Atlantic coast of Florida and came to the Bahamas with my father. Does that answer your question?"

It didn't take long before they had speared four lobsters. Carter twisted off the tails and threw the rest overboard since the claws had almost no meat. "I've never actually broiled lobster myself," Carter said. "Becca was such a marvel in the galley, but if you're not too fussy, I think I can manage. Rice-in-a-bag doesn't take a *Cordon Bleu* diploma. I'll melt some butter and lime, then open a bottle of *Pouilly-Fuisse*. If you concoct a salad from the stuff I bought in Nassau, I think we're set. Too bad we have to rush down to Georgetown."

"My goal is to find out about my brother and the longer we wait, the less likely I'll find anything."

"And you made a deal with Rollins," Carter added.

"Maybe when this is all over, we can come back here," Kat said.

"I'm not sure your husband would agree to that."

"There may be plenty of obstacles to cruising together, but Stewart isn't one of them. Remember when I told you he left a note the morning I flew to Bimini? Well, I didn't tell you the whole story." Kat leaned against the counter in the galley and poured each of them a glass of wine. "This wasn't only about Buddy interfering in our lives. I need to backtrack a bit.

"I told you that Stewart is a defense lawyer. He rescues people. That's how we met. I'd been charged with selling marijuana. It was a low point in my life, and Stewart saved me from possible jail time."

So that's why her name was in that first-time offender's article. Carter thought.

"I did spend a month in rehab as part of a plea bargain, but once I was out, we started dating. For several years our relationship worked, as long as I was dependent on him. But I was determined to accomplish something for myself, and once I had an established reputation as a free-lance reporter, things changed." Kat sipped her cold, dry wine. "Good choice."

"Thank you, but go on."

"Stewart couldn't handle my independence or my success. He was working hard to become a partner in his law firm. It's something he wanted to achieve and not an easy path. It seems we couldn't both be strong and confident at the same time. He started belittling me. Constantly told me I didn't have a real job, just traveling and writing from home. I don't want it to sound like it was entirely his fault."

"These things never are. Marriage takes compromise."

"True, but more importantly, I didn't live up to his expectations as a lawyer's wife. I admit, I hated that role. I didn't want to be 'The Wife'. We began arguing more, usually when my job took me away from my lawyer-wife duties. Our biggest fight was when I accepted that assignment writing about Hemmingway's time in Bimini. I missed the office Christmas party. He said I didn't support his career as Carolyn did. She's one of the partners. He took her home from that party, and I think that's when their affair began. That's when I realized my marriage was over." Kat was vigorously tearing lettuce.

"I was miserable for a week, and then I realized I was actually relieved. The fact that Stewart had an affair with Carolyn didn't surprise me, what did was that I didn't care. What brought us together didn't exist anymore. We had a marriage of convenience, maybe inertia. I didn't want to look back and know that this was all there was. I wanted an equal relationship, and our marriage never was going to be that. So, I didn't tell you the whole story, I did answer his note. I told him I had evidence of his affair with Carolyn and that as far as I was concerned, he could go ahead and draw up divorce papers."

"And that's why he wasn't so eager to come bail you out."

"Yeah. We're still living together, but it's just until he makes partner. Wouldn't look good if he was in the middle of a personal crisis. And he did help me when I needed it."

"Why didn't you tell me this earlier?" Carter asked.

"I wanted to make sure ..."

"What? Make sure that I wasn't going to take advantage of that isolated anchorage?"

"Something like that. I didn't know whose boat I had collapsed on but it had to be better than the alternative. Then the next morning, when I discovered you were alone, I didn't know what you might do when I told you why I was out there. But if you thought I was married and my husband was coming..."

"I guess it makes sense; me alone, you an attractive young woman."

The low clouds on the horizon turned from pink and orange to shades of gray as they sat with their wine in the cockpit. "Great meal, but I'm beat," Kat said. "I was so scared during that storm."

"After what you've been through, I didn't think a little ole storm would scare you."

"Snakes."

"What?"

"Poisonous snakes in particular. I'm afraid of those too."

"Venomous," Carter corrected. "Well, you're lucky. There aren't any venomous snakes in the Bahamas. Storms, yes. Snakes, no."

"I don't know how you do it. You stayed so calm," Kat said.

"I don't always. You witnessed that."

"You've earned the right for an occasional misstep." This was the first time either one had referred to the night in Nassau. "And now we're sitting here in this beautiful, calm harbor watching the sun set into the ocean. It doesn't get better than this."

"I agree. Reminds me of the last time I was here with Becca."

Kat slammed her plastic glass on the cockpit table, spilling wine on the teak surface. "Becca, Becca, Becca. I've tried to keep my mouth shut, but I've run out of patience. I'm sick of hearing about the Perfect Becca." Carter was unprepared for her sudden mood swing. He hadn't seen this coming.

"The way I see it," Kat snapped, "Becca was a self-centered bitch, and she doesn't deserve that pedestal you've put her on."

Carter drew in a deep breath to steady himself. It didn't work. With his eyes fixed angrily on Kat, he said, "From what you've just told me, you're certainly no marriage expert. We've been together, what, five days now? And you think you can judge my wife?"

"She left you alone to deal with Claire's death. It wasn't your fault! Aren't you even angry? She could have at least stayed with you through that painful period, but she coped out."

Carter was seething inside. "Oh, like you staying with Stewart until he makes partner, while you're sleeping with me?"

"*Slept.* Once. Stress relief."

Her words hurt, but more than that, she had split open his carefully constructed reality. He sat mute as Kat stomped down to the galley, came back with paper towels, and mopped up the wine on the table. "There. Is that what Becca would do?" She spun around, carried the towels and wine glass to the galley then locked herself in her cabin.

Alone, Carter rushed to the bow, collapsed against the rail to wait for the angry pressure in his chest to subside. During the night, Kat heard him pacing around on deck, but she didn't get up.

CHAPTER 19

Carter had finally fallen asleep in the early morning hours and the persistent banging on his cabin door woke him from a sound sleep. He flung open the door anticipating some additional post-storm crisis. Kat stood in the hallway; her hair wet from a shower.

"I couldn't wait any longer to apologize," she said with a faint smile. "I shouldn't have said those things last night. In my defense, exhaustion is partly to blame—and if I remember, we polished off two bottles of wine. Times like that my brain's censor shuts down and stuff comes out my mouth that shouldn't."

Carter ran his hand over his unshaven chin. "Well, you were right about one thing. Becca wasn't perfect. She smoked. She had diabetes and knew better. And she couldn't balance the checkbook."

"I made coffee. It's out on the cockpit table. Come on," Kat said.

They sat in the warm morning light, listening to the wind rustle the fronds of the palm trees and the occasional splash of small fish avoiding predators. A flying fish landed on the deck, and Kat tossed it back in the water. Finally, Carter broke the silence.

"That was the first time I let myself be angry with Becca. I had buried my anger, but boy was I angry last night."

"At me?"

"You and Becca."

"I heard you on deck," Kat said.

"Yeah. I even swam to shore to walk off some rage."

"God! I'm glad I didn't hear you go overboard. That would have truly frightened me."

"There's more I need to tell you," Carter said.

"You don't need to."

"I want to." Carter took a deep breath. "Becca didn't leave me. She killed herself."

"Oh, my God. I assumed…"

"Of course you would. I don't know why I let you believe that. Remember I told you I went to Nassau to pick up a boat? When I got back, Becca and Claire were in bed together. Claire had died, just as I knew. Her little bald head was snuggled up against her mother. She looked so peaceful. Then I discovered the awful truth. Becca had taken her own life along with Claire's." Carter massaged his forehead.

"Becca's depression over Claire made her blood sugar spikes worsen. She injected insulin as often as five times a day to control her blood sugar, but this was an intentional overdose. Becca left a note which I'll never forget. 'When Claire was born, she clutched a bit of my heart in her tiny fist. I can't live with that piece in heaven. Please be happy again.'" Carter's voice broke. "I knew Becca was depressed. So was I. Still, I should have seen this coming. I never should have gone to pick up that boat. If I had been there, I could have rushed her to the hospital. Saved her."

Kat reached across the table and rubbed the back of his hand. The weight of her hand didn't register. He was a world away.

"It was horrible. There was an investigation. The police took me in and questioned me. Where was I? Why had I gone away? For how long? Had I brought the insulin back from the Bahamas? I couldn't even grieve. God! I had just lost both my wife and daughter."

Carter found himself fighting for composure. "I don't think there's anything as painful as watching your child die. I wanted to die along with them. But neither Becca nor I have siblings, and Claire was the only grandchild. This was particularly hard on Becca's parents, but mine too. It broke my heart, and I didn't know how I was supposed to act, so I did the manly thing and blocked out my feelings."

Kat's hand was still on Carter's. She didn't want to break the contact.

"Now it's nightmares; they follow me everywhere. They're so vivid sometimes they leave me confused about what's real and what's not. Like when I heard you cry for help, I was sure it was Claire. Everyone said it would get easier, but it hasn't."

Carter cleared his throat. "I gave up the cottage and moved back on *Wind Chaser*. I got a few charters that winter and was beginning to pay down the loan. But then July came, and with the heat and threat of hurricanes, people don't charter boats. At least I convinced myself that was it. Truthfully, I wasn't good company. The joy had gone out of my life.

"The bank started calling, and I had no money to give them. I took odd jobs around the marina, and one day I was washing down a mega-yacht when a man in a suit carrying an expensive briefcase walked up and asked me where *Wind Chaser* was docked. He had repo man written all over him. He had no idea who I was, so I misdirected him, walked back to my boat, threw off the lines, and headed to the Bahamas. I knew it was going to end, but *Wind Chaser* was all I had left, and I wanted to keep something alive." Carter sighed and focused on Kat. "Then I anchored where I did, and you know the rest of the story."

"God, I was an asshole."

"I should have told you back in Nassau. I'm not sure why I let you think Becca left me. I didn't think we'd be together very long, so it didn't matter what you thought."

"I'm glad you told me," Kat said. "Maybe I won't make an ass of myself again. Please accept my apology."

Carter smiled. "Apology accepted, and I hardly think of you as an ass. You were great through that storm. I think you might catch on to this sailing thing."

Kat and Carter were distracted by the return of the ray. They watched until it skirted away, kicking up a cloud of sand with its wing.

Kat broke the spell. "Let's go do something. Maybe see that plantation?"

"Might as well, we've got to wait for high tide to get out of here and the time won't move any faster sitting here."

They took the dinghy to shore and walked along the firm sand beach until Carter spotted a low broken stone wall that marked an overgrown trail. As he pushed aside the branches, curly-tailed lizards scurried out of their path.

"I think this is it but watch your step. These islands are mostly limestone, it's jagged and collapses easily. You could twist an ankle. You've already got enough cuts and bruises, and you'd be no good to me as a crew member with a sprained ankle."

"Well, thanks for your concern."

"Hey, Rollins suggested that." Carter forged ahead through the undergrowth.

"Slow down," Kat called, "I'm tangled up in this briar."

"That's a chinny briar bush, be careful." Carter's warning was too late. Kat was already picking the painful stickers out. "Give me your hand. It's not serious, just painful, and even that will go away as soon as we remove the briars." Carter took her hand and picked out the spikes. Then gently kissed her palm. She snatched her hand back and started walking. Carter caught her by the shoulder. "Wait up. I'm sorry."

"It's not the time. We both have too much going on."

"Right. Sure. Come on. We're almost at the ruins."

"What happened to the plantation?"

"Like so many broken dreams in these islands, farming didn't work out."

"Where'd the people go?" Kat asked.

"No one knows, probably to other islands or the States. The buildings were abandoned. They finally decayed, and roofs and walls caved in."

"How sad."

"The end maybe, but not all of it," Carter said. "People from all walks of life were thrown together. Marriages took place among folks who in their old lives wouldn't even have spoken to each other. They shared a dream and everyone contributed."

Kat sat down on a crumbling stone foundation. "That part I get. I've always wanted to be equal partners with the men in my life. I haven't had that. I never had a chance with my father. He loves me, I know, but he's first and foremost The General. When he taught Buddy to shoot a gun, I learned too because I thought that would impress him. My brother and I weren't equal either; he was the needy one and got all the attention. Then I married Stewart, but that only worked as long as I was dependent on him. It feels like I've lived in the shadow of men all my life."

"And?"

Kat rubbed her palm where the briars had stabbed her. "I'm saying you're not the only one who has work to do."

"Come on. You need to see the house." Carter reached for Kat's hand, pulled her to her feet, and led the way through the ruins. "When we get to the top, you'll be able to see *Wind Chaser* in the anchorage." Carter stopped abruptly. A single cable cordoned off the top of the crest. A sign hanging on the wire read, "Keep Out, Private Property." Trees had been bulldozed, leaving their roots exposed. Rotting building materials, the remains of two bulldozers, a truck with flat tires, and a rusted generator were scattered across the barren land. A vacant trailer with a faded sign read, "Office". It stood in the sun surrounded by nothing but dirt and dust.

Carter stepped over the sagging wire and stopped. His stomach flipped. Kat caught up and stood beside him.

"What's going on?"

"The plantation house is gone. It stood right here." Carter pointed.

"Looks like someone bought up the island and planned some sort of development. I've seen this over and over. People tear up a place to fill unrealistic dreams, and once they destroy the natural beauty, their resources run out, and they leave it like this." His arm swept across the devastation. "Why do the Bahamas allow people to violate this paradise? Why can't they leave things alone?" He picked up a rock and hurled it at the trailer.

"Carter, stop. This isn't about you."

"It is. This island was mine. I need it to stay the same. No one has the right to change it." He continued to throw rocks until one broke a window. Finally, he squatted down, grabbed a handful of soil, and let it run through his fingers. "There's no place to picnic," he said quietly, his anger spent.

Kat knelt beside him. "Come on, let's head back down. We'll have our picnic on the beach."

"Another memory gone," Carter said. He stood up, wiped his hands on his shorts, and took a last look around.

Kat held his hand. "The past is not a place to stay. Maybe it's time for you to start new memories." They stepped back over the cable and headed down the path toward the boat.

Suddenly Carter froze. He heard the throbbing of a helicopter before he saw it and pulled Kat into the bush. They watched as it circled slowly around *Wind Chaser,* so low that one of the flotation cushions in the cockpit was blown into the water by the downdraft from the blades. The co-pilot leaned out and appeared to be photographing the transom with the boat's name.

"Coast Guard again?" Kat asked.

"No, their helicopters are white with an orange stripe and have the Coast Guard crest on the tail."

The pilot had spotted the dinghy pulled up on shore, and the helicopter swooped above the trail. "Stay down," Carter commanded. They covered their ears as the terrifying sounds of automatic weapon fire filled the air. Once the firing stopped and the helicopter gained altitude, Carter stepped out onto the trail with his hands in the air. A man leaned out, brandishing the weapon in his hand, motioning them to leave. The craft hovered at the top of the island, hoping to find a place to put down, but the abandoned machinery made landing impossible and the chopper sped away.

Kat came out of the bush, dusting off her hands and knees. "God, what were you thinking. They could have killed you!"

"That wasn't their intent."

"What was their intent?" She asked.

"To convince us to leave."

"How'd you know that?"

"They were firing into the air, not at us. You didn't see any bullets shredding the trees or bushes around us, did you?"

"I wouldn't know. I had my eyes shut and my ears covered."

"They only wanted to make a lot of noise to scare us."

"Well, they succeeded," Kat said over her shoulder as she stumbled down the rough path to the shore. Scrambling into the dinghy, she asked, "Do you think someone knows where we are?"

"How?" Carter asked.

"The Coast Guard location for starters," Kat said.

"Yeah, but that only announced where *Wind Chaser* was. Still doesn't clue anyone you're here."

On the way back to *Wind Chaser,* Carter detoured toward the boat cushion floating on the water.

"Can't we just leave it and get out of here?" Kat said. Their close call still shook her.

"We can't until high tide." Carter leaned over the side of the dinghy and scooped up the cushion.

Once they had the dinghy tied to *Wind Chaser's* stern, Kat said, "I'm worried about Manny,"

Carter shook his head. "I'm not. But what about Rollins?"

Kat wasn't about to tell Carter that Rollins distrusted Manny, so she let the question hang.

"Back in Nassau, you went into the bar pretending to be my nephew. Maybe your disguise wasn't as great as you thought," Carter said. "But as soon as the tide rises, we'll get out of here. We can pick up a mooring in Warderick Wells further down the Exumas, or if this weather holds, stay out in the ocean until Tuesday when we're to meet our protectors."

CHAPTER 20

Carter eased through the boats swinging at anchor in Elizabeth Harbor at Georgetown. More than one hundred snowbirds made this their winter destination and spent three or four months in the crowded harbor playing volleyball on the beach and socializing at impromptu pot-lucks in the evenings. Once they set their anchor, they didn't go anywhere until it is time to migrate north back to the States or Canada. It wasn't Carter's kind of place. .

"This harbor looks like a forest of silver birch trees," Kat said. "I don't think I've ever seen so many sailboats jammed into one anchorage. Don't they run into each other?"

"Sometimes." Carter was looking through his binoculars. "I'd hoped to dock at the marina, but there's nothing solid to tie up to."

Evidence of the storm was everywhere in the harbor. Not all of the area provided shelter from southeast wind, and this storm had taken many by surprise. Three boats lay washed up on shore, either having broken free of moorings or dragged anchor. Two more listed badly at the storm-damaged docks. Others had torn sails and tattered Biminis. There was some advantage to being in open water when a storm hit.

The Top and Bottom Marine Supply and Hardware Store was just a short walk from the dinghy dock. It was usually well-stocked, but today would be busy, and Carter hoped the parts he needed would still be available.

"Those agents don't arrive until tomorrow so I'm going into town to see if I can get the glass for the windshield and parts for the bilge pump."

"What about Isadore? Could he be here?"

"Not a chance. If he survived, with that wind direction, he'd wash up in Eleuthera, probably as far north as Spanish Wells."

Carter tied to the dinghy dock and made his way around palm fronds littering the road. He walked past the post office, its front window boarded over, the Peace and Plenty Hotel, the Two Turtles Bar, and paused in front of Victoria Primary School. Claire had attended classes at the school one winter while he overhauled *Wind Chaser's* engine. Children played outside, their young voices blending into one enthusiastic chorus. He pictured Claire running among them. She'd been so proud of her uniform.

At the marine store, Carter gave Nobbe the dimensions for the glass and picked up parts he needed. He started back along the dirt road that ran beside the harbor to the dock. From a distance, he saw her standing in the dinghy, hair in a ponytail. "Claire!" he called as he ran for the dinghy.

The little girl turned quickly toward him but seemed unfazed. "I'm Elizabeth. Dad and New Mom call me Lizzy, but I think that's a baby name. I like Elizabeth. I was pretending."

"Me too." Carter sat down and swung his legs over the side of the dock.

"I was pretending I was a sea captain. I've never been on a boat. Are you a captain? Is this yours?" Elizabeth ran her hand along the smooth rubber side of the dinghy and wiped her salty fingers on her shorts.

"Who's Claire? I've never been in the Bahamas before, don't you just love it? I'm collecting shells. You should see how many I have. We had a big storm day before yesterday. One of the shutters blew off the little blue house where we're staying. It's got lots of flowers and lizards with curly tails. They even come in my window. I have my own room with bunk beds. It's bright pink. Do you live here?"

Carter smiled listening to her enthusiastic small girl chatter. "No, I don't live here; I'm a boat captain. My sailboat's out there," he said, pointing toward *Wind Chaser.* "This is just the little boat I use to come to shore. It's called a dinghy."

"Who's Claire?" she asked again.

"Claire was my daughter. She's not here anymore; she got very sick."

"Oh, you're still sad, I can tell. It's okay to say she died. I know about these things. My Grandma Bea died last year, and Poppy is sad too. Now all he has are his horses, Pepper—that's his dog—and of course the barn cats, but they don't have names."

"Yes. She died. She was only nine. We sailed all over these islands. She could swim and dive too."

"Wow, she had the whole world. More than most kids ever have, even if they grow all the way up. I know she was happy. I bet she wouldn't have changed one day, even to have more days."

Carter was surprised at this insight from such a young child, even a precocious one. "You know, you're right. She did have an unusual life, and she loved the islands as much as you do right now."

Carter chatted easily with Elizabeth, telling her about his charter service and the things Claire loved about the islands. Her eyes widened as Carter recalled how Claire ran the dinghy, fed the iguanas on Allen's Cay, and snorkeled on the reefs.

An anxious voice interrupted them. "Lizzy. We've been looking for you. What are you doing in that boat?" Carter turned and watched an attractive young woman run down the dock. He knew she meant, who's this man you're talking to?

Visitors often didn't know how safe the out-islands were. Except for Nassau and Freeport, he and Becca had let Claire roam without any concern for her safety. Many times Claire spent the afternoon at the home of a new island friend and was invited to stay for dinner. It was the one time she'd get to watch TV. There was a reason that the Bahamas referred to these islands as Family Islands in their promotional material.

"It's okay," Carter said. "It's my dinghy. She wasn't doing anything wrong. Just pretending." The woman looked skeptically at Carter. "I'm Carter McDowell. I operate a charter sailboat service out of Fort Lauderdale." He pulled a card out of his wallet, hoping his credentials would assure her that he wasn't about to kidnap her daughter, even though the idea had some appeal.

"Mom, he has a big sailboat out there," Elizabeth said as Carter helped her out of the dinghy. "This is just his little boat. Isn't that cool? Two boats. He sails all over the place. He's a real sea captain. He told me all about it. Why don't we get a sailboat?"

"I'm sorry Mr. McDowell, Lizzy thinks the whole world belongs to her."

Elizabeth cupped her hand around her mouth and whispered to Carter, "See what I mean. She still calls me Lizzy."

Carter nodded. "Parents are like that. You'll always be her little girl, just like Claire will always be mine."

"Mom, can we go on Captain Carter's boat someday? He says lots of people take trips on it; it's what he does."

Elizabeth's mom smiled. "We'll talk about it."

Carter saluted and winked. "Hope we meet again someday, Elizabeth." He climbed into the dinghy, leaving her waving from the dock.

Weaving his way through the harbor, Carter's heart was lighter as he mulled over what the little girl had said. How much Claire had gotten out of her short life. He needed to think more like that. As he approached *Wind Chaser,* he saw Kat sitting at the table in the cockpit.

"That took a while, I was about to eat without you," she said.

"I ran into a little philosopher in town."

"I don't follow."

"It doesn't matter. Just another gal in my life who's helping me move on. What do we have for lunch? I'm hungry, and I want to get started on the repair of the bilge pump. Nobbe is bringing the glass out once it's cut. I'll need your help getting it in."

It was late afternoon before the glass was in and the bilge pump working. Carter felt content, a feeling that had been missing from his life.

"I have to let the sealant set, and tomorrow morning I'll go back into town to fill the propane tank. By the time the flight gets in with the agents everything should be ready, and we'll be set to go." Carter stretched and yawned. "I'm going to take a short nap. After that, if you want to go for a swim, we can dinghy over to Sand Dollar Beach."

CHAPTER 21

The sun was low in the sky when Carter woke. He'd slept longer than planned, too late for swimming. He didn't hear Kat moving about and assumed she was also napping. They both deserved it after the physical and emotional exhaustion of the past forty-eight hours. Carter decided to take the opportunity to show her she didn't have to assume the role of galley slave. He'd start dinner.

Setting up the cockpit table, Carter squinted over the stern into the late afternoon sun. The dinghy was gone! Dinghies were often stolen for the engines and boaters sprayed new outboards with dull gray paint so they appeared to be old, worn, and less appealing to potential thieves. But that was in Nassau. It never happened in Georgetown. Everyone left dinghies in the water tied to the stern. Then another thought flashed through his head. He immediately went below and tapped on Kat's door. No answer. He knocked again, louder. Nothing. As he opened her door, it was clear she was gone. This was the second time she had taken a risk and gone off without him. He didn't like it.

"Damn it!" he shouted, then he heard the outboard and saw her heading across the harbor.

"Where were you?" He asked as she threw him the line to tie off the dinghy. He tried to breathe normally. "Don't go off again like that. Wake me if you have to."

"I had something I needed to do. You said yourself, Isadore's not a threat. I didn't need you."

"Are you going to tell me?" Carter asked.

"Can I have some of that wine?"

Carter was still waiting for her to answer.

Kat twirled her sunglasses in her hand. "I didn't tell you everything I talked about with Rollins back in Nassau," Kat said. "He gave me the names of the other two geologists."

"Go on." Carter was impatiently tapping the table with a spoon.

"One of them lives here. That's where I was. After I talked to Rollins, I dug up information on these other two geologists that Oriental Minerals hired. It seems Woodside has a big-time gambling addiction and is in serious debt. I think that's why he moved here; out of reach of the loan sharks and no casinos in Georgetown to tempt him. Charles Russell, the other one, has an entirely different reason to need money, but that can wait. Tell me, doesn't it seem a little suspicious that Oriental Minerals hired guys who basically could be bought off? They just miscalculated with Buddy."

"I know Charlie. He lives on Sampson Cay. He keeps the generator and everything else that's important to the marina in working order. Didn't know he was a geologist."

"As soon as I told Woodside who I was and that I was investigating Buddy's disappearance, he yelled at me, claimed he knew nothing about the accident, and that filing his report, as he was required to do, finished his responsibility concerning any of this."

"Pretty defensive, I'd say."

"More than that, he said that if I came near him or his family again, he'd contact the police and press charges of harassment. Slammed the door in my face. Seems to me he'd want to help solve the disappearance of a colleague."

"Sounds like he's scared," Carter said.

"Every time I bring up Buddy, I get a dialog about these stupid reports. Right from the time of Rollins' dinner in Bimini."

"Please tell me you're not going back to see Woodside again."

"No, he's not going to talk to me. He made that clear, but I want to go to Sampson. Will you take me?"

"Can't you just bake cookies or something?" Carter asked with a slight smirk.

Kat stuck out her tongue.

"As I understood Rollins, I'm to be your charter service. Just promise you won't go alone to see Russell. Either take these agents that are coming or me. Better yet, all of us."

"These guys are geologists, not mafia."

"I don't care," Carter said. "You and I have guns; they could too. And it's a sure bet that Woodside has called Russell. He'll be expecting you. I don't know what you're uncovering, but it seems a lot of people don't want it disclosed."

"The phones are still out," Kat said. "If we go as soon as possible, Woodside may not have made contact."

"Are you sure you can trust Rollins? Maybe he's setting you up to save his ass."

"This is important to him."

"Well, it's your investigation. Just remember Rollins is a politician up for re-election. He's hardly an objective party. If it comes down to it, he might be willing to sacrifice both of us to win his election. He wouldn't be the first politician to make that kind of call."

"I trust him."

"If you say so." Carter shrugged and stopped fiddling with his spoon. "I've started dinner."

The next morning before nine, Carter dropped off the propane tank, checked on the flight arrival, and started back toward the dinghy. A hand grasped his shoulder so hard it made him wince. He heard a low voice.

"We need to talk." It was Manny.

Without turning, Carter said, "Last time you said that it didn't go so well."

"What you mean? You still got your boat and one of da best lookin' white gals I seen in thirty years. Wanna change places? I'm glad to see you made it through dat storm. Not everyone so lucky. We still lookin' for some boaters and a small plane dat went down. Let's you and me walk away from all these eyes and ears."

The two men walked in silence out on the little peninsula that ended at the concrete government dock. "We can sit here." Manny motioned to an overturned hull among other abandoned and derelict boats littering the shore. This was not the view the cruisers had from their boats in Elizabeth Harbor.

"I have some information you and Mz. Kat need to know. After dat storm, Isadore was picked up by a big Hatteras near Spanish Wells. Heard it on da radio. He rented a Sea Ray there and headed dis way. Good chance he's already here."

"Well, I was sure wrong about that."

"About what?"

"I told Kat I didn't think there was a chance in Hell that Isadore would make it down here. Are you sure? I haven't seen a Sea Ray in the harbor."

"There're lots of other spots to anchor if you don't want to be seen. Maybe he over near Stocking Island."

"Okay, but if he's here, why don't you pick him up?" Carter asked.

"Well, you know about small fish. We hopin' he'll lead us to whoever's got their hook in him. We just gonna follow him for now, but you been pretty casual wanderin' around dis island and I come to tell you, he's a real threat to you and Mz. Kat. I suggest as soon as you get those agents onboard, you put dat pedal to da metal and head up to Sampson Cay as fast as you can make dat sailboat go."

"Why? I thought Rollins wanted us to be conspicuous. Sampson is so isolated."

"True, but there's someone on Sampson Mz. Kat will want to talk to. One of the geologists who worked with her brother lives there. Name's Charles Russell. You know him?"

Carter nodded. "Thought he was a mechanic." He hoped his face didn't give anything away.

"He dat too. But my point is, if you evade Isadore again, we're hopin' the real culprits will figure out how incompetent he is and come after you themselves. So far, da guys Isadore's workin' for are intent on keepin' their identity secret. We want to land da big fish."

"Great. So we run from Isadore and into the arms of seriously bad guys."

"We hope so, but remember by then you have protection. Right now, you just listen. I've got something else to tell ya."

"Go on." Carter's eyes were on sandpipers skirting the water's edge.

"Piccolo wasn't killed when a timber fell on him. He was shot in da head."

Carter turned abruptly toward Manny. "Do you think she killed him?" Somehow he couldn't say Kat's name.

"Don't know for sure, but I don't think so. First she don't have any motive dat I know; she and Piccolo were friends from a long time back. And I don't think she had a gun until I issued it in Nassau. We had her backpack and nothing there except her computer, phone, and girl stuff. We didn't find anything in the remains of dat building either. We been over it a second time after da autopsy. Da caliber of da bullet was the same as police issue."

"Isadore?"

"Possibly."

"Why?"

Manny shrugged. "Maybe Piccolo saw him start dat fire. Or saw him with someone—like one of those Koreans."

"And you're still not bringing Isadore in?"

"Well, it's like I said, we're hopin' with you as bait, he'll lead us to da deep fishin' ground."

Carter wondered if the PM was protecting his son-in-law until the election was over. Had he ordered Manny to leave Isadore alone? No matter what Kat said, Carter wasn't trusting Rollins and now had suspicions about Manny. If the evil guys did show up, he doubted two agents would be enough.

"If Kat's not a suspect, can I tell her how Piccolo was killed? She feels so guilty about his death."

"I guess it don't matter, but keep it between yourselves. We don't know how she fits into all of dis, but someone is targetin' her." Manny continued, "Right now, you watch your back. I can't be with you. Da memorial service for Piccolo is Friday on Andros, and I need to be there, more reasons than one. While you here, best to lay low, maybe keep out in dis harbor on dat beautiful sailboat until you get dos agents onboard. Isadore and whoever he work for obviously got their own set of eyes and ears. They know you here."

CHAPTER 22

Carter tied the dinghy to *Wind Chaser* and called to Kat. "I saw Manny in town."

"Manny? How'd he know he'd find us here?"

"Well, I guess Rollins told him we were coming to pick up those agents. But listen, here's what he told me." Carter repeated his conversation with Manny.

"I should feel relieved that I'm not a murder suspect, but Piccolo died because of me, and Isadore lives. He's too dumb to die. What were the chances he'd make it someplace safe in that life raft?"

"That's what they're designed for."

"Did you tell Manny I knew about Russell?"

"No, he didn't seem to know that Rollins told you, so I thought it best to leave it at that. I also learned the plane is going to be late. We need to be at the dinghy dock at four this afternoon, and it will be after five before the propane tank is ready. The storm put everyone behind."

Just before four, Kat laughed as she lowered the binoculars. "That's got to be our spies sitting on the dinghy dock. Just like Rollins said, yellow duffle bags and all. Either this is what the Feds thinks sailors wear or they've got a sense of humor." She wiped the lenses of the binoculars and handed them to Carter.

"These two have eye-blinding bright Bermuda shorts, tacky t-shirts, pasty winter-white Langley skin, and boat shoes with socks." Kat continued, "No one wears socks. The guy's a bit chubby for my taste, but the woman's pretty. They're dressed more like twins than Buddy and I ever were. Definitely undercover as sailing novices. We'd do just as well without them."

"Can you keep your mouth closed and smile?"

"Of course." Kat pressed her lips together in a tight smile.

"Just because they don't know anything about sailing doesn't mean they're not experts in their field. I think their dress is fine. People often charter because they don't have any experience. It's how they learn. You didn't know much about sailing when you hopped onboard."

"At least I dressed for the part, bare feet and all."

Carter steered the dinghy through the choppy harbor; salt spray wet their faces. As they neared the shore, Kat waved and called to the couple. Carter brought the dinghy alongside and held it while Kat jumped off and tied up.

"Welcome to the Bahamas. Hope your flight was okay. This is Carter, your charter captain, and I'm Kat, I do the turn-down service and put the chocolates on your pillows."

The pair introduced themselves as Emma and Bill Hostetler.

"Is this all you have?" Kat asked, pointing to their duffle bags.

"That's it," Bill said. "Enough for a week."

"If we end up staying longer, we can wash on the boat, right?" Emma asked.

"Absolutely," Kat responded. "Jump overboard in your clothes and take a swim. I've done it; the salt makes them a bit stiff, but think of it as starch."

Emma looked at Kat, not sure whether to laugh or not.

Carter cut in. "What she means is you can wash a few things in the sink, but in general, we conserve our freshwater supply for showers and cooking. It's possible to get clothes washed on the islands. Lots of the marinas have laundromats, and if not, you can find someone in town who will do it if you ask around. Don't worry."

Kat jumped from the dock into the dinghy and reached back to help the couple board. "Watch your step; it can be a bit tricky if you're not used to inflatables."

Emma took Kat's hand and gingerly stepped into the dinghy.

"Sit on that back seat," Kat said. "Don't move. Okay, Bill, you're next." Bill fell onto the seat, rocking the boat.

"Neither of us has ever been on a sailboat before, but we like new adventures," Emma said, clinging to the sides. "Is it always this hot and humid?"

"Only from February to November. The rest of the year it's only hot, unless there's a hurricane." Kat gave her best pressed-lip smile as Carter started the engine and pointed the dinghy toward the anchorage where *Wind Chaser* swung. As they zigzagged out among the boats, waves splashed over the sides.

"Better hold those duffels on your lap so your clothes don't get wet," Carter said.

"Is it always this rough?" Bill asked.

Carter raised his voice over the outboard. "No, but this harbor is not very protected, and it can take the seas about forty-eight hours to calm down after a storm like we had."

"I brought some Dramamine just in case. I use it when I fly, but it makes me drowsy, so I hate to take it." Bill said.

Kat rolled her eyes. *Wonderful. Spooks who are either seasick or sleeping.*

As the agents climbed out of the dinghy onto *Wind Chaser's* deck, Carter whispered. "I saw that."

"You didn't say I couldn't roll my eyes," Kat whispered back.

Carter had moved to the bunk room so his guests could have the master cabin. "I'm assuming you want the large cabin. It has a double center-line berth."

"Oh, it's small," Emma said, looking over the cabin. "I've seen photos of cruise ships; I thought it would be bigger."

"Those photos are taken with wide-angle lenses and photoshopped. This, on the other hand, is truth in advertising," Kat said.

"*Wind Chaser's* a charter boat, not a cruise ship," Carter said. "But this cabin has a private head and shower. When you use the shower, please turn the water off when you soap up and on again to rinse." He continued, "Marine toilets can be a bit confusing. There're instructions posted on the wall to tell you how it works. It uses seawater to flush, and if you don't turn the valve off, it can flood the boat. And please remember nothing, absolutely nothing, goes down the toilet except toilet paper and what you've eaten."

"I'm sure we can manage," Bill replied.

"Okay, but call one of us if you have any problem, repairing a toilet is my least favorite job," Carter said. "I have to enter my repairs in the maintenance log then I'm going back to town to pick up the propane tank. By the way, we realize this was short notice, and I want you to know we appreciate you coming."

Carter walked through the main saloon. Kat whispered, "If you love me at all, don't leave me alone with them. How can you be so nice?"

"It's my business. If I wasn't nice, they wouldn't come back."

"Well, these two won't be coming back."

"Maybe not, but they might have friends who want to charter. If you get answers for Rollins, I'll have a boat available again."

Kat turned away as Carter sat down at the navigation station and pulled out his log book. Bill appeared from the master cabin and sat beside him.

"Carter, as Emma said, neither one of us have any boating experience. That wasn't a ruse. I'm sorry about that, but the agency had no experienced sailors available. But if you'll be patient with us on that score, I'm certain we can give you the protection you need."

"No problem. I often have people onboard who are inexperienced. If Kat gets testy, just ignore her. She gets that way with me too. It's been a rough forty-eight hours and we haven't had much sleep."

"No need to apologize and thanks for understanding," Bill said. "And there is one more thing. We aren't married. We didn't even know each other until we were given this assignment."

"So you don't want to share a cabin? Kat and I were thrown together by accident also, and it's the same situation." *Kat's going to murder me if I put her and Emma in the bunk room.* "*Wind Chaser* has three sleeping cabins. One has two bunks. You mind sharing with me?" Carter asked.

"I think that would be best," Bill said.

"No need to say more," Carter said. "But if the two of you change your minds, let me know. Your secret would be safe with us."

Kat wandered back into the main saloon as Carter said, "We can't leave until morning, so I thought we'd all go to Ernestine's for dinner. You should have some local color to take back with you."

"That's not why we're here," Bill said. "We'll follow the two of you and make it look like we're your charter, and you're showing us around the island."

"You do look like novices. No one would guess otherwise," Kat said, biting the inside of her cheek.

"Well, we're supposed to be conspicuous now that you're here," Carter said. "Ernestine's is a good place to start. It's popular with both cruisers and the islanders. Good Bahamian food and music. Have you been briefed on a man named Isadore Jones?"

"Yes, we've seen photos and had a complete briefing, by the Prime Minister, no less."

"Well, be prepared," Carter said. "We've good reason to believe he's somewhere on this island."

CHAPTER 23

"What time is it?" Kat asked the following morning as she joined Carter and Bill in the cockpit.

"Nine twenty-four. Or I should say zero nine two four," Bill smiled.

"Really? I thought it must be noon. I guess slogging along under power makes the time move slowly."

Carter sensed Bill was trying to be friendly, but Kat, being Kat, wasn't doing anything to make the trip easier.

"How long will it take to reach Sampson Cay?" Bill asked. "I'm feeling a little nauseous and when I knocked on Emma's door she said she hadn't slept well and has a headache and stomach cramps. Said she started feeling queasy after we got back from dinner last night."

"It's about a six-hour run. I can't put full sails up since we're heading north and into the wind. Sorry about that. Sails steady the boat."

"I think I'll go lie down."

"Good idea, either that or stay outside and focus on the horizon. That often helps. We won't be out of sight of land much. You'll soon get your sea-legs."

Within half an hour, Bill was back on deck, looking pale. Beads of sweat stood out on his forehead. He sat down in the cockpit and stared at the horizon.

"How's Emma?" Hardly had the words come out of Carter's mouth when she stumbled up the companionway stairs, leaned over the rail, and threw up.

She was shaking as she crumpled onto a cushion and stuck out her hands. "Look at this. My hands are so swollen, I can't even make a fist. They itch like mad, but if I rub them, they burn. It's driving me crazy. It's like the nerve endings are all mixed up."

"Hmm, nice nail polish," Kat said.

"Let me look," Carter said. Small blisters had formed between Emma's fingers. "You've got ciguatera. I've had it myself."

"What's that?"

"Fish poisoning."

"How'd I get it?"

"From eating reef fish contaminated with toxins that are on the coral. It's not poisonous to fish, only humans."

"What kind of fish?" Emma asked.

"Grouper, snapper, and barracuda, chiefly. Didn't you order grouper last night?"

"Yes. They said it was fresh. Caught that day."

"I'm sure it was. There's no reliable way to tell if fish are contaminated, the toxin is odorless and tasteless."

"You can always toss a piece to a cat. If the cat doesn't eat it, you shouldn't either," Kat added.

"Really?" Emma asked.

"No," Carter said, glaring at Kat. "That's one of many island tales."

"Is it serious?" Emma asked.

"It can be. It usually goes away in a week to ten days, but it's quite variable." Carter wasn't about to tell her that it could be months or even years and relapses were possible.

"You really should be where medical attention is available, in case it gets any worse," Kat added. Carter sensed Kat's intent.

"Will it?" Emma asked.

You couldn't get your hand around a gun if you had to. You'll just get in the way. Carter throttled back to idle.

"I eat grouper in the States. Why haven't I heard of this?" Emma asked, staring at her hands.

"You probably would if you lived in Florida. It's all about coral reefs and water temperatures," Carter said. "Outside of Florida, we don't have much coral along the east coast, and the water cools down in the winter, so ciguatera isn't common."

"Will it get worse?" Emma asked again.

"I don't want to scare you, but this is a nerve poison. Kat's right. I recommend we go back. There's no airport on Sampson. You'd have to first get to Staniel Cay by boat, then charter a small plane to Nassau, and change again there to the U.S. If I turn around now, you can catch the flight out of Georgetown directly to Fort Lauderdale."

Kat glanced at Bill. "Didn't you order grouper last night?"

Bill reluctantly turned his gaze from the horizon. "Yes."

Carter chimed in, "You said you felt a little nauseous, it might not be seasickness. The early symptoms are a lot alike, nausea, sweating, stomach cramps. Any blisters between your fingers?"

Bill examined his spread fingers and shook his head. "Don't see any."

"I think you're good. Just seasick," Carter said. "But it's best if you go back with Emma to be on the safe side."

"I'm sorry. We weren't the right choice for this assignment," Bill said sighing.

"It's not your fault," Carter said. "But at least with the wind behind us, I can get the sails up, and the ride will be smoother. Not much else I can do. I'm sorry this had to happen on your first sail." He turned to Kat, "Will you bring them some ibuprofen? It's in the ..."

"I remember."

After Carter swung *Wind Chaser* around, Bill and Emma retreated to their cabins. Kat stood beside Carter at the helm. "I'm not waiting for more agents. Rollins' plan failed. Time is of the essence, and I'm done sitting around. We'll head to Sampson Cay on our own."

"Well, this isn't Rollins fault. Just bad luck."

Carter had to ferry Bill and Emma to the dock and then on to the taxi. The question was, where would Kat be safe? He didn't want to leave her alone on *Wind Chaser* and going to shore didn't seem a good option. As he motored slowly among the boats at anchor, he spotted a Beneteau Oceanis with a green Bimini top and sail covers; the name *Serenity* boldly printed across the stern. A rowdy party was in progress.

"That's Steve and Jane Robinson." He turned to Kat. I think you should join their party while I escort Emma and Bill."

"And how do you plan to get me invited?" Kat asked.

"Watch." Carter dropped anchor as close as he safely could to *Serenity.* He and Kat were in the cockpit when Steve yelled over the water. "Hey Carter, Y'all come join us. Bring your crew and charter folks. It's my birthday."

"Thanks," Carter responded. "What can we bring?"

"We can always use more beer. Kalik or Sands will do unless you have some American beer," Steve answered.

Carter dropped Kat at the party, explaining he'd be back once he took his charter folks to shore. Words of sympathy followed Carter's explanation that one of his guests had ciguatera, and they were headed home. Carter knew it would be a long time before either of the spooks ate fish—any fish. While he was sorry for Emma, like Kat, he was glad to be rid of them. So far, they had only added complications.

Carter walked Bill and Emma to the Batelco telephone office, knowing he would find Woody with his rusty blue car and sometimes taxi. Woody's wife ran the phone and fax service and unless there was a plane coming in, Woody would either be there or across the street drinking Kalik and watching the ever-present game of dominos. Luckily for the agents, Woody was in the phone office propped on Rosie's desk.

Bill turned to Carter. "Should we see a doctor before we leave?"

"I know Emma's uncomfortable; honestly, there's not much that can be done. It has to run its course. Just hope it's a short one. The only thing that sends people to the hospital is if the poison affects their breathing muscles, but that's why I think you should be with her. If it makes you feel better, the government clinic is on the way to the airport; you might get Woody to stop and see if Doc. Rolle's there today. I don't remember which days he's in Georgetown."

Carter turned to Woody. "How 'bout taking my charter folks to the airport?"

"No problem, mon, but seem to me I just pick 'em up from der yesterday."

"Well, the wife has fish poisoning."

Woody peered at Emma's hands. "Oh Lordy, you be mighty uncomfortable for a while Mz. Emma. You might as well save your money and go on home, but we do hope you come back to our islands one day. Dis really don't happen very often. All my years eatin' fish, I've only had it, oh, maybe two, three times."

Emma groaned.

After they were in the taxi, Carter poked his head back in the telephone office. "Hey Rosie, are the phones up yet?"

"Nope." He waited for more information, but in typical Bahamian style, Rosie only answered the question he asked.

"How about tomorrow?"

"Tomorrow we see. Dat be another day." As far as Carter was concerned, that was a piece of good news. It was quite possible Russell didn't know they were on their way to Sampson.

Carter stepped back out into the sunshine to the loud slapping of dominos against the table, followed by enthusiastic cheering. This was the unique way Bahamians played the game; a game that seemed to have no end, only a change in players. He watched the group gathered under the Banyan tree; its distinctive twisted trunks and low spreading branches provided the shade both for the ongoing game and Momma Daisy's Bakery Van. The van smelled like heaven and sold the best pastries and bread on the island. Dr. Rolle was one of the players.

"Hey, Doc, I just sent someone to your office. The woman's got ciguatera. They're flying out, but they'd like to see you first."

Rolle continued to slap his dominos. "She breathin' okay?" he asked without looking up.

"Seems to be," Carter replied.

"Not much I can do then. But Cecilia in da office. If she need me, she know where to find me."

Rolle continued his game, so Carter headed to the dinghy dock. As he ducked around a tree, he froze. Isadore was stepping out of his dinghy. A powerboat would have stood out among all the sailboats and Carter hadn't spotted Isadore's Sea Ray. He must have picked up a mooring at Stocking Island as Manny suggested.

Once Isadore was out of sight, Carter slipped over to Isadore's dinghy, looking for a way to sabotage it. Unlike the trusting seasonal sailors, Isadore had chained and locked his dinghy to the dock. There was no way Carter could untie the painter and let it drift off with the current. Then he noticed Isadore's dinghy had an electric outboard engine. The high-tech battery was mounted on top of the motor. Carter stepped into the boat, unplugged the battery, quietly lowered it into the water, and watched it sink. *That will slow him down.*

Carter picked up Kat from the party aboard *Serenity* and made an excuse for their immediate departure. On the way back to *Wind Chaser* he told Kat he had seen Isadore and had dumped the battery pack from the outboard in the harbor.

"I'm proud of you. Didn't know you were capable of being so devious without my help," Kat grinned.

Carter ignored her. "We need to get out of here. With that electric outboard, he could easily come over in the night without being seen or heard."

"Are we heading to Sampson?" Kat asked.

"Are you sure you want to? We don't have support. We could go back to Nassau."

Kat shook her head. "I didn't find out anything here, and there's some reason Woodside is so defensive. I want to interview Russell."

"It's your call. I can dock *Wind Chaser* in the back harbor at

Sampson; there's little chance Isadore or anyone else will see her. I've slowed Isadore down, but he'll soon know *Wind Chaser's* no longer in the anchorage, and he'll be after us. We can hope by the time he gets to that Sea Ray we'll have the cover of darkness."

"We're sure getting our fair share of night sailing. And all along I was hoping to see the Exumas. Now all I see are moon and stars."

"Well, that's not all bad."

CHAPTER 24

Sampson Cay had the best hurricane hole in the Exumas. The few buildings were made from local gray limestone and gave the island a unique charm that Carter loved. The two-storied structure at the entrance was the home of Marie and Markus Peters, the marina owners, and their three children. It could be easily picked out through binoculars, and when it was directly off his starboard side, Carter turned east and headed into the harbor.

The front dock was used as an overnight stop by boaters traveling along the Exuma Bank. A narrow cut led to a natural harbor in the back, protected on all sides by land, and hidden from view. The current ran swiftly through this passage and skippers waited for slack tide to move from one dock to the other. Carter timed his arrival to pass directly into the back harbor, out of sight of other boats.

Up the hill from the marina was the only brightly painted building; a newly added all-inclusive store with basic food, gifts, and marine supplies. Reverse osmosis supplied the fresh drinking water. Fuel was available at the dock. A diesel generator was housed in another building far enough away from the marina and houses, so there was only a relatively inoffensive rumble. The small island was self-sufficient but depended on the generator that Charlie maintained. His wife, Ruby, ran the store and occasionally served in the dining room if extra help was needed. Each day the kitchen help, grounds and maintenance workers, and dock hands came over in runabouts from Staniel Cay, a short distance away. Sampson, like some of the cays in the Abacos, was a white outpost.

The marina offered family-style seating for dinner every night at seven. Carter knew they might meet intrepid sailors from anywhere in the world, but it was unlikely they would meet other vacationers because there was no land-based accommodation for rent.

The Russell cottage wasn't hard to find. It was the only other permanent home on the island. Carter and Kat walked up the crushed shell walkway and tapped on the screen door of the cottage. A thin woman opened it. It was hard to tell her age, her dark skin was wrinkled from life in the sun, but Kat guessed she was close to thirty.

Kat removed her sunglasses and held out her hand. "Hello, I'm Kat Deano, Are you Ruby Russell?"

"Yes." Ruby continued to hold the door but didn't offer her hand. "What you want?" Kat thought she smelled alcohol and saw Ruby's gaze go to Carter. "I seen you before."

Carter nodded. "Yes. I've stopped here lots of times on my sailboat."

"What you want?" she repeated, her eyes shifting to Kat.

"Dwight Edwards is my brother. He worked with your husband on that rare-earth mineral inquiry."

"I know who he is. Charlie call him, Buddy."

"Everybody does. Buddy's missing, and I'm trying to find out what happened. Is Charles at home?"

Tears formed in the woman's eyes. "You don't know?"

"Don't know what?"

"Charlie was killed when his plane went down during dat storm few days back."

"Oh God," Kat said.

"Come in." Ruby stepped back and held the door wide.

Kat and Carter followed her into the living room and sat on a floral print wicker sofa. Ruby plucked a child's stuffed rabbit from the chair and sat across from them. They waited for her to speak.

"Charlie was goin' to Nassau. Just got his pilot's license a few months back. You know dat pilot Eddie over on Staniel?"

"Eddie Bailey?" Carter asked.

"Yeah, him."

"He's flown some of my charters out of Nassau to the Exumas. Used him lots of times," Carter said.

"Dat not all he take back and forth. Wasn't makin' all dat money just from flyin' passengers in and out of Staniel. He have to go away for a while. Someone dat young with a twin-engine Cessna. He wasn't reliable, Charlie say. Anyway, Charlie had to fly for work, so he got a little single-engine thing."

Ruby retrieved a handkerchief from her pocket and blew her nose. "I'm sorry. I guess I need someone to talk to. Someone who maybe understand. I got no family here. After Charlie and me marry, we move here, but he da only reason I can stay. Markus depend on him. But now dat Charlie's gone, me and da boys will go to my family in Clarence Town, I guess. Dey gonna miss dis." Her voice trailed off as she fingered the satin ear of the little well-loved rabbit in her lap.

"He knew it was wrong what he did, but we needed dat money cause I was gettin' chemo and radiation in Miami. He did dis for me, for da boys. He say dey need their momma and he need his wife. We don't have no insurance, not for U.S. doctors."

"I know exactly what you mean," Carter said quietly.

"Charlie wasn't da same. Nervous all da time, not sleepin'. Jumpy. He was goin' to Nassau to make it right. To tell da truth. It was right after Buddy was here..."

Kat lit up. "Buddy was here? When?"

"Da day before da storm. They was up most of da night talkin'. Sometimes arguin'. I was afraid they wake da kids. Buddy say if Charlie go to Nassau and say da truth, he help Charlie pay da money back 'cause we used it all up. I hear Buddy say that report he write, they changed it. Forged his..."

Kat interrupted. "Do you know where Buddy is now?"

Ruby shook her head. "Don't know. He come in a little outboard cruiser. It got Andros on the stern, if dat mean anything. It maybe twenty-five feet, barely enough room for one person to sleep. He was gonna wait for Charlie to come back, but after da storm he left. He don't know 'bout Charlie. He gonna be broke up."

Kat fell against the back cushion and wiped perspiration from her forehead. "You did say the day *after* the storm, right?"

"Buddy's boat was in da back basin when dat storm hit and da water hardly even settle down when he left next day. Charlie wanted him to go to Nassau with him, but Buddy say no, it too dangerous. They already tried to kill him, and him goin' might put Charlie in danger. He say, best he just hide. Now my Charlie gone." Tears ran down Ruby's face. She took in a ragged breath.

"Charlie say he had to go right away. He had a mechanic go over da plane. Didn't have time to get Cecil over from Nassau. Dis some new guy who say da plane good to go. I don't know why he had to go so quick. Da weather turn bad, but I don't know if it was da storm or da plane bad. Probably won't never know."

"Did Charlie tell you why Oriental Minerals wanted them to say they found those deposits?" Kat asked.

"Don't know dat. Neither did Charlie or Buddy. I hear them talk about it. Wonderin'."

Kat pulled her wallet out of her backpack and handed Ruby a card. "I'm so sorry to hear about Charlie, but you've been a great help. If there's anything I can do, please call me." Kat wanted to say how relieved she was to know that Buddy was alive, but she couldn't say that to a woman who had just lost her husband.

"I hope you find your brother," Ruby said. "Maybe you can make dis right. Charlie shouldn't have taken dat money, but those men not doing right."

"Thanks. I'm going to try."

"And if you find Buddy? Tell him dis not his fault. Charlie do dis 'cause it be da right ting and dat make his dyin' more bearable."

Kat started toward the door. "Ruby, are the phones still out?"

"Yeah. Da tower in Staniel Cay got hit by lightnin' and come down. Two guys killed tryin' to get it back up. It gonna be awhile."

CHAPTER 25

As soon as they were out of sight of Ruby's house, Kat grabbed Carter. "Did you hear that? Buddy's alive. I knew it. I knew it in my heart!" She nearly vibrated with excitement.

It was ridiculous, but Carter was almost envious. "It's great," he said, squeezing her hand. "Finally, some good news."

"You know these islands, where do you think he might be?"

"There're 300 cays in the Exumas alone. That boat has a shoal draft. He can go places that *Wind Chaser* can't. He has plenty of hiding places, and since he doesn't even know we're looking, chances are we won't find him."

"Ruby said the boat had Andros written on the stern," Kat said. "I think we should skip Exumas and head straight to Andros."

"I have a question," Carter said. "Now that you know Buddy's alive, you're sure you still want to go ahead investigating all this?"

"Of course I do." Kat kicked at the gravel, making patterns in the dust with her shoe. "Okay." She took a deep breath. "Rollins told me the land the Koreans bought is on Andros."

"Damn. Am I ever going to know everything you and Rollins talked about?"

Kat sidestepped his question. "I think we should go to Andros and poke around. Rollins didn't want me to go until I had some hard evidence, but I think there's a good chance Buddy's there and now we know at least two of these reports were false. I'd say that's hard evidence."

"Are you going to call Rollins?"

"Not yet. I can find out more on my own. Less intimidating. But if we find anything, I'll call him. I made a deal. I would never have been able to find out about Buddy without Rollins' help. I owe him, and besides, someone's covering up something, so I'm not done here."

Carter tried to hide the relief he felt. If she quit, he would lose Rollins' offer to pay off his loan and keep his boat. Besides, he was enjoying her in ways he never thought he would again. "Have you ever been to Andros?"

"No."

"It's the biggest island in the Bahamas, but it's all chopped up by both salt and freshwater creeks. It could take days, weeks even, to cover it all."

"No, it won't. Rollins gave me the coordinates for the land. We can plot them on your chart. We'll know exactly where this is."

"Oh, so it's a 'we' thing."

Kat grinned. "Well, you did tell me not to go alone I recall, and our bodyguards abandoned ship."

Once they were back on the boat, Carter opened the navigation station drawer and flipped through his charts. He pulled out one that included Andros. Kat gave him the coordinates.

"It's pretty clever how Rollins disguised those numbers," he said. "He's no dummy. It's on South Andros. The bight that separates it from North Andros runs clear across the island." He pointed to the chart. "Not a lot down there. Mostly shallow water, spectacular blue holes, great bonefishing, and lots of lush, mosquito-laden marshes. There were a couple of dive resorts along the east side, but I'm not even sure if they're still open. I can't imagine why anyone would want that land if there aren't mineral deposits." Carter continued to study the charts as though they would provide answers.

"Maybe we'll find that out when we get there," Kat offered.

"It's a long way to Andros. Sure could have used Eddie's plane," Carter said as he put the chart back in its plastic case.

"Are you saying you're a pilot?"

"Small planes. I'm type certified for that twin engine. I've used it before."

"Is there anything you can't do?"

"Plenty. Right now, we need a fast boat. Something that will sleep two. Maybe Ruby can help. She knows everyone who comes over from Staniel. Someone's got to have something they'd rent. One advantage is neither Isadore nor anyone else would be looking for us on a powerboat."

Kat and Carter made their way back to the Russell's cottage. They stood in the kitchen watching Ruby fix lunch for the island's children and teacher. The one-room school, with a studio apartment, housed the teacher who was imported from the States. At noon each day, Ruby walked down to the school with a basket of food. As she worked Carter told her what they needed.

"Even better than gittin' something from Staniel, Markus have a Grady White Express with a 200-horsepower outboard," Ruby said. "He rent it out sometime."

"If we pick our weather it'll work," Carter said.

Ruby looked up. "It mighty cramped inside. Just one v-berth forward. You okay with dat?"

"It'll do just fine," Kat said.

Carter took a sudden interest in the children's drawings taped to the refrigerator. He could feel his face turning red.

"We've got a problem," Kat said, as they walked rapidly along the palm-shaded road back to the marina.

"I know. I'll sleep in the cockpit."

"No, not that. I don't want to tell Marie we're going to Andros. And what will you say about why you're leaving *Wind Chaser?*"

"I'll ask if I can leave her until I do some unspecified repair. But we'll need to have three days of calm weather to get over to Andros, including a fuel stop in Nassau and it doesn't look like that's going to happen anytime soon." Carter grabbed Kat's arm to slow her down.

"Wait a minute. When I was talking to Manny, he said he was taking the ferry from Potter's Cay to Fresh Creek on North Andros for a memorial service for Piccolo. We can set out for Nassau in Markus' boat and catch the ferry from there. Once we arrive at North Andros, we can figure out how to go down to South Andros. If I remember, there is air service, or we'll find someone with a shallow draft skiff to take us over. Let's find Marie. The first step is to rent Markus' boat."

Marie was in the dining room going over the reservations for the evening. "You guys coming to dinner? I got two sailboats out at anchor coming in and another at the front dock. It'll be a small group."

"Actually, that's not why we're here now. Any chance we can rent Markus' Grady White to make a run to Nassau?" Carter told a lie about needing parts.

"Come with me. Take a look at *Sparky.* She's already fueled, serviced, and ready when you are."

They stepped onboard. Carter checked the instruments while Kat looked over their cramped sleeping quarters. It made *Wind Chaser* look like the cruise ship the agent had imaged.

"Which side do you sleep on?" Kat dared to ask. She and Marie laughed. Carter found himself blushing for the second time that day.

Back in the dining room, as Carter shelled out the money for the rental, Marie asked, "So, you gonna eat with us tonight?"

Carter and Kat exchanged glances. Were they willing to risk being with a group?

Kat answered, "Sure. That'd be great."

"We got broiled lobster, fried grouper or barbecued chicken. My advice, go with the grouper, just caught today. Everything comes with peas and rice and 'slaw."

Carter answered for them both. "No. Thanks. We'll have lobster."

Kat and Carter enjoyed the boisterous camaraderie of the other sailors, none seemed overly interested in them. The three guys on the sailboat at the dock were from Australia and were sailing the Bahamas for the first time. They were not used to the shallow water and described the many times they had run aground. The couple on one of the boats at anchor told their funny story about their dinghy ride over to Big Major earlier in the day to see the swimming pigs. One of the pigs had stolen the red plastic gas can out of the boat, and they'd had to chase her down the beach to retrieve it. No one in the group had been as far south as Georgetown, so Carter answered questions about the boating services available there. They were typical sailors, swapping stories, drinking beer or rum, and eating local fare. Carter and Kat found themselves relishing their first relaxed taste of the islands since Mango Cay.

As dinner finished, Markus and Marie came in with a Goombay drum and guitar. The two of them sang island songs from a small stage on the far side of the room. Tables and chairs were quickly pushed back along the walls, and the sailors, dining room staff, and children were soon dancing to the distinctive Bahamian beat. Everyone changed partners and danced in groups, but when Markus sang *Island in the Sun*, Carter took Kat in his arms. Her skin was warm, and her hair smelled like the salt air. He could feel every change in her body as she moved under his hands. Carter didn't want the song to end. He wanted to hold on to this moment as long as he could. It had been a long time since he'd held a woman and she was a special one. He owed her a lot. Eventually, they realized they needed sleep since they planned to leave early in the morning.

When Markus and Marie took a break, Kat and Carter stood to say good-bye to their new friends. One of the Australians said. "We're leaving in the morning, mate. We're on *Sunshine;* it's a Moorings Charter. What's the name of your boat? If you're in the Exumas, we might meet up again. We'll keep a look out for you."

Carter knew that this was a real possibility. Cruisers often covered the same ground and would find themselves sharing other anchorages or docks. He was afraid sooner or later, he would tangle himself up with his lies. This wasn't his style. He needed to be careful. *"Silver Girl,"* Carter answered, stretching the truth further, "She's a Beneteau Oceanis 37. We're docked over on Staniel Cay, we came over in our dinghy. But we're heading north early tomorrow."

Carter stepped out of the shower, wrapped a towel around himself and opened the door to his cabin. Kat threw back the sheet and snatched his towel away. "No room for modesty on *Sparky,* but I want our first time to be on *Wind Chaser.*"

"It's not the first time as I recall," Carter said, smiling as he climbed in beside her.

"I told you, that wasn't love-making. That was survival sex. It could happen to anyone."

"You're sure this is what you want?"

"Shut up, Carter," she whispered, kissing him lightly.

Shining through the hatch, the moonlight lit her flushed face as he ran his hands over her breasts and down her stomach. Her nipples hardened as he ran his tongue around them. The music and dancing had been their foreplay, and now desire took over. Without hesitating, she wrapped her legs around him, drawing him deep inside. They made love with the urgency of new lovers and finally fell asleep spooned against each other.

Late in the night, Kat kissed him between the shoulder blades and rolled onto her back. "I'm not going to keep anything from you anymore."

Carter was suddenly wide awake. "Obviously," he laughed.

"That's not what I meant." She told him about Barracuda Bob and that Rollins suspected that the Koreans might be channeling money to his opposition to finance his defeat and give them free rein to put in a huge casino complex.

"My reputation and success are based on keeping my sources secret. I've never revealed a source to anyone—ever. Now you know everything."

"You're sure that's all?"

"Absolutely—well almost absolutely."

He rolled on top of her, pinned her arms above her head and tickled her with light kisses on her neck, arms, and breasts. This time they made love slowly, their bodies responding in a rhythm that already seemed familiar.

It would only take a few hours to reach Nassau in *Sparky*. Kat poured water through the coffee filter as she hummed the song stuck in her head from last night. So much had changed and she felt great. Carter was fully in her life; soon, Buddy would be too. And once they got to Andros, she was sure she would have answers for Rollins; it was all coming together.

She was so preoccupied that she almost missed the paper on the top step of the companionway stairs. Thinking it was the bill for docking, she finished making coffee before picking it up. When she opened it she was staring at Buddy. A chill ran down her arms. A note with a slightly out of focus photo was attached. He was sitting on a folding chair in a bare room, holding a copy of the *Nassau Guardian* turned to the front page. Kat hadn't seen a newspaper since they left Nassau, but she knew this was intended to show that the photo was recent. The picture proved nothing. Buddy always wore his University of Florida ring, one of his many obsessions. In this picture his fingers were bare. It had been photo-shopped. She scrambled out onto the deck and looked down the dock. No one was around; she didn't expect there would be. She sat down in the cockpit and read the typed note.

```
Ms. Deano,
You missed our rendezvous in Bimini. Don't do
that again if you want to see your brother
alive. Meet us at the south end of the runway
on Normans Cay at 3 a.m. Come alone. Leave
your friend in Sampson. Bring a list of ALL
names in the book you are writing. No
weapons. No cell phone. No recorder.
```

There was no signature. She read the message several times and examined the picture again.

Carter was still asleep when she opened the door to the master cabin and shook his shoulder. He pulled her down against his bare chest, kissing her hair, and running his hands down her back.

"Stop it," Kat said. She pulled his hands away and pushed the note and photo at him. Carter found himself staring at a likeness of her.

Carter scanned the letter and struggled to sit up. "Holy shit! Is this referring to the manuscript about that drug lord?"

"Yes. And the names Lehder gave me."

"Whose names?"

"Men in the business who never went to prison."

"Does Rollins know you're writing this?"

"I don't know. I didn't mention it, but I'm sure he knows all about Carlos' dealings in the Bahamas."

"Didn't you think he should know you're in contact with Lehder?" Carter asked.

"Why? Lehder's activities on Normans were more than thirty years ago. When Rollins and I met, it was the furthest thing from my mind. Buddy was my concern—and the threats to my life. As far as I knew, my writing had nothing to do with that. It's been a slow-moving project. I've had doubts all along it would ever get finished." Kat leaned against the door frame, her arms crossed. She watched Carter pick up wrinkled shorts from the floor and pull them on and followed him into the galley. "This note makes it clear there's a connection between Lehder and Buddy's disappearance."

"Wait a minute. I'm confused." Carter paused, the coffee pot in his hand. "I thought the attempt to kill Buddy had to do with the Koreans and rare-earth minerals."

"Apparently, I've been working under a wrong assumption."

"Where's Lehder now?" Carter asked.

"No comment."

"Last night you said you weren't holding anything back."

"He's in a U.S. Federal prison in WITSEC."

"What's that?"

"The U.S. witness protection program."

"If he's in WITSEC, how do you know this person you're communicating with is Lehder and not someone else?"

"Because he sends details that no one else would know. I've been able to track down some of the names he gave me; these guys are real."

"Let's take this coffee outside." Carter climbed the stairs holding both cups and set them on the cockpit table. "Do you want something to eat with that?"

Kat shook her head. "I've lost my appetite."

"Okay, next question. Why witness protection if he's in prison?"

"Lots of reasons. To name a few, Lehder made plenty of enemies along the way, people with long memories and histories of revenge killings. After he escaped from the raid on Normans Cay, someone ratted on him. He was caught in the jungles of Colombia and turned over to the U.S. He turned state's evidence and testified against Panama's Noriega with the hopes of a reduced sentence. In addition, he named other Colombian drug lords who had marked top U.S. officials for assassination. Lots of people went to prison. He's a dead man if his whereabouts are uncovered or if he ever leaves prison."

"You've said our government knew about all of this. Why didn't they intervene way back in the seventies?"

"It's a convoluted story."

"I've got time. Looks like we won't be going anywhere today."

Kat took a sip of her cooling coffee. "Even before the Bahamas gained their independence the U.S. established naval bases, known as AUTEC, on Andros. Their purpose was to test underwater weapon systems. Andros is the closest island to the Tongue of the Ocean and secluded. The water there is deep, nearly 6,000 feet in places, it's isolated from most ocean traffic, and…"

"Skip that part. I know the waters here. But it seems you're getting way off base from Lehder and drugs."

"Not really. In the late seventies, when Lehder was operating in the Bahamas, it was still an untested democracy. They didn't become a sovereign nation until 1973. Pindling, the first prime minister, was accused of accepting bribes from Carlos, but for the most part, he was pro-American and not a dictator. He ran on a platform guaranteeing voting rights for all Bahamians, not only the white landowners. But splinter groups formed among the black majority who thought Pindling was in the pocket of America. If Pindling was impeached, the Bahamas would have been ripe for a communist overthrow just like Cuba. Can you imagine the repercussions that might have followed if we wound up with a dictatorship here? If something like this happened in the Bahamas, it would have been a much bigger problem for the U.S. than drug dealers. At least that's how the thinking went."

"You've obviously done your research."

"I have to. I've built my professional reputation by getting it right."

"Okay, but could that happen in the Bahamas, as dependent as they are on U.S. money?"

"Sure, it could. Castro never let the loss of American money stop him."

"Point taken. But I still don't understand how this political stuff relates to our naval bases and the drug business."

Kat fiddled with her empty cup. "There were nine AUTEC bases on Andros; it was big business. The U.S. backed Pindling, but we walked a fine line. We didn't want to suggest he was openly ignoring the drug operators in his country. If we angered him, he might withdraw our lease for this costly high-tech research facility. Worse yet, if he were overthrown, not only would we lose a valuable ally, but the secret marine technology developed and tested at AUTEC might be used against us by some anti-American dictator. Think about it. What would happen if the technology had to do with firing nuclear weapons from submarines, and a hostile Bahamian dictatorship, just sixty miles off Florida's coast, had long-range missiles, or worse yet, nuclear capabilities?"

"So, we overlooked the drug thing to keep a friendly ally," Carter said.

"That's about it."

"Okay, but this is some thirty years later. Carlos is in prison and won't get out based on what you're saying. What's the issue now?"

"Lehder knows the names of people who continue to head up successful cocaine enterprises. Once the route through the Bahamas was shut down, many moved their operations to Puerto Rico, Mexico, and Central America. This is just a guess, but maybe some of these guys are afraid he'll expose them. Maybe Lehder's jealous that they're free and making money by piggybacking on his innovations. After all, he was a businessman, and what's he got to lose? Maybe he wants to settle some old scores or could be he's finally developed a conscience. I don't know."

"How do you think they found out about your book deal?" Carter asked.

"That's another thing I don't know, but in this culture, loyalty can be bought."

"Could this be a trap set up by Isadore?"

"You think he's that smart?" Kat asked.

"Well, either way, you're stepping into a mine-field. You're not going alone."

"Reread that note. If I don't show up alone, Buddy's dead. I've just found out he's alive. I'm going."

"And if you do, you and Buddy are dead."

"Not necessarily. If what they want is for me to withhold names, I have some power."

"Is this book done?"

"No, Lehder is writing the last chapter. That was our agreement, or I should say, his one condition. I don't know what the holdup is. He has stage four pancreatic cancer and wants this published before he dies. But frankly, that's not important to me now that I know Buddy's being held hostage because of me and this book. I have to go to Normans; Buddy might be there. How far is it?"

"God, you're stubborn."

"How far is it?" Kat asked again.

"About forty miles. It'll take us six hours on *Wind Chaser*."

"You can't take *Wind Chaser* in there. Remember what Manny said? She's too easily identified. If she steams in there, it'll be obvious I'm not alone."

"Alright, we go to plan B. We'll take the Grady White. It's got all the navigational equipment we need. That boat could do the run in two hours. It's got that cuddy cabin where I can hide."

"That boat's fine, but you're not going," Kat said sharply.

"So, you think you're going out there in the middle of the night, in a thirty-three-foot boat you've never operated to meet thugs on a runway on what used to be the coke capital of the northern hemisphere? You've never been to Normans Cay. It's tricky getting in."

"You said *Sparky* has navigation instruments, and I'll have your charts and spotlight."

"You're not leaving me behind," Carter said raising his voice.

"Yes, I am."

"Then you're not going either."

"You can't stop me." Kat crossed her arms and locked eyes with Carter.

"I can. I'll tell Marie you're not capable of handling Markus' boat."

"I can't believe you of all people would tell me not to go when I might have a chance to save my brother's life."

Carter visibly flinched.

"Sorry, that wasn't fair," Kat said, putting her hand on his arm.

"I wasn't in the right place to help Becca or Claire. Let me do this."

Kat sighed. She wasn't going to win. "Okay, but promise you'll stay hidden."

"Promise." Carter relaxed. At least he'd be nearby if something went wrong. "With *Sparky*, we can leave at midnight. I know Marie said the boat was ready, but since I have the time, I'm going to check *Sparky's* fluids and plot our course. Want to come?"

"No, I won't be any help. I'm going to download my manuscript onto a flash drive to give to these guys, not only the list of names. That will convince them I'm sincere."

CHAPTER 27

Late in the afternoon, Carter and Kat loaded their lifejackets and spotlight into *Sparky* and as soon as it was dark, crawled into bed on *Wind Chaser*. "I'm going to set the alarm for eleven," Kat said. "I'd like to have coffee before we set out." They curled up together for a short night's sleep.

At ten-fifteen, Kat gently lifted Carter's arm off her side, shut off the alarm, and eased out of the bunk. Quietly, she slipped on her clothes, grabbed her shoes, and stepped off *Wind Chaser*. She paused, listening to make sure Carter hadn't stirred. The only sounds were the occasional call of a night bird and the distant rumble of the island's generator. She walked barefoot down the concrete quay and over to the dock where *Sparky* was tied. Turning on the instruments, she found the route to Normans that Carter had loaded. She untied the lines and pushed away from the dock before starting the engine. She didn't want to risk waking Carter.

It was dark and overcast, no moon or stars, with a light easterly breeze. There was no point in checking the weather forecast because she had no choice. She was going. Following the course in the GPS, Kat threaded her way through the channel out of Sampson Cay and into deep water. Turning north, she opened up the 200-horsepower four-stroke Honda. The boat settled into a rough plane, bouncing off the tops of the waves. She kept her running lights off.

In her mind, Kat visualized what she remembered about Normans Cay while reading up on Lehder's location in the sailing guide. The island resembled an upside-down fishhook with its barb end curving around a lagoon. The shank of the hook composed a narrow four-mile-long island, white sandy beaches, and offshore, a virgin coral reef eleven miles long. An airstrip cut across the southern tip and a single road ran northward through dense trees and what was left of a string of houses.

The reef posed a problem. There were numerous shallows and isolated coral heads and everything Kat read cautioned against going in without proper light and the ability to read water depths. She approached the cay slowly, relying entirely on her instruments to give her depths and locations of the reef. It was tense and exhausting work.

Her stomach churned as she finally secured *Sparky* to the broken dock. She imagined someone was stalking her even though she didn't detect any sound or movement. The ride over had taken longer than she planned. It was ten minutes after three and everything was dark. She hurriedly worked her way through the scrub brush with her flashlight, not making any effort to remain unnoticed. She knew they'd find her. The moon broke through the clouds and made the derelict runway appear as an eerie chalk-white scar through the windblown trees. Suddenly she was grabbed from behind and a hood thrown over her head.

"Don't make a sound or you're dead." A Latino accent. Her hands were quickly tied behind her with a line that cut into her wrists as she stumbled between two of her captors over broken concrete. The hood disoriented her, but when they stopped, Kat imagined she was at the south end of the runway. The two men gripped her arms with such force that her hands tingled as a third man roughly patted her down and ran his hands under her shirt, searching for a wire. Finally, he pulled off her hood. Kat instinctively turned away from the bright light in her eyes. She could only see the outline of a pistol aimed at her and the silhouette of one man, but she was sure all three wore masks and gloves. These were professionals. *Stalker and crew,* Kat named them in her head. The tall one spoke.

"Where are the names?"

"Where's my brother?" The slap across her cheek was so sudden her head snapped back.

"I'm asking the questions. Don't piss me off," Stalker shouted into her face.

Kat's cheek burned. "In the right pocket of my shorts. Cut my hands loose. I'll get it for you."

Stalker laughed, "Are you shittin' me?" He reached into her pocket and pulled out the list, going over it with his flashlight. "Is this all?"

"Yes," Kat answered. "I brought you the entire manuscript on a flash drive in my other pocket."

"Okay, so you are a smart bitch." He pulled it out and with a quick motion, grabbed the back of her head with one hand and shoved the muzzle of the gun against her mouth, forcing her to open it.

She groaned and tasted blood. Tears stung her eyes.

"That's a silencer at the end of this barrel. No one on this island will hear anything, and it will be a long time before anyone comes down this way to even find your body. *Entiendes?*"

Kat nodded, her attempt at boldness gone.

"Now listen carefully. We have a good life. You have a good life. Publishing those names would fuckin' end all that. The U.S. can't ignore us if our names come out in a book. We got a nice little business going and don't intend to do time for things long past. Print those names or open your mouth about any of this, you're dead. We've got very long arms and equally long memories."

Kat kept her breath even. She could hear her heart pounding in her ears and wondered if her captors could see it beating through her shirt.

"No matter where you are, we'll find your pretty little white ass, and until we do, you'll always be lookin' over your shoulder. Do you know what it feels like to never let down your guard? Damn exhausting. Step out of line, and you and all your family will die in most painful ways." He took the pistol out of her mouth and turned to one of the others. "Cut her loose."

"I've got something to show you." He handed her a bunch of photos, aiming his flashlight so she could see.

Her hands shook as she flipped through them; his message was clear. There was one of Carter as he walked into the marine supply store in Georgetown, Buddy at the End of the World Bar, and another as he left Ruby's house on Sampson. One was of her stepping off the ferry in North Bimini, and a photo on Mango Cay; Carter, his hands in the air. The most chilling was a picture of her father's Mercedes in front of his hunting cabin in South Dakota.

"Keep 'em for your photo album. We've got more. And don't bother dusting them for prints. We're not stupid. Now, tell me what you're gonna do. Talk to me."

Kat swallowed and licked her dry lips. "I won't publish the name of anyone who has so far escaped prosecution."

"Or has escaped the attention of the fuckin' DEA or anyone else."

"Or escaped the attention of authorities. Will you take me to Buddy now?"

"When he's drunk he's got a real big mouth. How do you think we found out about your book?"

"Buddy can't hurt you. He's never read the manuscript. He doesn't even know where it's stored."

"Well now, if that's the truth, we don't have a problem. I just hope you're not shittin' me. It's up to you to make sure it stays that way. Ever watch a man die writhing on the ground with his kneecaps shot out and his intestines spilling out when a blade slices open his fuckin' gut? Not pretty. It takes a long time."

Kat doubled over and threw up.

"Fuck. I hate dealing with women."

Kat wiped her mouth with the back of her hand. She had one more fear. She tried to keep her voice from quivering, but she was shaking all over. "I'm not going to circulate those names, but Lehder is dying. He wants to get this out. If I don't do it, he'll supply someone else with those names."

"Tell us where he is. We have contacts on the inside. We can stop him."

"Lewisburg," she lied. She didn't know where he was, but this was a maximum security prison that was at least a possibility.

"Good. Meanwhile, buy time. Make Lehder think you're going to publish this like he wants. Better hope he dies soon. And this meeting never happened."

"Fine by me. Will you take me to Buddy?"

"He's not here, but don't get the wrong impression; we know where he is and who he's with. We can pick him up anytime we want. Part of our guarantee you don't rat on us." He crammed a wad of money into Kat's pocket. "You're workin' for us. Now get your shit together and get out of here. And don't come back to Normans under any circumstance."

Stalker turned off his flashlight. In the silent blackness, Kat couldn't tell if the men were still nearby. "What about Isadore?" she called. "He seems determined to kill me."

"Don't worry about his stupid ass. He's not your problem." She heard the men retreat into the bush.

Kat stood alone until her eyes adjusted to the night light. She wasn't sure she could even make it back to *Sparky*. She wanted to run but her legs didn't seem to be under her command. She had to stop twice to reorient. Eventually, she saw the boat bobbing against the dock. Her hands hardly cooperated as she untied the lines. Twice she dropped the key in the bottom of the boat before she was able to push it into the ignition. She should have brought Carter.

The men waited until they heard Kat's outboard start then headed through the woods to an abandoned house that had once been part of Carlos' vast estate. A hissing gasoline lantern illuminated the graffiti-marked walls. They kept their masks on.

"Did you convince her?" Manny asked.

"What do you think? Would these convince you?" Stalker pulled out another batch of photos, including Manny's family as well as Kat's. As Manny flipped through them, he stopped at one that showed him years ago. There were three people in the photo; Carlos, Ilse, and him. Ilse, the only woman he ever truly loved, was in the middle, an arm around each man. They were all laughing, and he and Carlos held drinks toasting something. That part he couldn't remember.

"Dat was a long time ago. Things are different," Manny said, hiding his trembling hands under the table.

"We know. But think of it as insurance. Wouldn't be so good if the PM got this photo of his chief of homicide or better yet if his opposition did. I don't expect you ever told Rollins about this fuckin' indiscretion. If I'm right, this would have kept you out of the police academy too."

"Look, I don't care where you do business; Panama, Puerto Rico, Mexico, you name it," Manny said. "My agreement was, you keep da powder out of da Bahamas, and I see your names don't come up. Ever. I done dat."

"And so you have, but now we have this new, pretty little *gringo*. We don't need the Bahamas, but we aren't gonna step back into the fuckin' past. And we know, sure as shit, she has a copy of that manuscript with our names, and yours, somewhere. So, your job is to make sure nothing happens to her, and that manuscript stays buried. But her brother? He's a loose cannon. Drinks and talks, talks and drinks. And remembers everything. Can probably recite our names in alphabetical order, yours included. We need you to take him out."

"Now hold on, I never agreed to anything like dat. Dis is da first time I ever seen da guy." Manny managed to hold the photo of Buddy steady.

"Not a problem." Stalker passed him two additional pictures.

"Who's da black guy he with?" Manny asked.

"We don't have a name, but I'm sure you can find that out. Look at that top picture closely. Not too many of your kind wear pilot uniforms. Carlos couldn't even hire Bahamian pilots when he needed them, and I'm sure his pay was better. Find this *piloto negro* and sure as shit, you'll find your target."

"Why don't you do dis yourselves? Why me?"

"I can give you a lot of reasons, but for starters, we don't fit in so well here. Light skin, Latino accents. We'd rather not make our faces known. Second, you can concoct reasons to be looking for the brother without raising suspicions. Just helping the pretty lady find her missing twin. Finally, you want to do this for us."

"Dat part of my life is over." Manny wiped the sweat running down the side of his face.

"Take a look at this before you fuck up." Stalker shoved another photo across the table. Manny held it under the light from the lantern. His heart raced, and his palms were clammy. It was Ilse in a bikini on a beach just as he remembered her, but this time her smile was fixed on a small child in a pink bathing suit, a ruffle across her tiny bottom. The photographer was intent on capturing Ilse so Manny couldn't see the little girl clearly. Her face was hidden by the shade of a floppy pink and white polka-dot beach hat, but he could see soft black curls and chubby light coffee-colored arms and legs. She appeared to be running into Ilse's outstretched arms. The two could not have looked more different, Ilse's straight blond hair, the child's dark curls.

Manny swallowed, his voice barely more than a whisper. "Is she mine?"

Stalker shrugged. "She's about thirty now. Pretty woman. Still lives with her mother, but plans to marry after she finishes up medical school. She's a smart girl. Make a fine doctor."

Manny contrasted this with the mess his son's life was in. Franklin was currently in prison doing fifteen years for dealing drugs. Franklin's wife wouldn't visit, and even though she cashed the checks Manny sent each month, she refused to let him have any contact with his only two grandbabies. For Manny, it was personal. Franklin, and all the young men like him, was the reason he fought so hard to keep drugs out of the Bahamas.

"What's her name?"

"Anna," Stalker answered.

"Where she live?"

"That can wait. We've other business to discuss."

"Look, she—Anna—doesn't have anything to do with dis."

"Well then, let's see that it stays that way. You take care of this brother, and we'll make sure your daughter becomes a doctor and goes on to marry that young man she's in love with."

Manny's stomach burned and he held the photo tightly. He wasn't sure he could let it go. "Can I keep dis picture?"

"Sure, might help you stay focused. We're done here now. We'll be in touch."

Manny sat at the table until he heard an engine start and fade into the distance. Then he put out the lantern, made a trail through the pines and scrub, and started toward the runway. Manny had docked his boat on the other side of the island, but he wasn't ready to leave. With the aid of his flashlight, he stumbled across the broken concrete and walked along the white-sand beach finally coming to the house that Carlos had owned, and Manny and Ilse occupied during the Colombian years. The house was in ruins, most of the roof destroyed by hurricanes. Manny sat down on the steps and listened to the familiar sound of the surf crashing and retreating on the beach, the backdrop for their lovemaking, his dreaming when he was such a naive fool.

CHAPTER 28

The sky was the bright side of gray by the time Kat tied *Sparky* to the dock and walked back to *Wind Chaser*. As exhausted as she was, the first thing she needed to do was face Carter. As she climbed onboard, she felt something sticky on her boat shoes. A trail of blood extended from the cockpit onto the dock. *God, they got here before I did.*

"Carter," she yelled, scrambling into the cabin. He was propped against the settee, blood on his face, chest, and shorts. She couldn't tell if he was breathing. He raised his head as she knelt. "Carter, it's me. Who did this?" He sat listlessly as she scanned the saloon. The place was in shambles, supplies and provisions littered the floor. Cautiously, she got up, opened the navigation station drawer, and pulled out her gun. Stepping over Carter, she searched the boat. No one. Whoever had attacked him was gone. Only Carter could tell her what had happened.

Kat eased herself down beside him and took his cut hand in hers. "Let me clean you up and get you in bed. You've got to help me. Grab the table. I can't pick you up myself." Wincing, he pulled himself up and leaned on her for the few steps to the shower. While Kat undressed him, he stood passively, muttering under his breath something she couldn't understand. It took all her remaining energy to lift his legs onto the bunk, and before she finished bandaging his ankle, he was asleep. Sooner or later, he would tell her everything. For now, whatever had happened was over, and they both needed sleep. She locked all the hatches, climbed into bed, and spooned against his back.

The late afternoon sun woke Carter. He squeezed his eyes shut but the bright light leaked through, preventing him from sinking back into the forgetfulness of sleep. For the first time since he had taken Kat onboard, he was depressed. He examined his cut hands and flexed his fingers, realizing it was more than a nightmare. He thought he remembered an intruder, being struck by the outboard gas can, and kicked in the side, but when he turned onto his back and probed his ribs, nothing hurt. Had he been attacked?

Carter had thrown out the medication the psychiatrist prescribed, hating the effect it had on him. He knew he needed to manage this by himself, avoiding situations that triggered these hallucinations and caused him to relive his sense of failure. He also knew it would take time. The question now was; what to tell Kat? Helping her investigation had given him purpose, and he had a real chance to hang onto *Wind Chaser*. He owed her that, but he couldn't trust her with her lies and manipulations. If this happened again, he wasn't sure he could pull himself out of it. The thought of losing his mind terrified him.

Being careful not to wake Kat, Carter swung his legs over the edge of the bunk and noticed the bandage on his ankle. He didn't remember that. Bracing against the wall, he limped into the pilot-house. He was shocked at the mess. *God, I must have been insane.* As much as he wanted to start cleaning up, he needed to check the cockpit – recalling another piece of the night's terror. Outside, there was no smell of gasoline, and the can remained strapped in its usual spot. Everything was in order, but the Glock that Manny had issued was near the helm. He scooped up an empty shell casing from the floor. Now, he knew what to tell her.

It wasn't long before Kat appeared. Her tone was cautious. "Carter, I need to tell you..."

"No, me first. Sit down. I don't know how to explain these spells I have. Since the day I discovered Becca and Claire, I've had nightmares. Sometimes, like last night, it's more than that. I hallucinate, sleep-walk—I guess that's what you'd call it. And at least at the time, I live it. My mind picks up pieces from the past and mixes them up with things happening now. Like when I heard your call for help out on The Bank. I was sure it was Claire. I see and hear things that aren't there. It happens when I feel powerless to help someone I'm responsible for. The nightmare always ends the same; I fail."

"Post-traumatic stress," Kat said.

Carter didn't react. "I need to tell you, so you'll know how real it was for me."

"I woke just after four. The alarm hadn't gone off. I turned to shake you, but my hand landed on the empty bunk. I panicked and ran through *Wind Chaser*, calling you. All I could think of was that Isadore had somehow gotten on the boat. I couldn't figure out how I slept through any sound of a struggle, but I was sure you were dead, and I had failed again.

"In one way it's not like a dream because it's a logical sequence of events, well, maybe not totally logical, but not spotty fragments that jump around like most dreams. I felt a thump against *Wind Chaser's* hull. I froze and sensed a slight rocking, the way the boat moves when someone is climbing onboard. Somehow I knew this was danger and everything depended on me. A voice begged me to hurry, but my legs were heavy with weighted-down helplessness. It felt as though I was running underwater. I pulled the Glock out of the navigation station drawer. It was so heavy that I struggled to lift it. The companionway stairs were an immense staircase, and I couldn't reach the top. I could make out the shadow of someone in the cockpit, and I smelled gasoline. Whoever this was intended to set the boat on fire. It was so similar to your experience at the Compleat Angler that I was sure it was Isadore."

Carter rubbed his eyes with his knuckles and continued. "He swung the outboard engine gas can, splashing me with fuel and I fired my gun. I don't know if I meant to kill him or not. Most of this took place in my head, but that part is real." Carter held out the gun and shell casing.

Kat sniffed the barrel. "It's been fired."

Carter's eyes darted around searching for anything to settle on while avoiding Kat. He was ashamed and embarrassed, but he needed her to understand how distorted his thoughts and actions had been—and how dangerous.

"He hit my arm with the metal fuel container. The pain numbed my hand, and I dropped my gun. I lunged as it skidded across the deck, but slipped in the gasoline and fell. I grabbed Isadore's ankle, but he was a moving target and kicked at my chest and side. Finally, a blow caught me under the rib cage and knocked the breath out of me. He vaulted over the rail, into his boat, and roared out of the harbor. I was sure this was about you with the same certainty that I knew the intruder was Isadore. I had to find you. I jumped from *Wind Chaser* and ran down the quay to the dock where *Sparky* was tied. She was gone."

"Did you really do that?"

"I'm not sure, but I think so. I ran to where the runabouts are tied. If anyone had been around, they certainly would have thought I was out of my mind, drunk, or stoned. I jumped down into a boat, cutting my hands as I jerked on the rusty chain. I braced my feet against the piling and pulled with all my strength. My foot slipped, and I gashed my ankle. I remember the blood everywhere. I'm guessing that part happened and that's how I cut up my hands and ankle. Then I realized you might be hiding. I staggered back to the boat and climbed over the rail. Like a madman, I exposed your hiding place and threw everything out searching. You saw the mess in the cabin. I must have passed out and hit my head on the table because that's all I remember until you found me."

Kat didn't realize she had been holding her breath. "I wasn't thinking about you," she said breathlessly, her eyes downcast.

Carter's head jerked up. "That's it. That's exactly right." Anger filled his voice. "That's why we can't work together anymore. You only have one focus. Find Buddy. I admire your determination, but not your willingness to walk all over people to get there. Me, Rollins, your husband, you don't think about anyone else, as long as it fits your agenda."

"I know you're angry, Carter, but we *have* to work together."

"Angry? Fuck! Pissed off is more like it. It's the same thing Becca did. She lied. Sent me off to Nassau already knowing what she planned to do. And you, you… It's too much of a rerun. I can't do this again." Carter's fists were clenched, his lips pressed tightly together.

"I'm sorry I lied."

Carter exploded, "'Sorry.' The perfect word. It's not only this once. I've lost track of all the times you've lied to me. You've even pulled me into thinking lying is okay. Well, that's not my style. I may not lead the exciting life of a roving reporter, but people can count on me, and I like it that way."

"Carter, listen. Rollins is waiting for us to solve the rare-earth mineral question; if we don't cooperate, the charges of arson and murder against me may resurface, and Rollins won't pay off your loan."

"Fuck that loan. The price isn't worth it. I'll work something out. You already knew what you were going to do when you agreed we'd go to Normans together. It was a bald-faced lie, and this time, it drove me over the edge. I fired that gun. I could have killed you." Carter was breathing hard. "But while we're on it, you're exaggerating any threat from Rollins. He doesn't dare go after you and have your daddy splash that recording all over the news."

Kat buried her face in her hands and shook her head, her words muffled. "There's no recording."

"You can't be serious?" Carter yelled.

Kat looked up and repeated her words. "There's no recording. My father didn't have a recorder."

"Shit. I can't believe this. How can you be so devious? Do you think Rollins has figured that out?"

"I don't know."

"Can he find out?"

"I don't know that either."

Carter stood up. "What are you going to do?" Kat said to his back. "Say something."

Carter's anger had run out. "I'm going for a walk until I can breathe normally." He climbed onto the dock and limped away from his boat, away from Kat.

Kat was sitting on the pier in front of Carrington's runabout, her feet dangling over the water, a plastic trash bag with her clothes and her backpack beside her. Carter sat down on the other side of her pack, keeping space between them. He wasn't ready to look at her.

"Tell me what happened on Normans."

Kat related every detail of her terrifying experience. By the time she was done, her voice was shaking.

"So, now what?" Carter asked.

"When Carrington gets off work he said he'd give me a lift over to Staniel Cay. From there, I'm going to Andros. I have to warn Buddy. I don't believe for one minute those guys won't go after him. I'm convinced Buddy is on Andros. I've said this before; I'm not your problem. You're not responsible for me."

The sun touched the horizon. Squawking seagulls and the slapping of waves against the dock filled the awkward silence.

"You *are* my problem," Carter said. "I might be able to walk away from you, but I can't walk away from the impact I would feel if you were killed. I do feel responsible, and I can't stand by and do nothing. It's not who I am. If something happened again…" He didn't trust his emotions enough to finish. He picked up her backpack and the bag with her clothes. "Come on. I want to put *Wind Chaser* back together before we leave in *Sparky* in the morning. I'm going to need your help."

CHAPTER 29

It would have been a perfect sail on *Wind Chaser,* southeast winds, and seas running two to three feet under scattered cumulus. But *Sparky* struggled and Kat and Carter were worn out from their uneasy truce and the relentless pounding of the boat by the time they reached the relative shelter of Nassau Harbor.

Carter had never been into Harbor Bay Yacht Basin; the water was too shallow for *Wind Chaser.* It was the low rent district, precisely what he needed. Carter weaved slowly among half-sunken derelict boats to the run-down docks with their decaying pilings. The few sailors docked here were liveaboards trying to stretch their money, but small Bahamian fishing smacks occupied most of the slips.

Carter signed in at the waterfront office, made arrangements to leave *Sparky,* and bought sandwiches for lunch. Kat planned to buy clothes suitable for Piccolo's memorial service. They both recognized the risk, but the East Bay Shopping Center was only a few blocks away, and Kat was determined not to let the threat of Isadore or the Colombians take over her life. This wasn't the tourist district where the cruise ship passengers shopped and ate. Except for the shopping center with its large, well-stocked grocery store, the street was lined with marinas, boatyards, and marine supply stores.

As she walked, Kat changed her pace and discreetly watched to see if anyone was trying to keep a measured distance. No one seemed interested in one more boater headed to the shopping center. She felt good being out and doing something normal, like shopping for clothes.

As she neared the stores, a black Chevrolet Suburban slowed down and matched her pace, causing drivers behind to blow their horns. Kat veered off the sidewalk and tried to duck into a Texaco Station, but the Suburban turned in front of her and stopped. Two men in dark suits jumped out and blocked her. The driver remained in the car, engine running.

"Are you Mary Katherine Deano?" one asked.

"What business is it of yours?"

The men flipped open IDs. U.S., DEA agents. Kat took her time examining the identification that declared them to be agents Joseph Jurgevich and Brian Scofield. "Yes, I'm Mrs. Deano."

"Take a ride with us," Brian said, motioning to the open back door. His voice was firm, and when he slipped his ID into his jacket pocket, he made sure his holster and handcuffs were visible.

Kat looked around and tried to keep her voice even. "Do you guys have any authority here?"

"You know we do."

"Hey mon, get your vehicle out of da driveway. You blockin' traffic, and I'm needin' gas." A man with long dreadlocks covered by a red, yellow, and green knitted cap, and gold chains around his neck, leaned out the window of a dark blue BMW sporting customized gold rims and hubcaps. "Come on, move it. Make your date with da pretty lady somewhere else."

Brian looked at Kat. "Get in."

The driver leaned on his horn. "You deaf? I said, move it."

"Hang on, pal. We're going," Brian barked.

The irate driver started to climb out of his car. "Des guys causin' you trouble?" He asked Kat.

"We're checking for drugs," Brian said, holding out his ID and walking toward the driver.

"Okay, mon, I'm good." The driver ducked back into his car.

Brian turned to Kat. "This is just a friendly discussion. We might be able to help you out. We're all Americans here."

Kat briefly considered running to the Rastaman, but if these agents were offering help, she needed to hear what they had to say.

"I want to make a phone call first." She wasn't going to go without letting Carter know.

"Don't do it, put it back in your pocket," Brian said, looking at his watch. "This won't take long; if we don't have you back at this exact spot in thirty minutes, you can make that call." He took her arm and pushed her towards the open rear door. "Slide over."

Kat glanced once more at the driver in the shiny BMW before she climbed in. Brian sat down beside her, Joseph got in the front seat, and the door locks clicked. As they turned around in the gas station, Kat heard the Rastafarian again.

"You assholes, you don't own dis place. Dis is da Bahamas." He screeched to a halt at the pump and flipped them the finger.

Brian tapped on the glass partition and spoke into a microphone. "Head toward Cable Beach."

"What are you so jumpy about?" Brian asked, turning to Kat.

"Well for starters, you blocked my way with your vehicle, produced some supposedly DEA identification, shoved me into the back seat, told me I couldn't use my cell phone while saying this is just a friendly drive and discussion. Now, how about telling me how you're going to help me. I was on my way to buy some clothes for a funeral; I can't imagine you wanted to help me pick a dress."

"Sassy aren't you? We want some information," Brian said. "As a loyal U.S. citizen, you shouldn't have any trouble providing it. Are you still involved with drugs?"

"Jesus, that was a onetime youthful indiscretion eight years ago."

"Then why the interest in Carlos Lehder?"

"Who says I'm interested?"

"Don't waste our time. We monitor incoming and outgoing emails on Corrlink. It's the only internet inmates can use. We know he contacted you."

"I'm writing his memoir."

"Why the interest?'

"Since you've obviously researched my past, you also know I'm an investigative reporter. The Bahamas are a special interest of mine. When Carlos contacted me, I was curious."

"We understand this book will contain the names of some big-time cocaine dealers who operated here and in the U.S. thirty years ago. We have reason to believe some of those men have been spotted back here recently. We want their names."

"Where'd you get that information?" Kat asked.

"Doesn't matter."

Kat stared. "You're bluffing. If you know they're here, then you know their names. There's nothing in my book that will help you."

"Word's out Carlos plans to name names. Do you know who Carlos plans to expose?"

"No," Kat lied.

"You're the daughter of General Mark Edwards, right? And Dwight David Edwards is your twin?"

"Obviously, you don't need me to confirm that."

"We understand the General's health isn't so good. A stroke, I recall."

"What's this about?"

"Is this your brother?" Brian pulled out a photo of Buddy that looked recent. He was kissing a black man who looked vaguely familiar.

Kat felt a knot in her stomach. *Do they know Buddy's alive?* "This doesn't prove anything. That picture could easily be photo-shopped."

"The General's views on homosexuality are well publicized. He openly opposed the 'don't ask, don't tell' policy… and with a black man? I'm guessing he's no more tolerant of interracial relationships."

Kat wasn't concealing her distress. The General would disown Buddy if he saw this. Even if he thought Buddy was dead, the shock could produce another stroke, a fatal one. Would she ever be able to stop protecting Buddy? She was annoyed at the arrogance of these guys, and her anger surfaced. "Damn-it, that's blackmail."

"There's another option. We can subpoena you and question you under oath."

"And you think those cartel guys won't come after me? Kill my family and me? Great choice."

"Nobody asked you to write that story. Besides, there's always witness protection."

"Not an attractive alternative." Kat needed some time and legal help to figure out her options. Could they extradite her? Even if they couldn't, she'd never be able to return to the States without being subpoenaed. Who was scarier, the Colombian cartel or the U.S. government?

"Why don't you go directly to Carlos?"

"He won't talk to us. He doesn't exactly have warm fuzzy feelings for the DEA. We were a big part of the sting that shut down his operation on Normans, and he claims we reneged on a plea bargain years ago."

"I know all that, and from the court documents I've read, he might be right on that score."

"We would have gotten Noriega anyway. The information he provided didn't give us anything we didn't already have."

"Why are you interested in these guys now?"

"We've been tracking the cocaine connection for years. This isn't new. But wide-spread drug operations are making border towns in Mexico, Texas, and Arizona nearly uninhabitable. In addition, we're getting pressure from both sides about the hordes of Central Americans fleeing drug-related violence, straining resources in Mexico while trying to get into the U.S.—legally or not. No border wall is going to stop that. We've got to get to the source. If we had names..."

"You know damn well once you go after them they're going to know where those names came from. You made the connection. They can too. You're not offering me any protection." Kat looked out the window as they passed the luxury hotels on Cable Beach. "This is all speculation on your part, but suppose I do have those names. My testimony would only be hearsay."

"It would be an important beginning. If it's the cartel you're afraid of, we can take care of that. You haven't heard what we can offer in witness protection. It could be very attractive."

"You don't have a history of keeping your promises." Kat knew that the U.S. had promised to reduce Carlos' sentence from one hundred thirty-five years to thirty-five years if he testified in the Noriega trial. After he did, nothing changed. "You're accusing my brother of being gay and threatening me with blackmail. After all that you expect me to believe some rosy picture of a new identity and location? You'd probably put me in Fargo, North Dakota or Chicken, Alaska. I'll take my chances without your help; thank you very much."

"Listen very carefully. You have two weeks to decide to cooperate. After that, we take a different approach; we'll extradite you from the Bahamas. We will get those names, but we prefer to have your cooperation. It will make it easier for everyone. Think about it. We'll be in touch." Brian rapped on the window and spoke again into a microphone. "Drop her back at the Texaco station."

As Kat climbed out of the Suburban, she added, "If you have anything on Buddy, I want it all destroyed before I'd even consider your offer." She slammed the door.

Kat was shaking, from fear or anger she didn't know. Was there any way she could stop the U.S. from extraditing her? She needed to talk to a Bahamian lawyer who specialized in such issues. She looked at her watch, two thirty-five. She and Carter planned to catch the ferry for Andros at nine the next morning. She stepped into the gas station and borrowed their phone book. Once outside, she sat down on the concrete stoop, her back against the hot building. There were four attorneys listed under Immigration and Naturalization. Pulling out her phone, she started down the list.

The third name she tried, the Honorable Winston Worthington-Atwater, M.P., had a four o'clock opening. *A member of parliament, that can't hurt.* His rate was four hundred dollars an hour. It didn't matter if it was U.S. or Bahamian dollars; the exchange rate was one to one. *God, Stewart is practicing in the wrong country, but it'll be an excellent use of the drug money forced on me.* She made the appointment, hurried through her shopping, and dashed back to the boat.

CHAPTER 30

At the marina, Kat climbed onto *Sparky* and threw the bag of clothes into the cuddy cabin with more force than necessary.

"This is exhausting. I can't even keep up with who my enemies are."

"What happened?"

As quickly as she could, she summarized her encounter and asked Carter to go with her to see the lawyer. The taxi dropped them off five minutes early near the U.S. Embassy, in front of an immaculate older house with white hurricane shutters propped outward, shading the windows. An elegant polished brass plate, on one of the wrought-iron gates, identified the office of the Honorable Worthington-Atwater. Kat pushed the buzzer below the plate, the gate swung open, and allowed them to walk up a brick path that wove through carefully landscaped gardens. An officious secretary greeted them at the door and directed them to a waiting room cooled by a ceiling fan. Flowering plants, in shades of pink, white, and purple stood on table tops and contrasted with the pale green walls.

"I guess his fees cover a gardener as well as office staff," Kat whispered.

At four-ten, the secretary returned and ushered Kat and Carter into Mr. Worthington-Atwater's walnut-paneled office. He was a tall, thin man of perhaps seventy, with a narrow face, rimless glasses, and a carefully trimmed mustache. Although dark-skinned, he seemed very much a British Colonialist. *A black Neville Chamberlain. I'd prefer a black Winston Churchill.* Kat thought.

Mr. Worthington-Atwater stood from behind his desk and motioned them to be seated on a brown leather couch. Kat glanced at the purple and yellow orchids on the side tables.

"Raising orchids is my hobby. Most people don't know this, but the best way to water orchids is to place three ice cubes in each pot once a week. It's a good thing I don't have any pets, my garden takes up all my spare time. It's quite a job in this climate, either too hot or too rainy. Take your pick."

Kat smiled but didn't comment; she was aware that the meter was ticking and started right in with her story. "I'm assuming everything I say here is confidential."

"Yes, of course. We have the same standards for client confidentiality that you would expect from an American lawyer. And if it makes you feel better, I attended law school in the U.S." Worthington-Atwater pointed to the diploma from Colombia Law School on the wall behind him.

Kat gave a quick background to establish her credentials and the reason she had come to the Bahamas. She didn't want the Honorable Worthington-Atwater to think she was just some paranoid neurotic taking up his time. She ended by describing the meeting with the Colombians on Normans and the threat from the DEA. As she promised Rollins, she didn't mention him at all.

Mr. Worthington-Atwater sat attentively, his chin resting on one hand. Before he spoke, he took off his glasses and wiped them on a white handkerchief from his breast pocket, then he nodded. "Yes, yes, you do have a problem—a potentially serious one. I am very familiar with the history of Normans and with the shameful behavior of Pindling's government. Even though as our first prime minister, he established racial equality and gained our independence from

England, this is a dark stain on our history. I think you are well advised to avoid testifying if at all possible. These drug people are dangerous, no morals at all.

"But as far as staying here without extradition, I don't think I have any positive news. I can slow down the process; make them take it to court. That would delay things for a few months, maybe a year, but it would be at considerable expense. The fact is, I have never known a Bahamian court to prevent the extradition of an American citizen. We take the view that if the U.S. wants to extradite one of its citizens, we should not interfere."

"No exceptions?" Kat asked.

"There are two. But they won't do you much good," Worthington-Atwater answered. "One is political asylum. From what you've told me, there is no valid reason for you to make that claim. And I must tell you; we have no American citizens who are here as political refugees.

"The second exception is equally unlikely to apply to you, diplomatic immunity. Diplomats include the prime minister, members of his cabinet and parliament, like me, and ambassadors. As long as we are in office, we cannot be prosecuted, even for a parking ticket, much less extradited. Unless of course, the extradition is surreptitious, done in violation of Bahamian law."

Kat perked up. "Did you say members of the Prime Minister's cabinet are in that category?"

"Yes, as you can see, it's very restrictive. I'm sorry. There are other countries that will not permit extradition. Belize is one that comes to mind. I can research that if you wish. As I said, I would advise you to avoid testifying against the cartel if at all possible."

"Thank you," Kat said, standing. "You've been very helpful. Don't research those other countries yet. I'll let you know if I need that."

Worthington-Atwater extended his hand. "It's been a pleasure meeting you and Captain McDowell. I'm sorry I don't have better options. If I can be of further service, please let me know."

Outside on the street, Kat suggested that they walk back to the marina past the cruise ships and the shops offering duty-free merchandise. It was inexplicable, but somehow, she felt less paranoid. "Let's find a good place to eat."

"We can stop at Luciano's of Chicago," Carter said. "They have beautiful waterfront dining. You're willing to risk it?"

"Sure. A condemned prisoner gets a last meal. Besides, there can't possibly be anything else bad happening today; my quota is filled."

CHAPTER 31

Right on schedule, the weather had changed, and Carter was relieved they would not be making their way to Andros on *Sparky*. Gray clouds filled the early morning skies, and wind whipped their hair as Kat and Carter made their way over the short causeway toward Potters Cay. One of the mangy, colorless potcakes panted close behind. Carter was familiar with these skittery, homeless dogs that frequented the docks and marinas in search of a handout. Brightly painted wooden food and fish stalls flanked the broken concrete sidewalk. Carter headed to Natty's Café. Not a cafe at all, but a take-out stand where Carter knew he would find the best sourdough biscuits in Nassau. Clusters of tables and mismatched chairs stretched along the row of stalls, but Carter and Kat would take their breakfast wrapped in waxed paper to eat on the ferry. No matter what they sold, all the open-air stalls smelled like fish, since this was the place where Bahamians came to buy the catch of the day. Business was already brisk; vendors were calling out their fresh stock; snapper, grouper, crab, and conch. Boats bobbed against the quay and the fishermen in rubber work boots, their bare chests already shining from exertion in the morning sun, hoisted net bags with catches from the night's run. Crowds of local customers noisily gathered, jostling for the best position to see what was being scaled and cleaned. This would determine what would be served in homes and restaurants later that day.

As they reached the café, Carter greeted Natty and bought bacon and egg sandwiches on warm biscuits smelling of yeast. On an impulse, he bought a third one and threw it to a nursing bitch, which produced a gang of snarling dogs that minutes ago had not been there. Not about to get into this turf war, Carter left the bitch to fend for herself. So much for his good deed.

Beyond the stalls, they headed toward the Bahamas Ferry office building where travelers bought tickets for Andros, Harbor Island, Eleuthera, and the Exumas. Ferries didn't run to each destination every day, and the sign listed the one to Andros on Tuesdays and Fridays. From the number of people in their line, and the bags they carried, it appeared that many were headed home for a long weekend, bringing items either not found on Andros, or available at a better price in Nassau.

Along with a few other white passengers, Kat and Carter were conspicuous as they approached. There was no way they would blend in with this crowd. The queue didn't seem to move, and as the time for departure approached, and the sun rose higher in the sky, tempers grew shorter. Carter watched three young children, oblivious to the growing irritability, playing tag zig zagging among the waiting passengers. It wasn't long before they knocked over baggage and bumped into people. The father whacked the tallest one on the head, grabbed the other two by their arms, and yelled at all of them, "Sit down." For a moment, all was quiet. Then the impatient voices of the adults filled the air again, and people pushed forward as though being closer would assure them of getting their tickets in time.

"What's the holdup?" Kat asked, shifting her duffle to her other shoulder.

"Nothing that I can see. We're just on island time."

Eventually, they reached the window and Carter bought round-trip tickets. Out of what was now becoming a habit, he scanned the crowd. A chill came over him.

"Don't turn around; Isadore's back there."

Kat stiffened. "He wouldn't try anything in this crowd, would he?"

Suddenly they heard a pop, then another. People started screaming, and the line disintegrated. Frightened mothers grabbed their crying children as a crowd formed. Sirens screamed in the distance; someone had already called the police. Carter and Kat forced their way to the front where Isadore was lying face down on the dirt in a pool of blood. Grabbing Kat's hand, he pulled her away.

Carter whispered into her ear, "We need to make ourselves scarce." They faded back into the crowd and kept their pace steady, moving toward the ferry.

Carter could feel Kat's tension as they walked up the steel loading ramp that accommodated both cars and passengers. While the crew directed cars to the parking on the bottom deck, people wove their way between the vehicles, up the stairs, and into the passenger lounge. The shooting was a police matter now, and it appeared the ferry would leave on time.

Kat and Carter stood at the stern rail and watched the loading; a pickup filled with lumber, a container truck, and a very pink Cadillac hearse, with a set of angel wings as the hood ornament, loaded along with cars of various descriptions. In addition to Piccolo's memorial service, it appeared there would be another funeral on Andros.

Kat focused on the shooting and how close they had come to being killed. "Why weren't passengers questioned before boarding? It certainly wouldn't have happened this way in the U.S." Her cell phone beeped, indicating a text message. "You owe us now." She held out her phone to Carter.

"Shit. This is getting worse," he said.

Kat turned away from the rail. "These exhaust fumes are choking me. Let's find seats."

Groups of swivel chairs around tables filled the spacious lounge. Everything was fastened to the floor. The sides of the ferry were glass. Had they been clean, it would have been possible to look out in any direction, but constant salt spray left the glass with a permanent haze. Passengers who wanted an unobstructed view climbed a short set of stairs to the open top deck. It provided a panorama when the weather and seas were calm, but today, with the wind kicking up the sea beyond the protected harbor, it would be uncomfortable.

Carter and Kat stood in line at the concession stand for coffee to drink with their biscuits. Lugging their duffels to a four-top table near the port side, they would view Nassau on departure. As the big diesel engines of the ferry warmed up, Captain Tyrone Farrington announced that, due to the sea conditions, the ship would take a longer route than usual, leaving by the east end of the harbor and going south around New Providence Island, the same exit Carter took when he slipped out of Nassau for the Exumas.

"So much for seeing Nassau. But you'll get to view Oprah Winfrey's house on Paradise Island. You were in hiding when we passed it on *Wind Chaser*," Carter said. Kat was picking at her biscuit.

"Did you know that before Paradise Island was developed, it was called Hog Island?" Carter continued, "The brains behind the name change thought 'Hog' might not be the best name for a gambling resort. Frankly, I think Hog Island's more appropriate." Carter was rambling, not noticing Kat's silence. The shooting had affected him too, but the message on Kat's phone even more.

As the ferry left the harbor and turned south, the bow plunged into the waves, tossing spray over the cabin top. Those who had started on the open top deck scrambled into the cabin, laughing and brushing water from their hair and clothes. One face was familiar.

"Stay here," Kat said. "That's Albury, the Minister of the Interior. I met him in Bimini."

Kat threaded among the passengers. "Mr. Albury, I'm surprised to see you on this ferry."

Albury held out his hand, his face expressionless. "A pleasure to see you again, Ms. Deano. What takes you to Andros? More articles about our islands?"

"No, I knew Peter Moxey. I'm headed to his memorial service."

"Ah, yes, terrible. You know he was shot and died in the fire the night of Rollins' fundraiser on Bimini? It remains under investigation."

"I know." Kat held his eyes as long as she could stand it. "And you? What brings you this way?" she finally asked.

"There's some property being developed on South Andros by a group of foreign investors, but every time I contact the company, they have some excuse why my visit would be most inconvenient. Makes me suspicious. I'm going to make an unannounced call. Nice to meet up with you again." Albury left Kat wondering; was this only idle chitchat?

When she sat down, Carter asked, "What was that about?"

"I'm not sure. Rollins told me Albury was the only other person who knew the site of the mining. I'm sure that's where he's headed. And I got the distinct impression he thought I was too."

"The only way he would assume that is if Rollins told him," Carter said.

"Maybe he's the leak Rollins is worried about. It wasn't exactly a warm greeting, and he certainly didn't act as though seeing me alive and well was any revelation. I wonder how much he knows."

A wave smacked the bow and water seeped through the ceiling tiles, dripping on many of the well-dressed passengers. People scattered, seeking drier seats. Two men, dressed in black slacks, white short-sleeved shirts, and dark ties seated themselves at the table with Kat and Carter. They introduced themselves as Mr. Clayton Powell and Mr. Ansil Edwins, the funeral director from Angel Wings Funeral Services and his assistant. Carter replied that they were friends of Peter Moxey and were going to his memorial service.

"I heard about him dyin'. I be bringin' Mz. Bethel home, but I grew up on Andros, and I know'd Petie and his mama too," Mr. Powell said. "It's so kind of you to come. His mama be comforted knowin' you care that much to join in da celebration of his passin'. Dis her second son to die. And Mz. Ida May's in a bad way. All she got left now is four daughters."

"I didn't know much about Pete's family," Carter said. "I knew him from the years he lived in Bimini. How'd his brother die?"

"Oh, he die as an infant. Long before Petie even born, but dat don't matter to da mama. As far as Ida May concerned, she has two chirren who pass before her, and dat's not da Lord's way."

"My daughter died," Carter said. "I know what you mean."

"I sorry for you, son. I know dat's hard. Was she just a bitty thing?"

"Nine. Her name was Claire. I miss her every day."

"I know you do. I know you do," Mr. Powell said, nodding. "But dis here funeral just might help you some. People in these islands celebrate life, not death. There's always time tomorrow to worry about da bad things. With families scattered all over, a funeral's cause for everyone to gather. There be lots of singin', eatin', and havin' fun tellin' stories and meetin' up. It go on for a long time, probably most of da weekend since people come from so far. It's good for da soul."

Carter smiled. "Somehow I think you're right."

"Oh, it will be, son. You see. Now, I got another job. I also be da choir director at da Jesus Be Praised Christian Fellowship Tabernacle. Dat's where Mz. Bethel go, and I see da singin' started already." Mr. Powell left the table and made his way across the rolling deck, directing as he went.

As they prepared to disembark, Kat spotted Manny. Everything that happened on Potter's Cay came back to her. She knew he planned to be onboard, but she hadn't seen him during the crossing and thought perhaps he had stayed behind because of the shooting. Someone called out to him and she thought she heard the name, Captain Lightbourne.

"What's Manny's full name?" Kat asked. "I've never heard you call him anything but Manny."

"Manford Lightbourne. Why?"

"Just wondered."

It was more than that. Manny's name was on Carlos' list and Kat sensed this could be useful information.

CHAPTER 32

One of the yachting guides described Fresh Creek as a dream destination. To Carter, it was anything but. Watching the current flowing rapidly through the creek, his mind flashed back to the one time he brought *Wind Chaser* into Lighthouse Marina. The tidal flow was formidable, and docking demanded a degree of seamanship not generally called for. He had waited for slack tide when the water's movement paused so he could tie up safely, and again when he pulled away from the dock. Sleep was almost impossible with the tidal current rocking the boat and slapping the hull. Sure enough, as they walked along the quay to the hotel, he saw two twin-engine sportfishing boats and one lone sailboat. From the expanse of barnacles and algae clinging to the waterline of the sailboat, it appeared the owner had given up moving on.

Kat and Carter walked up the stone steps from the quay to the hotel but found the door locked. They made their way around to the street side of the faded pink concrete block building. Perhaps at one time, the circular drive had been landscaped, but now it was surrounded by neglected hibiscus shrubs. Paper-thin Bougainvillea had climbed over every other plant, adding a chaotic hodgepodge of fragrant colors. Apparently, no one but the service trucks used the once graveled driveway. Giant palm fronds covered much of it and filled in the ruts formed by the frequent squalls. Lizards scurried out of the way as Carter opened the hotel door. Their footsteps echoed on the white tile floor of a spacious, empty lobby. With bare tan walls, the room possessed all the charm of a hospital waiting area. Two love seats with faded cushions stood flush against opposing walls. No conversation groups here.

No one was at the desk, so Carter rang the little round bell on the counter. A voice from a back room called, "Be wid'ya in a minute."

While they waited, Kat looked through the French doors that connected the lobby to the hotel restaurant. No one was seated, but she could see tables with peach-colored tablecloths, elaborately folded white linen napkins, and sparkling water glasses. A fresh hibiscus graced each table. Someone cared about this room. Her stomach growled and she hoped the food lived up to the décor.

The clerk finally appeared several minutes later. "What can I help you wid? Hope you not lookin' for a room. 'Cause wid des two funerals on da island, everythin' be jam up—crowded, what I mean."

"I called yesterday and whoever I talked to said to come on," Carter said.

"Who you talk to?"

"I didn't get her name."

"Probably Sassy. She don't know nothin', but she always say she do. Da truth is, we been booked for a week. You should have talked to Desirene. Desirene Peters, dat's me." The clerk pointed to the sign on the desk. "I'm da one who knows stuff here. If you want, I can call the resort at Small Hope Bay south of town, see if one of their villas available. Gonna cost you more."

"Well, we don't have much choice," Kat said.

"Nope, guess not." When no one answered at the resort, Desirene suggested they leave their duffels with her, have lunch, and come back. Maybe by then, she'd have an answer. Carter told her to reserve a villa if she reached anyone, and he and Kat headed across the lobby to the restaurant.

"You can't go in dat way," Desirene called after them. "Dat door locked."

"I thought you said to have lunch."

"I did, but dat door not open. You got to go around out by da marina side to dat door. It be open." Kat and Carter looked at each other, then left and made their way back around the hotel to the waterside.

"Why does this have to be so hard? They have connecting doors," Kat said, nearly stepping on a yowling, skinny cat who scurried into the bush. She was hot and hungry and worried once again about the shooting on Potters Cay and the recurring feeling she was being followed.

"It's the Bahamian way," Carter said. "Thought you'd be used to it by now. What's the hurry anyway, they probably don't serve until twelve, which means at least twelve-fifteen, and we might as well spend the time walking as sitting."

The waitress, dressed in a bright fuchsia Androsian print uniform, met them with a warm smile. Her name tag read, *Sassy*. "Da fish sandwich be good. Grouper. Just caught today."

With the agent's fish poisoning still fresh in her mind, Kat scanned the other items on the menu. Every time she asked about something, the waitress just shook her head.

Finally, Sassy laughed, "Now you know why we be called da out-islands. We out of everythin'. But we got da Grouper with Mama Dee's mac and cheese. Come with slaw. You like it."

Kat mostly pushed her fish around the plate with her fork, but Carter was willing to run the risk. He had been eating Grouper in the Bahamas for years without a problem and quickly finished both his and Kat's. Before they ordered dessert, Desirene came through the door from the hotel lobby. "I reach Joyette at Small Hope Bay, and she have a cottage. You like it."

"Thank you," Carter said.

"I thought that door was locked," Kat said.

"It unlocked now," Desirene said.

Kat waited for some explanation. None came. Instead, Desirene looked at Carter.

"You gonna need a car."

"I reserved one at Rooney's," Carter said.

"You sure bout dat? When he come by here dis mornin' for coffee, he say he all rented out."

"Well, he had one yesterday."

Desirene shrugged and walked back through the door leading to the hotel lobby. Kat shook her head. "There are some things about these islands I'll never get."

Having read of Andros' infamous mosquitoes, Kat and Carter coated themselves with repellent and went looking for Rooney's Garage and Car Rental, which they learned, was also the only gas station in town. They expected to find it on the main road, but since it looked like a deluge was looming, they decided to ask directions and stopped at a small blue cottage that advertised itself to be the Andros Conservatory and Trust. From the brochure they picked up as they stepped inside, ANCAT's mission was to preserve and protect the natural resources of Andros Island. Carter wondered if that included mosquitoes. After signing the guest registry, Carter asked the smiling hostess dressed, as expected, in a lavender Androsian batik dress, how to find Rooney's.

"It's easy," she said, wiping perspiration from her face with a handkerchief so heavy with perfume that Kat started sneezing.

"You got allergies, girl?" Kat simply nodded, her hand over her nose. "Well, lucky for you, I got dis other handkerchief I can give you," the hostess said, waving more perfume through the air.

"No, that's fine, but thank you," It was all Kat could manage as her sneezing continued.

"Well, then to get to Rooney's. Walk up to da paved road, cross over da bridge to da other side of Fresh Creek. Dat be Coakley Town, but we call da whole thing Fresh Creek. Just ask anyone. Or if no one around when you get to da other side of da creek, follow da road around da back of Sugar Shack at da first intersection. Sugar make good conch salad if you're hungry. You like it. Anyway, that be Chickcharnie Drive, if da sign still up. Turn back toward Fresh Creek, you see it through da trees—da creek I mean, not Rooney's. Keep goin', you come to it. Can't miss it, only gas pump around."

"Do you have a map?" Kat asked.

"No, but you can ask at da tourist office, it's just a five-minute walk, tuck up there in da trees by da Androsian Batik Factory. While you there, you can buy some nice shirts and dresses, napkins, tablecloths, and other house stuff. But I don't think they have maps. It's just one road, and everyone know da way."

"Come on," Carter said before Kat could argue with her. "I'm sure we'll find it. Thanks for your help."

"No help you mean," Kat said when they were out of earshot.

"Worse thing that will happen is we get rained on, and it won't be the first time we've been wet." The sky was turning dark.

A twenty-minute walk later, they stood in front of the gas pump looking at the one-room office, service station, and auto parts shop. It looked abandoned, but when they went inside, Rooney unfolded from a chair placed strategically in front of a fan. Soon they were in an elderly Nissan Sentra with the steering wheel on the left, wrong for driving on the left side of the road that was a hold-over from English rule. A sticker on the bumper conveyed the message that it had been bought in Florida. *Old, slow driver with blue hair. Honk loud.* The color was white and rust. As Carter pulled out of the station, the automatic transmission jerked, and the engine seemed to be running on only three of the four cylinders. The passenger window was permanently open, and from the noise, the muffler must have looked like Swiss cheese. Carter turned around and pulled back into the gas station. Rooney was still standing by the pump. Carter raised his voice over the engine noise.

"What number do I call if I break down?"

"It don't break down, and I close now dat all da cars gone. But here, I give you some engine oil to take along." Rooney handed Carter three quarts of cheap forty-weight oil through the car window.

"Well that's reassuring," Kat said as Carter drove off for the second time. "I wonder if there's a spare tire or a dead body in the trunk."

"What makes you think we'd get it open to find out?"

They drove south on a smooth, two-lane asphalt road that followed the east coast, blue smoke billowing behind. "Great smoke screen if we need to evade anyone," Kat said. "Hey, there's AUTEC, that's the naval station I told you about. I wonder if they give tours?"

"I hardly think so." Carter slowed to read the sign.

*Naval Underwater Warfare Station. Atlantic Test
and Evaluation Center.
Off-limits except to authorized personnel.
Stop at security gate and show identification.*

"Guess that excludes us unless my press ID would work."

"Do you have one with you?"

"Sure."

"I'd like to get to the resort before this storm breaks, and I'm not sure this car will restart if I turn it off," Carter said. "I wouldn't put any money on the windshield wipers working, your window doesn't close, and I don't think these roads are designed for drainage. I suggest we skip a tour."

Once past the AUTEC entrance, the road narrowed and turned to a mix of gravel, sand, and ground shell. Dust blew in the windows, driven by the wind. "Guess we know whose tax money paid for that pavement," Carter said.

In another ten miles, they reached the sign for Small Hope Bay Lodge and turned onto a mostly sand one-lane road cut through the wind-blown stubby pines which ended at a charming oceanfront resort. Individual cottages were spread out and nestled among the trees. The car's engine, so hesitant to run, now refused to stop after

Carter switched off the ignition. It gasped, turned several more revolutions, let out a wheeze, and finally shuddered and quit.

"Can't you do better than that?" Kat asked.

"Maybe it'll run for a woman. Tomorrow's your turn to drive. Don't forget to keep on the left side and remind me to check the oil before we start. With all that smoke from the exhaust, we didn't need the mosquito repellant."

An attractive central lodge housed the dining room, game room, and lounge. A posted sign said that except during hurricanes, meals were served alfresco on the patio overlooking the bay. According to their host, Andros had the second largest reef system in the Atlantic, and most guests were divers.

By the time they checked in, the rain had started in earnest, and they made a run to the porch of their cottage. Shaking the water from their hair and clothes, they were pleasantly surprised. The beachfront villa, like the central lodge, had rustic white plaster walls, and bare timbers cut from Andros mahogany. While there was no air conditioning, a ceiling fan and cross ventilation allowed the easterly ocean breeze to cool the room. The walls were decorated with bright green, aqua, and lavender batik wall hangings. Simple white butterflies adorned the sheer curtains and sea turtles covered the bedspread. All were the same hand-dyed fabrics made in the factory they'd passed in Fresh Creek.

CHAPTER 33

As Kat began to pull clothes from her duffle, there was a persistent banging on the cottage door. "Who could that be?" She pushed back the curtain and looked through the front window onto the screened porch. "It's Manny." She held the door open.

"Come in."

Manny remained on the porch. "Mz. Kat, da rain's stopped. How 'bout you and me take a walk down to da beach?"

It was hardly a question. His voice was firm and his expression unreadable. Kat glanced at her watch. "Sure." She called over her shoulder to Carter, "I'll be right back. I'm walking down to the beach with Manny."

Kat followed Manny down to the cupola at the water's edge. Water dripped from the corner spattering on the wood floorboards. "Why don't you take one of dem rockin' chairs." Manny pulled the other rocker to face her and gazed up at the domed ceiling.

Finally, his eyes met Kat's. "I'm goin' to get right to dis. I been doing a bit of research," he said. "Seems like you writin' a book 'bout Carlos Lehder. Dat right?"

Does everyone know about this damn book? Kat didn't respond to his question. "How'd you know we were here?"

"Desirene at da marina hotel where you had lunch told me, but dat's not what's important. I think you in over your head with dis book. You a smart gal and I know you can fire a gun, but you don't know how dangerous these guys are."

Kat flashed back to her nightmare rendezvous on Normans. *Oh, yes, I do!*

Manny's voice broke through. "You need to listen to me. We got dis drug ting mostly settled down and you in a position to start somethin' big up again. Not drugs, but somethin' more like a turf war."

"Do you know Isadore was killed on Potter's Cay this morning?" Kat asked.

"I do. Just stay with me on dis right now. Let's talk about Carlos. Say you are in touch with him and he give you names of men who turned on him, cause him to get caught, and because dey turned, dey never did a lick of time themselves. Dis book could start a very nasty fight between Carlos' supporters, who would love to kill da guys responsible for putting him in prison, and da guys on dat list who will defend themselves, I can guarantee dat. There be plenty of people who don't want all dis out." Manny leaned back in his chair.

"Den there's dis. If da guys, whose names you have, find out you about to expose them, da DEA have to come after them. Their only option is to get to you first. Shut you up for good. You followin' me?"

Kat could feel her stomach knot. She knew Manny's name was on that list and apparently, he did too.

"I want you to keep in mind an old Bahamian sayin'. 'If you sleep with da devil, your baby's gonna be born with horns.' Believe me I know. I don't know what Carlos tell you about his time on Normans, but if you got a few minutes, I might be able to give you some insight why you don't want to write dat book."

"I'm listening," Kat said.

It was Manny's turn to look to the past. The details were so clear, even after thirty years. "I spent da best and worst years of my life on Normans Cay, '78 to '82," he said. "People said it was dangerous, but I didn't care 'cause Carlos Lehder offered everythin', money, wild parties, and a house on da beach. Der was lots of liquor, weed, and coke. But most of all were da women. I never seen so many beautiful white women in all my life. They wore elegant gowns when da parties began, but by early mornin' they were usually naked, frolickin' in da surf. It embarrasses me to admit dis now, but even though I knew da girls were on Carlos' payroll, I had my eye on a tall blond German named, Ilse. She da only girl I ever loved. I heard da stories; if a man wavered in his loyalty to Carlos and revealed something in da middle of da night pillow talk, dat information went directly to Carlos. Da girl would earn a bonus and da man might meet up with an untimely accident. None of dis stopped me; I was young and, for the first and only time, da world was open to me."

"And was it?" Kat asked.

"Only for a while. I can still hear Ilse's charmin' accent. Carlos introduced her to me at one of his many all-night parties. She held out da back of her hand for me to kiss. Somethin' I'd only seen in a movie. She stood close and gazed directly into my eyes. Bahamian women don't do dat and I was taken in by dis direct sexual attention. She insisted dat I tell her all about growin' up in Clarence Town on Long Island. She paid attention to everythin' I said. As much as I wanted her, I didn't understand dat Carlos was givin' her to me. I knew da unwritten rules, I could dance with her, but not to music dat meant holdin' her close. Carlos loved John Lennon, and at three in the morning, da band played *Imagine.* Ilse wrapped herself around me and moved her hips in a way dat aroused and frightened me. Carlos was not to be toyed with, not when it came to business or women."

"What'd you do?" Kat asked.

"I told her dat I didn't want to take her back to Carlos. She spoke in a soft, seductive voice. 'You don't have to. You're my man.'"

"I was drunk and stoned, but I remember listenin' to da lyrics of dat song, 'Imagine all da people, livin' for today.' Dat's what everyone there was doin', and I couldn't visualize any life better than dis." Manny laughed. "I should have listened to da line, 'People think I'm a dreamer.' Da next day Ilse moved into my villa on da beach, or I should say da villa Carlos owned, and I occupied. Da short time we had together was a continual honeymoon. I still long for her."

"What was it like there? Other than access to drugs, women, and parties?"

"When I first came to Normans, I worked in da dive shop run by one of da few American residents. Novak was a professor of German whose passion was marine science. He led expeditions for da divers who came to explore da reefs and underwater caves. I had a knack for numbers and record-keepin' so I managed da inventory, scheduled dive groups, and kept da gear in workin' order. Carlos would often drop by 'cause he love to chat with Novak in German. Carlos could switch between German, Spanish, and English, and I hung around 'cause I wanted to be part of dis sophisticated world."

Kat stopped rocking. "Did you become part of it?"

"I thought so, at da time. Novak was difficult to work with, he always was angry at someone or somethin', so when I learned Carlos needed a personal bookkeeper, I jumped at da chance. Carlos needed someone to keep up with da work on Normans because he always was flyin' in and out on business. I was proud dat Carlos recognized my abilities and trusted me. I knew much of his business was illegal, but I was willin' to ignore how Carlos made his money to be part of dis inner circle. At twenty-four, I was makin' more in a year than my daddy did in ten. I never told my family what I did, but I sent money home to them on Long Island and to my cousins in Nassau, which later helped me survive."

"Why are you telling me this? I could turn you in even now."

"I know dat, but I also know you already had dat option 'cause you have a list and we both know my name's on it."

How does he know so much? First the book, and now this. Who was his contact? Kat wondered.

"I'm hopin' my story will convince you how deceitful des guys are.

I'm not a threat to you, but Carlos is. He'll turn on you if it serves his purpose."

"Go on."

"Carlos was constantly developin' dat island and da construction crews worked non-stop. As soon as one project wound down, another began. He built luxurious villas, broadened da marina entrance, and expanded da docks for big cargo ships. Dey lengthened da runway for large planes, and a Colombian flag flew from da control tower. Carlos installed lights and radar for around-the-clock take-off and landings. During my years there, bright runway lights and da drone of airplane engines became da rhythm of da night. Planes from South America flew in at night, off-loaded da cocaine into a warehouse, and refueled. Then dey turned around and flew back for another shipment. Smaller planes took da blow into out-of-the-way landing strips in da States. I knew all dis."

"And you didn't do anything?"

Manny shook his head. "Life was too good for dis young black man. If I snitched, I'd be dead. I was in deep. I kept da records of all da cash dat came in from da U.S., and da large sums of money dat went to Nassau. And I knew about da offshore accounts."

That's why he's on the list. He knows too much. What deal did he strike with Carlos to keep quiet all these years?

"I knew what dat money was," Manny continued. "Bribes to keep da Bahamian government happy and out of Carlos' hair. Da police made occasional raids, but Carlos always had plenty of warnin'."

"Didn't you expect to get caught one day?"

"If I'd stopped to think, yes, but I was willin' to believe dis would go on and on. Dis life was glamorous. Carlos had a bright red Excalibur. It was hardly necessary on a cay only four miles long, but I loved dat car, and when I saw Carlos spinnin' up da dust, a woman at his side, I imagined I would own one too. Other than da construction trucks, da only other vehicles on da island were jeeps driven by guards with automatic weapons and Doberman Pinschers. Dey patrolled da beach and da air stip. No plane was allowed to land, and no boat could anchor without Carlos' permission. It was his private empire."

"What happened to the people who had houses there?" Kat asked.

"Carlos was obsessed with expandin' da cocaine business and controllin' shipments into da States. He planned to own da entire island and most of da homeowners, who had built before Carlos came to Normans, were happy to accept his generous offers to buy them out. If dat didn't work, Carlos sabotaged their power and phone lines, contaminated da cisterns with animal carcasses, and threatened them."

Kat distractedly peeled paint flaking on the arm of her rocker. "Did you visit Carlos' house?"

"Oh, yes, often. Carlos and I would go over da financial records there. Everyone called his house The Volcano because an enormous stone fireplace rose in da very center of da vaulted ceiling livin' room. I never seen anythin' like it. Don't know why he had to have a fireplace in dis climate, but Carlos didn't need to be practical. In addition to da beautiful furniture, he had original paintings in every room, and expensive Persian wool carpets covered da highly varnished mahogany floors. Da wood was imported from Andros. It have da finest mahogany forests in da Bahamas. Da lumber mill's not far from here. I remember Carlos would throw his arm around me and we'd walk through da house overcrowded with furnishings.

"'All dis stuff comes from da finest European chateaus and castles,' he'd tell me, 'You need to learn about antiques. Learn to distinguish real from fake so I can send you on buyin' trips.' I was thrilled at dat. I was too embarrassed to tell him dat I'd never even been to most of da Bahama islands."

"I want to see his house," Kat said.

Manny shrugged. "Not much to see after da raid. It was burnt, and then hurricanes took off most of da roof." He wasn't going to let on he knew Kat had been there. "Maybe Carter will take you over to Normans."

"Maybe."

"I had dis fantasy. I imagined wearin' a beautiful silk suit exactly like da one Carlos wore. I would walk into da lounge at Graycliff. It's da finest restaurant in Nassau."

"I've heard about it," Kat said. "But I've never been there."

"Me neither, but my cousin work der as a waiter and told me all about it. In my dream, da maitre d' would bow slightly and say, 'Welcome to your island home, sir.' Da lovely blond Ilse would be at my side. We would sit together on a soft leather couch in da lounge like everyone does before dinner. I'd order champagne for Ilse, and for me, a handmade cigar rolled by an old Cuban who had escaped Batista's rule years ago. A waiter would bring da humidor for me to choose, cut da cigar, and light it by turnin' it slowly over two matches.

"As I enjoyed my smoke, Sean Connery, da island's most famous resident, would walk in wearin' a jet black tuxedo, a stunnin' woman on his arm. He would look at Ilse in her tight, silver sequined dress, diamonds at her neck, raise his eyebrow, smile his famous smile, and nod at me. After da cigar and champagne, da maitre d' would escort us into da dinin' room where uniformed waiters would serve warmed plates of steaks and lobster tails along with more champagne and wine."

At that moment, Kat felt sorry for Manny. This was an impossible dream, and he knew it too.

"At da end of da meal we would walk outside into da balmy night air, and da valet would ask, 'Taxi sir?' and wave to one of da black Lincoln Town Cars waitin'. Da taxi would drive us to da Nassau Yacht Haven where my speed boat, *Sun King*, would take us back to Normans in less than an hour. Ilse would snuggle against me, da coolin' wind blowin' her long, blond hair and I would look up into a sky full of stars and listen to da roar of da powerful engines. To finish da night, we would dive naked into da surf before fallin' into bed and making mad, passionate love."

Manny took a deep breath and slowly sank back in his chair.

CHAPTER 34

"What ended it all?" Kat asked.

"It was da night of July fourteenth, 1982. Won't forget dat. Da Bahamian government was finally forced to take action, and my dreams tumbled down. I woke to gunfire. I knew Carlos kept a huge supply of weapons on da island, but dis wasn't shootin' into da air dat accompanied da many drunken parties. Dis was different. Dis shootin' came from two distinct directions like opposin' armies. I turned to protect Ilse, but she wasn't in bed. I ran through da house and in da hallway tripped on a board in da floor dat had been pulled up. It was where I kept my money; all twelve thousand dollars was gone."

"She stole it?" Kat asked.

Manny nodded. "I heard engines sputter to life and da planes take off. Carlos knew dis day might come, and he had an escape plan all along. Ilse was part of it, but not me. For the first time, I had to admit, I'd bought into a dream dat never was mine. Now Ilse undoubtedly was on her way to Colombia with Carlos and my money."

"God! What did you do?" Kat asked.

"I grabbed da bread dat was left, a bottle of water, snuck out of da villa, and hid in da dense bush. I was so angry I shook. It wasn't about da loss of da big income and future. Two people had betrayed me. People I loved. Carlos, and more important, Ilse. I had been willin' to believe dat Carlos was my true friend. I believed Ilse when she said she loved me. Now I knew dat Ilse, like all da others, was just doing a job dat she had been paid to do. My life was worth nothin' to Carlos. And nothin' to Ilse. I was worth nothin'. I was a young, stupid, black, naïve chump. And not even an ethical chump."

Manny's fists were clenched in his lap. He was silent so long that Kat wasn't sure if he was going to finish. She was caught up in his story and wanted to hear it all. This was a memoir she'd love to write.

"How'd you get off the island?"

"I hid in da dense bush on da southern end until dat raid ended. Later, I made my way to a concrete-block building dat I knew was abandoned. It had been built to house da laboratory for da marine research center, but Novak left da island da year before, and it sat empty ever since. Da path was overgrown, and I was one of da few who even knew it existed. I would be safe there." Manny sighed.

"I sat against a damp wall for more than twenty-four hours. Sometimes I slept and sometimes cried. My shame, grief, and anger all mixed. When I finally got up da nerve to creep out, da island was completely silent; even da generator wasn't runnin'. I made my way around dead guard dogs, burned jeeps, trucks, and trashed villas. When I came to Carlos' Volcano, I stopped. Da door hung from its hinges. I wanted to walk through all da rooms one last time, but da ghost of Carlos paralyzed me. Everythin' I wanted was gone. Friends I thought I had and da life I wanted to live. I was depressed. Maybe lost is a better word. Lost. Alone. Betrayed."

Manny looked so pained retelling his past that Kat wished she could put her arms around him.

"I continued through da bush, stayin' off da road. I hadn't seen a soul since leavin' my hideout, but I couldn't shake da feeling dat I wasn't alone. I needed to get off dat island. When I reached da dock, I saw all da seaworthy boats were gone, but I could see a rubber dinghy with a small outboard bobbin' out in da lagoon. I prayed dat all da commotion had scared off da hammerheads dat congregate there every year. I didn't know which scared me more, stayin' on da island or gettin' in dat water with da sharks. But by now, my anger took over. I wasn't goin' to take da rap for someone who betrayed me. I tied my shoestrings together, put my sneakers around my neck, and waded cautiously into da lagoon."

"At least you were still thinking."

Manny shrugged. "Dat outboard was ancient and battered. A fuel can sat in the bottom of da dinghy. I shook da can and guessed I might have 'bout two gallons of gasoline. I was worried someone might still be around so I paddled with my hands for as long as I could before riskin' any noise from da engine. Once out of da lagoon, da outgoin' current pushed me away from da cay."

Kat's foot had fallen asleep and she longed to shift in her chair, but she was afraid it would break the spell.

"Then, I had another problem. When I pulled da rope starter nothin' happened. I was being swept out to sea without oars or tools for a repair, if I could even figure out what was wrong. I was frantic, so I pumped da primin' bulb and pulled dat rope starter 'til my arm ached. When I gave up, I realized my feet were stingin'. I hadn't even smelled it in my panic, but there was gasoline in da bottom of da boat. Someone had installed a small fuel filter in da hose between da primin' bulb and da engine. When I pumped da bulb again, I saw fuel run out where da hose was clamped. I found a coin in my pocket dat fit da screw at da hose clamp. I couldn't fully tighten it, but when I squeezed da bulb, da leak was less. A few pulls on da rope starter and da old engine sputtered and more or less came to life. I could get it to run at about half throttle by repeatedly pumpin' da bulb. It was a balancin' act, a little gasoline spewed out with each pump and I didn't want to use it all up before I reached Highbourne."

Kat was now jiggling her foot. "That's where you stopped?"

Manny nodded. "It was hours later when dat dinghy sputtered into Highbourne Cay. I was relieved, but I didn't feel safe. Late dat afternoon, I hitched a ride on a supply boat headed for Nassau and walked to my cousin's house, a place I would be safe 'til dis all die

down. My glory days were over. But I had one small pleasure."
Manny's voice sharpened, a sense of satisfaction in his words.

"Da glory days were over for Carlos Lehder too. Like so many powerful men, da cocaine king had taken unnecessary chances. He viewed himself as invincible. But he flew too close to da sun."

"I know what happened after that." Kat picked up the story. "Carlos was caught in the jungles of Colombia, in 1987, extradited to the U.S., and will spend the remainder of his life, under an assumed name, in an undisclosed prison."

"Dat may be da best place for him. Many would line up to kill him if he's ever paroled. I wouldn't mind doin' it myself." Manny rubbed the tension from the back of his neck.

"To me, betrayal seems more of a crime than all da cocaine traffickin'. I never told anyone about my time on Normans. Not even my wife. You da first. Now it's comin' back to bite me."

"Maybe it's you who should have listened to the Bahamian saying about sleeping with the devil," Kat said.

Manny smiled sadly. "You right, but it's thirty years too late for dat."

"What happened to Ilse?" Kat asked.

"I never heard from my dream girl again." Manny fingered the photo he had in his pocket; the one of Ilse with the little girl. Anna, his little girl, no, his grown daughter. A young woman who soon would be a doctor.

"Ilse would be over fifty now," Manny said. "I do think about her and wonder: what would she look like? Where is she? Is she happy?" *And my daughter, who will die if I don't take out Buddy.*

Manny looked at the young woman across from him now. He liked Kat. She was gutsy, persistent, and willing to risk her own life for the truth. Not cowardly like him. Carter was one lucky man. Manny hated what he was going to do, but he couldn't, wouldn't, lose his daughter a second time. He knew the pain of betrayal and he wished there was a way that he could do this and not betray Kat and Carter. Maybe he was no better than Carlos. If he could convince Kat to give this writing up, maybe then he could convince his Colombian friends to leave her, Buddy, Anna, and him alone.

"Do you see why I'm tellin' you dis?" he asked. "Des guys will use you up and throw you away. Carlos can't be trusted. I was loyal to him, and after all those years, he turned on me. I hope you get dis from da story I told you. You'd be better off to throw out dis manuscript and forget it."

"I can't do that." She thought about the death threats from the Colombians to everyone she loved and the threat of exposure by the DEA.

"Then do with dis what you want," Manny's voice was flat.

"There's nothing to be gained by telling the DEA or anyone else about your involvement," Kat offered. "I'm convinced you've had nothing to do with this life since or you wouldn't have told me." They both looked at the setting sun reflected in the surf.

"Back to dis mornin'," Manny said. "Isadore was on Potter's Cay to take you out. I was watchin', expectin' him. When I saw him gettin' a bead on you through dat crowd, I shot over his head because I was afraid of hittin' some innocent. But someone else not bothered by dat and der was a second shot dat killed him. If you know who fired it, I'd like to know."

"I don't know." Kat's response lacked conviction.

"Never mind. I'm pretty sure I know anyway, but I wanted to hear it from you. I was followin' Isadore. But we didn't want him dead. He was da only lead to what might be goin' on with the Koreans, and he might have had information 'bout your brother too."

"Do you think so?"

"Dis ting with your brother, you don't need to say anything, but I got a good feelin' dat he's alive and dat part of the reason you here, is because you know dat too."

Kat whirled around to face Manny. "We're here for Piccolo's funeral, like you. I have to change for dinner."

Manny stood up when Kat did. "You think about what I tell you. I be here 'till Tuesday. Ferry don't go back 'till then. We can talk again if you decide there's somethin' I should know."

"Are you staying here at the lodge?"

"No, I'm stayin' at my cousin Rupert's house. But I'll see you at da service. I like you Mz. Kat, Carter too. I wouldn't want anything to happen to either of you. If you do any investigatin' while you here, I'm goin' be with you."

Kat walked away as Manny called after her. "Tink about what I say. Ditch dat manuscript and stop da contact with Carlos. Dat writin' is dangerous."

"No," Kat called back. "Publishing is dangerous."

CHAPTER 35

Kat hadn't slept well. Her dreams mixed with Manny's sad and frightening story. Rising before daylight, she sat on the sandy beach listening to the waves gently roll in and out, the only reliably constant for the moment. Manny's warning and her options filled her head, but she couldn't see any good outcome. As the sun rose, she stood, brushing the sand from her shorts and headed back to the cottage. She didn't want Carter to wake and find her missing. For now, she had to put aside her troubles. Today her focus was the memorial service for Piccolo Pete.

It wasn't hard for Kat and Carter to find Ida May's house once they reached Johnson Town. Hand-lettered signs pointed the way, but it was just as easy to follow the cars heading down a dusty road. After bumping across a wood plank bridge spanning a narrow creek, they turned onto a side road lined with houses painted blue, green, or pink. At one time they had been the bright shades that Bahamians believed warded off evil spirits; now they were faded by the sun.

Haphazardly parked rusty pick-up trucks and cars surrounded Ida

May's house. The salt air quickly aged even new cars. Carter parked beside the road, and they walked along with other guests, most of them carrying covered dishes.

"I should have picked up something," Kat said.

"Store bought food can't compete with this."

Ida May's house was a blue box with peeling white trim and a small porch across the front. She was the proud owner of an air conditioner which hung out of a side window. It was propped up by a two-by-four and rattled like their rental car. Conch shells lined the sand walkway and formed borders around scraggly bushes. There were a few flowers near the door, struggling to survive, but no grass. Someone had raked the sand clean. Everything appeared ready for guests.

Kat and Carter made their way among tables covered with Bahamian comfort food; fried and barbecued chicken, conch fritters, peas and rice, macaroni and cheese, Johnnycake, and coleslaw. A separate table held sweet desserts; key lime pie, guava duff, and cakes of all kinds, and more food was arriving. No one would go hungry even if the gathering went on all weekend. Kalik and sodas filled picnic coolers. Many of the men had small bottles of rum in their back pockets, discreetly pouring it into plastic cups. Before the weekend was over, discretion wouldn't be necessary.

An elderly woman pounded out spirituals from a bright blue upright piano located in the yard. Additional guitars, banjos, and both steel and goombay drums rested against the railings. Guests sang, clapped, and swayed to the beat that underscored the melodies they all seemed to know. The music and singing would go on all day and most of the night. Carter was sure that Piccolo would have approved.

Many of the women were in Sunday dress with full white skirts, colorful blouses, and wide-brimmed hats adorned with bright artificial flowers. To Kat, it looked more like an Easter parade than a funeral. Older folks sat in assorted lawn chairs, cooling themselves with cardboard fans advertising the local funeral home. Little boys, with their shirt tails hanging out, ran through the yard, chasing chickens and dogs, and grabbing food from the table as they streaked past. Teenagers tried to act bored, but no one was immune to the air of celebration. Kat and Carter had no idea when any actual service would begin, but it didn't seem to matter; somehow, it would all come together.

"I'd like to find Piccolo's mother. I need to talk to her, make sure I'm welcome," Kat said.

"She's probably in the house. We'll ask someone," Carter said, squeezing Kat's hand. He hadn't considered the possibility of not being welcome. There were a few white faces in the mix, but from their dialect Carter heard in passing, he knew they were Bahamians. Given the circumstances, maybe Kat was right; they needed to be clear on this.

"I want to talk to her, tell her about me, what happened," Kat said.

As Carter had surmised, Mrs. Moxey was in the slightly cooler house. Large pots on the stove smelled of fish chowder and souse made from pig's feet and other parts Carter didn't want to contemplate. Mrs. Moxey sat in an overstuffed chair on the living-room side of the open space. Two babies sat on her lap, and another young child hung on her knee. Several attractive women surrounding her were talking and laughing. Carter caught parts of the conversation that recalled Piccolo's childhood pranks. He expected these stories would become part of the remembrances.

"Excuse me, Mrs. Moxey, we want to introduce ourselves. I'm Carter McDowell, and this is Mary Katherine Deano."

"I know who you is. Kat, you is called." Ida May's cloudy eyes focused on Kat. "Petie talked 'bout both of you. I'm pleased you come here for dis day."

Ida May balanced the babies on her lap and held out her hands to Kat and Carter. "Sit down. Let me pass these young 'uns to der mamas."

"You have beautiful grandchildren, Mrs. Moxey," Kat said.

"Oh, Lordy, these are my great-grandbabies," Ida May said. "These beauties standing here are my grandbabies; now they have chirren of der own. And please call me Ida May. All my friends do."

Carter was relieved they were being included as friends. Maybe Kat was wrong and this was going to be alright.

"Are Pete's children here?" Kat asked.

"I expect they are or will be. Some he claim is his and others he don't, but they all here today." Ida May laughed and then looked directly into Kat's eyes. "But dat's not what you come to say to me, is it child?"

Kat shook her head and sat down on a stool in front of Ida May's chair. She took a deep breath. "I'm sure you know I was accused of Peter's death. I want to tell you, he died saving my life. He was a hero." Tears ran down Kat's face, and she bit her lip to keep it from trembling. "I didn't kill him, but I feel responsible for his death."

"I'm glad you came and say dat to me directly, child." Ida May's voice was smooth and soft. "But you just hush about dat. You don't git dis old without knowin' loss and grief. Ida May handed Kat an embroidered handkerchief she pulled from her pocket. "It does comfort me knowin' he died helpin' someone, and he always be a hero in my eyes. But child, I know'd his dyin' weren't caused by you. Des ole eyes don't see much on da outside anymore, but dat don't stop me seein' on da inside. Even before Preacher Moss come and told me. I know'd, I know'd exactly when he die. A big ole black crow landed in my tree and wouldn't stop dat terrible racket dey make. I know'd then." She paused and wiped her eyes.

"I remember Petie's stories of you as a little ting watchin' out for your brother after your Mama die. I know'd you not kill my Petie. It wrong da way he die and somethin' bad got to be put right. You and me both know dis. But I worry cause more bad tings might be comin' along with it. I feel it. It wake me up at night, just like dat ole crow did. I work with da potions I got from an old Obeah woman my mama knew on Cat Island, but I don't seem to have no power over it." Ida May's tone was somber. She tipped her head back, rocked side to side, and chanted in a language Kat didn't understand. Then suddenly she sat up and smiled. "Now, you go out der and enjoy dis last time we all have together with Petie. Go on now. We talk again before dis day over. I know you got more on your mind and I help you any way I can."

As Kat and Carter started for the door, Ida May made one more request of Kat. "I'd sure appreciate it if you say somethin' about my Petie when da time comes. Lots of folks give testimony, but you know'd him in a way none of us did."

"I'd be happy to, Ms. Ida May," Kat said. "But do you think people want to hear from me?"

"Sure dey do. No one hold anythin' against you. And if dey do, dey need to answer to me. Now, go on outside and let dat music get inside you."

While Kat and Carter were in Ida May's cottage, Manny was in the yard, making his rounds, talking to guests. Suddenly he found himself in front of a man who looked a lot like the black pilot in the photo that the Colombians had shown him, a picture in which the man was linking arms with Buddy. The man wasn't in a uniform today, but Manny was sure it was the same person.

"You look familiar," Manny said. "You a pilot?"

"Yes, I fly for Western Air. Name's Elliot Glover." He extended his hand to Manny.

"I think I was on one of your flights a couple of weeks ago. Western Air's bout da only airline I still like," Manny said, not offering his name. "Must have been on dat flight from Nassau to Fresh Creek."

"No, I fly into the Congo Town airstrip on South Andros. I have a little beachside cottage down there. Like the quiet. Not many people there, you know."

"Yeah. I guess it's better than Nassau for a family. My son got into big trouble in Nassau."

"Don't have any family. Just spend my time bonefishing along with a little freediving."

"Boy, you like to take risks. Flyin' and freedivin'. You dive da blue holes?"

"No," Elliot answered. "I wouldn't even dive those with tanks. If you're not paying attention, when the tide goes out, you can get sucked down. It's not for me. But I'm just a half-mile down the beach from Jared's Fish Camp, nothing between him and me. He cleans my fish in exchange for the use of my boat when I'm working. I love bonefishing, but I hate cleaning them."

"I know da place. I stay there when I come over to fish," Manny replied.

At that moment Carter and Kat stepped out of Ida May's cottage. Kat recognized Elliot and ran to him, calling his name. He grabbed her, lifted her off her feet, and swung her around in his arms.

"God, Elliot. It's been forever."

"A million years," Elliot said. "You look great, tanned, and healthy. Life must be going your way."

"I'm nearly as dark as you," Kat laughed placing her arm against his light coffee-colored one. She'd never given it a second thought when they were kids, but now she wondered how much white blood would turn up in his family tree if he searched Ancestry dot com. She started to say more but spotted Manny behind Elliot. "Hey, Manny. I see you've met my childhood friend."

Elliot held Kat's eyes. "Since you've come this far, I hope you'll take the time to come down to South Andros after the service. Everyone will tell you there's nothing there, but you'll be surprised by what you find. You can fly back with me, that alone should make it worth your while."

"I'd like that. I have a few days. Give us time to catch up. I didn't even know you were a pilot. See how out of date I am?"

"I'll leave you two to reminisce," Manny said. Neither Kat nor Elliot acknowledged his departure.

CHAPTER 36

Manny had the information he needed; where Buddy was and that he was alone. He didn't have much time and he needed to think clearly. Putting a hole in Buddy's head with his service revolver wasn't an option. It could easily lead right back to him. In his years as captain of the homicide unit, many murders went unsolved. That's what this one had to be.

Manny looked back. Carter had caught up with Kat talking with Elliot. Their animation and laughter spoke of a camaraderie Manny envied. His resolve wavered, but only for a moment. He reminded himself of the choice, an alcoholic geologist—a loose cannon—versus his brilliant daughter who was about to become a doctor.

Jared's Fish Camp was perfect. It wouldn't be suspicious; he'd stayed there before. "Just comin' to fish." Jared always left gloves and knives at the fish cleaning station at the end of the dock. Nothing traceable to Manny. He had never done anything like this, but he had to eliminate this hold over him for good. If he hurried and was cautious, this could work. He needed someone with a flat-bottomed skiff to carry him inside the reef to Driggs Hill on South Andros. Then, he'd rent a car at the airport and make his way to Elliot's place.

Manny had disappeared, but any additional conversation between Kat and Elliot was interrupted when a noisy pick-up truck arrived loaded with folding chairs from Ida May's church. Kat, Carter, and Elliot were recruited to set up the chairs facing the porch.

"We'll talk more after the service," Elliot said. "Come find me. I'll be standing at the back. I sit too much in my work."

Children sat cross-legged on the ground, and Kat and Carter joined the other adults sitting in rows. The music stopped, and the crowd quietened as a tall, thin man with a graying mustache stepped up onto the porch. Even in the heat, he dressed in a dark suit, white shirt, and black bowtie.

"I want to welcome all of you to dis service for Peter Purcell Moxey. I'm Preacher Moss, the pastor at Zion Baptist Church here in Johnson Town. I know'd Petie, as we call him, for 'bout all his life. He was a good boy and a good man. Always lookin' out for others." This was followed by "amen" from the audience.

Kat stopped listening, mulling over what she would say. The testimonies had begun, and she would soon be asked to speak. When the preacher called her name, she walked to the makeshift pulpit. Without preparation, she began. "My name is Kat Deano, and I want you all to know that more than once, Peter Moxey saved my life. The last time he did, he died doing it. He is my hero."

"Amen. Dat's right. You know it," guests called out.

"My brother and I spent a lot of time wandering around and getting into trouble on Bimini while our father fished. Piccolo Pete, as Peter was known on Bimini, always seemed to be around to rescue us." Kat looked over the audience, catching Elliot's eye. She knew the story would tell itself. "I could tell you lots of stories about Peter, but this one shows just the kind of man he was and why he has always had a special place in my heart.

"Even though we knew how to run the outboard and were strong swimmers, our father wouldn't let us take the dinghy out when he fished on his boat. It was a hard and fast rule. But this day, the sun was shining, a light breeze blowing, and Bimini Bay was so flat it looked like you could walk on it. The temptation was too much. Buddy, my twin brother, and I had a special friend on Bimini, Elliot, who is here today. He was always around whenever we wanted to plan some adventure, so as usual; it was the three of us that day." Kat looked directly at Elliot, who was shaking his head and smiling in remembrance.

"For those of you who don't know, there is a small island in the middle of Bimini Bay. Just the kind of place for children with imaginations. There's nothing there except a tangle of mangrove trees and the shorebirds that nest in them. We had named it Black Beard Island. I don't think anyone on Bimini calls it anything. We had an ongoing game of pirates, and the only thing we fought about was who was going to be the leader. Elliot said he should be since Bimini was his home, Buddy said he should be because he had read all the books about pirates. I thought I should be because I was sure my real name was Anne Bonny, one of the most famous women pirates. Elliot insisted that I was too small to be a real pirate and Buddy argued that our mother had never given me the name Anne Bonny and the only reason I knew anything about her, was that he told me."

Kat leaned on the podium, waiting until the laughter died down. "Well, this particular day, one of us—I don't remember which one—decided it was the perfect time to search for the gold that we were sure Black Beard had buried on our little island in Bimini Bay. The fastest way to get there was to borrow our father's dinghy. He was already out fishing. If we were back before he returned, he would never know. The trip out worked fine, but we didn't find any gold. However, when we were ready to come back we couldn't start the outboard and in our haste to get to the island, we had forgotten to bring oars.

"It was getting late, and we knew we had to get back to the marina or our exploring days were numbered. The three of us draped over the sides of the dinghy, paddling with our hands. Only we hadn't paid attention to the tide, and soon the current was quickly carrying us out of the bay, no matter how hard we paddled." Kat looked out over the crowd. Several were smiling.

"Fortunately for us, Piccolo Pete was fishing from the dock at Brown's Marina. When we spotted him, we stood up, yelled, and waved frantically. He jumped in a boat and towed us in. We got a good tongue lashing, but by the time our father returned on his boat, we were just four friends sitting on the end of the dock with fishing lines in the water. Piccolo never told on us; he was that kind of a friend. There's hardly an adventure that I can recall from those days that did not involve him one way or another. I will miss him terribly."

"Amen," the audience called out again.

As Kat walked back to her seat, several people took her hand, nodding and thanking her. A woman with bushy gray hair sticking out from around her hat and a dark, sun-weathered face grabbed Kat's arm and pulled her close. "I know you here to bring an end to dis trouble on our island." She put something in Kat's palm and closed her hand around it. "Dis take care of you. Keep it wid you tomorrow. You find what you afta and bring it to an end."

Kat was stunned. What did she mean? How did anyone know why she was here? She hadn't even told Ida May. Once Kat reached Carter, she leaned over and whispered, "I need to talk to Elliot."

"You okay?" Carter's brow wrinkled with concern. "Want me to come?" Kat shook her head and made her way to the back where Elliot was leaning against a tree.

"Walk with me," Elliot said quietly.

Once on the road, Kat and Elliot walked hand and hand. "What a surprise," Kat said. "I had no idea you would be here. I'm so glad to see you. Where have you been all these years? What are you doing now? How long have you lived on South Andros?"

Elliot laughed. "Slow down. To start, I've lived on South Andros since I finished high school. I went to flight school, and I've been a pilot for Western Air for the last seven years."

"I remember your interest in airplanes," Kat said. "You were always hanging around Chalks airstrip when we weren't getting into trouble. You've even lost your accent."

"Matters who I'm talking to. Commercial pilots have to speak the Queen's English to communicate with the control tower. Don't think they'd be able to translate the Bahamian dialect."

"Are you married now? Kids?"

"No to both." Elliot stopped in the road. "Kat, Buddy's at my house."

Kat gasped and threw herself at Elliot, wrapping her arms around him. "You've just given me the best news possible." She stepped back, wiping tears. "How'd he know where to find you?"

"Lucky coincidence," Elliot replied. "He was on my plane from Bimini when he came over to do that job for Oriental Minerals. We were equally surprised."

"I know he was thrilled to see you after all these years. You two were so tight, I often felt like a third wheel. How long has it been?"

"Too long, but that's not what's important right now. He needs to see you. You're the reason I came to the service. I mean, I wanted to pay my respects, but I also planned to make contact with you."

"You knew I'd be here?"

"Buddy's been in touch with Ruby and knew you'd asked for help in getting a boat to come over to Andros." Elliot smiled, "He knows you pretty well. He says your thoughts and movements are inside his head. Some twin thing. By the way, he heard about Charlie. It upset him as you can imagine. Anyway, I flew a friend's Cessna over earlier today. Brought some of Pete's folks from South Andros, but they're staying the night, so I can take you back with me."

"Now?"

"Well, once this is all over."

Kat didn't know how much to tell Elliot. They were old friends, but lots of years had passed without any contact. Elliot sensed her hesitation.

"Maybe it would help if I told you that Buddy's been with me since the boating incident. I know he's in hiding. He filled me in."

"But he was on Sampson a few days ago."

"Yes, in my boat. He also made a trip to Georgetown and tried to talk to that other geologist."

"Woodside."

"Right. Other than that, he's been here. Kat, he's not drinking. That was something I insisted on, and so far he's kept his word."

"I hope he does, but don't be too disappointed if he doesn't. He's made a lot of promises that he hasn't kept," Kat said. "I love him, but he's wired differently. And that doesn't excuse his drinking."

"I know Buddy better than you think. His quirkiness doesn't bother me. To me, he's special."

Kat didn't know quite how to respond. Elliot hadn't seen Buddy in years, but she was gratified he appeared so committed. "Carter and I were heading to South Andros this evening. I looked up a place called South Andros Beach Club and made reservations there. Do you have room for two on that plane?"

"Not a problem. Take your time. Here's my cell phone number." He handed her his card. "Give me a call when you're ready. I'll hang out here most of the day. We can meet up at the airport; it's three miles south of town."

CHAPTER 37

It was after three. Preacher Moss and the testimonies were finally over. Guests were leaving their seats and mingling in groups. Kat slipped back into her chair beside Carter, her eyes sparkled.

"Buddy's at Elliot's house." Kat repeated her conversation with Elliot and his offer to fly them to South Andros. We need to turn this car in and meet him at the airport."

"I know you're eager to see your brother, but before we go, we need to talk to Ida May," Carter said.

Kat let out an audible sigh.

"Can you wait just another ten minutes? It may be our only chance to see if Ida May knows anything about what's happening on South Andros, or someone we can call on for help. Then we'll pick up our stuff at Small Hope Bay, turn this car in, and see if Rooney will give us a lift to the airport."

Someone pointed them around the house. Shaded by low sheltering branches of an immense gumbo-limbo tree, Ida May rested in a rocking chair, her eyes closed. She seemed to be alone for the first time. Kat wasn't sure if they should interrupt her solitude, but she opened her eyes and smiled as they approached.

"Do you know da red peelin' bark of dis here tree best for takin' the itch out of poisonwood? Jist make sure you know da difference in da two trees. Dey look a lot alike. Dat poisonwood a terrible ting. Ten times worse den poison ivy. Drive a person crazy scratchin' day and night. Now, you git yourselves a couple of dos chairs and tell me what's on your mind."

Carter got right to the point. "We've heard Koreans are heading up some big project on South Andros. I wonder if you know anything about it."

"Capt'n Carter, first you gotta know, da chickcharnie be mighty upset about what's goin' on down der. Might be minin', might be drugs, might be somethin' altogether different. I don't know, but I know dis. You need to be careful. You too Mz. Kat. Platinum say one of dos men walk into da propeller of a plane and it spread his head all 'round. Dat's how bad upset da chickcharnie be. Dey got a big ole fence with razor wire at da top and guard dogs, Platinum say."

Carter wasn't sure he was following her conversation. "Who's Platinum?"

"He my cousin's boy."

"Does he know how we can get into the area where this work is going on?" Carter asked.

"Probably. He know jist about everythin' goin' on down dere. But I have to tell you, he my kin and I love him, but he not factually reliable. He change his story more often than he change his underwear. He did some time in Nassau jail so maybe he be okay now."

"Can you give us his phone number?" Kat asked.

"Ain't got a phone, ain't got much of anything, but I can give you directions to his house."

"That'd be great. We'd like to see if he'd help us. It's pretty important."

"Don't I know. Don't I know." Ida May nodded her head. "You got somethin' to write on?"

"Just a minute." Kat fumbled in her purse for a pad and pen.

"Okay, den here go. You have to walk part way to his house, he built dis little ting from one of those old stone foundations right where Wide Creek settlement used to be. Dey all move out when electricity go in on da main road. Houses fell down over da years. I wouldn't want to be dere by myself. Spooky. All overgrown with poisonwood and dos vines dat wrap around you if you sit still too long. Is how da chickcharnie keep you out. Got to know your way dere." Ida May looked at Kat who was staring at her, the pen motionless. "You writin' dis down?"

"Yes, ma'am."

"Okay den. After you get to Kemp's Bay, you drive on south. Cross dat first bridge at Deep Creek, dat not da same as Wide Creek. Deep Creek be a proper town wid a church and all. Take da first road to da right. It got a name, but nobody call it by a name. It just da old settlement road. You see it. Run right along Wide Creek. Pretty soon dat road turn to dirt, but you keep going down dat dirt. It git smaller and smaller 'til it no more than a path with weeds grow'd up in da middle. Finally, you leave your car and walk. It not so far from der. What's left of dos ole houses come up on da right. First da old church, then da houses. You see one with a roof, dat be Platinum's. Don't know where he got dat material for a roof. He ain't got electricity or water and no phone like I say, but he choose to live like dat. His daddy say he can come up here and live with him. He could be helpin' his daddy out but no, dat Platinum won't budge." Ida May finally took a breath. "And when you see him, you tell him Ida May say to help you. He know I have powerful potions and if he don't help, I'll jist have to work it on him. He know what I mean."

"What do you think of this?" Kat asked, holding out the clay figure in her hand.

"Where you git dat, child?"

"One of the women at the service gave it to me. She was wearing a purple hat."

"A big ole fat woman?" Ida May asked.

Kat nodded.

"Dat be Mz. Cordella. She know some of da old-timey witchcraft. I think you lucky. She musta have a vision, see something special in you to give you dat. It be a token. A good one. She not so generous always.

I'd do as she say, carry it wid you. And I thank you again for comin' here. It mean a lot to me."

"It did to me too," Kat said, tucking the little figure in her pocket. "Knowing I was so welcome helped a lot." Kat leaned forward and kissed Ida May on the cheek.

"You two go on now. I know you got some work to do. Jist be careful. I think dis be a dangerous job you takin' on. I do what I can from here to keep you safe."

Once they reached the car, Carter said, "Finally I get to meet Buddy. Your excitement shows. You were twitching all over the entire time we talked to Ida May."

Kat's eyes widened. "Really? Do you think she noticed? From what Elliot said, he's fine. But I need to see for myself. He's good with facts, but not so good with people or emotional issues. And, you know what? We may be about to put this all together."

"Yeah, if Platinum and the chickcharnies are on our side." Carter started the car, backed onto the road, and headed to Small Hope Bay Lodge.

"Okay, tell me about these chickcharnies. I didn't want to ask Ida May. She seemed convinced of their power, and I was afraid we'd never get back to the directions to Platinum's house."

"It's best you know 'bout da chickcharnie before we git to South Andros," Carter said, imitating Ida May. "They're these little elfish creatures that live in the forest here. If you ever see two pine trees sort of knotted together at the top, that's a chickcharnie nest. They spend their days hanging upside down by their tail in the branches of the pines. They're easy to recognize; they have bright red eyes, three fingers and toes, and can turn their head all the way around. They're very mischievous and quite powerful, but also very sensitive. If you do see one, don't offend it by laughing or poking fun at it. Bad things will happen to you—like that fellow who lost his head in the plane's prop.

But if you're respectful, you'll be blessed with good luck. We can use some of that."

"Do people believe this?"

"Matters who you talk to. Lots of the old-timers do. Seems like Ida May does, probably your Ms. Cordella too. My theory is, a long time ago, some parents made up the tale as a way to keep the kids from walking out into the bush and getting lost. Like most myths, it probably has some basis in reality." Carter swerved around three dogs lying in the middle of the road.

As they'd hoped, for a small additional charge, Rooney gave them a lift to the airport. Kat had called Elliot, and he was waiting.

"Have you ever been to South Andros Beach Club?" Elliot asked.

"No, but it looks charming from their website," Kat answered.

"Well, it is, in a non-conventional way. It's owned by a young couple from Vermont, Jesse and Chelsea Backman. Seems they came to dive and fell in love with South Andros. It's not exactly what you might think of as a beach club. It's more of a combination blue hole dive operation and bonefishing lodge. There are a couple of cottages, but don't expect anything fancy. Remember you're on South Andros. People come here seeking solitude, fishing, and diving. Life is simple. No casinos, fancy restaurants, or nightlife. But the club's got character, and you never know who you'll meet."

CHAPTER 38

Elliot taxied down on the single airstrip at the Congo Town International Airport. It was so similar to Kat's arrival on South Bimini, she flashed back to what now seemed like a million years ago. In reality, it had been less than three weeks. As they walked through the one-room terminal, Kat wondered; what made this airport international? She read the arrivals and departures; like Bimini, there was a direct flight twice a week from Florida.

The sun hung low in the sky as they walked across the employees' lot to Elliot's car. "It's about thirty minutes to my place," he said. "It's south of the beach club. I called Buddy, but he didn't pick up. This is the hour he usually walks the beach; it's his substitute for Happy Hour. We'll drop your bags at the club. By that time, Buddy should be back at the house."

Kat was lost in her thoughts as they rode along. At last, she would have confirmation that Buddy was okay. She had so many questions for him. Elliot interrupted her solitude.

"Is there any reason someone would be following you?"

"Why are you asking?" Kat turned in her seat, checking behind.

"That car has been back there since we left the airport," Elliot said.

"Why does that surprise you?" Kat asked. "You said there was only one road."

"Well, it pulled out of the car rental lot, but the commercial flight from Nassau landed more than two hours ago, and there's no reason anyone would hang around the airport. There's not even a snack or drinks machine. Someone is keeping their distance even when I change my speed. Seems a little strange."

"Are you worried about someone coming after Buddy?" Kat asked.

"From what he's told me, yeah a little."

Elliot turned at the hand painted sign announcing the South Andros Beach Club. As he headed up the sandy drive, he heard the other car accelerate on the road.

"While you get your duffels, I'll see where Jesse is," Elliot said. "He may be on the beach with the dogs or still out with a dive group. But no matter, you can leave your stuff in the house. Chelsea will be there. She'll already have started dinner. Wait until you taste her bread and cake. She bakes every day."

Elliot walked on ahead, and Carter opened the trunk to pull their duffels out. "What have you told Elliot?" Carter asked.

"Not much. Buddy told him about the rare-earth mineral hoax and the falsified report. He knows about the boating accident and that I've come here looking for Buddy. My instincts are to trust Elliot, it's clear he cares about Buddy, and he's taking a risk hiding him in his house. Just the same, maybe it's better not to tell him more."

"I think it may be more than that."

"More than what?"

"His feelings toward Buddy."

"So you think that photo the DEA agent had was real? You don't know much about twins if you think I wouldn't have known this. We always knew everything about each other, even without talking." Kat slammed the car's trunk and walked ahead of Carter toward the lobby.

Elliot was right about the character of the beach club. Once a sprawling beachfront house, two separate cottages, with views and sounds of the ocean surf, now flanked each side. They entered what had been the living room and now served as a lounge for guests, with TV, comfortable slightly worn rattan furniture, a stack of board games, shelves of well-used books, and a dusty computer. A faded note stuck on the screen read, "No service today." The tape was discolored and peeling, barely holding up the paper sign. Colorful beach-scene murals with jumping dolphins and seabirds covered the walls. The painted concrete floor made sense, given all the sandy bare feet that tramped through. Someone put a lot of personal effort into the place. The kitchen, at the far end, opened to the living room and screened porch dining area. It would be fashionable in an upscale restaurant. Here, it was where the kitchen had always been, and cooking was not for show. The tantalizing smell of baking bread made up for the slightly scruffy interior. Elliot confirmed that Jesse had the dogs on the beach, Chelsea told them to leave their luggage by the porch door, and she'd put it in their room. They didn't waste any more time. Kat wanted to see Buddy.

Manny saw the brake lights come on and Elliot turn into the South Andros Beach Club. Undoubtedly, Elliot would take Kat to see Buddy before dinner. Right now would be the ideal time to find Buddy alone and the best chance he'd have to save his daughter. As Elliot's car disappeared, Manny accelerated hard, only slowing when he turned into Jared's fish camp, a coral and teal blue one-storied concrete building with the style and charm of an old-fashioned motel.

Manny slipped around to the side and down the dock to the fish cleaning station. In the fading light, he spotted two men drinking beer in the combination bar and dining room. The men couldn't see the dock or him, and no one sat in the chairs outside. At the fish station, he found what he wanted and quickly put on a pair of thick gloves, took a knife, and slipped it into his pocket. He would have preferred one of Elliot's kitchen knives, it would be less traceable, but he didn't have a flashlight and didn't know if he would be able to locate a knife in the dark kitchen. He wished there was more time to think this through, but time was against him.

Manny slipped off his shoes, hid them in the grassy dunes, and walked into the water knowing the surf would keep his secret. The glow from a television illuminated the first house along the beach. He hoped this was Elliot's house and that in the dark, he hadn't missed one set further back among the palms. The screen door on the porch was unlocked; no one ever locked doors here. There was no reason to. The wind had come up and the noise of the surf, TV, and the breeze blowing the palm fronds muffled the squeaking of the screen door. Stepping into the shadows of the room, he could see someone asleep on the couch.

Silently, Manny moved closer. It had to be Buddy; he looked so much like Kat. Standing over him, Manny pulled the knife out of his pocket. Sweat ran down his face as he hesitated. He had been trained for all kinds of self-defense. He knew how to use a knife against an assailant, precisely the angle to enter the chest and puncture the heart, but he had never deliberately killed another person. Could he do this? He blinked and saw the man who stood in the way of his daughter's future.

A light swept across the room. Manny spun around and focused on the headlights of a car pulling into the drive. It had to be Elliot's car; Manny had waited too long, the opportunity lost. He slipped out the same way he had come in. The flood of relief and anxiety made him stumble in the crashing surf back to the fish camp. Grabbing his shoes, he left the gloves and knife on the cleaning station and made his way up the dock as quickly as his uncooperative legs allowed. When would he have another chance? He had no alternative plan. He had to convince Kat to give this up. He'd drive back to the beach club and talk to her again.

CHAPTER 39

Elliot turned the car off in his driveway. "I fly tomorrow, but if you're willing to be here by nine, you guys can take my car back to the club tonight."

"We can be here as early as you want," Carter said as they followed Elliot into the living room.

Kat's voice broke, "He's asleep. Let me wake him." She stood over Buddy, watching him sleep so peacefully. Then she reached down, gently kissed his cheek, and whispered in his ear. "It's Anne Bonny. I've come to free you."

Buddy's eyes were suddenly wide; he grabbed her, pulled her down on top of him, and hugged her, kissing her hair. They spoke over each other, "Oh my God, I am so glad to see you."

"I didn't know if I'd ever see you again," Kat sobbed, her voice muffled by his chest. Eventually, she pushed herself up and stared into his face. Buddy wiped tears from her cheek and smoothed her hair.

"Shush, shush. It's okay now. I'm fine," he said. "And I found Elliot too. Can you imagine after all these years?" He struggled to sit up without letting her go.

"You're okay? Really okay?" Kat asked, her arms still around him.

"Yes, really. But I could use a little breathing room."

Kat laughed. "Sorry, I wasn't sure this day would ever come. I thought I had lost you." She blinked back tears.

"Can we walk the beach?" Buddy asked.

"I'd like that."

Buddy stood up, hugged Elliot, and thanked him for bringing Kat.

Kat watched the way they looked into each other's eyes. Was Carter right? Was this more than a renewed friendship? The only thing that bothered her was that she hadn't known. She realized she hadn't introduced Carter.

"Buddy, this is Carter. He's a big part of finding you." The two men shook hands.

"Thanks for helping Kat."

"No problem," Carter said. "All I did was steer the boat. With her determination, she could have done this alone."

Buddy grabbed Kat's hand. "Come on, let's walk."

Elliot watched as they walked with their arms around each other toward the beach.

"I think we just became background," Carter said, walking up behind Elliot. "Where do you think this leaves you and me? We could both lose here."

"I suppose. We'll have to wait and see. I don't want to lose Buddy now that we've finally reconnected."

"I don't have siblings. I've only known this kind of love once in my life," Carter said.

"As long as I've known these two, they've always had a special bond, almost telepathic. Want a beer while we wait?"

Once on the beach, Kat started. "Me first. You look great. How are you handling all of this? Elliot says you're not drinking."

"True. And I don't plan to again. Ever. He's too important to me."

"Okay, let's start there. Tell me about Elliot."

"It's simple. I love him. Have since we were kids. He's the best thing that has ever happened to me—other than having you as a sister."

"I had no idea. Why didn't you share this with me?" The hurt sounded in her voice, but Buddy didn't notice. "When did this start?"

"I don't know. When are you old enough to fall in love? It started on Bimini. Elliot and I would sneak off, but I lived in fear that The General would find out. At the very least he would have sent me off to military school. I wouldn't have survived that—the bullying, the conformity. And I hate to think what he would have done to Elliot. One day when The General was particularly angry with me, he told me that as weird as I was, at least I wasn't queer. What would you have done?"

Kat gazed at the starlit night. "Look, a shooting star. Do you remember, Mom always said it was a little bit of heaven streaking across the sky."

"It's not a star. It's the visible path of a meteoroid as it burns and vaporizes entering the atmosphere. They're more visible here without the glow of city lights."

"Buddy, focus. We were talking about you and Elliot. I wish you had told me. You didn't need to carry the burden of that secret alone. It wouldn't have mattered to me."

"No, probably not, but I didn't want you to have to lie to The General if the subject ever came up, even though you are good at lying," Buddy added with a grin.

"One of us has to be. You sure aren't. So, what happened? When did you guys split?"

"It was my decision. I didn't see any way to go on. It was too risky, and I was still trying to be a normal teenager. We couldn't exactly run away together, two young boys, one white, one black. We were, I don't know, maybe fourteen, fifteen. I was a coward. I told Elliot that I didn't want to see him anymore. Worst mistake of my life."

"You weren't a coward. You were a kid."

"I did find him on Facebook a few years ago. But I was afraid to friend him. I thought he wouldn't friend me back and I couldn't face that rejection. I learned he was a pilot, but on his profile page, he only listed the Bahamas as his home, no town, no island. It was a complete accident when we met on that flight from Bimini, that or fate. He doesn't usually do that run, but someone was sick, and he was subbing in." Buddy stopped and looked at Kat. "I'm not leaving Elliot. I don't care what The General thinks. I know he'll never accept me, but now that I have Elliot I can face The General's rejection. It's time for me to live my own life."

Kat took Buddy's hand. "Daddy does love you."

"Yeah, probably, but I wish he could accept me. Maybe it would be best if he thought I died in that accident. I have no plans to return to Florida. I finally know where I belong. I've found my happy place. Does that make sense to you?"

"It does."

"Now, what about you?" Buddy asked. "How'd you find me?"

Kat wasn't ready to share her ordeals with Buddy yet. That could come later. "You know me. Once my curiosity is aroused, I don't quit. Too many things didn't add up." She smiled. "Let's go back. We both have people we love waiting for us."

"Hmm, Stewart?"

"That was over long before I even came to the Bahamas. I just hadn't made a move."

"Fine by me. I never did like the way that asshole treated you. Always putting you down. He seemed to think he was the reason for your success. This Carter guy seems okay. Probably has his own baggage."

"More than you know."

On the walk back, Kat said, "Buddy, I need to get into that compound where you were working, find out what's going on."

"I'm with you. From the beginning, I was suspicious," Buddy said. "The Bahamas are primarily limestone. This is not the geological strata that contain dysprosium. It's mostly mined from ion-adsorption clay ores found chiefly in southern China. But I was curious, so I accepted their offer. I need to warn you. They're intent on keeping this secret. There's no way in that I know. They have it fenced and locked up with gates and guards with dogs."

"I have the name of someone who may know how to get in."

"Pick me up tomorrow morning. I want to go with you. I know the layout there, and if you get in, I can help."

"Okay, and about Elliot, I'd prefer you not to tell him what we're doing. Deniability is safer."

CHAPTER 40

Carter and Kat set out for the Beach Club in Elliot's Honda. "Boy, this sure beats that rental thing we had in Fresh Creek." Kat was silent; her head back, resting with her eyes closed. "Hey, Buddy's fine." Carter continued, "Are you sure you want to go tomorrow? No one will blame you if you quit now."

"I'm not quitting. More than ever, I'm convinced whatever is going on is related to the attempt on Buddy's life."

"This is your investigation, but I don't need to remind you that these guys are probably behind the attempt on your life too."

"Well then, don't remind me."

"I don't think they'll exactly put out the welcome mat. We need Manny's help, someone with authority here."

"Seems like you trust Manny more than Rollins. What if this is about drugs again and Manny is part of it."

"Believe me, he isn't," Carter said.

"You can't be sure."

"There are some things I know," Carter said.

"Manny's name is on that list I have from Carlos," Kat said.

Carter was unsettled by the information Kat revealed. It didn't match what he knew about Manny. "That can't be right. I've known him for as long as I've been sailing here. He's got a personal vendetta about drugs. His son is in prison in Nassau over dealing. It's why he signed on for the narcotic squad when he joined the police force. I'm not sure he's happy with the move to homicide, even though it was a promotion to captain. He's fanatical when it comes to keeping drugs out of the Bahamas."

"Well, people change. Remember my past."

They argued about Manny all the way back. Finally, Kat relented, "Okay, he was assigned to help. Maybe he will be useful, but we have to find a way to contact him."

"As far as I know, he's still on North Andros, probably at his cousin's until Tuesday—the day the ferry comes."

Manny was leaning on the counter separating the kitchen from the lounge, nursing a beer when Kat and Carter walked into the beach club.

"Well, why am I not surprised to see you here?" Kat asked, barely concealing her sarcasm.

"Where else would you be stayin'?" Manny asked. "We gotta talk about why you come down here." Manny pointed across the room to wicker chairs grouped near the bookshelves. "Let's sit over there."

"Is something wrong, Manny? You seem kind of…," Kat began.

"Nothin' wrong," Manny said too quickly.

While Carter ordered beers for them, Kat told Manny she had located Buddy.

"I suspected as much," Manny said. "And what he have to tell you?"

Kat sensed Manny was barely listening as though she was telling him things he already knew. But she described the falsified reports and that the site where Buddy had worked was on South Andros.

"So, I'm not at all sure what this is about," Kat said. "But I plan to get into that property and see. Somehow I think it's all tied to Carlos Lehder."

"Dat seems a bit far-fetched. Why don't you drop dat? You found your brother. Isn't dat why you came?"

"Maybe it's the reporter in me, but I'm convinced something is being covered up. Rollins assigned you to help me find Buddy and get to the bottom of that boating tragedy. If there is something that he should know, I want to give him that in exchange."

"He didn't exactly put me on dis to help you. His real interest was to find out what role Isadore had in all of it – whose side he on. I think Rollins' more interested in not bein' embarrassed by somethin' dat could ruin his re-election chances. But now Isadore dead and he can't keep dat shootin' out of da papers. Da opposition goin' to be tryin' to prove some corruption on Rollins' part, you can be sure of dat."

"Okay, then let's see what we can find out tomorrow. Maybe we can give him some ammunition to strike back against those charges," Kat said.

"How you plan to get in der?" Manny asked.

As Carter set their beers down, he told Manny their plan to find Platinum.

"I know da guy. Like Ida May said, he not very reliable. But she also right, if anyone know dis island, he does. He had weed growin' all over da place and most of it we never would have found if we hadn't made him take us. Da interior of dis island's solid with chinny briar and scrubby trees, poisonwood even. Not tall ones, just thick. Easy to get lost back in dat bush if you don't know your way."

"Or if the chickcharnie kidnap you," Kat said.

"Dat what we call an old granny tale. Told to keep da grandbabies safe. Ain't no such ting as a chickcharnie. Don't pay attention to dat. Just island folklore."

"We need to pick up a rental car and get Elliot's car back by nine tomorrow morning," Carter said. "Where can we meet up?"

"No need for a car. I got one. You stop by Jared's Fish Camp in the mornin'. Dat's where I'm stayin'. I'll be ready. You can lead da way to dis guy's house. From there we'll take my car. I'll be happy to meet dis brother of yours finally." Manny stood up. "You enjoy your dinner now. See you in da mornin'."

Kat stared at Manny's back as he left the club. "Did he seem distracted to you?" she asked Carter. "He didn't even make eye contact with me."

"I didn't notice anything. Maybe he feels displaced, like he should be the one setting this up, not some girl reporter from the U.S." Carter said with a sly smile.

CHAPTER 41

Chelsea wiped her hands on her apron as she approached Carter and Kat. "Capt'n Carter, we sit family-style for dinner, I'd like to seat you beside one of our return guests. Senator Coggins. Is that okay?"

"Senator who?"

Chelsea laughed. "That's exactly why I'm putting you there. He wants some island flavor, not some Florida import who's here for a few days. He doesn't want to be recognized, at least that's what he says so, please don't bring up U.S. politics."

"He doesn't know any politics," Kat stuck in.

"Perfect," Chelsea said. "Just treat the senator as one of the big game fishing guys. That's what he wants."

"Carter doesn't know anything about big game fishing either," Kat added.

"Better yet." Chelsea headed back to the kitchen.

Kat turned to Carter. "Okay, here's a brief. Walter Coggins, Texas Republican, a key member of the U.S. Senate Committee on Energy and Natural Resources. Supporter of fracking. Opposed to most alternative energy."

"How do you know all that?"

"I read."

"Well, it's more than I need to know if I'm not even supposed to recognize him."

"Just so you're prepared," Kat said. "I'm going to sit directly across from you. I can pretend stupidity."

"Thanks a lot."

"You're welcome. I wouldn't want you to have to carry this off all on your own, and I can kick you under the table if he says something important."

"Won't you ever stop being the reporter?" Carter asked.

"Reporters like to ruffle feathers. A few well-placed questions and I can make him talk about things he never thought he would."

"Unlikely. Chelsea says he doesn't want to be recognized."

"Oh, come on. Have you ever known a politician who seriously doesn't want to be recognized? And I can be very charming."

"So I've witnessed. Like talking back to Prime Minister Rollins?"

Kat stuck out her tongue.

"Do you mind?" Carter asked, pointing to the seat beside Senator Coggins.

"No, please. I'm Walt Coggins. You from Andros?" Coggins asked, extending his hand.

"It's Carter. And no, I'm not from Andros, but I've spent most of the last seventeen years in the islands. I run a charter boat service."

Carter scrutinized his distinguished-looking dinner mate's carefully groomed, swept-back gray hair, pressed khaki shorts, and a navy short-sleeved shirt with the name *Carpe Diem* stitched above the pocket. He looked more like a man who had stepped out of the pages of *Motoryacht* magazine than off a fishing boat. His persona came complete with the practiced smile of a seasoned politician.

"And is this lovely lady your wife?" Coggins asked as Kat sat down opposite Carter.

"No, this is Kat. She's my first mate."

Even from her place across the table, Kat could smell alcohol on Coggins' breath. She visualized the well-stocked bar on his yacht.

"Well, aren't we both lucky. This is Willow, my first mate." Coggins finally introduced the tanned blond woman on the other side of him. "I'm more of a fisherman myself. That little jewel out in the harbor is mine."

Carter looked across the patio to the bay. There was only one sport fishing boat. He estimated it was nearly eighty feet.

Willow? Really? Kat smiled politely at the woman opposite her then turned to the senator. "So, Walt are you here to get some out-island flavor?"

"Exactly. And to find some relief from reporters." Coggins rattled the ice in his drink. Willow took her cue and headed to the bar to refresh his drink. Carter's eyes followed the leggy blond as Coggins continued. "When I'm not fishing, I'm busy being a U.S. senator and reporters follow me everywhere."

"I thought I recognized you," Kat said, pushing her sunglasses up onto her head. "I've seen you on TV, but I didn't want to say anything." She winked at Coggins. "Figured you wanted your privacy."

Well that didn't take long. Carter was sure Coggins sucked in his stomach and sat up straighter.

"Well, thank you, miss. It certainly can be tiring. Have to watch everything I say when the press is around. Can't relax and be myself."

"Well, now you can," Kat continued. "It's unlikely you'll find any reporters here. Nothing happens down here worth covering unless someone gets worked up about undersized lobster."

Carter suppressed the urge to kick Kat under the table. This wasn't idle conversation. Kat had gone into action.

"Are you planning to fish along Andros?" Kat asked.

"Definitely. I'm dropping Willow here for the next two days so she can dive. I've rented one of the private villas for her. Not as fancy as my yacht, but the best I can do around here."

Carter had the impression that Willow was more than crew. He had never known hired crew to be given time off in the middle of a job.

"I don't like to fish," Willow said, trying to become part of the conversation. "But I do love to dive."

"Me too," Carter said, "But not this trip."

Kat ignored the exchange between Carter and Willow and addressed Coggins. "Fishing is better in Bimini or Chub Cay. But if it's isolation you want, this is the place. It's even isolated from fish. I love to fish, and here I don't even have to interrupt my fishing to reel anything in."

This was news to Carter. Kat had never expressed any interest in fishing but her remark produced an over-enthusiastic laugh from Coggins who reached across the table to squeeze her arm.

"Maybe we can exchange mates for the next couple of days," Coggins said.

Kat shook her head. "Not this time. We're here for a funeral."

"Sorry to hear that. I don't know how much fishing I'll get in either. This is a working vacation. I sit on the Senate Committee on Energy and Natural Resources, and a couple of weeks ago the Bahamian Prime Minister announced plans for North Korea to mine rare-earth minerals in the Bahamas. You probably don't know, but these metals are important for hybrid vehicles and clean energy. This could have a big impact on my oil-producing constituents, and since I represent Texas, I need to stay on top of this."

Carter agreed; Kat was right. Was it her charm, his ego, or the scotch that had loosened his tongue? Carter's impression was this was a guy who couldn't keep a secret even sober. Kat had the senator's attention and Carter was willing to sit back and let her carry the conversation.

"Are you saying the PM announced there are rare-earth minerals on Andros?" Kat asked.

"No, no, he didn't say where," Coggins leaned toward Kat and tapped his temple. "I put two and two together. I had an option on a large tract of land about twenty miles south of here, and suddenly it's off the market. No one will say why."

"Well, I don't know about rocks, the only thing I've ever seen here are bonefish, chickcharnies, and mosquitoes," Kat said. "Should I be on the lookout for them?"

Coggins laughed and held out his empty glass to Willow. "And, darlin', tell them I want the best scotch they have, not this watered-down crap." Turning back to Kat, Coggins picked up where he left off.

"There's nothing to see. As I said, they have to be mined. Actually, they're not so rare. But what is rare are large deposits. Right now, China has the corner on the market with eighty percent of the world's supply. Extracting and processing rare-earths is labor-intensive and expensive, and up until now, the U.S. hasn't invested in this. However, there are rumors of a joint venture between a U.S. chemical firm and an Australian mining company setting up a processing plant right in my backyard. If large deposits were extracted here and then shipped to Texas for processing, it would be a big boost for those alternative energy tree huggers."

"Wouldn't that be a good thing?" Kat asked.

How in good conscious can she continue to lead Coggins on? Carter wondered.

"Not where I come from," Coggins answered. "Oil is the backbone of the Texas economy. We don't drive electric or hybrids in Texas and we don't put solar panels on our homes. But if you're interested, let me give you a great source. There's a reporter who writes about the Bahamas. Freelance. Mary Katherine… something. I forgot her last name. Knows a lot. Even did some interesting pieces on Hemingway, but that was a while back. I assigned one of my aids to follow everything she writes."

Kat turned suddenly to Willow, offering her Chelsea's dinner rolls. Coggins didn't notice; he was distracted by the sound of an outboard. A polished center console tender was heading in from his yacht.

"Wonder what's wrong?" Coggins grabbed the tabletop as he stood.

"A problem?" Carter responded.

"That's my captain. I told him I'd radio when I wanted a pickup. I'm not ready to go back. We haven't even had dessert, coffee, or brandy. Maybe my guest decided to come in after all." Coggins leaned heavily on the table and whispered. "He wants a low profile, but I'm going to share this with you two. Franklin Albury's onboard. Does that name mean anything to you?"

Kat shook her head. "Don't think so."

Carter had to work hard to keep his expression neutral. He didn't dare make eye contact with Kat.

Coggins plopped down into his chair, grinning. "Well, he's the Minister of Finance. No, wait. Minister of Interior."

"Well, Walt, you must be important to have someone of that rank as your guest," Kat said, trying to avoid Coggins' breath.

Carter watched Coggins' captain tie the yacht's tender to the dock. As the man turned toward the patio, Carter recognized Tucker Bain, a competent Bahamian captain and friend. "Hey, Tucker." Carter waved as Tucker made his way up from the beach. "What a surprise. Sit and have a beer."

"Good to see you too, mon. What brings you to dis neck of da woods?" Tucker leaned across the table and shook Carter's hand. "I'll take a rain check on dat beer. I came to talk to da senator about a problem with his boat."

"Yacht," Coggins asserted. "I hired you to deal with maintenance problems. I'd like to finish this peaceful dinner with my new friends."

"What is it, Tuck?" Carter asked. "Anything I can help with?" Carter knew that Tucker wouldn't have interrupted the senator unless the problem was urgent.

"Da boat has a leakin' through-hull valve," Tucker answered. He turned back to the senator. "I came to ask where you keep da through-hull plugs. I've looked in da locker where you said parts were stowed, but I didn't find any. I need to plug dat through-hull. I can't get in der to see what's wrong or how serious dis is 'til I plug it."

"Well, look again. You're wrong. My boat is well-maintained. I had it gone over in Florida before I hired you. My American captain said everything was up to standards and his training is top-notch. I only hire the best in the business."

"No sir, you're wrong on two accounts. Your boat doesn't meet standards and you don't have any plugs onboard," Tucker said. Carter could tell from Tucker's voice that this was not the first time he had collided with the Senator.

Tucker turned to Carter. "Do you have extra plugs on *Wind Chaser?*"

"Yes, but *Wind Chaser's* not here. We came over on the ferry. Dudley Marine in Nassau will be your closest source."

Tucker nodded. "My thoughts exactly." He turned back to Coggins. "Sir, if I call Dudley now, we can get some flown in tomorrow. If I remember, there's a plane dat comes early in da mornin'. I'll find Jesse. He'll know da flight schedule. If I can get them early enough, we can be underway by da afternoon."

"I wish I could lend a hand, but I'm tied up tomorrow," Carter said.

"Thanks, but I can do this," Tucker responded.

"Now just a minute. This is my decision." Coggins' face was red. "Both you guys are making a big deal out of a piss-ant hill. My yacht is in fine shape. We can take care of any problem after our cruise is over. I've got important work here, and I'm not going to be delayed by some little thing like this."

"Senator, maybe you didn't hear me," Tucker protested. "Your boat —yacht—is takin' on water. Dat means it's sinkin'. You hired me to captain. Safety for da boat and crew is my responsibility. I can get those plugs from Nassau tomorrow, but meantime, under des circumstances, I'm not takin' *Carpe Diem* anywhere."

"You may be captain, but I'm the owner." Coggins voice was louder than it needed to be. "And I say we're heading south in the morning. That's an order."

"I'm not," Tucker replied. "I'm done here. I'll get my tings off your boat. You're on your own with dis. When I return, I'll leave da center console at da dock so you can get back to your God-damn sinkin' yacht." Tucker hurried toward the dock.

"Damn him," Coggins swore. "He's been trouble from the start. Just one conflict after another. Thinks he knows more about my yacht than I do. According to him, he knows the best routes, where coral heads are, even where I can drop anchor. I should have brought my captain from the States. But no, I thought I'd be doing these guys a favor hiring one of their own. Put a little money back into these islands, and this is the thanks I get. These guys down here don't want to do any work." Coggins turned to Carter. "Want a job?"

"No, I don't. Besides, I have a lot of confidence in Tuck. If he says that boat isn't seaworthy, I suggest you listen to him. Your best bet is to apologize and let him fix things before you go anywhere. It's not going to hold you up more than a day." Carter wasn't usually this bold, but Coggins' remarks about Tucker pissed him off.

"I should have known you'd side with him. You're all alike. Jealous. That's what this is all about." Coggins threw up his hands, spilling his scotch. Willow scrambled to mop it up. "Jealous about what I've accomplished in my life and waiting for a chance to attack me. I see it all the time in politics. Always have to watch my own back. No one else does. I don't need any advice from you. I can manage my yacht myself." Coggins pushed back his chair, knocking it over. "Come on Willow."

"I'll stay in the villa tonight so you can get an early start tomorrow," Willow said, politely. She seemed embarrassed by Coggins' outburst.

"Good choice," Carter said under his breath.

Willow turned to Kat and Carter. "It was nice to meet you both."

Coggins staggered to the door. As he tripped on the threshold, Willow caught his arm.

"Well, the Senator sure showed his true colors. What did Chelsea say about him not wanting to be recognized?" Kat flinched as Coggins slammed the door to the lodge. "A reporter would be thrilled to have heard that tirade."

"I just hope he doesn't let it interfere with his judgment," Carter said.

"It already has," Kat said. "He's going to miss out on Chelsea's coconut cake."

The next morning, Carter and Kat grabbed mugs of coffee from the kitchen and walked down the path to the beach. Carter waved to Willow who sat on her porch decked out in a black bikini.

"So what was that not-so-subtle hint about her *private villa?*" Kat asked. "It certainly wasn't directed at me. I'd hardly call these rooms *villas*. And that name? Willow? Is that some stage name to go with her personal trainer toned body and bottle-blond hair?"

Carter decided it wise to dodge Kat's questions. He turned his attention to Coggins on *Carpe Diem's* bridge deck, preparing for departure. He heard the diesels fire up.

"Well, there he goes," Carter said. "Hungover for sure and a disaster waiting to happen. I hope we don't read about him in the newspaper."

"And he's got Albury onboard."

"As far as I know, there's no place to anchor or dock further south," Carter continued. "And sooner or later he's got to come back and pick up Willow. I'm glad we won't be here when he does. Come on. We've got to meet Manny and take Elliot's car back."

CHAPTER 42

The gravel crunched under the tires as Carter pulled into Jared's Fish Camp. Outside of his room, Manny balanced on a rickety plastic chair that looked as though it could collapse at any moment.

"I think it best if you park down the road and stay in your car until Elliot leaves," Kat said to Manny. "I know you met him at the memorial service, but I'd rather not have to explain why you're with us."

Dressed in his pilot's uniform, Elliot was leaning against the back porch railing.

"Wow. What is it about a man in uniform?" Kat asked, handing him the car keys.

"I'm glad you can spend the day with Buddy, but I'm sorry I have to work," Elliot said, hugging Kat. "Promise me you'll come back now that we've reconnected."

"Not a difficult promise since Buddy is staying." Kat was still stunned that she hadn't picked up on the relationship between Elliot and Buddy when they were teenagers. All this time she considered herself the perceptive twin, but she'd never had a clue about this.

Once Elliot's car was out of sight, Manny pulled into the driveway.

Together, he and Kat walked into the house where Buddy and Carter were discussing the plan for the day.

Manny interrupted, "I know how to get to Platinum's. It's not very far, but then nothin' is on dis island since all the towns are up and down along dis east side. No one wants to live in da interior, nothin' there 'cept poisonwood, mosquitoes, and blue holes. I'll be out at the car."

"Carter already warned me about poisonwood," Kat said to Manny's back. "I suppose you're going to tell me there are chickcharnie too."

Buddy broke in, "No, that's island folklore based on a three-foot-tall *Tyto pollens* owl that couldn't fly. They're actually a relative of the common barn owl. They were native to Andros, and coexisted with the population until the sixteenth century when European settlers cut down the forests for the timber. That destroyed the owls' habitat. They are probably extinct now or live only in the dense interior of Andros. It's said the chickcharnie can turn its head all the way around, that part of the tale most likely started with the *Tyto pollens*." Kat rolled her eyes impatiently, but Buddy didn't notice.

"Bats hang upside down, and there are lots of various species of bats in the caves on Andros, so that was easy to add to the tale of the chickcharnie. Put it all together, mix in some rich island folklore, and you've got a great legend. Oh, they like bright colors and sparkly things. Too bad you don't have a bracelet or necklace you could leave for them. They'd like that. If you walk in the bush here, you'd see jewelry and even aluminum pie pans hanging in the trees that people have left behind." Buddy glanced at Carter and stopped.

"You talk like a walking encyclopedia," Carter said. "How do you know all this stuff? I'd give anything to have half your smarts."

"And I'd give anything to have your insights. Whatever makes my brain different doesn't include catching on to subtlety or humor like everyone else. I like facts, numbers. They're reliable and consistent. It's people I don't understand. I take everything literally, even when I know I should read between the lines, and sometimes I'm really wrong. I thought Oriental Minerals wanted to know if there were rare-earth minerals on Andros."

"Interesting. I never thought about it. I assumed insight and intelligence went together," Carter said.

"It's not about intellectual ability; it's called emotional intelligence. Look it up sometime. It's a different part of the brain. Describes perfectly what I'm missing. Believe me, living without it is a real handicap. People pick up on my social ineptness, that and my fixation on details. Just stop me if I go off on a tangent. Kat's used to it, but I know I can be annoying."

"Does your attention to detail extend to directions? That may come in handy when we're trying to find our way around this compound—if we get in."

"No problem. Another one of my weird skills," Buddy said, with a grin. "I've got eidetic memory." Looking at Carter's puzzled expression, Buddy continued. "Photographic memory. I could draw you a map more up to date than Google Earth based on the time I wasted scratching for non-existent minerals."

Manny drove south, crossed the one-lane bridge at Deep Creek, and turned onto the dirt road beside it.

"I'd hardly call this a creek, it's so wide," Carter said, looking over the flowing water.

"Wide, but shallow. Dat's why it's good for bonefishin'," Manny said. They stopped the car once the road was no more than a sandy path. Weeds grew up in the center. "We have to walk from here, but it's not far."

Through the dense bush, they spotted the remains of the church steeple and then the crumbled foundations of several houses. Carter spotted one with a roof. "That's got to be Platinum's. That tin looks like it wouldn't withstand blowing rain, let alone a tropical storm."

They stepped around cans and beer bottles scattered outside, and Manny banged on a flimsy door. There was no answer. Manny pushed it open to the unmistakable smells of marijuana and citronella. Platinum was leaning back in the only chair, teetering on two legs, a half-smile on his face, his eyes unfocused. It all changed when Platinum recognized Manny. He tried to hide his roach under his foot and began waving his hand in front of his face as if that would dispel the distinctive odor.

"I swear, I ain't growin' no more. I need dis for my pain. Doctor say."

"What doctor, da bush doctor?" Manny asked.

"I ain't goin' back to jail."

"Well, you lucky dis time. 'Cause dat's not why I'm here." Manny's dialect had become stronger during his exchange with Platinum. "My friends and I need you' help."

"Sure ting. Anything you ask. Platinum's you' man."

"We need to get past dat fence south of here."

"Don't know nothin' bout dat. Never seen no fence. I swear, I not involved in any of dat."

"Any of what?" Manny asked, stepping closer to Platinum.

Platinum tried to scoot back in his chair. "All dat stuff what dey protectin' with dat fence and dogs."

"You said you didn't know anything about a fence," Carter said.

Platinum's eyes darted from one of his guests to another. Kat stepped forward. "Look at this Platinum." Kat held out the token she'd been given. His eyes widened. "We've been to see Ms. Ida May. She sent you this message. She said, if you don't help us, she will put her spell on you and get the chickcharnie after you. She said to tell you, you won't like what she does. Something about your manhood falling off, if I recall."

Platinum pointed at Kat's hand with a tobacco stained finger. "Put dat ting away and tell her not to do dat. It 'bout all I got. But she right 'bout da chickcharnie. Dey all upset. If I help you, can you settle dem down? Dey da reason I have ta smoke da weed. It's da pain dey cause me. My back and legs. Can't hardly walk. Can't catch no fish. I be in a bad way."

"I see you in a bad way," Manny said. "Maybe another bit of time in Nassau set you right. You think so?"

"In fact, I jist remember, I can take you to a cave dat goes right into dat property, right to da marina dey build. But it be dark and wet in there, and bats. You got flashlights?"

"Where can we get some?" Carter asked.

"Da store in Deep Creek," Platinum said.

"Manny and I'll go," Buddy said. "You two can stay with Platinum."

"No need for dat," Platinum said, wiggling nervously in his chair. "You can't go in der 'till low tide. Dat won't be 'till dis evenin'. I put a line down dere dat lead straight to a big ole blue hole right in da middle of dat cave. If you careful, you can walk on da ledge all da way around dat hole 'cept when da tide is high, den da water come almost up to da ceiling, and if you slip and fall in, you get sucked right down by dat monster, Lusca, and never come back." Platinum's ramblings changed course.

"Say, I hungry. Can you pick me up somethin' while you in Deep Creek? Don't matter what, jist somethin' for a hungry man."

"Now you're not thinkin' of goin' anywhere are you?" Manny asked, pocketing the roach Platinum had crushed out on the floor. "'Cause if you are, you know I'll hunt you down personally and see to it you spend a long time in Nassau when I catch up wid you. Big ole José still in der and he lookin' for a cellmate. He' mean and ornery as he was when you be his buddy."

Platinum's entire body was jiggling. "No sir, I be right here. Right here in dis ole chair when you and your friends come back. I ain't goin' nowhere."

"That's perfect, Platinum," Manny said.

"And you bring ole Platinum something to eat? Man can't be a good guide if he hungry. Best you wear jeans and jackets. Oh, and water, you gonna need dat."

"Seems like you and Platinum had a previous encounter," Kat said, as they walked to the car.

"He was caught growin' and sellin' weed. Sellin' to kids. I can't abide dat. Da narc squad burnt down most of his crop he planted in da bush. You couldn't even see them from a helicopter; it's dat dense back in there. But he did his time. I hope he's tellin' da truth about not growin'. I don't care if he uses it, just don't want him sellin'."

When they reached the car, Manny banged on the fender, "Shit."

"What's wrong?" Carter asked, coming up behind him.

"Flat tire."

"Do you think it was intentional?" Kat asked.

"I doubt it. Probably picked up a nail or somethin' on da road." Manny bent down to examine the tire. "Doesn't look like it was slashed or anything. I hope there's a spare. These rentals aren't always very reliable."

"Tell me about it," Carter said. "Did you see that thing we rented from Rooney in Fresh Creek? It ran mostly on three cylinders and was held together by rust."

Manny opened the trunk. "We're in luck. There's a tire here, and it looks like it even has air," he said, pounding his fist against the spare. "Now if there's a jack…" Their luck had run out.

"I'll call Jesse, see if someone can bring us one," Kat said, pulling out her phone. "Great, no service."

"I'll walk up to the highway," Buddy said. "See if I get reception there."

Carter grabbed his arm. "I don't think that's a good idea. It'd be our luck that the guy who picks you up would recognize you."

"I'll go with him," Manny offered. Together they started down the road.

"Wait." Kat ran after them. "I think Carter's got a point. Buddy needs to stay hidden. He's the only one who can testify against Oriental Minerals."

"Okay, I'll go alone, I can thumb a ride," Manny said. "Done all the time on des islands."

CHAPTER 43

Less than an hour later, Manny arrived in a gaudy, custom painted, purple transportation van. Unlike Kat's van from the airport on South Bimini, this one was covered with decals that advertised Viola's Transportation Service. The driver handed each of them her card and introduced herself as Viola Lloyd.

"What you all doin' back here anyway? No one back here but dat weed-tokin' Platinum. If you see him, don't believe half what he tell you. He say most anythin'. Told me once dat da AUTEC base was testin' nuclear weapons for submarines and dey plan to kill all the Bahamians by poisonin' da fish with radiation. Dat weed make him paranoid, among other things, is what I say. Dat base been closed down long time now and we all still here. Da only base even close to us before you get all da way up to North Andros be on Mangrove Cay and it take a boat even to get to dat one. Dat Platinum, he make up all kinds of tings. Don't pay him no mind."

"Let's get this tire changed," Carter said to Manny and Buddy.

Viola looked at Kat. "Did you come down dis road to find da old settlement? If you want a real tour, you call on Viola. My number right der on da card. I do weddings, funerals, proms, sightseein' tours, and transportation to da airport. Anytime you need me. Courteous and reliable, like it say. And I make jewelry too. How 'bout it Missy, you want to see what Viola got? Seems we got some time and shoppin' take your mind off dis heat and da pesky gnats."

Kat walked with her to the back of the van where Viola pulled out a dozen little gold foil-topped boxes with necklaces, earrings, and bracelets. Kat picked out a bracelet made of tiny shells and silver beads.

"Oh, now dat be a special one, cost a little bit more, but it be a good luck bracelet. Keep you safe from all kinds of spirits dat roam Andros. We do have 'em, you know. Plus, da chickcharnie like pretty shiny tings. Kind of small though, look like I made it just for a skinny gal like you."

"I'm going to wear it as an anklet. I think it's exactly what I need if you're right about it bringing good luck," Kat said, fastening it around her ankle.

"Oh, it does, you see," Viola said, nodding vigorously.

It took them longer than expected to find the store in the small settlement of Deep Creek. After slowly driving the length of the gravel road that separated the ocean on one side from houses on the other, they turned around and stopped to ask a woman sitting on her porch shucking corn. She pointed to a green house and told them to walk through the yard; the store was in the back.

The hand-painted sign above the door read; The Store. If We Don't Have It, You Don't Need it. The screen door was open, so they stepped inside. No one was around.

"It's evident why it's called The Store. Look at this." Buddy strolled around. "We can buy screwdrivers, wrenches, a whole assortment of nails and screws, and fishing lures. I don't see flashlights, but over here is beef jerky, Campbell tomato soup, Vienna sausages, and Kraft mac and cheese. I love that stuff!"

Buddy continued to pace around. "Hey, we might need some of these; Goody's extra strength headache powder, Ludden's cough drops, and Philips milk of magnesium." From across the room, he called. "There's no order to this. The school supplies, pencils, notebooks and stuff are all mixed in with greeting cards, wrapping paper, and Christmas decorations. How can anyone do inventory?" A distant slamming door stopped Buddy's meandering. Supporting himself with a single crutch, the store owner crossed the yard. "Need somethin'?"

"You have flashlights? Manny asked.

"You lucky," the man said, stepping inside. "Da supply boat come in yesterday so I not only got flashlights, I got batteries too. If you come a day ago, I be all out of da batteries."

The shopkeeper reached under the counter and stacked flashlights and batteries on top. There was only one type of flashlight, and the faded print made it look as though they had been part of the inventory forever. Buddy blew the dust off the cardboard. "I can't find the date of manufacture or a price," he said, turning the package over in his hand.

"Doesn't matter," Carter said. "There's no other option."

Buddy continued reading. "The battery life is rated at ten hours, but that might not be ten continuous hours, and battery life varies with temperature."

"We'll buy extra batteries," Carter said. Now that he understood a bit more about Buddy, he didn't want to show his exasperation with Buddy's obsession with details. It didn't matter what the package said, it was this or nothing. Carter paid an excessive price, given the quality. Things were expensive since everything was imported, but he suspected the owner was taking advantage of them.

Heading back to the car, Carter asked, "Manny, do you think Platinum is telling the truth about a cave going all the way into the compound?"

"We won't know for sure until we try it, but there are extensive caves on Andros. People from da University of Florida come here all da time to map da layout of caves and study bats dat live in them."

Kat piped up. "Bats?"

"Yeah, Platinum was right about dat. Da Bahamas have lots of different kinds dat aren't found anywhere else."

"There are nine hundred species of bats worldwide," Buddy said. "Fifteen different types have been identified on Andros, but funnel-ear bats are the ones native to the Bahamas. The deep caves are their favorite habitat, cool and damp. They're very agile flyers and are rarely caught in nets, which is why so little is known about their natural history."

"Do they carry rabies?" Kat looked slightly uncomfortable.

"Prevalence of rabies in bats is overstated," Buddy answered. "They're usually flying about at night to find insects to eat. They have no interest in humans, but keep your movements slow and deliberate so the bats can sense your position. And if we do see a bat colony don't shine your flashlight directly at them. That startles them, and you'll have the whole group flying at you." No one was paying much attention, but Buddy persisted as they headed back to the car.

"You really should be more worried about the fault lines along the inside of these caves. This island is mostly limestone, which is soft and erodes easily. The walls are made up of formations of calcium carbonate, which can shift or dislodge and trap you inside the cave. And watch your step; the floor will have lots of sinkholes along with slippery bat guano."

Eventually, Kat said, "Buddy stop. I'm not about to give up this investigation, but this is definitely too much information."

Platinum was sitting on the broken front steps when they arrived. Carter handed him a couple of the sandwiches that Chelsea had fixed for them when they told her they were going to explore the island. Platinum didn't speak, simply stood up and went into the woods while munching on a sandwich following a path that looked like someone hacked it out with a machete. The four trudged, single-file, behind.

They hadn't walked more than ten minutes when Platinum

stopped and pointed. "It be der." The entrance to the cave was hidden by brush and natural rock. "Someone got to clear it." Platinum sat down on an outcropping of rock and started on a second sandwich.

"You sure about this?" Carter asked.

"I know'd what I know'd," Platinum said.

Carter and Manny pulled the brush away until they could see the concealed opening. It was so narrow that only one person could pass through at a time.

Platinum pointed toward the hole. "Got to duck down to git in. But it git into a big ole

room once you inside. There's a gate at da far end where it git narrow again. Big ole rusty thing. You see it. I tie a line to dat gate so from there on, jist make sure you follow it right around dat blue hole. Dis cave curve around a bit and der is one split in dat path, but you have my line to follow so you don't git mixed up which one to take. If you move along steady like, it take you 'bout an hour to git through. Most of da way you can stand straight up."

"Did the Koreans put the gate in there?" Kat asked.

"Ain't no Korean here. Des guys speak Spanish," Platinum said.

"How you know Spanish?" Manny asked.

"I know'd cause ole José talkin' to hisself all da time in lock up. Mutterin'. Sometimes shoutin'. Keep me awake all night. I wanted to punch him. But he too big. I know'd what I sayin'.'"

"Really?" Kat remembered both Ida May and Viola's words. 'He not factually reliable.'

"Yup. Ain't no Koreans. Anyway, dat gate old, made of iron or somethin', and rusty." Platinum was repeating himself. "Maybe da rum runners or wreckers built it. But maybe not. Who know? Dis is as far as I go. Oh, when you git to da other end, watch out for da net."

"Anyone else know about this cave?" Manny asked.

"Nope, jist me."

Platinum rose unsteadily to his feet, wiped his hands on his pants, and turned away. They weren't going to find out anything more.

CHAPTER 44

Inside, they stood upright in a large vaulted cathedral-like room. It was eerily silent. Shining their flashlights around, they could see impressive mineral icicles hanging from the ceiling and pillars rising from the floor.

"This is indescribable. I've never seen anything like it," Kat said. Her flashlight reflected on the imposing structures. "Looks like they're centuries old."

"More than that," Buddy related. "Limestone stalactites grow less than an inch every thousand years as the water containing dissolved calcium bicarbonate drips from cracks in the ceiling. Many caves, particularly limestone ones, contain impressive geologic curiosities. The brilliant hues come from additional minerals in them."

"Interesting," Carter said. "All I know is, if it continues like this, it should be an easy walk through this mineral maze."

"Don't count on it," Buddy added. "Caves vary from spacious domed grottos with skylights to dark, tight passages and long winding shafts. We're lucky this one is dry. Most of the caves on Andros are under water and can only be accessed by divers with scuba gear."

"I can see what entices people to explore caves," Kat said. She continued to shine her light around the walls and ceiling, highlighting the magnificent structures.

"Spelunker," Buddy said.

"What?" Kat asked.

"Cavers are called spelunkers."

"It's like a backdrop for a sci-fi movie," Kat said, still trying to give words to what she saw.

"Or a psychological thriller," Buddy added. "Caving can be dangerous. I wish we were better equipped."

"Well, we're not. It's only about an hour walk according to Platinum." Kat turned to Manny. "What do you know about these wreckers Platinum was talking about?"

Before Manny could answer, Buddy burst in. "Beginning in the sixteen hundreds, shipwrecking was a lucrative occupation in the Bahamas. In some locations, islanders built lighthouses or lit fires on the beach to purposely lure ships onto the coral reefs so they could plunder the wrecked ships. Legitimate salvage operations wiped out wrecking by the end of the nineteenth century when the Bahamian government cracked down."

"Dat's all fine, but we're not here for a history lesson," Manny said.

"I'm wondering who put this gate down here," Kat said.

"It's possible this cave might've been used to hide confiscated goods," Buddy said.

Kat led as they wound through the pillars and columns. "I'd feel better if you walk behind me so I can test the surface," Carter said. "I'd hate to lose you down a sinkhole."

"No, sinkholes aren't that big, only blue holes, but anyone of us could sprain an ankle," Buddy interjected. "Oh, wait, you're kidding, right?"

"Yeah, I was, but I don't want her to get hurt because then she'd expect me to carry her the rest of the way on my back and if she falls and gets bat guano all over her, she'd stink as bad as this cave does."

"I'd carry her," Buddy said.

"You needn't worry. I'm perfectly capable of walking on my own," Kat said.

"Manny, any idea what Platinum meant about a net?" Carter asked.

Manny had remained quiet while the others kept up their nervous chatter. Now he answered Carter's question. "Maybe it was left behind by one of da research teams who came to study bats. Lot of what Platinum say don't make sense. Most likely he got tangled up in some vines."

When they reached the far side of the vaulted room, Carter said, "Well, so far Platinum has been correct." He pointed to a thick line tied near the bottom of the gate leading into the tunnel. Turning to Manny, he asked, "Platinum said the men here aren't Koreans, what do you think about that?"

"Okay, I'm going out on a limb here," Kat added. "Platinum said they spoke Spanish. Do you think they could be Colombians, and this is about a new drug operation?"

"If it's drugs, why were the Koreans involved at all? Why the rare-earth mineral ruse?" Carter asked.

"I can answer dat," Manny said. "There's no way a bunch of Colombians could come in here and buy up a big chunk of land. They already caused enough trouble in years past. Rollins never would agree to dat. Da Koreans could be a front. Make it look legit."

"How in the world would the Koreans link with the Colombians, if that's what this is?" Carter asked.

Kat was the one who answered. "Ever since Kim Jong-Un took over from his father, North Korea has been discreetly seeking trade partners outside Asia. They already have an embassy in Brazil, and they trade with Cuba. It doesn't seem so impossible that they have made contacts in Colombia as well."

Carter was beginning to see similarities between Kat and Buddy. It was evident that they both could absorb a lot of information and recall all the details. The difference was Kat found a profession that allowed her to benefit from her remarkable ability.

"So, back to my question, do you think we're about to uncover a Colombian-backed drug operation?" Kat asked.

"We'll know more after we get in and have a look around," Manny said. "Let's keep movin'."

"Do you suppose this cave has a name?" Kat's voice echoed off the walls.

"I'm sure it did once. Someone put that gate in here," Buddy said. This floor is smooth; limestone is naturally rough and jagged. I'd say it's been worn down by lots of people walking on it."

"Recently?" Kat asked.

"Maybe the people who lived in da settlement used it before they all moved out," Manny offered. "There are lots of strange beliefs surroundin' caves. Some old-timer probably could tell you."

"Here's an example," Buddy recited as they made their way along the shaft. "Preacher's Cave on Eleuthera was a burial ground used by the Lucayan Indians. They believed caves were the gateway to the afterlife. A team of archeologists recovered bones and artifacts dating back to the eighth century. Other myths and legends have been interpreted from the petroglyphs on the walls."

"You spend a lot of time on da computer, don't you?" Manny asked.

"Yeah, it's amazing what you can find. But, you have to sort through the fake stuff and do your research. Hunt down the source."

"And you remember everythin' you read?"

"Doesn't everyone? Buddy answered.

"Not like you," Manny replied.

"Do you really think Platinum put this line in here?" Carter asked.

"More likely it's someone from the Andros Conservatory and Trust," Buddy said. "I read one of their projects is to identify and document the location of all the blue holes on Andros."

"If that's the case, how many others might know about this passage?" Kat asked.

"Hard to say. But it's most likely Platinum's not the only one," Buddy answered.

"Do you think whoever is in that compound knows this way in?" Carter asked. "Maybe Platinum showed them. Could he be setting us up?"

"He knows how much trouble he'd be in if he tried to pull somethin' like dat," Manny said.

"There's something else," Buddy said. "Platinum talked about a marina. There wasn't a marina anywhere where I was working. If someone put one in, they were in an awful hurry to get it up and running."

They walked single file through the tunnel until they gathered at a wide-open area surrounding dark blue water.

"This must be the blue hole Platinum mentioned," Carter said. "We can walk along the ledge now, but if Platinum was right that water covers this when the tide changes, we won't get through at high tide."

"When is high tide?" Kat asked as she tossed bits of limestone in the still water.

"I checked the tide table earlier. We have plenty of time," Carter answered.

Once around the blue hole, the passage narrowed and was dark. Kat was not looking forward to ducking through tight spaces. "I'd hate to think what I might see if I had better light," she said. "This stinks."

"Probably bats," Buddy said.

"Whatever it is, I've decided spelunking is coming off my bucket list," Kat responded.

"Did you have it on your bucket list?" Buddy asked.

"No, but this trip will certainly be my last," Kat said. "I hope Platinum wasn't stoned when he marked this route—if he was the one who did. He doesn't impress me as a person who could focus long enough to complete any job. And what would be his motivation?"

"Maybe that's the answer," Buddy said. "He couldn't be sure he'd find his way back out if he didn't."

Fifteen minutes passed before they confronted a dead end. "Now what?" Kat asked. The ceiling had collapsed and filled the low passageway. The line disappeared under the debris.

"This is what I meant about these limestone walls," Buddy said. "They're unstable. Cavers get trapped this way."

"If we want to go on, we're going to have to dig this out," Carter said. Let's give it a try." They slipped off their backpacks and placed two flashlights on top to light the area. No one said anything as they began digging with their hands, but Carter was sure he wasn't the only one wondering if someone intentionally blocked the passage. Carter climbed up on the loose rock and tugged at a large boulder wedged near the ceiling. Suddenly it came away, and he fell backward. Debris showered down on his head and shoulders and pinned him under a new pile of stone.

"Carter," Kat screamed.

"I'm alright, but my arm is trapped. Go easy," he said as the others dug at the rocks to free him. His arm had been crushed and bruised.

"Should we go back?" Kat asked as Manny examined Carter's arm.

"Can you wiggle your fingers? Wrist?" Manny asked. Carter winced as he made a fist. "I don't think it's broken, but it's up to Carter. I can cut a sling from da backpack material if you want."

"I'll be okay, but I'm not going to be much help. Just fix me up something, Manny."

Manny tied the sling around Carter's neck. "Dat's not going to stop any swellin'. You sure you want to go on? A crush injury can be mighty painful."

"Damn," Buddy said. "I knew I should have picked up some of those Goody's Extra Strength headache powders. It's acetaminophen. An analgesic would help Carter right now."

Carter's arm throbbed, but he said, "I'm good. If we turn back now, we'll have to wait through an entire tide cycle, and we won't get through tonight." Carter could now only watch as the others cleared enough of the rock away to create a small opening.

Once through the rubble, Manny called out, "Hold up. There's no more line."

"You sure?" Kat asked shinning her flashlight bean along the walls and floor.

A blocked passage and no more lead-line. Carter thought. Aloud he said, "Maybe it's buried under the debris and we'll find it again further on."

"Do we turn back?" Kat asked again. "I don't want to get lost back in here."

"I say we go on," Carter answered. "We've come this far and it looks like this is a straight shot." Carter shinned his flashlight into the dark cavern ahead.

Walking slowly as they kicked at the loose stones searching for the line they passed openings on both sides, disappearing into the inky darkness. Finally, they came to a split in the tunnel.

"So, Platinum was right about this branching and we don't have anything to lead us. What's everyone's best guess which fork we take?" Carter asked. "They look equally good—or bad."

"I have a navigation app with a compass on my phone," Buddy said.

"Of course you do," Kat said, not at all surprised.

"But, I don't have any service," Buddy said, looking at his phone. "My internal sense of direction says go right."

"Well, I'd bet on your directional sense over the flip of a coin," Carter said. "Right it is. It's now eleven-thirty so if we have to come back, we'll know how long it takes to return to this point."

"Are we on the right path?" Kat asked after twenty minutes. "Shouldn't we be at the end by now?"

Manny called back from the lead, "I think I see light ahead."

The opening was only about two feet wide and like the other end was blocked by branches. "Stay here," Buddy whispered to everyone. "I was here before, let me get oriented."

The moonlight outlined ten or twelve tall poles that reflected light. As Buddy crawled forward, he realized he was looking across a harbor at the masts of twelve cruising sailboats. The boats were lined up against a long concrete dock that ran parallel to the other shore. No one was around. Overhead a camouflage net blocked the view from aerial surveillance.

Returning to the others, he spoke softly, "I found Platinum's net. It's not what we thought. It's a camouflage tent covering a bunch of sailboats. They weren't here when I was excavating."

"This doesn't fit any hypothesis we've come up with so far. Sailboats are too slow to use for drug trafficking," Carter said.

"And not useful for transporting heavy loads of unrefined minerals," Buddy added.

"Could they be setting up a casino-marina complex like Rollins' hypothesized?" Kat asked.

"That doesn't sound like anything to kill people over," Buddy said.

Carter cut in. "You know, I'm rethinking what I said. Sailboats might be an ingenious way to transport contraband into the States because they aren't suspect. All the times I've sailed in and out of Florida, I've never been boarded. If these guys are using sailboats to carry drugs, I think they have a brilliant plan. We need to get back to Rollins and tell him what we've found."

Manny shook his head. "Not yet. We don't have proof of what dis is. Maybe there's a logical explanation. Makin' some false accusation would be embarrassin'—for everyone. We need to get on one of those boats and take pictures. If we're lucky, there're already drugs onboard. Then we'd have our proof."

"Too risky," Carter said. "There may be an alarm, someone sleeping onboard, a guard dog, or a night watchman. Any of these things could get you killed."

"I think you're overstatin' da risk."

"Well, it's your call," Carter said.

"I'd go, but I don't swim," Manny said.

"Oh yeah? The hell you don't. I remember clearly, you said you swam in that lagoon on Normans." Kat's anger was evident.

"I was lyin'."

"And how many other parts of your story were made up?" Kat asked.

"Look, I don't know what you're arguing over," Buddy said. "Manny says he can't swim, Carter can't go with that arm, so that leaves me and I'm quite capable of swimming over there, you know that, Kat."

"No, you won't," Kat said firmly. "We can go back to Rollins with the information we have. Now that we know a way in, we can lead an investigation team back."

"Not enough," Manny said, shaking his head. "Rollins isn't going to make a move without solid evidence. He told you dat himself."

"Then I'll go. I'm the one that made a deal with him," Kat said.

Carter, Buddy, and Manny all spoke over each other, objecting.

"Kat," Buddy said, "Listen to me, all my life you've protected me. I know that. Let me do this for you." Without waiting for her answer, Buddy took off his backpack, pulled out the sandwich, handed it to Kat, and dropped his flashlight and iPhone into the plastic zippered sandwich bag. He stripped to his jockey shorts, held the plastic bag between his teeth, and waded into the dark water. Struggling against the current, Buddy swam toward the first boat with breaststrokes that didn't break the glassy surface. The others watched him grab the stern ladder, pull himself onto the swim platform, and climb into the cockpit. No alarm sounded.

CHAPTER 45

Buddy felt the urgency, but he had to be careful and quiet. Staying low, he crept across the cockpit to the companionway hatch. A padlock hung on the outside. Knowing he would be exposed, he crawled across the cabin top to the forward hatch. As expected, it was locked. No one was inside. He cupped his hand around the end of the flashlight, letting only a tiny beam of light through and searched the outside lockers. He found what he was looking for, the handle for the manual bilge pump. The padlock at the companionway was secure, but the attachment for the hasp wasn't; one end was attached to fiberglass on the cabin top and the other to the wood of the hatch door. He slipped the stainless-steel bilge pump handle through the shank of the padlock and twisted with all his strength. The fiberglass splintered, and the hasp pulled loose with a cracking noise. Buddy froze, but the sound hadn't alerted anyone. He held his breath as he pushed back the hatch cover, ready to dive back into the water. No alarm, so he quietly slipped into the cabin and pulled the hatch closed.

Stepping around wooden boxes in the main saloon, Buddy made his way forward. In the first sleeping cabin, the bunks had been removed, and there were large tanks. The second cabin housed just one tank, leaving enough room for a person to sleep. Flexible tubes hooked to the containers. From the acrid smell of diesel permeating the interior, Buddy was sure the tanks held extra fuel for a long-range voyage. Retreating to the saloon, he shined his flashlight on the wooden boxes. He could see a mass of electrical wire attached to them and traced the wires to the navigation station, an analog timer, and the chartplotter.

Buddy knew that this sophisticated nautical GPS could be interfaced with an autopilot and programmed to steer a boat from one waypoint to the next even if no one was onboard. He pried open one crate. Staring at red bricks, his heart raced. Explosives! Often his work required dynamite and as much as he wanted to dive back into the water, if he was right about the plan, he needed solid evidence.

At the navigation station, Buddy turned the timer away from zero as a safety measure and checked to be sure all the circuit breakers, except for the chartplotter, were off. Scrolling through the various waypoints of the active route, he eventually came to the mouth of the Potomac River. A chill went through him as he realized the purpose of this setup. He didn't need to see anything more.

Careful to leave everything exactly as he found it, he switched off the flashlight and waited for his eyes to adjust to the darkness before slipping out. He turned the broken hasp so that it was unlikely to be noticed from the dock. Someone would have to board the boat to discover his break-in. That was the best he could do. There was no need to risk going on any of the other boats, he could deduce the rest of the operation, and he was confident of their destinations.

The details of the plan spun around in his head as he slipped back into the water and swam to shore. Briars scratched his legs as he crept quietly barefooted. He was so focused on the implications of his discovery, that he was disoriented. It was the first time his sense of direction failed him. He took a chance and quickly flashed his light twice with the hopes Kat was watching and would remember the game they'd played as children when they were supposed to be in their rooms sleeping. When she flashed back, he let out a sigh of relief. He had his bearings and made his way to the others. Kat was outside, sitting on a fallen tree.

"You were gone so long, I was beginning to worry," she said.

"Let's go back into the cave. It's too risky to talk out here, and I have a lot to tell everyone."

"What'd you find?" Kat asked while she rubbed his arms to warm him.

Buddy took a deep breath. "Those boats are filled with explosives and if I've interpreted the data correctly, they're headed for major ports on the east coast. The chartplotter on that first boat was interfaced with the autopilot and programmed for the Potomac. It's brilliant. The boats can be coordinated to reach different destinations at the same time."

"It's more than brilliant," Carter said. "Blowing something up with that setup doesn't even have to be a suicide mission because no one has to be onboard by the time it reaches its destination."

No one spoke as the ramifications sunk in.

"Are you sure of dis?" Manny asked.

"I verified everything I could. Still, it's only a hypothesis, but it's so logical it's scary," Buddy said.

"This has to be Carlos," Kat said. "It fits everything I know about him. He was suspected of masterminding the bombing of the U.S. Embassy in Bogotá. But there was never any proof. He covers his tracks carefully. Who would suspect he'd ally with Korea—or that he even could? If Carlos is still the egomaniac he used to be, he can get his revenge on the American government before he dies. He's said all along, he wanted to write the last chapter and I had to agree not to edit any of it. I'm certain that chapter will contain all the details that we now know; how he planned and carried out this attack. I'm sure he intends to release it only after he dies. Then as he burns in Hell, he'll do so laughing." Kat remembered Manny's words. *Carlos will use you, then throw you away.*

"It's not like you to jump to conclusions," Carter said. "Just because Platinum said there are Spanish-speaking people here now, how can you be sure? We haven't seen anyone." Carter turned to Manny. "Could Carlos coordinate something like this from prison?"

"It's possible with da right amount of money and influence. Lots of drug lords keep up a very active business from da inside. I guess it depends on just how isolated he is."

"Well, he was able to contact me, and after the initial email, his notes came by snail mail, each time with a different postal code and no return address. He's got a network somewhere." Kat turned to Buddy. "Did you get pictures?"

Buddy stared at her. "I forgot. I got caught up in the details and magnitude of all this."

"Those sailboats have radios dat would reach AUTEC," Manny said.

"We can't risk that," Carter said. "They may seem casual about security, but I'm sure someone here is monitoring the radio. We've got to go back and get in touch with Rollins, and it's coming up on high tide."

"Let's go," Manny said. "I don't want those boats goin' out of here on my watch."

Buddy hadn't moved. "There's one other thing I'm worried about. I had to break the lock's hasp to get in that boat. As soon as anyone gets onboard, it will be obvious that someone breached their perimeter."

CHAPTER 46

"I think we'd better conserve our flashlights," Manny said. "This trip back could take a while and we don't know if we can get around that blue hole now that the tide has come up." They set out single file behind Manny. The dim light of his flashlight made it impossible to identify any familiar markers. Water dripped down the inside walls, hitting the floor, adding a nerve-racking irregular sound in the shadows.

As they moved slowly past a colony of bats hanging from the ceiling, Kat said quietly, "I don't think this is right. I would have definitely remembered a bat colony. Could we have missed the fork in the dark and be heading the wrong way?"

"Look ahead," Manny said. There was the slightest illusion of light coming through a small opening.

"Where do you think we are?" Carter asked, "It's certainly not the way we came in. No gate. No grotto."

"It's my mistake, I'll go look." Manny crawled out into the mist of an early rainy morning. He could see a fence not more than fifty feet away. *Shit!* They were still inside the compound! A chill ran down his spine when he spotted a guard holding the leash of a Doberman with one hand and smoking a cigarette with the other. The dog strained against the leash and let out a bark. The guard turned and spotted Manny as he ran back into the cave. Manny grabbed the flashlight Kat was holding and switched it off. Pulling out his pistol, he turned to face the entrance. If the guard was stupid enough to enter the cave, he would be in clear silhouette with the dim morning light behind him, and he would be dead. Then another thought occurred to Manny; a single guard would have a radio. Manny stepped outside again and could see that the guard held a small unit to his mouth. He wasn't as stupid as Manny hoped; he was calling for backup. Manny stood up, making himself a target, and watched the man aim his gun. Manny had a bead on him and shot him through the chest. The dog, now free, charged, his teeth digging into Manny's arm. Screaming, he dropped his gun.

As soon as Buddy heard the shot, he ran outside and scooped up Manny's gun as the dog took his second charge, this time for Manny's neck. Buddy's single shot killed the dog instantly. All was quiet except for Manny's heavy breathing. He was shaking, but got up slowly, cradling his bleeding arm. "I'm glad your daddy taught you to shoot. You saved my life." His voice quivered.

"You'd have done the same for me," Buddy said. Manny couldn't answer.

Buddy picked up the radio and listened. Nothing. If the guard had gotten a transmission through, or if anyone had heard the shots, surely there would be someone on the radio. Or would there? He called Kat and Carter.

"Help me pull this guy into the cave, the dog too." The three of them struggled to drag first the guard and then the dog through the entrance.

Carter shined his flashlight on the dead guard's face. "Not Korean. I'd say South American, and based on what we're surmising, probably Colombian."

Kat voiced the thoughts that occupied everyone's mind. "How long do we have before someone discovers the guard missing? What if someone heard those shots or has already discovered the broken hasp on that sailboat? We're out of time and out of options."

"I've thought of one more," Buddy said. "I can rewire that boat I was on. Take the current directly from the battery through the timer and to the explosives. With the timer set for eighteen minutes, I'll have time to swim back, and we'll all be protected in the cave when those boats go up."

"That's too dangerous," Kat said.

"This can work. Hear me out. The boats are close together, and one would start a chain reaction. The explosion would be heard all over South Andros. The AUTEC base on Mangrove Cay is operational, and it isn't that far away. They have sophisticated equipment to detect ground-shaking events—earthquakes and explosions."

"How do you know that?" Carter asked.

"Trust me, I do. We're sure to get their attention, and we hide in the cave until help arrives."

"What if there are guards and dogs around the marina?" Kat asked.

"I did it before, and I didn't see any."

"It's daytime," Kat said.

"I'll have the cover of this rain. We can hope those guards would rather stay dry than patrol."

"We don't even know if setting a timer will make the charges blow," Carter argued. "There may be some redundancy. Maybe it's wired to the chartplotter to blow when the boat arrives at its destination. Or maybe there's some inertia device to go off on collision, like a car's airbag. We don't know what we're dealing with here."

"I can set a timer to go off at a pre-determined time, and I'm going to change the wiring to bypass all that."

"Let me go," Carter said. "I can do that rewiring as well as Buddy. Had to do enough of it on *Wind Chaser* over the years."

"Not with one hand, you can't," Buddy said. "I'm the only one to do this."

Kat was panicked. She turned on Manny. "This is your job. You're the law enforcement here. Buddy is in this by accident. Do something." She was shaking Manny by his shoulders. "God damn it, what the hell good are you?"

"Kat, calm down, the longer we sit here, the more danger we're in," Buddy said, putting his arm around her. "Manny saved us from that guard. Risked his life. He's injured, he can't help now. I can do this safely, and I'm a big reason we're in this mess."

Kat took a deep breath. "But if it hadn't been for you, this never would have come to light, and those boats might have sailed out of here and blown up half of the East Coast."

"Well then, either I'm a hero or an idiot," Buddy said. "We're wasting time. My turn to lead. I can retrace our path back to the marina."

When they reached the opening near the marina, Carter said, "I'm going to see if I can spot any guards or dogs. It's the least I can do."

Carter crawled back in a few minutes later. "No one. I suspect they don't know that anyone can get past their fence and no one has discovered a missing guard."

Buddy put his flashlight back in a sandwich bag along with Manny's knife. He wasn't sure if he'd need the flashlight or not, but it was a dark day, and he didn't know how much light there'd be in the cabin to do the work he needed. They watched while he slid as quietly as possible into the water and started toward the sailboats.

"Come on, let's get back in da cave," Manny said.

"I'm waiting for Buddy," Kat said, wiping water from her face.

"I'll wait with you." Carter put his arm around her. The rain was steady now, and they couldn't see Buddy. They could only imagine the steps he was taking to rewire the explosives.

The silence was suddenly interrupted by diesel engines as a big motor yacht entered the harbor. A flare lit up the gray sky. Kat squinted through the rain. "Is Buddy in danger?"

"I don't know," Carter said, standing up. As the engines idled, they listened to Coggins shout over the still harbor.

"Anyone here? I'm taking on water. Need to tie up and get help."

"Shit! Where'd he come from?" Carter asked. Then they spotted a launch with bright lights headed fast toward the motor yacht.

"Oh God, he's alerted the guards. Buddy, stay below. Please stay below," Kat pleaded.

"This area is off-limits." A Latino accent on a loud hailer. "Leave immediately. Repeat. Leave immediately."

"I'm sinking. I need help," Coggins hollered.

The launch fired warning shots over the yacht's bow. "Turn that boat around. Now."

Carter and Kat watched in horror as Coggins began the slow process of turning the big yacht around in the tight harbor.

"Don't hit those sailboats!" boomed the amplified Latino voice. Men started emptying the barracks, running to protect their boats. They were disorganized, some were armed, some were not, but Carter realized there was now no chance of Buddy carrying out his plan. If he set off the explosives, it would be a suicide mission. If he didn't, they would all be captured and killed.

"Buddy, Buddy!" Kat screamed and ran toward the boat basin. Carter sprinted after her. Ignoring his injury, he grabbed her with one hand, and stumbled back to the cave as she hit and scratched, him, struggling to be free.

Even in the protection of the cave, the series of deafening explosions knocked them flat and made the outside brighter than a midday sun. Carter wrapped around Kat, huddled against one wall, protecting her from stones falling from the cave's ceiling. After the explosions stopped, they didn't move. Carter could feel Kat's sobs even though the noise temporarily deafened him.

Carter knew it was all over. His entire arm throbbed, maybe it was broken, but for the moment the pain protected him from the gut-wrenching agony that waited outside the cave. The fiery explosions would have killed Buddy, Coggins, Albury, and the Colombians. They were the only survivors.

Kat escaped Carter's embrace and scrambled across the cave, screaming. Her fists had the force of desperation as she beat on Manny. "You son-of-a-bitch. You coward. Coward. Buddy's dead. It's your fault." Manny didn't try to defend himself. Finally, Carter pulled her away and held her against his chest until her rage subsided.

CHAPTER 47

The AUTEC base, a few miles north on Mangrove Cay, detected the ground-shaking event on their seismographic equipment. Not knowing if this was an earthquake or explosion, in less than five minutes three small, heavily armed U.S. Navy cutters roared out of the AUTEC channel and turned south.

The AUTEC commanding officer placed a call to the Bahamian Defense Force, located in a restricted area of Coral Harbor, on the southern tip of New Providence Island, and another call to Prime Minister Rollins. Four Bahamian police intercept boats left at full throttle from Coral Harbor, along with two helicopters.

The helicopters arrived first and circled the still-burning wreckage. The pilot looked for a clearing to land. "Man, look at dis," he said to the medic. "I never seen nothin' like it, I didn't think der was anythin' back here. There's an airstrip. Wonder what they're doin' here?"

"Don't know," the medic said. "All I know is, we're to offer medical assistance and evacuate any American survivors. Don't know what shape they be in. I'm followin' orders." From the ground, Kat, Carter, and Manny watched the helicopter put down. Kat was in a daze as Carter helped her board. Before he climbed in, he pulled Manny aside.

"I don't know if I'm making the right decision here, but now that Buddy's dead, my only concern is Kat's safety. I don't have time to give you the details, but for the protection of everyone, let's say we were never here. You alone uncovered this. Say what you want. It's your investigation."

Manny nodded, slammed the helicopter's door behind Carter, and gave him a weak salute. *So the fiction begins.*

Before Kat fell into an exhausted sleep, she said, "Look, I still have my anklet. I meant to leave it for the chickcharnie."

"It's okay, I think everything you did will keep them happy for a very long time," Carter said, stroking her hair.

By the time the helicopter reached cruising altitude, Carter was also asleep. Kat's head was against his chest, his arm wrapped around her. Even the noise of the helicopter didn't disturb them. The pilot phoned Rollins as he had been instructed. He didn't use his radio.

"I have two Americans, a man, and a woman. Da medic say da man maybe have a broken arm. Other than dat, they dirty, wet, and smelly. Do you want names?"

"Negative on names," came the reply. "Get them back here as quickly as you can. I'll take it from there."

"Roger that. Heading to Nassau."

The helicopter set down on a heliport in the center of Nassau and the pilot reached around and shook Carter. "We're here."

"Where?" Carter blinked and looked around.

"Princess Margaret Hospital."

"We don't need medical attention. Just a hot shower, a bed, and clean clothes will do," Carter said.

"I know. Had to borrow the hospital's heliport," the pilot said. "I'm followin' orders direct from the Prime Minister. Dat black Lincoln over there is waitin' to take you to da British Colonial Hotel. Prime Minister Rollins said to tell you not to talk to anyone, not da press, not anyone before he meet you there. And dat's an order. I don't know what dis is all about and I don't wanna know. I never even seen you, and dat's my orders too."

Carter and Kat ducked under the whirling helicopter blades and walked towards a black, unmarked car with dark windows that sat on the side of the pad, its engine idling. The medic ran up behind Carter. "Here's a splint for dat arm. Best you put it on after you clean up. Put some ice on it too. Keep da swellin' down. Good luck, mon."

A man in a dark suit, standing outside the Lincoln, flashed his police ID, opened the rear door for them and scooted into the driver's seat. Without speaking, he pulled into the afternoon traffic, heading the few blocks to Nassau's only five-star hotel.

Kat pulled out the little figure she'd had with her all along, her lucky token, Ms. Cordella had said. She rubbed it against her cheek. "I should have given it to Buddy. Maybe he would have survived. But he's dead." She fingered the token in her hand, sad beyond tears.

"Yes," Carter said softly, stroking her hand. Carter knew no words would take away the pain. She needed to grieve.

CHAPTER 48

Their Lincoln bypassed the elaborate yellow façade and front entrance of The British Colonial Hotel with its uniformed doormen. He pulled around the side to a wide roll-up door and inserted a keycard into a box on a post. The door opened to reveal a space with a loading platform for commercial vehicles. Pulling in next to a laundry truck, the driver led Kat and Carter down a back corridor to an elevator, remaining silent until the doors closed.

"I know dis isn't elegant, but it's very private; da way da PM wants it. Dis is da entrance he use when he needs to be discreet or when his special visitors need to be. Movie and TV stars, heads of state, and sport celebrities, all been in dis elevator before you. It'll take you up to da Presidential Suite."

The elevator went directly to the top where a security guard waited. He opened the double door to the suite that occupied the entire floor. "I think you'll find everything you need here, food and drinks," said the officer. Looking them over, he continued, "You'll have time to shower and clean up before da PM gets here. Do you have other clothes in Nassau?"

"Yes," Carter said. "They're on a small powerboat named *Sparky,* docked at Harbor Bay Yacht Basin." Carter didn't add that the rest of their clothes were still at the South Andros Beach Club. He handed the officer the keys to *Sparky.*

"I'll send someone to get your tings from da Yacht Basin now and send them up to you. Meanwhile, you'll find robes in da closets nearest each bathroom."

"And one more ting, for security, I need to pat you down."

"No problem," Carter said, holding out his arms.

"Is dis a cell phone," he asked when he felt Carter's pocket.

"Yes," Carter said, pulling it out. The officer took it from him.

"And Mz. do you have one too?"

"Yes, but why are our phones being confiscated?" Kat asked.

"I don't know, but da Prime Minister was very particular 'bout dat. I'll return with your clothes. Now, rest up a bit." The officer quietly closed the door behind himself.

Kat pulled back the curtains of the large picture windows, and looked across ornately landscaped gardens surrounding a pool and extending to the harbor. "He'll never see any of this." The words caught in her throat and tears rolled down her cheeks. Carter came up behind her and held her against his chest, a place that shared her loss. As her breathing calmed, she turned and wandered over to the table, cut some cheese, twisted off some grapes and added crackers to a plate. She gave a sad laugh.

"After we got in that limo, I had the feeling I needed to call Buddy, tell him everything that happened. I can't do that. Ever."

Carter felt his own eyes sting and well up. He knew the feeling. In his head, he still caught himself talking to Becca. "No matter where you are, or what you're doing, Buddy will always be a part of you."

"I'm going to get in that Jacuzzi tub." Kat's voice was drained of emotion. "I want to be alone right now, but check on me now and then to make sure I don't fall asleep in there."

"I won't be far away; I'm going to shower as soon as I finish this beer. Want one or a glass of wine?"

"I think, for now, I'd better stick with water, or I definitely won't be awake when Rollins comes."

Carter saw her tear up again. "Are you sure you're going to be alright talking to him?"

"I want to get this over."

Rollins was in their suite a few minutes before six. "I'm relieved to see you both again. When I got word of the explosion, well, I wasn't at all sure you had survived."

"Buddy's dead." Kat's voice was choked by sorrow. Her hair was still wet, and her eyes red. The stress of the last twenty-four hours showed on her face.

"I know. Manny told me." Rollins reached over and took her hand. "I'm truly sorry. He made the ultimate sacrifice, and after all you've been through; to lose him now is more than anyone should have to bear." Rollins took off his glasses and pinched the bridge of his nose. "Unfortunately, I must ask you to talk about what happened. Can you do that? The reporters are all over this. Please turn that TV to channel four."

Carter hit the remote in time to hear the anchor on the Nassau station. "There is breaking news as we come on the air. There has been a major explosion on South Andros. Details are still coming in. We turn now to Captain Manford Lightbourne on the scene in Andros."

Manny looked years older as he stood in front of the camera. Someone had supplied clean bandages for his arm and neck, but he still wore his dirty civilian clothes. He read from a statement clasped in his hand.

"Da Bahamian Defense Force, under da direction of Prime Minister Rollins, has intercepted an alleged terrorist plot aimed against U.S. eastern seaboard ports, which was being planned right here on South Andros. Da explosives have been set off, and there's no longer any threat. Unfortunately, it appears there are no survivors. Dat's all I can tell you now." Reporters fired questions at him, but he turned away from the camera.

The station cut back to the anchor in the studio. "We will report details as they become available during the evening. Prime Minister Rollins is currently briefing the U.S. Department of Homeland Security and will address the people of the Bahamas at eight this evening. But right now, we'll go to the Honorable Michael Buckley, the candidate of the Bahamas National Movement, in his Lyford Cay office."

The television screen showed Buckley seated in a plush black leather chair with a banner behind him proclaiming, "The Next Prime Minister. A Man You Can Believe."

"I should have known Buckley would make himself available. Wonder what spin he's going to put on this," Rollins said.

Buckley began by shaking his head and pursing his lips. "Like everyone, I am, of course, stunned but thrilled by the exposure of this horrific plot, but the timing of this raid, just three days before the election, is designed for political gain. Rollins endangered Bahamian and American lives in a vain attempt to boost his re-election chances. When I am Prime Minister, I promise a full investigation of this sordid affair."

The television screen went back to the anchor. "We will bring you updates as they become available. Stay tuned for the Prime Minister at eight."

"In other news, U.S. Senator Walter Coggins with the Honorable Franklin Albury onboard left South Andros Beach Club on the senator's eighty-foot motor yacht yesterday morning at approximately seven o'clock. The boat is now overdue and is reported missing. The vessel is white with blue trim and a tuna tower. The name on the stern is *Carpe Diem*. Everyone is requested to keep a sharp lookout for this vessel and report any sightings to BASRA at 242-333-4100 or on marine radio channel sixteen. We now take you to Captain Tucker Bain, who was..."

Rollins switched off the television and looked at Kat for a moment before speaking. "Mrs. Deano, is this your memory of what happened on South Andros?"

Kat's focus was back but she didn't answer directly. "There's more you need to know." As quickly as she could, she told Rollins everything, including Carlos Lehder's memoir she was writing, the Colombian cartel's threat if she publicized the names of the drug lords she received from Lehder, and the DEA's warning to extradite her from the Bahamas and put her under oath to reveal those names.

Rollins listened without interrupting. "It seems you are truly between a rock and a hard place."

"Yes, I am. But so are you. One of the names on that list would be a major political disaster for you if it, and his story, came out. I have a proposal."

"Go on."

"I want your help to stay in the Bahamas. I can't be deported and put under oath, and you can't afford that either."

"I don't see how that's possible, as much as I'd like to help. We have a very close relationship with the U.S., and there are very few exceptions to our extradition agreement with them."

"True, but there are a few. I've talked to the Honorable Winston Worthington-Atwater. He described one possibility."

Rollins stared at her. "Are you prepared to accept Bahamian citizenship?"

"Yes."

"Just let me say, if I am re-elected, my current Minister of Tourism will not be part of my new cabinet. Now, is your memory the same as Manny's on this?"

"Yes, exactly."

Rollins turned to Carter, who so far had been silent. "I was about to make the final payment on your boat loan. We need to do whatever we can to promote cruising here."

"Are there no survivors except for Kat, Manny, and me?" Carter asked.

"Manny wasn't exactly accurate on that," Rollins said. "A few guards who were on patrol around the perimeter survived. We've already picked them up and interrogated them. They are Colombians, by the way. But they were all too far away to witness anything and claim they were only hired to guard the marina compound. They will spend the rest of their lives in prison, but this is mostly a move to satisfy the U.S. government since these men were so far down the chain of command they can't provide any useful information. So you, Mrs. Deano, and Captain Lightbourne are the only three witnesses we have."

Carter looked into Kat's eyes. "My memory matches Manny's."

"Yes, yes, indeed," Rollins said and turned back to Kat. "Don't worry about extradition. At least not legal extradition and I don't think the U.S. would try anything surreptitiously after we have exposed and blocked this potential attack against their ports. Now, until this election is over, I suggest you stay right here. Cross your fingers I win. I'll have your meals sent in. If anything happens, you can always get in touch with Barracuda Bob." Rollins smiled at Kat. "I'll be in touch as soon as the election is over. Now, I have a TV interview to prepare for."

They shook hands. As Rollins pulled their cell phones out of his briefcase, he said. "Sorry, I had to erase all your photos." He turned to Carter. "I'll send a car in the morning so you can get that wrist x-rayed. No need to give anyone your name. Now, both of you get some sleep."

CHAPTER 49

The foiled terrorist plot was the lead story on the U.S. as well as the Bahamian news, and as much as he attempted to avoid the attention, Manford Lightbourne became an instant hero.

Prime Minister Rollins was trailing at the polls before the raid on South Andros, but after continued news coverage, he won re-election by a slim margin. His constituents recognized the benefits of the favorable publicity about the raid. The islands were dependent on American tourism. Rollins kept his promise, over objections from members of his party, appointing Kat to his cabinet.

Kat heard nothing further from Carlos Lehder, even though there had never been any concrete evidence linking him to the South Andros plot. She didn't know if he was still alive. She had no intention of publishing his memoir. Given the possible final chapter, there was no need for enemies of the U.S. to make him into a martyr. She destroyed her written copy of Carlos' list of names and deleted them from her hard drive; however, the names, like everything she read, were indelibly etched in her memory.

Kat blocked out her grief by immersing herself into her new role. Carter knew about the hollowness under her heart and that at unsuspecting moments she would be ambushed by guilt and grief. He also knew she would find her way through this. She was that strong. The best he could do for her now, was give her time and space. His presence was an acute and painful reminder. He joined a regatta heading to Cuba.

CHAPTER 50

Nearly a year later, a groundbreaking ceremony was about to begin on Bimini. Bleachers had been set up on the vacant land where the Compleat Angler had been, where Papa Hemingway had worked and played, and where Piccolo Pete had died. Ida May sat beside Hemingway's descendants in the front row, mopping the perspiration from her face with a handkerchief. All of them had contributed money to a new Hemingway Museum, an extension of the recently completed high school library. Kat had donated the money the cartel had given her.

Rollins and most of his cabinet were already seated on the platform. Kat was standing

in front of the stage, anxiously scanning the crowd. A gentle breeze rustled the palms and blew her hair around her face.

Spotting Carter winding his way among the seats toward the stage, she smiled and ran to him. They locked in a silent embrace as she smelled the salt on his skin. "I was hoping you'd be here. God, you look good." She looked at his sun-bleached, still too long hair and his tanned skin.

"You've let your hair grow out. I like it," Carter said, smoothing the soft curls. How's the job?"

Kat shrugged.

"I know you're great at it. You can put a positive spin on things, stand up to the best or worst of them, and lie when you need to," Carter said, grinning.

Kat laughed. "Well, I've got wonderful people to work with and great islands to promote. Just have to keep the riff-raff out. The biggest complaint I receive from tourists is taxi drivers who never have change and conveniently forget the posted rates. But fixing that won't be enough. The bigger job is to convince tour companies that the Bahamas are not a haven for criminals or terrorists. And I've got to be twice as effective as anyone else. Even before my confirmation hearing, there were rumblings about the position being filled by a young, white woman. I'm not sure how Rollins pulled that off. I accepted this post for two years, and God, I miss you. Are you continuing your charter business?"

Carter nodded. "Part of the reason I'm here is to pick up a young family, the Talbots. They have a ten-year-old daughter."

"Good for you," Kat said. "I think so much about our time together and your patience with me and my search for Buddy. Who would have ever thought what the three of us would end up accomplishing? I wish the whole world could know what a hero Buddy was. But at least for now, that remains our secret. And just after he found the peace and happiness he was looking for." She continued, "My consolation is that I see Elliot every time he flies into Nassau. We had dinner just a few nights ago. It helps to have Elliot to talk to. It keeps Buddy close, but it also makes me feel his absence more acutely."

"How is Elliot?"

"Sad, lonely, trying to focus on the time he and Buddy had together. It's not easy for him. He doesn't have anyone, other than me, with whom he can share the depth of his grief and the love he lost."

"As Ms. Ida May told us, if you live long enough, loss comes to everyone's life. And the grief really never ends. It's the price of love," Carter said. "But as we both know, loss can set a new course. I'd lost all sense of direction. I'd quit searching, nearly quit everything, until you came along. I was bogged down by the heavy weight of my past. I have a long way to go, but I feel like I've found my way out of uncharted water now and I have you to thank for that."

"Well, you couldn't go on the way you were."

"You're right. I was on a very destructive path."

"Moving forward is not a straight line," Kat continued. "I'm really on my own now. No Buddy, no Stewart. I'm making a promise to myself. I'm going to be an equal partner in any relationship I make from now on." Kat paused and glanced over the gathering guests. "I'm struggling to say something, and I was hoping you'd give me a lead, but you haven't. So, here goes. I committed to Rollins for two years but any chance you'll need a first mate in another year? That you'd want me?"

"Rollins has given you diplomatic immunity. I can't offer that."

"There's something you don't know."

"Now, why doesn't that surprise me?" Carter smiled.

"Please, listen. You heard about Manny, right?"

Carter nodded. "I was in the Dominican Republic. Had to have *Wind Chaser* hauled out. I pulled up the *Nassau Guardian* online and was sad to read his obituary."

"There's more. Right after the election, Manny's son, Franklin, was released from prison by executive order. He remained in Manny's custody and under probation. The court required Franklin's wife to permit his two young children to visit him regularly at Manny's house. I often joined them, and I can tell you, the thing that brought joy to Manny was the laughter of his grandchildren when they shared his home. Then four months ago, Franklin found his father dead in their Nassau home. The cause of death was a bullet to his head. Ballistic tests indicated that the bullet came from Manny's service pistol, found next to his body."

"None of that was in the obituary."

"No, of course not. But, Manny took the fall for me. I don't know all the details yet, but he had the names of those Colombians. About a month before he died, he met with the DEA here in Nassau and struck some kind of a deal. The names are out. Manny made sure of that. The DEA has started rounding these guys up, so I'm off the hook, but Manny shouldn't have died. It should have been me."

"I hardly think you're the suicidal type."

"You don't think his death was a suicide, do you?" Kat asked.

Carter couldn't think of any appropriate response.

"Rollins has promised a full investigation," Kat said. "But back to my question. Do you want me as your first mate or not?"

Carter glanced toward the bay, squinting into the late afternoon sun before returning his focus to Kat. "I don't know. Both you and Becca used me. I'm still a little short in the trust department. Becca knew her plans when she pushed me to bring that boat back from Nassau. And you—well, you know that part."

"Yes, if it makes any difference, I feel like we met in wartime. I'd like the chance to see where we could go in peacetime."

"Me too," Carter said, letting his hand linger on her cheek. "The next time I'm in Nassau, I'll call you. We'll have dinner." Carter had learned to trust himself. He was determined to do this his own way.

Kat pulled him close with a kiss that was deep and intimate. "Remember that." They both stood frozen until Carter turned, gave her the thumbs up over his shoulder, and called, "I'll be back." He faded into the crowd, headed toward Brown's Marina.

Running her hands through her hair, trying to compose herself, Kat stepped onto the platform and took her seat beside Rollins.

Rollins turned to her. "Are you sure you want to remain in my cabinet?"

"For now," Kat said, wiping her eyes.

Back on *Wind Chaser,* Carter fixed a Caesar salad, broiled lobster tails, and opened a bottle of dry, chilled white wine for his guests. As the four of them dined in the cockpit, the little girl chatted enthusiastically. A radiant red sun sank on the horizon and as the stars came out, fireworks started, signaling the end of the dedication ceremony. Carter tossed back his head as laughter bubbled up. For a split second, he didn't know if explosions came from the dazzling night sky or from deep inside his heart.

ACKNOWLEDGMENTS AND
AUTHOR NOTES

This is a work of fiction so don't look on your charts for all the cays and islands mentioned here. However, many persons and places are real, and when they fit the story, I included authentic details which sailors and Bahamians will recognize. At the same time, I have taken the liberty to embellish characters and locations as only an author of fiction is allowed to do, and the blame falls on me if anyone is offended.

Even though I based much of this novel on personal experiences gathered while sailing the Bahamas over forty years, it also required a great deal of research. That list is extensive, but I want to mention a few titles that stand out with their varying interpretations of Bahamian history and culture and make entertaining reading: *History of Bimini,* by Ashley B. Saunders, *Turning the Tide: One Man Against the Medellin Cartel,* by Sidney D. Kirkpatrick, *Blow,* by Bruce Porter, *Pindling: The Life and Times of the First Prime Minister of the Bahamas,* by Michael Craton, *The Tales of Andros, An Island in the Sun,* by Diann Hanna-Wilson and *Folk Tales of Andros Island, Bahamas,* by Elsie Worthington Clews Parsons. I borrowed ideas from all of these perspectives, and leave it to you to decide how much is true.

Along the way, I heard firsthand stories from many Bahamians and kept them in my sailing journal. I interviewed George Jung, Carlos Lehder's partner in crime, by email while he was incarcerated (the real one, not Johnny Depp, although that might have been fun too) and gained his perspective of the Medellin cartel years.

Writers always say that many people contributed to the completion of a book, and I would be remiss not to mention some of them—first, my husband, Ed Howle, my writing partner and inspiration. We discussed every scene, character, dialog, and plot sequence. He read every draft and revision. I relied on him for his expertise in all sailing matters; after all, he taught me to sail. His effort equaled mine throughout the writing process, and in my mind, I think of him as my co-author.

Uncharted had its beginning years ago at the Salt Cay Writers workshop in the Bahamas with its knowledgeable and supportive faculty and talented participants. My thanks to organizer and author, Karen Dionne and faculty members author, Robert Goolrick, and editor, Chuck Adams who started me down this path. I am grateful to my first readers who provided valuable feedback and bolstered my confidence. From there, I could acknowledge all the agents who rejected the manuscript, including the few who dropped in an occasional positive word that convinced me to continue this discouraging process. Rather than bore you with that long list, I will cut to the end when I finally found what I was looking for.

SisterShip Press focuses on writing built around life on the water. Fortunately, it came with a compassionate editor, seasoned sailor, and writer. Working with Shelley Wright convinced me that the hard work and thoroughness of an editor does not get enough praise. It is a daunting task and takes endless red pencils and a delicate hand.

I am indebted to Shelley for her seemingly limitless insights, perseverance, humor, and boundless enthusiasm throughout the process needed to shape my story into a publishable, engaging novel. She patiently read my many drafts and knows these characters, their actions, and emotions as intimately as I do.

Shelley was assisted by Jackie Parry whose attention to detail and technical advice was invaluable, particularly as I struggled with the chapters describing the storm and grounding. The changes she suggested made this section, at once, realistic and readable.

I am forever grateful to both of them for their ability to express thoughtful, critical remarks as supportive suggestions in order to protect my fragile writer's ego. Thank you, Shelley and Jackie.

To successfully release the book to the public takes people with skills beyond writing. I am indebted to Ann Clermont, fellow writer and creative web designer for constructing my amazing website, www.janethowleauthor.com and to Annie Seaton, a well-established author and designer of the stunning cover. These pieces are important parts of engaging readers and without the expertise of these two women, my writing might still be lost among the many titles available.

Janet M. Howle

The author can be contacted at
www.janethowleauthor.com

Facebook: Janet Howle - author

Instagram: Janetmhowle